Praise for the Immortal's Blood series

'An intriguing premise . . . an intricate, fast-paced story . . . Humphreys packs gods, deicide, warring tribes and some impressive world-building into just over 300 pages' *Guardian*

'Humphreys' plot, prose, and characters give this book a sense of quality and gravity without skimping on fun and readability' *Grimdark Magazine*

'Wonderful characters and great world-building, in Humphreys' special brand of addictive storytelling'
Diana Gabaldon, author of the award-winning *Outlander* series

'Brilliant: smoothly-written, engaging, fascinating. The kid can write. The world is wonderful – I wish I'd thought of it'
Conn Iggulden, author of the *Emperor* and *Conqueror* series

'Insanely gripping and thoroughly unusual'
Morning Star

'Chris Humphreys skilfully weaves together several different storylines without any feeling like they're rushed over and still manages to keep the momentum of the plot' *The Book Bundle*

By Chris Humphreys from Gollancz:

Smoke in the Glass
The Coming of the Dark

THE COMING OF THE DARK

Chris Humphreys

This paperback edition published in Great Britain in 2021

First published in Great Britain in 2020 by Gollancz
an imprint of The Orion Publishing Group Ltd
Carmelite House, 50 Victoria Embankment
London EC4Y 0DZ

An Hachette UK Company

1 3 5 7 9 10 8 6 4 2

A CIP catalogue record for this book
is available from the British Library.

ISBN (Mass Market Paperback) 978 1 473 22607 4
ISBN (eBook) 978 1 473 22608 1

Typeset by Deltatype Ltd, Birkenhead, Merseyside

Printed in Great Britain by Clays Ltd, Elcograf S.p.A.

www.gollancz.co.uk

To Reith

Dramatis Personae

Corinthium:
Ferros
Lara
Roxanna
Makron
Lucan
Streone
Petros, head groom
Severos, brothel owner
Gronigen, Wattenwolden sergeant
Bavringen, speedy Wattenwolden
Doukas, Governor of Cuerdocia
Sepoloumos, young officer
Rablania, Cuerdocian woman
Mikos, Cuerdocian shipwright
Andronikos, legendary hero, mortal
Danlos, sailor
Olankios, immortal and general from Balbek
Sofran, Saphardi general
Malthoros, officer
Bratan, soldier/messenger

Soldiers of the Ninth Balbek Riders:
Demetrios
Haldan
Eurokos
Glaman
Mikos

Saghaz-a (Land of the Four Tribes):
Anazat, High Monk
Gistrane, Huntress
Karima, Huntress
Korshak, Horse Lord
Maranne, child nurse
Bezan, Monk
Karania, leader of the Huntresses
Baromolak, King of the Horse Lords
Framilor, captain of the Seafarers
Lanane, Atisha's attendant
Pershak, Horse Lord guard
Ramaskor, Seafarer envoy
Ganator, Seafarer envoy

Ometepe:
Atisha
Intitepe
Fant – dog
Toman, head of Intitepe's guard
Sekantor the Savage, pirat
Muna, governess of the City of Women
Besema
Yutil

Midgarth:

Luck
Freya
Hovard
Bjorn Swift-Sword
Einar the Black
Agnetha
Stromvar, Dragon Lord
Gytta, Luck's wife
Ulrich the Smith
Peki Asarko
Petr the Red
Soren, Bjorn's second in command
Beornoth, Freya's helmsman
Torval, guard
Ture, sea captain
Tiny Elric, Ulrich's son

Sirene

Two letters found in the vaults of the Keep, castle of the Warrior Monks of Saghaz-a. The first, written by Makron, renegade of Corinthium (also known as Smoke, the Prophet) to Anazat, leader of the Warrior Monks. The second, Anazat's reply …

Hail, lord,

Though I would prefer to communicate as we usually do, through smoke in the glass, I understand your need for something formal to take to the leaders of the Four Tribes of Saghaz-a: those Horse Lords, Huntresses, Seafarers, and your own Monks, all formerly the most bitter of foes who fought each other for hundreds of years before the revelation of the coming of the One – Praise her! Praise him! – united them. Still, I understand your cautions, and how difficult it must be to keep them united; how they require written facts rather than your mere reporting of a conversation. Thus have I written this on a separate page for you to dispose of, allowing you to share what follows.

Honourable leaders of Saghaz-a,
I have learned that a young officer, Ferros of the Ninth
Balbek Riders, was brought to Corinthium as soon as he was
killed and reborn, becoming the empire's newest immortal.
The powers there – Lucan, current leader of the Council of
Lives, and his daughter, our most dangerous immortal enemy,
Roxanna – believe that this Ferros has the abilities to lead
the fight against me. So, in the Sanctum on the Hill, he was
educated – and corrupted; seduced by Roxanna to bind him
to her will. This despite the presence of a wife, Lara. My spies
in the city report that in despair this young woman joined a
suicide cult to try to force her own immortality. She failed, of
course, and is dead.

Ferros has now been sent to deal with me and defeat the
uprising of tribes I have arranged in the empire's border
province of Cuerdocia. He is as formidable as they think
him, and has discovered the massing of our army beyond
the mountains for the invasion which they did not know of
until now. As I write this, and with a small troop, he pins my
force of Horse Lords in the narrow tunnel between Saghaz-a
and Cuerdocia, which was only one week from completion.
Nevertheless, I am confident of breaking through within days,
to invade the southern part of Corinthium's empire, as we
planned. I will inform you, through the glass, when we achieve
this.

Please let me know how fare our other plans – and most
especially let me hear of the One.

Praise her! Praise him! Praise the One!

Anazat's reply:

My lord Makron,

Between the Horse Lords' skills and courage as warriors and your intelligence I am confident that the southern invasion will happen as planned.

You asked for information. The preparations in the north for the invasion of Midgarth are almost complete. As you know, over the years we have seriously weakened them by sending assassins over the mountains and killing a number of their immortals. We have two of their so-called gods in our thrall: Peki Asarko, a despicable yet powerful leader, Lord of the Lake of Souls. He is still in Midgarth, undermining it; while I have their sole truly dangerous god, Luck of Askaug, as a prisoner in the Keep. He came seeking knowledge of us, and is certainly getting it. Both these Midgarthians are now slaves to the drug, Sirene. They journey with her when I allow them, and are sinking further into her embrace by the day. Soon they will be helpless to do anything other than obey our will.

There are gods in Midgarth who are still formidable warriors. Their names are Hovard, Bjorn Swiftsword, Stromvar Dragon Lord and perhaps the cleverest of them all, Freya. Still, they do not know the size of the fleet we are assembling. The Seafarers will launch the northern invasion, as you launch yours, when the two moons meet in the sky on what we in Saghaz-a call the Entwining.

You ask also of the One. There we have true joy. The baby that is neither boy nor girl but both was indeed born, as

3

prophesied to us, in that far-off, savage island of Ometepe. My spies there report this: the child's father, Intitepe – their ruler and god and the only immortal male in that land, because he has slain all the others – tried to murder the child because of a prophecy that said that just as he killed his father, and his seven sons, so a son of his would one day kill him. He failed, for the mother, Atisha, was sent in error first to the City of Women in the south of the country. There revolt against his tyranny exploded. He is now dealing with a country in flames, and we will not be troubled by him again.

Meanwhile mother and child have been rescued by Korshak, Horse Lord, and by Gistrane, Huntress. They are bringing the One to us by speedy vessel, reaching us before the invasions commence.

So the time is near, brother. When the two moons marry again in the sky, then will come the end of the dominion of the immortal and the beginning of the dominion of man. Every man and woman of the Four Tribes, together with devotees like yourself, in every other land, will conquer the world – united under the banner of the child born to bring us into the light.

Praise her! Praise him! Praise the One!

From the end of *Smoke in the Glass* ...

The two men left at the gate had run out of arrows, and blades had driven them back. Six huge men were there, swinging vast double-handed swords. Ferros threw one javelin, Gandalos another, both hit, then both ran forward. Four fought four at the cave entrance.

Their enemy were hampered by the lack of space, their weapons suited to plain, not cave. Their steel drew sparks as they dragged points across the ceiling, trying for the high cut. So Ferros stepped close and opened a man's stomach with a slice, Gandalos stabbed another through the eye, the other soldiers killed as swiftly and, for a moment, there were just the four of them there, heaving breaths.

Until another man stepped through the entrance and made it five. He did not have a sword. He had a bow. And it was aimed at Ferros's chest.

There was an instant, just a small one, during which Ferros thought he might do something. Knew that the hesitation had probably cost him a life. This one anyway.

But Gandalos did not hesitate. Just stepped in front of Ferros and took the arrow through his throat.

'No!' cried Ferros, catching his comrade's body as he fell, lowering him to the ground, aware of the two other soldiers as they stepped up and killed the bowman. Focused on the light as it left the young man's eyes.

Then he heard the voice. Recognised it immediately. Which meant that he must have been struck too, without even feeling

5

it. He was dead, had to be. Because the person who spoke was dead as well.

'Rise, my love. Rise and fight,' she said.

He looked up at her. She looked down at him, in the moment before she bent and snatched up Gandalos's sword. For more of the enemy had burst into the cave and she turned to take them on.

'Lara?'

I

Resurrection

Four weeks earlier, in the city of Corinthium ...

She woke with grave dirt in her mouth and a dead man's arm across her chest.

Crying out, Lara swallowed soil. Choked, spat, took in more with a desperate breath, spat again. She was in complete darkness, with the stench of death, putrid and gamy, filling her nostrils as much as the earth did, and the weight of both pressing her from all sides. It told her she was not alone in the dark. That part of what pinned her was a body. That perhaps there was more than one.

Though she'd never been a worshipper, she knew the stories of the afterlife, its joys and its horrors. Simbala ruled Death, and she was known to be a capricious god, assigning some to happiness, some to eternal terror. It was clear that her failure to worship had condemned her to that second fate – to rot for ever in this fetid darkness. She had sought immortality and found it only in a living grave.

Lara wept. She screamed, but her tears and cries were swallowed in mud. She began to move all her limbs at once, arms and legs shifting the earth that encased her, fingers and toes clawing it aside. But any gap she made, where breath came easier for a

7

moment, was soon filled, and earth closed round her again. The other bodies – two, she was sure of that now – came and went as if drowning in a sea beside her, seeking to pull her down with them ever deeper into the fathomless dark. Movement did nothing, changed nothing. Screams went unheard, prayers unanswered. Gradually she stilled, until her only movement was the sobbing and tears and snot that would not cease, and the breaths she somehow managed to take to stay alive.

Alive.

It was the thought-word that stopped her. Why was eternal death her only option? What if there was something else? She realised that there already was – because the bodies beside her, her grave companions, were just that ... bodies, only moving when her movements made them. They did not claw, scream, weep as she did. She explored them with one hand. One was a man, one a woman. The man had an ... *irregular* face. It took her a while to remember the youth who'd stood beside her at Simbala's altar with half his face eaten away by disease. This was him beside her. The woman, then, had to be the old one who'd sought immortality to stay with her younger lover.

So there were differences in this pit, between the sentient and the senseless dead. And in difference, surely, *surely*, Lara thought, there must be choice?

She forced a hand up to her mouth, began to slowly push the earth aside. It was crumbly, but she was able to form it when she spat on it, moulding a tiny cave for herself where breath came a little easier. With breath came ... not rest, the panic and terror were there, a collapse of earth away – but at least the ability to think for more than a few seconds at a time, to wonder ...

What if I am not dead? And whoever buried me thought that I was?

She thought back. The last thing she remembered before

waking here ... was the dagger slash that took her life. Back in that cave in Corinthium, where Carellia had brought her for the ritual of the suicide cult of Simbala. She had offered her throat ... to the woman behind the mask, who she had thought was her friend but had been replaced by her enemy. By Roxanna, the immortal. She did not understand how Roxanna had transformed into Carellia in the ceremony. She did understand why she'd done it. For Roxanna was her rival for the love of a man, her man. Ferros.

And now she believes that she has succeeded, Lara thought. Fury seized her, cold as any grave. With fury came clarity and then the realisation that she did now have a choice: accept this fate, this living death. Or choose another.

She was buried. She could not know how deep in the ground. She could only know that somewhere above her was a surface. And while she had even this little breath, she could climb up to that.

The first task was to discover which way was up.

The only thing that could still move, other than her limbs, was her mouth. She couldn't see but she could feel. The pressure in her head made her guess that she was facing downwards but since being killed no doubt made everything different, she had to be sure. So she used her lips to gather some of the clay-like mud before her, took it in, rolled it into a ball with her spit, forced both hands up to cup around her mouth and pushed the ball out with her tongue. It landed on her left little finger. Tried it again. Same result.

As far as she could tell then, she was lying on her left side, facing down. So the surface was behind her, to her right. She could not know how far. She could only try to reach it.

It took a while to turn herself over. When she was on her back, sure she was facing upwards, she began to dig beneath her with her heels and above with her hands, forcing the earth away.

9

Slowly, so slowly she thought she barely moved, she got herself nearly turned and pointing up. Then, as slowly, she forced her arms above her and began to part the earth over her head.

It took another age. Again and again she stopped, certain she had no strength left to continue. Did continue, she knew not how long. Time had no meaning in a grave. She kept going and at some point the earth changed, loosened, became drier, less like clay, more crumbly. With a burst of energy she felt might be her last she began to claw her way up, faster, her legs scissoring beneath her as if she were swimming. Until there was a lighter type of darkness.

Until Lara burst from her grave.

She lay on the surface, sobbing. It took her a while to notice anything other than that she was free. Gradually, her senses returned. She felt the cold of lying on the wet earth, made wetter and colder by the rain that fell. She was still clothed in what she'd worn for the ceremony, a light dress that gave little protection. Though it was deep night, she could see where she was by torches mounted in small guard turrets on a tall wall about sixty paces away – the land wall of Corinthium. So she was lying on ground outside the city. She did not know who had taken her there, or why. Whether it was the cult itself, getting rid of its failures, or the authorities ridding the city of heretics and criminals. She was both, now. She was also alive – and that was the greatest puzzle of all.

She sat up, touched her throat. The last thing she remembered from the ceremony was the dagger being slashed down … by Roxanna, the immortal, who had somehow taken the place of Lara's friend, Carellia. She remembered the eyes glittering in triumph beneath the mask, just before the agony of steel opening her throat, and the death that followed it. Yet she had not died – and the skin that she touched now was not a gaping wound, but one that was … healing.

Lara's eyes shot wide open. She brought both hands up to her mouth and gasped. Everything else – the cold rain, the taste of earth in her mouth, her ceaseless shuddering – all disappeared, shoved aside by the power of a new truth.

She was immortal! The suicide cult, that had produced only three immortals since the founding of the city, had now produced a fourth.

Her.

It was wonderful. It was terrible. Her life was over. And she would live for ever.

When her racking sobs finally ceased, she became aware that, immortal or not, she was cold, starving, exhausted. She needed shelter, water, food.

There were lighted windows facing the city walls; people who could not squeeze their way into Corinthium but wanted to live close to it had set up clusters of shacks. Forcing herself to her feet, Lara staggered towards the mortals.

Four days later ...

'Tomko?'

Lara turned to the man who'd called. 'Sir?'

The head groom, Petros, threw her a curry comb. 'Give Serrana a good going over.' He leaned and spat into a pile of straw. 'It's the fucking queen who's riding 'er, so you better make her fucking beautiful, or you'll fucking catch it.'

'Sir,' Lara said again, and went to the stall where the tawpan mare waited. Gentling her with clicks in the throat, she slipped a bridle over her head and led her out into the yard and over into a patch of sunlight. The rains had finally ceased, and a winter sun returned. Sheltered by its walls from the chill easterly winds, the sunny side of the yard was almost hot. Though Lara had found that, having experienced the coldness of a grave, nothing kept her warm for long.

Exercise helped, and she went hard at Serrana's long and luxuriant coat. The mare loved it, while Lara had always loved horses and the care of them. For the first few moments of the combing, she could lose herself in the scent and the feel. Imagine herself back in Balbek, preparing her own mare, Saipha, for a morning ride. Think of herself as she'd been, when she'd been both mortal and happy. When she'd had only one purpose – to be with and to please her man. Before her purpose had become to kill the woman who had stolen that man and had tried to kill her ... no, had *succeeded* in killing her. The mortal her.

The thought made her cease combing and Serrana's eyelashes unfolded, her look plainly saying *don't stop*. She began again, though less vigorously than before. She was distracted, first by her thoughts – and then by the open window above her. For through it she now heard voices – one of which was his.

Ferros.

She'd first heard it the day before, soon after she'd bluffed her way into the stables of the Sanctum by the luck of claiming and calming a runaway horse which had escaped from the yard, and dashed past her shortly after she'd taken up position on the street outside its gates. She'd recognised fortune's touch, and seized it, throwing herself across the horse bareback when it slowed near a broken wagon, calming it with gentle touches of the bridle, her thigh, her soft words. Petros, the head groom, had been impressed with 'the lad', Tomko – for Lara had borrowed boy's clothing from the first people who'd sheltered her outside Corinthium's walls, and decided it was safer to remain as one. When she'd told him she was an orphan looking for a job, and had nowhere to live, he'd taken pity on her, taken her on, and in. For all his gruffness and foul language he was a kind man, who'd lost his own young son to the sea three years before.

When she'd first heard Ferros in that room above, she'd yearned to run straight into his arms. For he was weeping, something she'd not witnessed in her tough soldier in their five years together. Laughter always, tears never. And she knew, because she could hear her name cried out, that he wept for her, for her death, knew she could take that misery away by going to him and saying, 'I live, love. More. I live, like you, for ever.' But as she'd tried to figure out a way from the stables up into that room, into his arms, she'd heard *her* voice, 'the fucking queen's' as Petros had just called her. Heard her *comforting*, sensed her *taking* Ferros into her arms, holding him, consoling him. Loving him. The immortal who'd killed her. The immortal who she'd vowed to kill.

So she'd stopped herself. For one, she knew that she was not a killer, did not know the way of it. Not yet. While she had directly experienced that Roxanna was gifted in those skills. But even more limiting than that was her ignorance of immortality. How could she kill someone who could not die? Who would be born again, even as she herself had been born again, birthed from a grave? Who had also instantly taken the place of her friend in the suicide ceremony by some act of dark magic? Roxanna was more than an immortal. She was a witch. So Lara had taken a breath, returned to her duties, swallowed her yearning. For now. She needed to free herself from ignorance before she acted. How, she did not know. But she assumed that since Simbala had chosen her – for Lara now believed in the gods as she never truly had before – that the goddess would continue to place opportunities before her, just as she had with the runaway horse.

Besides – and this was also a true and real thing – Ferros had betrayed her with this fucking queen. She knew, she could sense it, she could smell his betrayal through the window, its scent in her nostrils stronger than the mare's that she combed.

It was no longer a question of taking him back. It was not simply about revenge. He must earn his right to be with her with more than his tears, prove that it was her that he chose, above any other. Vengeance needed to wait for that. Wait for opportunity and a further blessing of the goddess.

Which came, even on the thought – on the opening of the door from the palace into the yard. Came on a voice she recognised, the first voice she and Ferros had heard in the city when they'd stepped onto the dock from the ship that had brought them from Balbek, six weeks before.

'Petros? Petros?' The voice of a man, high-pitched. 'They have closed the Heaven Road for winds. And I must be in Sevrapol in two hours.'

'A palanquin, Lord Streone?' enquired Petros, emerging from the stables, rubbing his hands on a cloth.

'Of course! Immediately. And your twelve strongest bearers. None of those limping dullards you fobbed me off with last week.'

Lara looked at the man, remembered him, though she and Ferros had not been sure that he was 'him' at all, such was the amount of make-up he'd worn, his high voice, and the multicoloured fabrics that had swathed his vast body. Later Ferros had told her, in their room above the tavern, that Streone was indeed a man, a famous actor, poet and singer and something more than that: the Innovator of the Great Spectacles, producer of the huge celebrations, or pageants, staged throughout the year, but especially at last week's feast of Simbala.

Then Ferros had told her something else – that Streone was also one of the immortal elite. So she realised, as she continued making the mare's coat glossy and smooth while the palanquin was readied, that Streone would have all the knowledge she required. All she had to do was find a way to make him tell her ... everything.

When his vehicle was ready, Streone slipped into its cushioned, silk-walled interior, and twelve hefty men, three on each corner pole, bent and lifted. As it was carried from the yard, Lara led Serrana back to her stall. Petros would want her to ready the mare for riding. But he would just have to do that himself.

Quietly, Lara slipped through the gates.

It was easy enough to hang back and follow the palanquin. Though the streets were quiet on Agueros, the highest hill of the city, because only immortals and those who tended them lived upon it, each hill below got ever more crowded. The main street that was the spine of the city, the Stradun, was three palanquins wide, and well paved. She'd heard that ancient regulations demanded that it be kept clear, for the rapid movement of the elites through Corinthium. But if those laws had ever been observed it was a long time past. As more and more people came to live in the city, all space was colonised. Market stalls were set up before almost every shop front and people milled before them, while carts and wagons brought goods to service them. All traffic slowed and often blocked the way. The red banner at the crown of the vehicle's silk roof was meant to guarantee swift passage. But people found ways of ignoring it until they were forced aside by bellows from the palanquin's leader at the head of the left pole, or by blows from the baton he carried. It was why, one hundred years before, the elites had created the Heaven Road. They could cruise above the people, and mock them from on high.

Lara followed close, concealment unnecessary. She was just another street kid, an orphan of the city, of which there were many. Though if they knew who she was ... she'd heard her name called out many times at crossroads in the three days since her resurrection. The suicide cults were ruthlessly persecuted, and the names of any of those who'd killed themselves proclaimed and reviled. Leaders of the group had been executed and their bodies hung by their heels, dripping blood, on government office walls. She'd wondered if her friend, Carellia the whore, was one of them. Except it wasn't Carellia who had slit her throat, it was Roxanna. This Lara knew. It was something she would never forget – the eyes glittering triumphant beneath the mask as the dagger slashed down. For now that memory was only horror. To make it something else she needed answers. Answers that could be provided by the man in the palanquin.

It took almost two hours to reach their destination, the fourth hill of Corinthium and so about the midpoint between Agueros and the harbour. Because of its centrality, Sevrapol had become known for entertainment, and people would come from all over the city to partake in its delights, which ranged from the classical plays that were performed in the elegant theatres that lined this part of the Stradun – no stalls before their gilded entranceways – to less refined activities in the alleys that wound off on every side. In those every appetite was catered for – taverns, ox-roast halls, cockpits and dog pits for the fighting of those creatures and the wagering upon them. Bawdy ballads were sung, and clothes stripped slowly off, in houses beside brothels. Everywhere wine and ale flowed, with men and women shouting their competing wares, luring fresh customers. She and Ferros had walked up there once in their first week in the city and clung to each other, wide-eyed provincial folk stunned by the sensual assault of the place.

But that was then – and this is now, thought Lara, stepping into a shuttered shop's doorway, as the palanquin halted before one of those marble-columned theatre fronts and was finally set down. Now she was not intimidated at all by the noise and the hustle. Dying will do that to you, she thought, chewing her lower lip.

She couldn't hear what Streone said to the head poleman.

Wait, she assumed, as the bearers all bowed then moved away in twos and threes in search of refreshment. Streone went off alone – not, she was surprised to see, into the plush theatre. Instead, he pulled his scarf in front of his face, a hood over his head, and entered one of the alleys.

She hurried to catch up, saw him as he turned the first corner ahead. She hadn't noticed before, in her one swift glance in the stable yard, but the Great Innovator was not dressed in the peacock finery of their very first encounter. When she and Ferros had met him on the docks, they'd had that doubt as to his gender. There was no question he was a man here, shod in sturdy boots and with a rough-woven cloak covering basic breeches and jacket. When she'd caught up, was just five paces behind him, he turned. Before she stepped into a doorway she saw that he also sported none of the face paint he'd worn then.

Just as well for him, she thought, as she noted the alley's inhabitants. The deeper into Sevrapol they got, the narrower the way became; the darker too, with house roofs almost conjoined above, blocking out the sky. Hard-faced men watched her a little longer as she passed, gauging. Cries came from open doorways. Some were faked pleasure, some fear, some drunken laughter. She avoided the eyes of the men that stared at her, clutched the dagger at her waist a little harder. Prayed that she would not be forced to use it, since she did not truly know how.

Streone halted before a plain brown door and looked each way up the alley before knocking. What are you about, she wondered, as she shifted to the other side of the alley so she could see both man and door. A hatch opened in it, she glimpsed a mouth, shaping words. Streone murmured a reply, the door opened, and he slipped inside.

Lara crossed the alley, pressed the door. It was locked. She didn't knock – Streone must have spoken some kind of password that she couldn't know. But she also couldn't stay where she was and wait for him. She'd noticed one man in a doorway further down, with the sallow complexion of a drinker and hunger in eyes that he kept on her. As he moved towards her, she slipped into another alley to her right, even darker than the one she'd left. Its wall was part of the same house that Streone had gone into and it ran down to yet another alley that had to be the house's rear. She took it, even as she heard footsteps behind her, praying that it wasn't a dead end, that she wouldn't be trapped.

It was ... but she wasn't. There was a heap of broken furniture and wooden crates against the wall, beneath a window ledge. Without even considering it, she scrambled up the pile, stretched, leaped. Her fingers gripped the ledge, as the pile gave way. But she held on, pulled herself up and through the window which, miraculously, was open. She saw that she was in a bedroom, unoccupied, but lamplit and reeking of cheap scent. As she lowered herself to the floor she heard a slurred curse through the open window.

She waited. In the alley, the man muttered, moved away. Ahead, the door of the bedroom was ajar, and through it she heard voices. One was high-pitched. She recognised it. So, creeping forward, she put her hand to the door frame and listened.

'All is ready?' Streone asked.

The voice that answered was deeper, gentle; a man, well spoken. 'All, Lord Streone.'

'And has he ...' there was a hesitation. 'Has he said anything to you about what ... about what must be done now?'

'Nothing, lord. Why would he speak to me? It's you he wants.'

This was not said gently. Streone coughed. 'Very well,' he said more firmly. 'Leave me. Wait elsewhere. I will begin.'

'Lord.'

Someone came out of the room on the floor below. Lara

slipped back into the shadows behind the door, looking about for a place to hide in case this was the man's destination. But she heard him go the other way. When another door closed somewhere below, she stepped out, and softly descended the stairs to the lower landing.

There were two doors there, one fully open and giving onto another scented bedroom, also empty and draped, like the one above, in gaudy silks, with a basin and jug on a stand. Though she had never been in one she had a sense that she was standing in a brothel. The second door was old, with frayed wood and peeling paint. The man who'd left had pulled it closed but, warped as it was, it had not fully shut.

She bent to listen at the gap, heard Streone sigh deeply. Something came into her nostrils, an acrid smoke that made her gag.

Though her every instinct made her want to turn away, she knew she could not. Answers lay within the room. Slowly, she pushed the door open enough to thrust her head in.

Streone was sitting in one corner, facing into it and partly away from her. Before him, on a stand that in the other room would have held a jug and basin, Lara could see a glass globe the size of a small watermelon. Smoke swirled within it, smoke which, even as she watched, cleared – and a man's head appeared. A man with a beard, long hair, deep-set eyes. She raised her hand to her mouth to contain her gasp – what witchcraft was this? – as the man within the smoke spoke.

'Streone,' he said.

'Makron.'

'All is well?'

'All is not well.' Streone's voice rose higher in complaint. 'I do not like this place you force me to come to. It is,' he shuddered, 'filthy.'

'I told you before – a globe must never be used in the Sanctum.

Lucan has too many eyes and ears there. He must never know we can talk like this.'

'But you also promised that if I came here, today there would be more ... more of this.' Streone picked up a glass vial, turned it upside down. 'But this is the last of it.'

'I sent more. But my first vessel was attacked by the pirates of Omersh and had to turn back to Cuerdocia.' Full, sensual lips shaped a smile. 'I cannot control pirates, Streone.'

'Nevertheless—'

'More is on the way. I have sent it in three separate ships. Perhaps all will arrive at once and you will have ... plenty.' As Streone went to complain again, the man barked, 'Enough!' and then continued, 'Now tell me of the Sanctum.'

Lara shifted slightly, so she could see more of Streone's face as well as the other man's. There was something hypnotic about that other. He lulled her. She accepted what was plainly dark magic: a man speaking within a globe of smoke. She also knew she would never want to look into that man's eyes for long.

'Someone has come. A new-birthed immortal. Lucan and his daughter are very excited by him. They say he is special. To me he seems just another rough soldier—'

'The cavalryman of Balbek? I have heard of him. Why are they so excited?'

'They think he is the one foretold.'

'Foretold to do what?'

Streone cleared his throat. 'Uh hum. To deal with you, Makron.'

'*Deal* with me?' The man laughed. 'He would have to be very special indeed.' He nodded. 'What else?'

'He came with a wife.' Lara leaned closer as Streone continued, 'But she joined a suicide cult.'

Makron frowned. 'That seems strange. Besides, I thought they were long suppressed.'

'They were. But they spring up. The ceremony was discovered, all participants killed—'

'Wait!' The man in the globe stared above Streone, raised a hand, rubbed either side of his beard. 'Roxanna did this.'

'What do you mean?'

'There are no coincidences. Roxanna would have wished to get rid of this wife. She only knows one way of controlling a man. Seducing him. Bewitching him. A rival would prevent that.'

'As you would know, lord.'

The sunken gaze returned to Streone. No trace of a smile now. 'As I would know.' He nodded, then continued, 'So this girl is out of the way. What next?'

'They are letting the soldier mourn for a week. And then he and Roxanna are sailing for Cuerdocia.'

'To deal with me.' It wasn't a question and Streone simply nodded. 'I need you to delay them. My work here is not yet complete. I have one tribe yet to bring to our side. It will take a little time more.'

'How would you advise I delay them? They are far more powerful than I.'

'Oh come, Streone.' Makron laughed. 'You may be soft and foolish as yourself. But you have the ability to possess, as we all do. You'll simply have to possess someone … *stronger* to do your bidding.'

'I can do that, yes.' Streone shook his head. 'But someone as strong as Lucan? As Roxanna?'

'No. But you will have surprise on your side. They will not be expecting it … from you.' He looked suddenly to the side. He nodded, turned back and his eyes narrowed. 'Do it. Delay them. One of my ships will arrive within two weeks – with Sirene. The next time we meet, I expect a report of your triumphs.'

'Lord, wait, I—'

But Makron didn't wait. Smoke swirled in the globe, and the face was gone. Streone slumped back. He lifted the glass vial he still held, tipped it again. Nothing came from it. He sniffed at it, sighed, corked it and threw it into the satchel at his waist.

Lara didn't understand much of what had passed between the two men. She did not understand *how* it had passed. But then, everything she'd understood of the world had changed from the moment she'd woken up in her grave.

She had been awed by the city, by its inhabitants; been hesitant in her dealings with them in a way she never would have been back home in Balbek. No more. She needed to understand, now. Right now. The man rising from his chair would help her do that.

'Streone,' she said.

He yelped, staggered back, banging into the stand, which tipped. With another cry he grabbed the globe, just before it fell. 'You fool!' he shouted. 'Look what you nearly made me do!' He replaced the globe on the stand, turned back. 'I told Severos that I would call when I was done. Why did he send you?'

'No one sent me. I came by myself.'

'What are you talking about, boy?' Streone leaned closer, his expression puzzled. 'Do I know you?'

'We've met.'

'Met? Met where?' He peered at Lara. 'No, I don't know you.' He frowned. 'But did you ... how long were you standing there?'

'Long enough.'

'You mean you saw ... ?' Frown turned to fury. 'You interfering little fool. You are going to have to answer some questions now.'

He stepped forward, his big hands reaching. Lara stepped back. 'I'll answer yours,' she said, drawing her dagger, 'if you answer mine.'

Streone looked down, focusing on the blade. Then he looked

up. 'Oh, young man, you don't know what you have done. And Makron did say I would need to start using the gift again to do his bidding. May as well start with you.'

'What gift?' she said.

He took a step backwards, laughed. 'Come here, you,' he said, opening his arms wide.

Streone did not move, remained on the other side of the room. And yet Lara felt as if he'd rushed across and ... *crashed* into her. She felt as if his whole bulk had hit her, and she reeled back into the wall as if struck. But there was something else too, in his touch of her. He had touched the *whole* of her. Inside and out. Tried to penetrate her, occupy her ...

... *possess* her.

It was what the man in the smoke had said, one of the many things she had not understood. She understood it now, all of it. The one touch had told her, not in her mind, far deeper than that – in her whole being. Now she knew why Carellia had become Roxanna – or rather, how. How Roxanna had taken the old whore over to do her bidding.

Possession. It was an ability. Like the healing of all wounds, birth after death. Yet not only did she understand it, she understood in that same ferocious moment of total contact that she could do it, use it. Become anyone she chose. For a time. She would not know for how long until she tried. Something in that first touch told her it could not last long. But while it lasted it would be ... extraordinary.

All this she understood in seconds, those few while she looked across the room at Streone. He had not moved, was still across the room. Though the fury on his face had changed to shock. 'But you're ... you're ... immortal too! You have to be, or I'd be in you now.'

She raised her hands, the one with the dagger, the one without. Looked at them in wonder. 'I really am.'

'Wait! I do know you,' he gasped. 'You are … the suicide!' He broke off. 'It's impossible. And yet?' He shook his head, and his voice deepened. 'You'll come with me. You'll come with me to the Sanctum. Right now.'

It wasn't that he shouted this last that made her know she wouldn't. She knew that already. She might have learned, in an instant, the secret power, the true power of immortality. But the woman who'd killed her was in the Sanctum. And Roxanna had three hundred years' experience of this … wonder. Lara was not ready to face her, not yet.

'No,' she said.

'You will come!' He began screaming, 'Severos! Severos! Quickly! Bring rope.'

Lara turned to flee. Streone, for a big man, moved fast across the room. 'No, you don't,' he cried, seizing her shoulder. 'You'll stay here.'

Lara whipped back. 'What?' Streone said, his eyes widening.

Lara stepped away. Both looked down – at the dagger sticking from his chest. 'Fool,' he moaned, as he sank to the floor.

There were raised voices below, boots on the stairs. Lara ran out and up, back into the bedroom she'd first entered. Was out the window, lowering herself from its ledge, even as men came shouting into the room.

She dropped, ran down the alleys and then into the crowds on the Stradun. If any pursued her, they would not find her now.

She walked, with no destination. She was not sure what to do next. A decision would arrive when it must, she felt. For now, she was content to sit with what she'd discovered, the astonishing things that she had learned. The first: that she could kill, if she needed to. Even if Streone would be reborn soon enough, she had not considered that when she put her knife into his heart.

The second was this astounding ability, as astounding as immortality itself. That she would also need to sit with for a while. Then, as with her destination, she would decide what she would do.

Four weeks later ... in the caves of Cuerdocia

'Rise, my love. Rise and fight.'

Ferros looked up at her. She looked down at him, in the moment before she bent and snatched up dead Gandalos's sword. For more enemies had burst into the cave and she turned to take them on.

'Lara?'

But there was no time to do anything other than gasp her name. Not with five more men there, bent on their deaths. He rose just as Lara lunged, driving her sword straight at the leading man's belly. He parried it, yelping, swinging his own sword down hard, staggering back, his body penning the others for a moment in the narrow tunnel entrance. A moment Ferros seized, grabbing a dropped shield by its centre strap, slamming it into the staggering man's chest, knocking him further backwards into the men who followed him. They were a tangle of limbs and blades, he, Lara, and the two other soldiers, a rising whirl of steel. It took only moments, and then there was just them, with the dying and the dead adding to the flesh pile before the inner cave's entrance.

Then others were with them, ten of his soldiers rushing forward, these with javelins and shields, snapping into a wall of leather and metal. No enemy now came and, seeing the pause, Ferros seized Lara's arm, pulled her back towards the cave-mouth, then out.

The clouds had cleared, the rains had gone, and in the two moons' light – waxing Horned Saipha, waning Blue Revlas – he

25

could at last see her clearly. Yet seeing did not help him believe.

He reached a hand, laid fingers on her cheek, as if touch could make her real. 'How? How?'

'You can guess the how.'

'So you ... you ...' He shook his head. 'You did not die.'

'I did. As you did. Then I was reborn. As you were.'

'Oh, my love!' He grabbed her then, pulled her tight into his chest. 'I thought I'd lost you. I mourned—'

'I know.' She pulled away so she could see his eyes. 'I watched you in the temples, crying out my name. Before you boarded the ship.'

'You ... watched me? You were there? Then why did you not—' Confusion furrowed his brow. 'You saw my pain. I thought you were gone for ever. Worse, that I had caused you to die.' His voice rose. 'Why did you not come to me then?'

'Why? You know why.' She stepped from the shelter of his arms. 'Because of who was with you. Because of ... *her*.'

'Roxanna?' He swallowed. 'She gave me sympathy ...'

'Oh, is that what she gave you?'

'Lara, I—' He raised a hand to her in supplication, then let it fall. 'I thought you were dead.'

'Not when you first fucked her, you didn't.'

He winced at the hard edge of her voice. 'It's true, I was ... bewitched.'

'Of course. Poor boy. You couldn't help yourself. It wasn't your fault.'

The savagery in her tone made him step away. 'You weren't there. You can't know,' he said, lowering his eyes.

'I wasn't there.' She sought his eyes. 'And neither was she.'

His gaze jerked up to her. 'What do you mean?'

'After you did ... whatever you did ... she came to the suicide ceremony. She ... took over the priestess.' She ran her tongue over her lips. 'It was Roxanna who killed me.'

26

He stepped away. 'No. I do not believe it. How would she do that?'

'You know how. It comes with immortality. The ... *bonus*.' Lara spat the word. 'Like I just did with Gandalos.'

'Gandalos?' Ferros looked back into the cave. 'You possessed him. Used him.'

'As if you haven't done it already.'

His gaze sharpened. 'I have not. Why would I? It is barbaric.'

'You haven't? Truly?' She shook her head. 'But, Ferros, it is not barbaric. Well, it is. But it is also ... *wonderful*.'

Ferros started to reply – and then shouts distracted him. Both from the caves, where the clash of steel on steel could again be heard. And on the plain ahead, where cavalrymen were galloping hard towards them. It was the twenty who'd led the Assani away, while Ferros and his men had chased the prophet, Smoke, into the mountain. He'd lost a few in there – Gandalos was one. But with the fifteen who'd survived, he had thirty-five men now – all Wattenwolden too, hardened fighters from the northern forests of the empire. Enough to hold the narrow entrance behind him for a time – long enough, he hoped, for Roxanna to return from Tarfona, bringing its garrison to help him prevent the invasion he'd seen was coming.

The troop's sergeant was at the head of the column that reined in. 'Straight in,' Ferros called, pointing at the cave. 'Javelins and shields.'

The men obeyed, dismounted, rushed in. It would be tight for that many men in the cave; none of the enemy would be able to force their way past. For now. He turned back to Lara, hesitated. What could he say to her? What to ask, how to explain? 'Lara,' he began.

'This is not the time, Ferros. There are too many things between us now. I will rest for a while, and then I will join you in the fight.'

'As ...' He looked at the three men the troop had left to tether the horses. 'You will not—'

She followed his gaze. 'I will not. Gandalos was an exception, to stay close to you. I only ... *possess* enemies, unless my need is very great. As it was to get on a boat to follow you to this land. And you would know, if you were not so afraid, that possession is hard on the body. It cannot be done time after time.'

Afraid? It was not a word his old Lara would have used of him. And it was another thing he could not deal with now. 'Rest. I would prefer it if you did not fight. There is no need – in there, we have enough.'

He turned to go – and she took his arm, delaying him. 'Know this, Ferros. When she returns, I will be ... someone else, for a time. I do not want her to know me. Not yet. I still do not know what I am going to do. And you must swear to me that you will not tell her.'

Another realm of questions opened before him. None could be asked now. 'I swear it. And now I must go. We will talk later.'

He turned and ran into the cave. Lara staggered, and placed her hand against the rock face. It did cost one, possession, the coming and the going of it. But her weakness was more than that. Suddenly being with him again, the man who'd been her everything for so long. Being with him, and being so furious with him. She was different, in every possible way. And that included her love for him. It was there, but it was different too. In what lay ahead, she would have to discover just how different.

There was a sudden loud increase of noise, funnelling out from the cave as if it were a mouth. Men with swords, she thought, pulling her own weapon from its scabbard. Noting the blood staining its shiny planes.

I can be one of those.

2

The Vision

It was a week before Luck was summoned again. He thought that strange. That the leader of the monks – Anazat was his name, Luck had discovered – had not wanted to interrogate him further and immediately. Until he realised that what the monk had told him when he first arrived was true: he was not there as a prisoner, but as an 'honoured guest'. They'd declared a truce, and neither would break it until both did.

He tested it, of course he did. First, he slept for a day and a night. On the second morning he'd woken ravenous. Fresh food – cured meats, cheese, bread, fruits, most of which were new to him – awaited on a table, along with a jug of juice and another filled with clear mountain water. Hot water had been poured into a trough with walls that came to his mid-thigh so he stripped, used cloths and the scented contents of a small glass bottle to wash and rinse himself, finally ridding himself of a stench that was near as bad as that of the hibernating bear he'd woken and possessed on the other side of the mountain. He did not wish to put his old clothes back on for the same reason – then saw that he did not need to, for someone had hung a robe on the back of the door. It was cut like the one he'd seen Anazat and his acolytes wear, of soft wool – though when he slipped it on, he discovered it was lined in linen. It was the

29

most comfortable thing he'd ever worn. It fitted him perfectly, as did the deerskin, fleece-lined shoes he also found. The right one had an extra sole, because his right leg was shorter than the left. It was clear that while he slept he had been carefully studied.

I will study in my turn, and test the bounds of this ... liberty, he thought. Just because a cage does not have bars, does not mean it is not a cage.

Yet seek as he might, he could not find any bars. He explored the fortress – or 'the Keep', as its residents called it. Wandered from the huge kitchens in the depths, to the eyries in the tops of the guard towers. There were people everywhere – monks in cowls, cooks and servants, armed sentries – all were similar, most of what would have been mid-height in Midgarth. All had dark hair – the little of it that he could see, for all had their heads shaved, save for a small circle of black about the crown. None of them challenged him, nor asked his purpose there. Answered any questions he asked – if they could, for most could not speak his language. Though even these conveyed to him the same simple answer from servant to soldier – each had been called, to worship, and to serve.

The question of what, or whom exactly, he would save for Anazat.

Still, that summons did not come. On his second day of exploration, one monk revealed that the head monk was not even there, had gone out into the world to deal with matters of 'high import'. So Luck, wondering what orders had been left, tested the cage still further – by walking through the Keep's main gate, descending a little way down the switchbacked road that led to the valley far below. Got three hundred paces to realise that no one followed him, or sought to bring him back.

He was ... free. Which irked him, once he'd accepted it. For Anazat knew he wasn't going anywhere. Anazat had set a hook with exactly the bait this 'fish' would eagerly seize: the promise of knowledge. Had rightly guessed that Luck had always craved that. So when he returned to the castle, he arranged for an elderly monk, Perakach, to start to teach him this 'writing' that Anazat had showed him when he'd first arrived. Symbols on a page that others could read and interpret? He'd recognised the power in it immediately. And speaking the written words aloud, gently corrected in pronunciation by his tutor, he began on that first day and the ones that followed to learn to speak the language of the place too. The language's name was *tolanpa-sen* – which meant 'the one word'. He'd learned there were other peoples in this world, this vast world. Four 'tribes', Perakach told him. *Tolanpa-sen* was the common tongue they used to speak to each other.

In only one thing was he restricted. This he discovered on the fourth morning when, after long hours spent deciphering written words, and saying them, in Perakach's cell, he decided to visit the stables again. He had always liked horses and was amazed by the contrast between the small, shaggy-coated ones he knew in Midgarth and the huge, sleek beasts most rode in Saghaz-a. He indicated to a groom that he would like to take one for a ride. Again he was not denied – so he went back to his cell, to put on his old breeches and doublet, clothes which were better suited for a ride than a robe. They'd been taken the day before, cleaned, patched and returned, and now hung from hooks, above something new – all the belongings he'd brought from Midgarth.

Someone had found his boat-sled in the woods. The vessel itself was not there but everything else was – his cooking pot, the knife Hovard had given him, his short axe, his one change of clothes – even his slingshot with its bag of smoothed killing stones. But what held his gaze was the seeing globe, that he'd taken from the assassin back in Midgarth. Smoke swirled within it. Only one thing was missing, as he discovered while conducting an ever more frantic search – the vial of the liquid drug that he would pour upon the glass to see. To travel.

He felt instant hunger. Truly it had never fully gone away since that first time, a nag always at the edge of his mind. He'd tried to ignore it, resist its lure. Now, seeing the globe without the means to use it, he wanted to, suddenly, immediately.

So he would.

He leaned into the corridor. 'Anyone there?'

Though he never had any sense of being followed, someone somehow was always within earshot. 'Sir?' came the reply and, a moment later, a young man appeared, a cleaning cloth in hand. All who'd been assigned to his care did speak some of his language. It was one of the duties for those who lived at the Keep, he'd discovered – to learn the tongues of other lands.

'I want something,' Luck said.

'Anything, sir.'

'Bring me a vial of Sirene.'

The young man's eyebrows – plucked to the thinnest of lines to match the circlet of hair about his crown – shot high. 'Is not … possible.'

'But you just said anything.'

'I … you wait, please.' The young man bobbed a bow, then ran back along the corridor and disappeared down the stairs.

Luck went back into his cell, lay down for a moment, couldn't stay prone, rose, went to the window. Both above and below him, swallows dived, swooping into the eaves, small sticks in their beaks. I'd like to soar again, Luck thought, but in a different way.

'Sir?'

It was a deeper, lower voice that turned him to the cell's entrance. A big man stood there, one he'd never seen before; older, the hair that circled his crown entirely grey. 'You need something?'

This man spoke Luck's language almost as well as Anazat, with a light accent. Luck gestured to the globe he'd placed on the small table. 'Yes. Bring me Sirene, please.'

'That is not possible.'

'I thought anything was possible. For me.' Luck took a step forward, aware that his voice had risen slightly in pitch. He felt anxious, feared denial. Centred his voice before he spoke again. 'Did Anazat not tell you to give me everything I desire? I desire this.'

'I like to help,' the man said, coming further in, hands raised in a gesture of calm. 'In this, I cannot.'

'Will not!'

'Cannot,' the man repeated. 'Sirene is locked away. Only Anazat has key. He is not here.'

'You're lying!' Luck could not help his shout. 'Anazat wants me to do this!'

'Sir, please.' The monk stepped nearer. 'Sirene is not to be approached casually. Especially by someone who is … inexperienced with her. She is not … controllable. She will—' He broke off. 'You need a guide.'

'I don't want a guide.' He looked up into the man's eyes, his voice dropping to a growl. 'And I *wish* to lose control.'

'Trust me,' the man laid his hand on Luck's arm, 'you do not.'

Luck was about to throw the man's arm off, to shout more, demand. But this close to him, he noticed something he hadn't before – his eyes, if not fully black, were shaded in it, muddying the whites there. This man had … experienced Sirene too. And Luck saw things in his eyes that he knew were a mirror for his own – craving, yes. But sadness too. Deep, unquenchable sadness. He stepped back. 'What is your name?' he asked, more quietly.

The man bowed. 'Toparak.'

'You know of what you speak, don't you?'

'I ... know.'

There was an infinity of sadness in the pause between words. It calmed Luck, suddenly. The craving did not leave him entirely but it loosed its tight hold on him. For he recognised, from his brief experiences with her so far, that sadness would be part of any encounter he had with Sirene.

The man noted the calming, and his tension eased too. 'Anazat returns tomorrow. Then, I think, you will ... *voyage* again.'

Again, there were other things in the pause. Envy perhaps. Sadness. Luck nodded. 'Very well.'

The man straightened, stepped back. 'Is there anything else I can do for you, sir?'

'Yes. You can tell me if you ride.'

'Ride?' For the first time the man smiled, and some of his pain left him. 'I was born on a horse. I come from the Sea of Grass, where the horse is life. But I haven't ridden in ... a long time.'

'Neither have I,' said Luck. 'Join me, and show me some of the world beyond these walls.'

'I will.'

Toparak was a good guide – in everything. The tack required to control the large horses of Saghaz-a was quite different from the simple harness that Luck used in Midgarth, and he altered it further to suit his weaknesses at leg and shoulder. The horse was different too, and though he mounted a grey gelding, while Toparak took a black stallion, Luck's horse was still far livelier than anything he'd ridden back home. Yet he had done more than simply ride, of course. He had possessed horses, a score of times over the centuries. Knew them in a way no mortal rider, however gifted, ever could. And though there were differences of temperament, a horse's desires, unlike a man's, were usually fairly clear: do what must be done, before getting back to a warm stable, and hay.

Toparak, who indeed looked like someone who'd ridden before he walked, having given a few simple tips, was impressed. 'You can sit a horse, sir,' he said, running his tongue over his lips. 'But can you race one?'

Challenge given, accepted. Neither man had spurs, neither needed them, a tap of heels, an easing of reins, a cry of 'Yah!' and the two were off, side by side down a forest trail that ran from a side gate of the Keep. There were dead-fall trunks to jump, avenues of melting snow to skid along.

They left the forest, riding hard along a track that took them ever higher up the mountain. They reined in at last on a shelf of stone that jutted out over the valley, now far, far below them. It was an even better view of the world than back at the fortress. The spring sun was upon the land. In the distance to his left, he could see men in the bell tower, the rest of the Keep hidden by folds of land. In the clear air he could pick out clefts and fissures in the far distant range of mountains opposite the one on which they sat their horses, as well as other features of the valley below. A wide river flowed through it between vast fields, all bordered in stone walls. Ploughmen moved oxen across some, while large herds of cattle stood on others of verdant green. Luck whistled as he leaned forward to pat his mount's neck. It was so different from Midgarth, where forests and rocky scapes covered most of the land, and such soil as existed was hard to work. 'It is rich, your land. Bountiful.'

'Now it is,' replied Toparak, 'but if you had sat your horse at this place but thirty years ago, you would have seen only ruin.'

'Anazat told me a little of that when I first arrived,' said Luck. 'Tell me more.'

The other man turned to him. Into his eyes, that had been sparkling with the pleasure of the ride, came that sorrow Luck had noticed before. Along with something else. It took him only a moment to recognise it, because he saw it sometimes when he gazed into the seeing waters at himself.

It was shame.

Toparak spoke again. 'That time I never think about. That time never leaves me, especially in sleep.'

'You suffered?'

'Yes, but that is not what haunts me. What does is the suffering I caused.' He looked to the south, past Luck, who kept his own gaze on the man's eyes, for he could always read truths there. 'If you rode hard for three weeks, these two mountain ranges would sink into a vast plain – the Sea of Grass.'

'You told me you were born there.'

'I was. In my language my people are called *taramazak*. The nearest in your words would be ...' He looked above Luck for a moment. '"Those who hunt from the horse".'

'What do you hunt?'

'For centuries we hunted the ...' He paused. 'I do not know a word for this animal in your tongue. Maybe you do not have it. It is like bull and cow, but much bigger, faster. With big horns and a thick coat. We call it *azama-klosh*. It moves in herds so vast they make the world thunder.' He shook his head. 'At least, it did once, so I am told.'

Luck considered this. There was indeed no beast in Midgarth that sounded like it. 'Once?'

'By the time I was born, the great herds were already past. They were smaller – yet we hunted them still as we always had, because it was all the *taramazak* knew. And then they became smaller still. Some of my people wanted to stop, to tame the beasts, breed them. But most wanted the old ways to stay, the wandering ways, and if we could not find what we needed on the Sea of Grass, we would look for it elsewhere.' He waved his hand over the land below. 'Here.' He nodded. 'The raids began

36

in the time of my grandfathers. I came here for the first time forty years ago. When I had thirteen summers.'

Luck was still watching the man closely. Saw that shame again replace the sorrow. 'It was the first time you killed a man, wasn't it?'

Toparak looked at him. 'Man. Woman. Child. And killing was only one thing I learned.' He shrugged, then turned away again. 'But by the time I came the people here had learned how to fight us. They had united under the priests in these mountains. Under the women warriors who live upon those.' He nodded across the valley. 'And along the river you see here, came ships from the north, filled with the strangest warriors of all. They were ... *bought* by the people we'd sought to subdue. And they did not stop once they'd stopped us here. In the time of my father's youth, they sailed south to our lands, into the Sea of Grass, and burned all they could not steal.'

'Anazat calls them the Seafarers.'

'That is the name they are called by now. We called them the *pazamor-ash*.' He looked into the sky. 'Devils of the flood.' He looked at Luck. 'Do you have devils in your world?'

Luck thought for a moment of Peki Asarko, Lord of the Lake of Souls. The rogue immortal who flayed then displayed those he killed. 'Oh yes,' he replied softly, 'we have them.'

'We thought we were savage. But the devils of the flood?' Toparak shook his head. 'They only began to slaughter us less when they started to kill the other tribes as well. Then all fought all. And Saghaz-a burned.'

Luck saw that the pain was not just in the man's eyes. It ... vibrated off him now, in waves of sorrow, loss, guilt. Though he could only possess beasts, never another man, something about being 'other' gave him a strong sense of another's suffering. He felt Toparak's pain, in his head and heart.

37

So it was to relieve both of them that he then asked, 'And yet it all changed?'

'It changed.' Whatever Luck had done worked. The sorrow left the eyes, replaced by a kind of wonder. '*He* came.'

Luck thought back, to his first conversation with Anazat. '"The one before the one"?'

'*Azana-kesh*. Yes.' Toparak smiled. 'He'd come many years before, to all the peoples. Many had not believed his message, of the One that is to come. Some did. Enough did. And kept that belief like a small flame saved to light the next night's fire. Slowly, that flame caught, spread. Slowly, the suffering in all lands became too great, and people in all lands sought another answer. Found it in the message *azana-kesh* had left. Found it in the One.'

'The child. She who is he, both and neither?'

Toparak simply nodded. 'The One.' He smiled, and it dispelled the last of the sorrow from his face. 'You have other questions, do you not?'

'At least one thousand.'

'I am not the one to answer them. I have not ... voyaged enough, in the realms unseen.' He gestured to his eyes, where Luck had noticed the faint darkening. 'One day, I hope these will be black. That I will be allowed to see the deeper mysteries. One day. Meantime, he will have your thousand answers.'

'He?'

Toparak swivelled in his saddle, and pointed to the bell tower, peaking over the trees on the next ridge. Luck looked, and saw that now a thin column of smoke was rising from it. The smoke was not grey or black but a distinct and deep scarlet.

'Anazat has returned,' Toparak said and, with a reluctance that was palpable, turned his horse's head back to the path.

*

38

Anazat awaited him in the same room that the god had first flown into as a raven. There was no greeting, no enquiry as to his welfare, no talk of his absence. There was only a directness that spoke to Luck's craving.

'I am told you demanded Sirene,' Anazat said.

'I requested it, yes.' Luck came and stood before the man, who had his back to the alcove which contained the seeing globe. 'You told me I could have anything I wanted. Go anywhere I chose. I wish to go,' he gestured behind the man, 'in there.'

Anazat glanced back at the glass on its plinth behind him. In his turning, Luck was able to see it. As ever, smoke swirled within. He felt an instant hunger.

The monk turned back, blocking the view again. 'It is not to be voyaged in alone. Not till you are more experienced in *her* ways.'

'So you would still control what I see?'

'I told you before, Midgarthian. Sirene cannot be controlled.' This reply was snapped and Luck noticed what he hadn't before – the dark bags under the man's eyes. His slumped shoulders. Whatever he had been doing away from the castle had exhausted him. Anazat continued, 'It is best you have someone with you, the first few times at least. There are dangers, along with the delights. And I am not,' he took a long breath, 'fit for the journey right now. Later in the week. In a few days perhaps.'

'Listen to me, priest.' Luck took a step closer, till he could stare up into the man's black eyes. His voice was low as he continued. 'I have lived for nearly four hundred years. As man, as beast. I have seen things – done things! – of which you could only dream. Alone. Always alone. I never needed anyone to hold my hand and I do not need you to do so now.'

A light came into the blackness. The man's jaw and shoulders set and his voice, when it came, was a whisper. 'You think not? You think because you are a so-called god in your land, you can be one in the smoke?' He shrugged. 'Very well. Since you demand it, you will meet Sirene. But when she takes you,' a faint smile came, 'try to remember that I warned you not to go.'

'When she takes me?' Luck echoed. But Anazat had already turned to the alcove, and if he heard the question he did not respond. Instead he tied a scarf around his own mouth, then lowered himself with a grunt into the far chair. The word came muffled from beneath the scarf as he waved at the chair opposite him. 'Sit.'

For a moment, Luck did not move. It wasn't the fear of what he was about to do that made him hesitate. It was the look in the priest's eyes, in the timbre of his voice. Caution had gone. And it was replaced by ... well, Luck read it as a kind of glee. He had forced the man to this, to what he already understood and the god had only glimpsed. Whatever lay ahead now, there would be terror in it, that much Luck could see. But he had climbed the unclimbable mountain to learn – and terror was ever part of any education.

'Let us begin,' he said, and sat.

'We already have,' Anazat replied and, leaning far away, he pulled a vial from his robes and tipped a great glug of viscous liquid onto the globe.

Luck remembered where only a few drops had taken him before. Anazat had poured far more than that. But he wasn't going to avoid the thing he most sought. He leaned forward, inhaled deeply ...

Everything went. All light, all sound, all touch, all scent, all sensation. Not as if he'd been suddenly thrown into a dark and windowless cell; he wasn't floating, or falling – there was simply no sense of movement at all. There was no body to move.

No*body*, Luck thought – then realised that thought had been absent too. With that first one, he felt that perhaps it had been missing for a while. Though time, of course, had no meaning either. When all laws of nature were suspended, how could it?

That second thought – a question – cascaded into others, and some awareness came with them. Not physically, Luck still felt nothing of himself, no flesh where thought could be contained. It was more that he sensed a place beyond him, beyond the darkness and the falling …

'Falling!' he screamed, because he was now – though when he folded onto ground that had appeared suddenly beneath him he did so without any pain. He clutched himself and waited nonetheless, his eyes – he could feel them again – clenched shut. He didn't open them, didn't want to. He was frightened of the nothingness he'd just emerged from, didn't want to return to it any time soon.

He could prevent himself seeing, but there was nothing to be done about all the other senses, fully and instantly restored. The earth under him – he was lying on it, limbs sprawled, one cheek pressed into what felt like damp grass. Smelled like it too – fresh, and after rain. Then he felt warmth, sunshine on his skin. Heard a buzzing that grew slowly nearer, then shot fast away.

Luck opened his eyes and sat up.

The figure was a dozen paces away. Man or woman he could not tell, for the person had their back to him and was covered in a robe that flowed from crown to toe – and which changed colour even as Luck watched it. An earth brown shifted to lake blue which changed in its turn to orange. But then he realised that it was only one part of the shifting, that the land itself – trees, flowers, the grass he lay on, the sky he lifted his head and gazed up into – also failed to stay as one thing, as what they were.

He looked down – and the person turned. A loose cowl obscured half a face. He could make out part of a nose; a single, closed eye. Like the world around, the features of the face shifted and the skin changed colour, going from a white paler than milk to the blackness of ... of a monk's eye.

The last time Luck had entered the smoke within the glass, the monk had been with him. 'Anazat?' he called, his voice sounding strange to him, the word appearing to have form beyond sound as it moved through the air away from him, waves pushing towards the shrouded face. When they reached it, they transformed the skin, settled it, into a dark brown. Not Anazat then. And when the one eye slowly opened, there was no blackness within it. A pure white surround, with its centre the dark blue of a midsummer midnight in his land, when the sun never set.

The world settled. The colours were what they were now, vivid, but unchanging. And when he spoke again, this time his words had no physical form, except sound.

'Who are you?'

The reply was simple and it was a woman who spoke it, though her voice was low enough to be a man's. 'I am Sirene,' she said.

She said. Anazat had referred to the drug as *she* before. He'd thought it a mere way of speaking – his own people would call their ships 'she', because Inge-gerd, goddess of seas and rivers, of all waters, would better protect one of her own sex. He was also aware that everything here was held together by Sirene; that nothing existed beyond her. His ... *other* was here, the one that could travel beyond his body, here in the world of the drug which worked on his mind. His body was back at the Keep.

And yet ... The way she looked at him from the one eye he could see? The slight smile on the scarlet lips? Was there a mischief in their curl? He was suddenly uncertain, about everything.

'But who is Sirene?' he blurted.

'Anyone. Everyone.' She laughed, and vanished.

42

Beyond where she'd stood, he now saw that the land dipped, a faint trail running across the grass, leading down an avenue of beech trees in full leaf. He took one hesitant step forward, then another, and then he was walking. Yet something was different, and it took him a while to realise what it was.

He did not limp. It was as if his short left leg had lengthened to match his right. For the first time in his life he walked as others did, descending through a sun-dappled glade into a valley that could have been in Midgarth. He raised his right arm, and marvelled that it was the same length and strength as his left.

He was halfway down the path when he heard the singing.

He halted, so suddenly he lurched, stumbled. He recognised the song, even from the few notes. It was from his land, an ancient one that told of love sought, found, lost, regained. But it wasn't that which made the tears start to his eyes. Those came because he recognised the singer.

He ran out of the trees into a garden. It was beautiful, filled with flowers, wild and tamed, with beds of herbs for food, for healing. In one corner was a bower and on its bench, framed by fecund buds, sat a woman. As he entered she rose, smiled, held out her hand. 'Welcome, my love,' she said. 'I knew that you would come, sooner or later.'

Sobbing, Luck fell to his knees before Gytta, his wife of forty years. Dead for ten.

Her hand was on his head. That caress, that touch. He'd remembered the *fact* of her touching him. But he had forgotten the feeling of it. Had wept one whole night five years before, when he realised he had. Now her hand was on him again, he wondered how he had ever lived without it.

He looked up at her. She smiled, the smile that had first beguiled him, not only with its look but with its sound, some folds of her face making it, like a small sigh. He studied her, the

43

face he'd so missed. So different from the last time he'd seen it, thinned and wrinkled from the disease that consumed her. Different too from the first, when he'd met her at a fair in the deep south near Lorken, and she'd sold him a lotion to soothe the pain that sometimes came to his hunched shoulder. Then she'd been scarce twenty. When she died, she'd been sixty. Her age now was from the years in between, perhaps halfway. He could tell that by the laugh lines deepening about her eyes, the silver criss-crossing in her fair hair, like the warp and weft in the tapestries she'd weave. This was the age she'd been when they'd gone to live alone up in the mountains. A time of peace, of exploration – her of herbs, him of the wonders of the world and all its creatures. A time of love. Twenty years, gone in a click of his fingers. They'd only returned to Askaug when she'd gotten too ill, and he thought that someone, some healer somewhere, could yet save her.

He rose to his feet. They were of a height, for she was small for a woman of Midgarth. She reached and wiped his tears away. He took her hand, kissed it. 'My love,' he murmured, closing his eyes. 'I know this is only a dream. But it is one I could stay in for ever.'

'A dream?' She laughed, the sound as gentle as a stream in the forest. 'Why do you call it that?'

'A vision, then.' He squeezed her hand. 'Different, better than any other. For I can touch you, smell you.' He leaned into her hair, inhaled the meadow freshness of it.

She stepped away from him, her eyes searching his. 'So you think I am another one of your visions, Luck?'

He looked beyond her, at the garden, the vividness of its flowers, the softness of its light.

'Yes, my love. You are part of the vision. Sirene has shown you to me. For you,' tears started into his eyes again as he spoke it, 'for you are dead.'

'I am.' She reached then, took his face in both her hands, drew him close. 'But, my love,' she said, staring deep into his eyes, 'where did you think I'd gone?'

He stared at her. Over the centuries of his life, he'd changed his mind many times about what happened after death. In his youngest days, he'd believed what his people did. That mortal or god, when they died, went to a world where they could do what warriors and most gods in Midgarth liked best: to feast and fight for ever. Where those women who did not fight – most women – gathered and did what they preferred – gossiping and weaving mostly, he'd thought. But he soon believed no more, for his body was not shaped for the war all others appeared to love, his stomach and brain not suited to drinking; while the women he knew would sit idle and 'gossip' no more, indeed less, than any man. After that, and especially after Gytta died, he believed only in oblivion. Mainly because to imagine her somewhere else without him hurt too much.

He looked at her, held in the time when he'd loved her perhaps best of all. He placed his hands over hers, against his face. 'You went to your rest, my love. And left me to the torment that was life without you.'

She turned and walked away into the garden, hands to each side, fingers brushing against the crimson, white, pink and yellow flowers, that lolled their huge-petalled heads into her path. 'So you believe that all you see now is fantasy? That nothing here is real?'

He looked at her, silhouetted against the sunlight. 'Nothing.'

She turned back to him, sharply, and her voice when it came had lost its softness. 'You could not be more wrong.' She shot out her hand and pointed behind him. 'Sirene is not a vision. Sirene is the power of the world.'

He swivelled round – and there, standing at the head of the path he'd come down, was his guide. He could still only see part of the face, shrouded as it was. The one white eye, the half-smile. Then, from the folds of her robes, she raised a hand, and beckoned.

He felt it, like a grip at his chest, pulling him forward. He resisted, planting his feet. 'I will not leave,' he said, turning back. 'Now I have found you once more, I will never let you go.'

'Ah, my love!' Gytta's voice was gentle again. 'On that, you have no choice.'

The tug from behind was powerful. It swivelled him, and he stumbled but dug in again. 'I can,' he yelled. 'I always have. The choice that all have, men or gods. I can die, and join you here.'

'You could die. Yet even then, you would not join me here. That choice is not yours. That choice is ... hers.'

He looked ahead, to the cowled figure. The hand still reaching for him. He threw himself onto his knees, thrust his own hands into the earth. 'No!' he screamed. 'Please!'

Gytta's hand was in his hair again. For a moment, the force pulling him away lessened. He did not turn around but closed his eyes, as her lips touched his ear, as her voice softly came again. 'Listen to me, my love. You cannot stay, and you cannot die, because you are needed. Midgarth needs you, and the people who love you there. The entire world needs you.' Her lips pressed gently into his head, and as the world around him dissolved, she added, 'For you may be the only one who can stop what is coming.'

'What *is* coming?' he cried.

'Winter with no spring. Night without end.' Her voice faded as she spoke, till the last words were scarcely there. 'The Dark,' she whispered.

Her touch was gone, the garden where she lived, gone. He fell again, fell as he had arrived, through a blackness that wasn't there and was everything, everywhere. Only a breeze came ... yet there were words on it. 'Remember about love,' the breeze whispered, 'but learn everything you can about hate.'

Blackness ended in pain. He hit the floor, landing on his side. His head thumped onto the flagstones and he heard a cry, as the world returned in a vividness that was a different kind of pain.

Anazat was bending over him. 'You fell from your chair. Are you all right?'

'Send me back,' Luck moaned.

'Back? Come, sit up.' Anazat helped him to sit, then go onto his knees, then rise, finally helping him sink again into his chair.

Luck saw the glass vial before him. Sirene was within it, and beyond it. He grabbed at it, but even as his fingers wrapped around it, others as cold and hard as iron wrapped around his wrist. 'Let it go,' Anazat grunted, squeezing, and Luck had no choice but to release.

'Send me back,' he groaned again.

'There is no back.' The monk took the vial and put it into a box on the table which he locked, keeping the key in his hand. Then he too sat and looked at Luck. 'As long as I have been with her – and it takes many, many journeys to get eyes as black as mine,' they gleamed as he spoke, 'Sirene has never taken me to the same place twice. Besides, a second dose as strong as I gave you today would kill you. Maybe in a week you may be strong enough to try again.'

'Good.' Luck placed the heels of his hands into his eyes and pressed. It did nothing to shift the agony there. 'Then I could go back.'

'I told you, there is no back where you can go.' He took his lower lip between his teeth, appraised the god. 'So Sirene gave you something special?'

It was not something he would discuss. For all the agony in his head that nearly prevented all thought, Luck realised that he had finally found the bars in a cage that had appeared to have

47

none. Anazat was his gaoler and his gatekeeper – as long as he had the key to the box on the table, which held the liquid in the vial.

He stood, swayed, gripped the table before him, steadied. 'I'll tell you one thing I got. Advice.'

He stumbled to the door, gripped its edge as Anazat said, 'What advice?'

He did not turn, or speak, just thought it as he left the room. *That I need to learn about hate.*

Anazat called something else, but he did not hear what it was.

Luck staggered along corridors and down the stairwells of the Keep, pausing often to lean his head against cold stone and close his eyes. When at last he reached his cell, he plunged onto the bed. But if he thought that sleep would come, he was wrong. His body felt like it had been through battle. His mind whirled. 'Gytta! Gytta?' He murmured her name again and again, in joy, in sorrow, as a question. He knew Sirene had taken him there. He had so many questions about the drug, about the woman in the cowl. But was the world he'd returned to any more real than the one he'd left? He, who'd spent so much of his life beyond the veil of things as they seem, doubted that the tang of wood smoke in the air had any more substance than the scent from the flowers in his wife's garden. The touch of her hand had been as real as the mattress he pressed down on now.

And all the while her question tormented him: 'But, love – where did you think I'd gone?' Because, despite what Anazat said, about never going to the same place twice, if Gytta was somewhere in the world, or in the world beyond, there had to be a way to reach her.

Yet she'd also said to him that he might be the one to save this world. A burden he had no wish to shoulder. For now, he wished nothing more than to lie there and dream.

And then he realised he did want something else. Realised it in the tweet of a bird on his window ledge. With the spring, this one, or others of its breed, had started to come again and again. He left crumbs from his bread for the purpose of seeing them. It was of a type unknown in Midgarth – the size of a sparrow yet blue-grey not brown, and with a head that was all black, like a cowl that reached to the shoulders.

Luck knew what he wanted then – to escape his mind and lose himself in flight. And perhaps, he thought, I can fly up to Anazat's cell in the tower and discover where he keeps the key to the cage, the one of escape. Of Sirene.

Luck sat up. He'd learned to do this, to possess a beast, at the same time he'd learned his first words. It was as easy as a thought, as a breath, as a look. So he looked at the bird, who looked at him ...

It was as if he'd been picked up and thrown against a wall. He yelped, fell back onto the bed, sat straight up. The bird had not moved, just stared back. He focused on it, drove his will forward ...

Again, he felt as if he'd run head first into something hard. This time, though, the bird shook itself from beak to tail, chirped, and flew away.

Luck fell, sobbing, back onto the bed. And then he began to laugh, a terrible wrenching laugh that had no humour, only bitterness about it. Everything has a price, he thought. And the price Sirene had charged him was the very thing that made him a god. The power of possession, of transformation. Yet he knew, even as the laughter turned to tears, that he would give up that power for ever, give it up joyfully along with his so-called life, to feel Gytta's hand pushing through his hair but one more time.

3
Voyager

Despair.

It had gripped Atisha from the moment that she had been captured by Korshak, the Horse Lord, and Gistrane, the Huntress. Held her as they took her and her baby from the valley where the air globe, her escape from the City of Women, had crashed. Possessed her as they walked beside her and led her to the coast. She had no alternative but to do what they demanded of her. No choice but to leave Fant on the shore and board the ship that sailed, two days after her capture, away from Ometepe. His howls then and in her memory only added to her despair.

They could speak some of her language, though their accents were strange. Yet it was not about her, she soon realised. It was all about her child. If they treated her with respect, even kindness, they *worshipped* Poum.

From the moment of conception her child had been under threat. Firstly from Intitepe, the fire god, the father who sought to throw the child – the son he thought *he* was, the son prophesied to slay him – into the volcano. Now from these strangers who also threatened, if in a different way. They were taking Poum to some place far away. She was the mother of the child and so came too. But she was irrelevant, she knew. She was the child's feeder, comforter, that was all. She had no power, could not say no, nor hold back in any way. And, for the three weeks of the voyage so far, that had filled her with the greatest despair of all.

Yet the despair went in a moment, when she realised that she did have power still. The power of her will, expressed when she sent three arrows straight into the heart of the target set up on the ship's prow.

Like all simple moments, it was the climax of all the moments and realisations that had gone before it. But Gistrane, the Huntress, didn't recognise it, just grunted a brief approval in the guttural common language of the Four Tribes – *tolan-pa-sen*, they called it – that Atisha had insisted on learning from her first coming aboard.

Their target was a bale of hay, circles within circles painted onto it, the widest the length of her arm, the smallest the size of her two hands joined at fingertip. A sail had been hung behind to trap and save the blunted arrows they shot. Vast, yet she had still managed to lose a dozen arrows to the wind which came gusting from behind them and pushed the ship, with its three masts and huge sails, fast along. By the end of the first week of practice, she had contrived to at least hit the canvas. By the end of the second, half her arrows found the hay bale, though only one made the outermost circle. It was halfway through the third week that calmer seas, less crosswind, a steadier hand and a settling eye sent more and more arrows ever closer towards the smallest circle – and one finally into it.

Gistrane grunted, spoke. 'Better. Now do it again.'

Atisha duly nocked, drew, shot, sent the second arrow in beside the first. 'One more,' came the command. She placed the arrow, shot it, saw it nestle in beside the others. Gistrane's grunt had a little more surprise in it this time.

That was the moment when she felt all her despair lift. Laying

51

the bow beneath the guard rail on the raised rear deck, Atisha said, 'Now tell me more of your land.'

Three weeks, and already she knew perhaps as much of the Huntress's language as Gistrane knew of hers. It was another skill Atisha had discovered she possessed, this thing of tongues. Between her learning of Gistrane's language, and the Huntress's knowledge of hers, they were able to understand each other well enough.

'Everywhere we go, people are wishing to see you, paza.' It meant 'little doe' in *tolanpa-sen* and though Gistrane was indeed much taller than Atisha, she still resented the title. Though she never showed resentment. It would not get her what she wanted.

'Everywhere?'

'Yes, not fear it. It begin slowly. We dock, there will be crowd to greet you. See you. They spread the word of your coming through land.'

They are not there to greet me, Atisha thought. They are there for Poum. And they will wish to see ... what makes the child different. They will wish to see that Poum is neither sex, and both. For that, she'd learned, was their prophecy, their reason for ... everything. Why they sailed across the wide world. Why they planned on conquering it all.

The One.

The thought of a naked Poum, exposed to an ecstatic, yelling crowd, made Atisha shudder. Again, it was nothing she need share. Instead she asked, 'And then?'

'Then?'

'Where do *we* go next?'

'To rest for time at Keep.'

'What is keep?'

'Like,' Gistrane crinkled her brows, seeking a comparison, 'like palace at Toluc, but stronger. Centre of worship, where these men live.' She pointed at the monk, who had emerged from below decks and staggered over to the rail to vomit into the sea. She and Poum had mastered their stomachs in the first few days; he still had not by this, the fourth week.

'Where is?'

'Is ...' Gistrane shrugged. 'Perhaps middle of Saghaz-a. Halfway between Seafarers' land where we come and Sea of Grass where Korshak and brothers live. In the mountains, across valley from where we dwell.'

'The Huntresses?'

'Yes.' Gistrane narrowed her eyes. 'Ah, paza! I show you beauty of forests, you never wish to leave.'

'Only women there?'

'Only. Why we want men? Men one use only. To breed with and give us daughters.'

'And if you have sons?'

'Returned to world of men. Most go to Keep, to be trained as monks.' She smiled. 'To keep them would be to keep a baby snake that one day grow big and bite us.'

There was strangeness all over the world around birth. Though how could any woman willingly give up a child? It made her wonder if any Huntress wanted to give birth, knowing that a boy babe would be taken from her immediately. Did none ever think to fight, as Atisha had thought to fight in the Palace of Waters if Poum had been a boy?

It was Poum she focused on again, for Poum that she needed more knowledge. 'How long stay we at Keep?'

'Little.' Gistrane spread the fingers of one hand then closed them three times. 'Maybe?' she said. 'You recover from the voyage. Poum – praise her, praise him! – grow stronger. And then more must see you across our land. From seas, to mountains, to forests, to Sea of Grass. See you before day of when two moons meet.'

'What happens that day?'

Gistrane smiled and stretched her arms wide. 'We conquer the world.' She grabbed Atisha's hand. 'For the One! Listen to prophecy, paza.'

Atisha had had enough of prophecies – the one that made Intitepe wish to kill her child. This one that had Poum saving the world. But she was spared the listening by a familiar wail from the main deck – one that brought her breast milk surging out, darkening the front of her dress.

Gistrane had a servant with her, an older woman named Maranne. She looked after Poum while Atisha learned the way of the bow – and learned of her enemies. She was holding the squirming babe now. Poum may be 'the One', Atisha thought, and the object of all these people's hopes, but a baby, any baby, still needs to feed.

A steep stair led from the narrow, raised rear deck to the long main one. Atisha descended it backwards then turned to take the child. 'Here now, my sweet, my love,' she crooned, loosening the folds of her dress. Then she looked up, and saw that she was regarded from all around. Sailors, with faces burned by weather and scarred with blade, who looked like they would slit their mothers' throats for a jug of fermented asses' milk, stared at her with wide, wondering eyes; eyes that were filled with a fervent joy. No, stared that way at Poum.

Atisha did not wish an audience for this intimate act. There was a door set in the rear deck's housing, which led to their small cabin below. The seasick monk, wiping his mouth on his sleeve, was just going through it. Atisha followed, descended another narrow stair, one hand on the guide railing. When she reached the deck below, she was about to turn left, to her cabin. But from her right she heard the monk spitting and, for no reason she understood, went that way instead. Poum had found a breast and was contentedly sucking. Atisha was not needed anywhere in particular. But she suddenly realised that, of the three who were her main captors, Gistrane she knew best, while Korshak, the Horse Lord, had a strange combination of worship of Poum and lust towards her that prevented much conversation. Only the monk was completely unknown to her. Now she had discovered that the monks were to be her captors in this place called Keep, it was time to change that.

He had gone into his cabin, one even smaller than her own. Perhaps that was why he left the door open, for the closed, windowless space would make him even sicker than he already was. She saw him sitting on what passed for his bed, his back to her. She was about to speak, to question, when a foul smell of burning came to her nostrils, as his words did to her ears.

He called out what sounded like a name but one she didn't know. *Leidanasa*, she thought, something like that.

She peered through the gap between door and frame. The monk now had his back to the cabin's sea wall, his legs stretched before him. Between them was ... a glass globe about the size of the man's head. Smoke moved within it, then suddenly cleared – and a face appeared within the glass.

Atisha gave a little gasp. Poum, startled, removed her mouth from the breast and looked up. The monk had not heard so, gently, Atisha reattached her child, bent forward, listened.

The man within the glass – similar to the monk, with shaven head, though older and with much blacker eyes, blacker teeth – talked rapidly, too fast for her young knowledge. Some words came, the sentences falling at their ends which told her that the monk in the cabin was being questioned – the way in Saghaz-a, and the opposite of her own tongue in Ometepe. She caught some things. 'Baby' was clear, and the monk used the word for 'growing'. Then she thought the man asked about the arrival, and the monk before her replied that it was two weeks away, adding something about 'strong winds'. This seemed to satisfy the man in the glass, who then again spoke too fast for her comprehension, questions no more, instructions, the monk replying with assenting grunts. He asked one question himself, the word 'gathering' clear. The man in the glass gave what she thought was a smile and answered with 'thousands'. Then he was gone.

The monk lay there, staring at the globe. She was about to turn away, when he did a strange thing – uncorked a small vial and poured some of the liquid upon the glass, stoppering it again fast. Then a sizzling came, vapour rose, and the man leaned in, inhaled deep, then slumped back onto his bunk, black eyes glazing. Both she and Poum began to cough. She turned rapidly away. Her eyes streamed and as she made her way to her own cabin, Poum started to cry. A breast soothed again.

Not so Atisha, who lay down and stared up at the ceiling, her head spinning. There was so much she didn't understand about this new world she was being plunged towards. This seeing glass, how it enabled people to speak over distances she could only guess at, was just the latest confusion. She was also aware that even though it had made her choke, there was something about the liquid the monk had used, the smoke that had risen from it, that was … desirable. One breath and she felt that. Something else to watch, to avoid.

She shifted Poum to the other breast, and stared up through the wood of her ceiling, beyond it. Saw again the man who'd spoken – commanded – with his black eyes and his overwhelming certainty. Another man planning to use her, as men had always done.

One especially.

Intitepe. Lord of lords, fire god, king, lover. She tried not to think of him too much, though she could not stop him coming in her dreams. He who she'd worshipped, with her body, with all her belief; he who had tried to kill her and the child they'd made. Well, she had defied him. And she would defy this black-eyed man when the time came.

She thought back to when she'd sent three arrows through a small painted circle. She imagined that circle right over Intitepe's heart, drew back the bowstring and let her arrow fly.

The Fire King felt a stab in his chest, as if something had penetrated his heart. It made him think of Atisha.

Where are you now? he wondered, rubbing at the cramp. Though he knew, if not her exact location, at least the method by which she travelled. Villagers had reported a mother and baby boarding a sailing ship – much like the two that floated at anchor beyond the reef, about three hundred paces from shore.

He parted the leaves of the bush that concealed him from any watchers on the water and studied the vessels again. So different from those of his people, which were not wooden like those before him but woven from reeds – huge canoes truly, with benches for paddlers and a sail that could catch the wind but take them only in the direction it blew. These two must somehow be able to also move against the wind. How else had they arrived on his shores, sailing south, when the winds had changed to blow north, in that sudden switch his people called 'the breath of god'?

He would learn all that when he took them. 'Bring him,' he said, and Toman, who had taken over as captain of his guard when One-Eared Salpe was killed, rose, bowed, and ran.

While he waited, Intitepe studied the water. Gentle waves foamed briefly as they broke on the reef, then curled onto the beach with a sigh. So different from the roars and smashing of only the day before. The storm had blown itself out. But its suddenness had badly damaged the vessels he studied – though their rigging was unknown to him, he could see broken spars and shredded sails. And it had scattered the fleet that they were part of, the one sent to invade his land.

All this he'd learned from the man he awaited now. But what he wanted most was news of Atisha. He'd last seen her leaving the City of Women in something he would never have believed if he'd been told about it – a basket that flew beneath the clouds.

The City of Women! He spat between leaves onto the sand. He hadn't been sure that Atisha had been in that basket at first so he'd stayed, led his men to storm the city when the bridge had been completed the next morning. There he'd discovered that most of the inhabitants were gone – any who were able to climb down the cliffs in the night, and kill the guards he'd left to watch them. He found only the most ancient, the infirm and the deranged; those he'd wished to see, to punish in as slow and public a way as possible, had vanished.

Besema, Norvara and Yutil. Each had been 'the One' in his marana years before, his closest companion and lover. Each had betrayed him, and the great gift he'd given them of his love, with their defiance – especially that bitch Besema, who Muna said had been their leader. Muna, who he'd appointed the governess of the city and who had failed to stop the revolt. Once he'd learned all she could tell him – including what she'd heard of Atisha's flight – he'd punished her failure. The crows would have cleaned her bones of flesh by now at the base of the cliff he'd personally thrown her over – the same cliff it appeared that Besema, who had to have eighty years of life behind her, had managed to climb down!

I will catch her eventually, he thought, spitting again. And no swift plunge of a death for her when I do.

Someone coughed. He turned. Toman threw the prisoner down before him. The man whimpered, curled up into a ball, clutching to his chest an oozing stump, all that remained of his right hand. He'd been reluctant to answer Intitepe's questions to begin with. Once he'd been held to the flames for a while, he was not reluctant at all.

The Fire King studied him again. He'd been surprised by his look – by the roundness of his eyes, nearly as much as by their blackness; by his pale skin and black teeth and the circlet of hair around his shaved head. Quite different from that other man, who'd pursued him, after the fight against the rebels had gone so badly wrong, on his giant beast – a *horse*, this fellow had named it. He'd been huge, like his mount, with a topknot of long dark hair, and eyes of blue ice.

He had learned a lot about these invaders, once the man – he called himself by a word that sounded like 'munke', which in Ometepe was a type of basket – started talking. Indeed it was hard to keep him to subjects that Intitepe wished to hear about. More fire helped to focus the man's mind.

The world! He'd always thought it was contained within the waters that surrounded Ometepe. Seas that no one could sail far into, and certainly not through. Even he, the greatest sailor who'd ever lived, who during his hundredth year had sailed around the entire island, mapping it, had never got more than three days beyond sight of land. Yet these people – that horseman, this munke-man, others – had managed it. Managed it for years, it seemed. Others like the one who whimpered before him had come, lived hidden, and learned – the munke spoke Bunami, the main language of the land, nearly as well as Intitepe. And he'd explained, through his weeping, that they'd done all that for two reasons: conquest and prophecy.

I know about both of those, Intitepe had thought.

Now, he shoved his foot onto the remains of the man's burned hand, who cried out, tried to curl even more into himself. 'Tell me,' Intitepe said.

'Anything! Anything, king!' the man sobbed.

'Tell me everything about the ships I see before me.'

'Everything?' The man's black eyes stared up, bewildered. 'If my lord would tell me why he needs to—'

'You ask me why?' Intitepe stood, bent down. 'Do you want me to bring the flames to you again, munke? Burn your other hand off?'

'No, no, please no!' The man struggled up to his knees. 'I only ask because there is so much to do with ships and I know very little of how they work. I ... I ... I do not wish to ... to bore you, lord.'

'Then do not. Tell me ... how many men are on board, how many of them are fighters, where they will be sleeping, what weapons they use, what guard they set.' He straightened. 'Tell me that, so you may live another night.'

The man spoke. It was hard to stop him, and much wasn't necessary to Intitepe's needs. But the Fire King listened, and when he'd heard enough he turned to the soldier crouched nearby and gave his quiet commands.

Later, in the depths of the night, in that dark, sleepiest hour before the dawn, they set out. He was in the first and largest of the three canoes, at the front, only the munke before him and that only because the man waved a lantern of a type Intitepe had never seen before, which sheltered the flame within a box of beaten metal and something hard and clear that he called 'glass'. It was a signal, one that would reassure any guard. There were five paddlers on each side of his canoe, three a side on each of the others. His ten were working hard, because of the weight of the thirty men spread between them, lying under cloth. Beneath Intitepe's cloak he was in his full armour – links of hardwood slats, from neck to thigh, lined in iron. At the belt round his waist were his stone-tipped club and obsidian long dagger.

He fingered them, and smiled. They had served him well, as he moved through Ometepe, putting out the widespread fires of rebellion. And using fire to do it, as well as rock, arrow and blade. He was the Fire King, after all. All who'd dared to oppose him had learned the folly of that on pyres across the land. Though he'd been surprised at how well the untrained peasants had fought. Desperation and the certainty of their coming punishments drove them. It had been fine. He had rediscovered the joy of the fight, lost these three hundred years. And his soldiers, who'd grown fat and idle, had found it again too. Those who lived, at least, his best in the canoes around him now. The only true annoyance was that he hadn't caught up with that bitch Besema.

He stared ahead. The fact that there were two ships presented a problem. He would need them both. He would need others when they found their way to shore, if his plans were to be fulfilled. But the munke had been happy to share the system of signals they used at night, for danger or reassurance. Lights and calls. Men could be persuaded to make both, like the munke had done.

Two sentries, one at each end of each ship. Four men in all, awake. If they all were. They had arrived safe that evening after a long and stormy voyage. No one had yet come ashore.

The prow of the canoe nudged into the side of the nearer, smaller vessel. Wooden steps with ropes either side were directly before them. A man appeared and peered down. The munke called up to him, his tone reassuring, though of course Intitepe could not understand the words. But the munke knew how slowly he would die if he betrayed the Fire King now.

He followed the man up the ladder. Climbed after him over the wooden wall. The sentry was questioning the munke and turned to look as Intitepe stepped near. He made some noise that could have been a question. Made more as the dagger opened his throat. But the Fire King held him close to kill him, and the sound didn't travel. Lowering the dying man to the deck, Intitepe leaned back and softly called, 'Come.'

His men swarmed up and over. They'd been told where they needed to go and did. Men died, quietly. The munke had said that this was a ship with supplies for the invasion, weapons and food, while the other had some soldiers too. More soldier transports were following, apparently. Intitepe looked forward to seeing them.

Toman ran up. 'All safe, my king.'

'How many?'

'Ten. Ten who will not see another sunrise.' Toman grinned, wiping blood on his cloak. 'They were very surprised.'

'Any munke?'

'The black-eyed ones? Two. Both safe.'

'Good.'

'And the ones chained below to the benches? Slit their throats?'

Intitepe had been surprised to hear that these invaders kept prisoners they called 'slavs', or something like it. They were worked to death – at oars, which moved the ships when there was no wind; or in mines ashore; any task the munke or their allies, who sailed ships or rode horses, did not wish to perform. Some were rebels. Some criminals. That's when he knew these people were barbarians. No one was slav in Ometepe. You obeyed Intitepe or you burned.

'Leave them.' He peered at the other boat a short distance away. 'One canoe and its men to stay here.'

Commands were whispered, passed on. They re-embarked, his men under the cloths, the munke again before him. He was weeping quite hard now, which annoyed Intitepe. 'Quiet!' he barked, jabbing the man in his stump. He yelped, loudly – and immediately, from the vessel they were making for, came a voice shouting a question. 'Tell him!' whispered Intitepe but the munke just cried out again in agony, and the man ahead started to ring a bell.

Throwing the munke into the water, Intitepe yelled, 'Fast!' Men came out from under the cloths on both canoes, seized more paddles, drove their vessels forward. But on the ship ahead, that bell still sounded and men were shouting and running.

There was no need for silence now. 'Faster!' cried Intitepe. Then something hit him in the chest and he looked down to see an arrow in the slats of his armour. 'Bows!' he yelled, and three men in each canoe seized theirs, began to shoot. But the men on the deck ahead had the advantage, and five of his men tumbled into the waves, shafts in their chests.

There was some rigging low-slung at the front of the ship, away from the falling arrows. He urged his paddlers there, then swung himself up into the ropes, followed by his men. Scrambling up, he pushed himself over the front wall of the ship onto the deck. Arrows passed his face, glanced off his shoulder. He could not wait for all his men to arrive. There could be no delay. 'Forward,' he yelled, and ran alone into the people ahead.

Three of them had bows, two had spears, and two others drawn swords – ones far longer than any in Ometepe. Among the munke's pained ramblings, he had told of these weapons, how kings would pay fortunes for them, how exquisite they were as a tool for dealing death. Ever since he'd heard, Intitepe had wanted one. So, swooping his dagger and club like the arms of a windmill, he made straight for those men. A spearman lunged at him. He swivelled to the side, let the thrust go past him, brought Skull-crusher hard down onto the man's head. Another man aimed his spear tip at Intitepe's face. He ducked, then slashed Slake-thirst's obsidian edge across the man's throat. Behind him, more of his men were running in with cries. The defenders turned to them. These men with swords were straight ahead.

One was small, black-eyed. A munke. He had a shorter sword with a straight blade. The other was tall, with a topknot of hair falling to his waist. He was like the man who had chased Intitepe into the forest after his defeat by the rebels. His sword was long and curved. A Horse Lord, his prisoner had named him, for the beast he rode. That meant that below these decks there might be horses too. Intitepe wanted one of those almost as much as he wanted a sword.

The two men were in fighting stance, waiting for him to come. So he halted, listening to the sounds of death from behind him. He did not need to look. Every time a warrior of Ometepe took a life he cried, 'Mine!' It meant all the life power that had been in an enemy was now absorbed into his conqueror. There were many such cries, then fewer, then none, and he was aware of his men gathering behind him. Beyond the two sword-men, the crew of his other canoe had gained the deck, killed whoever opposed them, were grouping behind his foes. Intitepe halted their advance with a raised hand. The Horse Lord placed his back to the munke's to face them.

Beside their lord, two of Intitepe's bowmen nocked and aimed.

'Wait.'

His quiet command was instantly obeyed. A near silence came, the only noises the creak of the wooden ship, and the whimpers of dying men. Until the munke spoke, his accent worse than his burned friend's, but the words clear enough.

'Do not kill we.'

'Why not?' Intitepe replied.

'We ... help you.'

'You came to help?' Intitepe smiled. 'I hear you came to conquer us.'

'Who this told you?'

Intitepe looked past the munke to a shivering heap upon the deck. His men must have pulled the burned one from the water. 'He did.' The one before him turned. His black eyes were wide when he turned back. Intitepe spoke before he could. 'He told me many things. Of how, when you have conquered us, you seek to make a child of mine your god.'

The Horse Lord grunted something. Intitepe moved so he could see his face. 'You speak our tongue?'

The man shrugged. 'Little.'

'Then I speak slowly.' Intitepe took a small step forward. 'You will put down these swords. Then you will lie down before me, kiss my feet, and beg for your lives.'

The Horse Lord may have spoken only a little – but he understood. Fury came to his ice-blue eyes. With a great cry, he raised his sword high, ran forward. 'Wait,' Intitepe said again to his bowmen. Then he bent, jumped, landed right before the charging lord. Hundreds of years of fighting had given him an instinct for weapons, even strange ones, and he could see that this sword, this magnificent blade, would work well at a distance. From atop one of the man's beasts, his blows would be unstoppable. But close to?

It was a gamble. But he was right. The lord was near on top of him, trying to stop, trying to pull back his sword and sweep it down from its height. Too late. Too late, because Intitepe leaned sideways, then put the tip of Slake-thirst's far shorter blade all the way through the Horse Lord's throat.

His curved sword clattered onto the deck. Blood poured over Intitepe's hand, but he crouched, stepped closer, held the taller, dying man above him while his hands flapped at the stone in his throat, wrapped around it, could not extract it. Intitepe held him there till he died and only when he had did he draw out his dagger.

The Horse Lord fell, his blood pooling around him on the deck. The munke straight away laid down his sword, followed it to lie before Intitepe and kiss his feet. The Fire King looked all around him, at the living and the dead. At the ships that were now his. At a world, with dawn just touching the horizon.

'Mine!' he said, and smiled.

The sun had barely crested the horizon when he gathered everyone on the deck of the larger ship. He'd learned it was called the *Sea Hawk*, after a bird that lived in that other world. His new munke, Bezan, had told him that. The old one had died, suddenly, soon after he was snatched from the water. It was no matter, he had three now, and each spoke his tongue to a fair degree.

Bezan had also told him that five more ships, scattered by the huge storm, were due to rendezvous in this bay whenever they could. It was where the invader had first come to his land, where the fishermen's rebellion, now ended, had begun. Five ships, all of which he wanted, if he was to do what he wished to do. So he needed to give his orders, without delay.

The *Sea Hawk*, which he'd swiftly toured, was an extraordinary vessel, so different from the simple boats his people sailed. Even the largest, his own ship, the *Serpent*, was a small canoe compared to this. The power that its sails could harness, which could move it in any direction, even against the wind – these were skills he would learn. That he must learn.

Now he stood on the raised rear deck of the ship, and looked at the people crammed onto the main deck below him. His own warriors formed a loose circle around them, bows to hand, arrows notched, strings slack. Intitepe was certain that they would not need to be tightened, shot. The crews he'd captured were cowed. The blood dripping onto their heads from their dead comrades, hanging from their ankles in the rigging, had done that.

But they were only half the people who stared up at him, waiting. The other half were in rags, their ankles and wrists raw from where chains had held them, all with the white faces of those who had not seen the sun for many a day. As they hadn't. For these were the slavs that the first munke had talked about – criminals and war prisoners condemned to row these boats when wind could not move them. Intitepe still thought the system inhumane. But he could see its uses – what free man would willingly spend his life shackled to a bench, out of the light?

He looked down at them. Everyone stared at the blood-slick deck, dread on all their faces, avoiding his eyes. All ... save one.

One slav was staring up at him. And he was grinning. An idiot, Intitepe thought. Or merely a fool, to meet the eye of a god. Intitepe was about to take a bow and shoot him himself when the idiot did something else. He shouted out a word. He mangled it. But it was a word from Intitepe's realm.

'Beer!' the man cried.

Everyone around the man moved away from him, staring in terror. And Intitepe ... smiled. It was absurd, that word here, now. Beside him, Toman drew back the bowstring, and aimed for the man's heart. The slav did not flinch, just kept smiling. 'Kill?' Toman asked.

'Wait.' Intitepe turned to Bezan, cowering at his side. 'Who is that man?' he asked.

The munke peered. 'Very bad man, lord,' he muttered. 'His name is Sekantor the Savage. He is pirate.'

'What is pirat?'

'Is ...' Bezan swallowed. 'Sea captain. Sea thief. Sekantor famous fighter. Cruel. Drunk.'

Intitepe signalled with his eyes. Two of his men went and grabbed an arm each of this pirat, pushed and pulled him up the steep stair to the rear deck, hurling him down before Intitepe who bent a little to look into an eye that was afire. A single eye, he realised, shining blue in the weathered face, for the other was puckered, a blade-slash across it. 'Ask him why he wants beer?'

The munke muttered. Sekantor laughed and replied. The munke translated, one of his eyes twitching. 'I am sorry, lord. He say because ... because he is thirsty.'

Intitepe couldn't help it – he laughed too. There was something about the man. He didn't stare in terror as most men did. Terror bored Intitepe. He used it, of course. But often over the centuries he had discovered that terrified men worked less well than those who had self-interest. 'Do you have beer on this ship?' he asked.

'We do, lord. We munke brew it. Better than water for voyage.'

'Bring some.' As Bezan turned away, he added, 'Bring for two.'

The munke called down to one of his fellows on the main deck. The man ran off, disappearing down stairs. Came back carefully bringing two large leathern tankards, spilling liquid as he came. He passed them up the steep stair to Bezan who brought them before the king.

'Give him one. Tell him not to taste it yet or he dies.'

Bezan spoke, then handed one tankard to Sekantor, who licked his lips but did not drink. Intitepe took the other vessel. 'Ask him how much he wants this drink?'

'He say, more than his life.'

'So he would give his life for this beer?'

'He says yes. He die happy.'

'Then,' Intitepe said, laying the Horse Lord's curved sword on the pirat's shoulder with one hand, and raising his own mug with the other, 'let us drink.'

The munke told him. Sekantor smiled. He locked his one eye on Intitepe's two, raised his mug, then spoke a long sentence – a toast, the Fire King guessed. Then, as the munke began to translate – a toast indeed, to an unheard-of thing: women who give sex for gold – the pirat gave a final shout, lifted the mug – and drained it.

Intitepe raised his, began to drink, spluttered, drank more – the taste was extraordinary, like nothing he'd ever known. The beers of his land were all made from wheat, were pale, had one sweet flavour. He'd always preferred the harvest of the grape. But this ... it was rich, deep, full of spices, none of which he'd savoured before. He drank on, pleasure in every moment, almost finished the mug, immediately craved another. He could see why a man would die for it, and die happy.

Sekantor the Savage was looking at him now. For the first time he wasn't smiling. He squinted at the blade still resting on his shoulder, then shrugged, lowered the tankard, and closed his eye.

Intitepe looked at the mug in his one hand, the sword in his other. Both looked ... shinier. 'Ask him how good a sailor he is.'

The munke asked. Sekantor didn't open his eye, though his brow wrinkled. He murmured something, and the munke said, 'He say he is the best at sailing in the world.'

'And is he also the best at thievery?'

Words passed. 'He say he even better at that.'

'Then ask him how he would steal the ships that are still to come?'

The munke murmured. Now Sekantor opened his one eye and looked straight at Intitepe before he spoke rapidly.

'He would do three things. The first would be, on these two ships, to make the sailors the slavs and the slavs the sailors.'

Intitepe smiled. He liked simple solutions. To have men on the deck who could sail, and men on the benches who could row, one group that he'd freed and so would have a little loyalty, another that he'd fought and so would be good to have chained up ... it was simply perfect. 'The second?' he said.

Sekantor spoke, a short sentence. The munke questioned him angrily, and Sekantor just repeated what he'd said. 'I sorry, lord. But pirate say you should make him captain.'

Intitepe nodded. 'And the third?'

Again Sekantor spoke. Again, the munke queried. 'Tell me what he said,' growled Intitepe.

'I sorry again, lord. It is him, he—'

'Tell me.'

The munke swallowed. 'He say you go to captain's cabin, you drink more beer, and then he show you how you easy steal ships that come.'

Intitepe looked into the tankard. There was yet some liquid in it, and he drank it off. It was still delicious. 'Tell him ... we will.'

The munke gasped, then spoke. Sekantor tipped back his head and laughed again. Then he kneeled down, and placed his forehead onto Intitepe's feet.

The fire god looked again to the horizon where he hoped to see sails appear shortly. What then, he wondered?

For four hundred years, aside from the occasional peasant rebellion, his realm had been at peace. It been savage at its beginning, though, when he had fought and beaten and killed every rival – his father, his seven sons. Finally Saroc, prophet-king and last male immortal. But all that was a long faded memory of glory. And though he'd learned to live with peace, though he thought he'd been content with a life making love to the women in his marana, in discovering the secrets of plants and stars, he now realised that truly he had never been happy. He was bred for adventure. For war. There were new lands to conquer, new adventures to be had. New enemies to kill.

He raised the wondrous curved sword he'd taken. The first sunbeams of the day glistened in its planes. Dawn had come, and the world was beginning all over again.

'It is the last of it, little doe,' the woman said. 'See! See for yourself. How pretty you look!'

She stepped away, and Atisha looked at herself in the glass. Yet another wonder of the new world she had entered. Back home, no woman or man ever got a clear view of themselves, for their only reflection was in the shifting surface of water. But in what they called a mirror, she could see the whole of herself.

And she wasn't pleased.

It wasn't just the reality of who she was – a young woman, pleasant enough in looks, she supposed, nothing remarkable. Intitepe had chosen her for his marana not for her beauty but for her questing, questioning mind. That had lured him, rather than her face or body. She knew that she was skinnier than she'd ever been: worry and then the four-week voyage with foul food had done that. But the women who tended her, dressed her, painted her face and did her hair, were not interested in what was real. They wanted only illusion.

She stared. The long dress she wore, buttoned from neck to ankle, was so tight she could only move in a sort of shuffle. Her hair had been washed, straightened with tongs, its curliness taken out, so it hung in two straight brown shanks down to her shoulders. Colours had been applied to her face, lightening her browner skin, till she was almost as pale as the women who tended her, who had come aboard the day before as soon as they docked. They had also used paint to make her eyes huge – necessary, they told her, so more in the crowds could see her.

The crowds, she thought, and shuddered. They'd been mentioned, though not truly talked about. As if they were trying not to startle 'the doe', their paza. But by the little she'd understood, she was being presented to a world and its people who knew of her coming, had been awaiting her for years.

No, she thought again, not me.

She looked across, to the cradle where Poum slept, though she was awake now, her fingers in her mouth, crooning in the way she had when she was fed, and content.

Atisha looked, straight at the core of her child, who'd thrown off her loose coverings again. She'd tried to think of Poum as 'she'. For it was a boy, a son, that Intitepe feared, that he wanted to slay; in a girl there was safety. But truly there was nothing there to define her child either way. There was the round and the straight. The soft and the hard. Atisha had kept hoping that all would entirely change. That Poum would be a daughter in fact as well as desire. But nothing had altered.

And of course, nothing altering was exactly what her captors wanted. Every one of them that she had encountered, from the hardened Horse Lord Korshak, to these three women sent aboard; every sailor on the ship and the monk with his black eyes – all did nothing but gaze upon Poum and her difference in rapture. No, worse. They gazed in worship.

My poor little one, Atisha thought. From her birth the child had been cursed with prophecy. In Ometepe, a king thought that *he* was the son born to slay him. In Saghaz-a, the child was born to save all humanity because *she* was he and her.

Poum was not clothed and would not be. Poum was naked to show the world who she-he was. Perhaps there is a better way to think of him-her? Atisha thought. Perhaps I should embrace them ... both? Perhaps Poum is ... *they*?

Yet whatever *they* were, they were her baby. So when the knock came on the door, and Korshak stepped in to say, 'It is time,' it was Atisha who went quickly to the cradle and lifted Poum from it, before any of the women could.

There had been noise beyond the ship's wooden walls from

the moment Atisha woke to hear it. A constant murmur like you would find near a hive. Yet she knew that this sound was made by humans, not bees. Sometimes another noise would come – a trumpet sound, or a drum struck. Voices had begun a chant that was like a song, men and women in harmony, singing and repeating one word, that word which had been the first she'd learned of the complex language of which she now had a basic grasp.

One.

Wrapping Poum in the soft blanket *they* lay upon, she pulled her baby to her chest, did not move despite Korshak waving in the doorway. The cabin, this wooden world she'd occupied on the four-week voyage from Ometepe, seemed just then the only safe place to be.

'Come, paza,' said the woman who'd painted her face. 'The world is waiting.'

Instead of daunting her, Atisha suddenly found the words had the opposite effect. She had never been frightened of the world. Where she came from there were friends and enemies everywhere. People both good and bad. She could only assume it was the same in this land she'd arrived in – and that there was someone in it who would help her.

'Then let us not keep it waiting,' she said and, as much as the tightness of the dress allowed, she swept out of the room.

She'd dressed in the cabin of the master of the ship. Its door gave straight onto the main deck. This was lined with trumpeters, all in the black robes of the monks. The moment she appeared, they raised their instruments and blew one long, single, triumphant note. Yet even before the sound had faded from the air, something four times as loud overwhelmed it.

Thousands of people screaming that word.

'One!'

She stepped back, as if she had been struck. In her arms,

Poum's eyes went wide in shock, though *they* did not cry. Squinting against powerful sunlight, Atisha looked out onto this new world.

Their ship was one of several drawn up at a long wooden dock. Many others rested at anchor in the bay, bounded by a curved crescent of land, like a curl of ox horns that nearly met at a gap where, she noticed, sea mists roiled. Behind the dock the land rose sharply, buildings large and smaller on terraces that ran the length of the ox horns, all around the bay.

Each flat rooftop, any open space and every ship was packed with people. They were doing the screaming.

'One!' the word crashed down upon her and Poum again and again, before fading like an echo.

She looked away from the mob, to the relative quietness before her. Directly opposite the cabin, standing in front of that line of trumpeters, were four figures – three men and a woman.

The tallest was another Horse Lord, like Korshak. This man also wore the kirtle that reached from shoulder to mid-thigh. But his was elaborate, with the straps that ran its length adorned with gems, and with breast- and backplates of that polished metal – steel, it was called – instead of leather. His helmet was steel too, but decorated with renderings of eagles, and real bird feathers iridescent in the crest. As she looked at him, he swept the helmet off and bowed deep.

The second man was a Seafarer, as she'd learned the sailors were termed. Again he was like the men she'd sailed with in attire, but outdoing them in ostentation. His blouse was purple and suffused in silk trim. His breeches were velvet, with silver thread running in bands up the sides. His hat was covered in lace, which fell in shimmers as he swept it from his head in another bow to her.

The one woman was a sober contrast, in blouse and breeches of deepest forest green. Unadorned, save for a large brooch of shining silver on the left of the chest – a beast, half woman half horse, drawing back a bow. She had no hat. When she bowed, her hair fell thick and unbound to her waist. Her eyes held the keenest look of all.

The last man was also soberly dressed – a monk, though his plush robes were not a dull black but shot through with the deepest purple. His eyes were beyond black too – she'd become almost used to the eyes of the monk who'd come with her and was her main tutor in language. His eyes were dark – but this man's? They appeared of a bottomless depth. He alone came forward, and also bowed, though it was the merest inclination of his head. Then he began to speak – in her language, and almost without accent.

'Fairest. Purest. Mother of the One and of us all. Welcome to your land.'

He spoke loudly, as if Atisha was standing far away, rather than just before him. Spoke for others too then. Spoke slowly, his words being translated and repeated from deck to dock, and spreading around the port like the twittering of starlings. He places himself at the heart of this, she thought. He who claims to know me and my world best.

He lowered his voice so only those near could hear. 'We are the leaders of the Four Tribes. Four who are now one people.' He turned slightly, and each of those behind him tipped their heads when he spoke their names. 'Karania the Huntress. Baromolak of the Horse Lords. Framilor, Seafarer.' He turned back. 'And I am Anazat, head of the order of monks at the Keep.' He gestured to the dock, and the ramp that had been set from ship to shore. 'Will you come?' he said.

'Do I have a choice?' Atisha muttered, but if he heard, if he understood, Anazat did not react, just stood with arm still outstretched.

If the noise had been loud when she came from the cabin, it

was louder when she placed her foot upon the shore. Poum did startle then, began to cry. Clutching *them* to her chest, Atisha followed Anazat, as she was followed by the other leaders, along a roadway that wound steeply up the hill. It was lined by Seafarers, horse warriors, monks and Huntresses, arms linked and holding back the crowds of townsfolk who pressed forward, stretching out their arms, acclaiming her. No, acclaiming the one whom she carried.

Eventually, they reached a white building, the largest there and in the very middle of the slopes. Climbed a staircase up one side, came into a large room. Beyond it was a wide, roofless terrace which they led her onto. Now she could look all the way around – the cliffs that circled the bay, the ships upon it, the vessel she'd arrived on still at the dock. Every space, apart from the waves themselves, was filled with people. There were still mists at the harbour mouth, a bank of sea fog that seemed held back from the bay itself. The clouds above had parted and joined many times in their walk. Now, they parted again and the sun shone, dazzling them all.

Anazat stepped close. 'It is time,' he said.

'Time for what?'

'To show the truth.' He gestured to Poum, still crying and squirming in her arms. 'Show the world what it has been waiting for, yearning for.'

'No.' Atisha was surprised at how firmly she said it.

Anazat leaned closer, whispered. 'If you do not, I will.'

She could sense other monks moving nearer. She looked around, seeking pity, help. But everyone was stone to her, staring only at Poum, waiting. Everywhere, there were only her enemies.

Then she looked down – and saw him. She had not noticed him before. Was it because he was the smallest man there? No, she thought, not that. Perhaps it was because he had not tried

76

to be seen, lost among the taller men and women and him so different, with his red-gold hair, his one bulky shoulder, his awkward stance. Yet in the moment of seeing she found what she'd sought, what she had not seen once since the day she'd sailed from Ometepe. There'd been worship, desire, hunger, wonder – but never compassion. Which she saw now in this small man's eyes.

'Who are you?' she asked in the tongue of her captors.

He replied in the same, and it sounded as strange in his mouth as it had in hers. 'My name is Luck,' he said. 'And I think you must do what *they* ask.'

'They?' she said, catching a note in the word.

'Our enemy,' he said, just before Anazat snapped an order, and two monks dragged the small man away, into the crowd, out of her sight.

There was at least one other here who knew his enemy. And he had given her a moment of hope. She turned, and began to unfold Poum's blanket.

Suddenly another trumpet sounded. It was very different from any she'd heard so far. Its note was so deep she felt the vibration of it through the floor, through her feet, up inside her. A murmur arose all around and, like everyone on the terrace, she looked to the source of the sound, beyond the dock to the mouth of the bay ...

... and saw four sea serpents burst from the mist.

77

4

Raiders from the Sea

Hovard, his hand on the sea serpent's neck, stared ahead ... and gasped.

He'd known this world would be different. The coasts they'd sailed and rowed along had changed from the rocky, barren promontories of northern Midgarth, softened gradually into lush forests and finally to tall chalk cliffs surmounted by grassy banks. The change began after the Maelstrom, that clash of wind and wave and submerged rock that had always marked their furthest point north. No one in their history had made it past the Maelstrom, though many had died trying. Hovard's mortal parents, Bryn and Marka, had been some of the first, and that had been four hundred years before. Stromvar had tried twice in his life, been wrecked twice, lost all his crew and only made it home each time by possessing once a whale and once a walrus. He had been known as the Walrus for a time, though never to his face. Two of their present fleet, which had set out three weeks before, had been lost to the Maelstrom. Mortals all, for the gods were on the four others. Chance, combined perhaps with greater experience, had saved them.

He swivelled to look at those ships now. At each single mast a different coloured pennant flew, and at each prow there stood a god. Freya sailed nearest him. Stromvar was beyond her, with

Bjorn on the far left. Those two were, as ever, pushing ahead. Racing each other to glory.

Is that what awaits us here? Hovard wondered, turning back to the sight that had taken his breath, this enormous town, bigger than five Askaugs. He knew he hadn't set out for glory but for knowledge. To learn of this enemy – who they were, how strong they were, in what style they fought – had been decided upon at the Moot on Galahur, once Hovard had proved his right to command by killing the monster Ut the Slayer. Waiting for death to come to them, like sheep penned close to the butcher block, was not the Midgarthian way. And though he'd tried to persuade one of the other three to remain behind, as they'd tried to persuade him, none would. So the preparations to defend the land had been left to other gods to organise, the northerner Petr the Red and Einar the Black, from the southern forests, taking the lead.

We are here now, all of us, Hovard thought. And to learn anything, we must fight.

He swung from the prow and dropped onto the platform behind it. Raised above the deck, some hated it – Bjorn prominent among them – because it spoiled the lines of the graceful sea creature, part otter, part shark, that was the Midgarth longboat. But Luck had designed it, to support a weapon he'd invented, derived from the only weapon he was any good with: the slingshot. Dried ox gut was stretched and wound tight around a pole, with a leather sack on its end in which a shaped stone the size of a large man's head was placed. Though he had never built one, his brother had left charcoal sketches on hide. Sensing they might need something of the kind, Hovard had set men to create it. And even Bjorn had been impressed by the destruction this new weapon could cause – especially after Hovard added a refinement.

To be unleashed, when? Hovard peered ahead. There were

crowds everywhere he looked, more people gathered in one place than he'd ever seen, equal to the entire population of Askaug, Lorken and the Seven Isles at least. But since his eyes were ever good, he saw that most were just people, townsfolk. It was on board the vessels, these strange, high-sided, many-masted ships, that men with weapons stood, startled, no doubt, by what had sprung suddenly out of the mist. What Hovard recognised was an invasion force, its destination their motherland. So they would stop them here, some of them anyway, before the enemy headed to Midgarth's shores.

One of those vessels, nearest the opening of the bay, was directly ahead now, perhaps three hundred paces away if water were land. He could hear the shouting on board, saw the anchor being hauled up.

Hovard cupped his hands, and bellowed back to the rowers. 'Hold left! Pull right!'

The serpent head bore to the right. Turning back, sighting, changing the elevation slightly, Hovard spoke to the man beside him. Ulrich the smith was a mortal suited to the task Hovard had given him because contained in the metal barrel before him was something he worked with every day. 'Now, Ulrich.'

The smith prised the lid off the container, leaned away from the sudden, intense heat that rose from it, took up a torch and thrust it in. It caught; he handed it to Hovard who lit the oil-impregnated sacking on the projectile in his sling before flinging the brand into the sea. Fire was dangerous on a wooden ship – as he hoped his enemies were about to find out.

Pulling out the holding pin, he threw himself face down onto the platform.

The sling uncurled, faster and faster, whirring through the air like a thousand bees. He could feel the shock when the rope reached its end, through his belly where it touched the wood; heard the unfolding, the whoosh of stone departing through air. Raised his head, watched its trajectory, a fiery comet with a trail of smoke that smashed through the railings on the enemy's deck. He was near enough now to hear the screams.

It was followed closely by others. Freya's blazing stone also found its mark on a different vessel. Stromvar and Bjorn shot too, though without fire for now, because their task was different. Then, swinging their prows, they pursued their unlit stones towards the largest warship in the bay. Following the plan. As was Freya. He could see her, leaning hard on her rudder, her ship heading back towards him, both of them aiming for the dock ahead.

While he was looking he was winding. With the sling latched again against its springs, he took another shrouded rock from the pile, placed it into the sling, and nodded at Ulrich.

Grinning, the smith passed him another brand.

Bjorn glanced at Stromvar's longship. Somehow it had got half a boat length ahead. Turning back from his perch on the prow he yelled, 'Double time!' and his benchmen responded. It was early to go to double time, his men could not keep it up for long. But they were nearly there, at their target – and he so badly wanted to win. It was always a race, between him and Stromvar. Over the centuries that they had fought each other in single combat, it was a race to see who could defeat the other – kill the other – three times in a row. Both had only ever managed it twice. Here, the race was to see who would have the glory of being the first god on an enemy's deck. Not a native enemy. The first from beyond their seas.

He looked past the Dragon Lord's vessel. Hovard and Freya's ships were pulling hard for the dock. Even as he watched, two stones flew from them almost simultaneously, describing high and fiery arcs before smashing into two of the tall white buildings ahead. Before them, upon the dock and in the crowded roads behind it that switchbacked up the steep hillside, he could see the results of those shots – crowds of people scattering like ants whose nest has been poked by boys. Screams came on the offshore wind. Whatever was in the struck buildings had to be tinder dry, for smoke was already swirling high into the sky.

He looked again at his rival. Stromvar had called for double time too. But Bjorn had caught up and he saw that this race, at least, would be won by neither – for the enemy ship was only three boat lengths ahead now. 'Pull ... and brace!' he yelled. As the men behind him obeyed, gave one last great heave and shipped their oars, Bjorn wrapped his arms around the sling-shot's mount a moment before the serpent prow, with its chest of oak carved to a point and strengthened with bars of iron, smashed into the wooden walls of the enemy.

Everyone was flung hard forward. But all were braced – and up the next moment, their first weapons to hand. Bows. Arrows flew up – and down. Shocked the enemy may have been but they were also fighters. Yet there were not enough of them and they were cleared from their railing by a storm of steel-tipped shafts.

There was netting hanging over the ship's side, rungs of rope the size of fingers. Convenient if you were painting the vessel, or bringing men aboard. Less so if you didn't wish an enemy to join you on your deck. In a swift glance left, Bjorn saw that Stromvar was about to do exactly that.

'Seven Isles!' the Dragon Lord yelled.

'With me! Askaug!' Bjorn cried, leaping at the netting, seizing hold, climbing. Some arrows still flew from behind him, keeping the enemy clear. Only a few, because only the best archers had that task. The rest of his men knew theirs – to follow their leader aboard.

He reached the top, peered over – and flung himself sideways as a man thrust a spear straight at his face. The man's own face came close, and Bjorn flung himself back, using momentum and the give of the rope to drive his forehead into the man's nose. He tumbled back and, swinging again, Bjorn got his feet onto the rim of the wooden wall and, in the next instant, stood up upon it. Using the instant after to draw his sword, Sever-Life, from his waist and yank his smaller, sea-fight shield off his back.

Now was not the time for thinking. Now was the time for fighting. He'd been doing it for close to four hundred years and he had never grown tired of it. The opposite.

As he balanced on the wall, three more men came at him, two with swords, one with a spear. Since the long weapon arrived first, he dealt with it first – swept his shield down and used its edge to knock the thrust away. Swept a cut into the man's neck as he stumbled past. Knew it had bitten, turned to the next threats, one sword thrust, the other slashed. Parried the first with Sever-Life, turning his wrist up as he did and jabbing the point into the man's eye, before bringing it hard down and across to meet the force of the next man's cut. This third had stepped close – too close, and Bjorn punched his small shield straight into his eyes.

Three foes down – and a pause. Some of his own men were beside him now – Tiny Elric, apprentice smith, and bigger even than his father and master Ulrich, was wielding a weapon chosen from his trade, a huge smelting hammer. The giant leaped down onto the deck and, sweeping it in huge arcs, carved a space around him that more and still more of his comrades filled.

There were plenty of the enemy on the deck – decks, Bjorn remembered, glancing left and right, for at each end of the vessel a low tower stood. Near the front one, he saw Stromvar – unmistakable for his vast height, as tall as Elric, as well as for the noise he was making, roars of laughter as men ran at him and men died. The Dragon Lord was wielding twin axes, each one of which an ordinary man would use with both hands. The arc they scythed before him created an empty space of steel-whirred air and he and his crew advanced into it, heading for the raised deck above the prow.

Which left, as was planned, the aft tower for Bjorn. Still aloft, he looked down and saw that his boarding crew were all aboard, gathered on the part of the deck that Tiny Elric had cleared with his hammer. Bjorn jumped down, raised Sever-Life and his shield high, and yelled, 'With me!'

They drove forward in the spear-blade formation, a steel wedge used to smash an enemy's shield wall. He and the smith were the tip, and at first it was easy. Few of the enemy had had time to don armour, they were a scattered mob, and the spear-blade thrust through them, the only difficulty the bodies tripping the feet, and the deck slickening with blood. But then Bjorn heard the cries behind him, looked back and saw two of his own men reel from the wedge, arrows in their shoulders. He looked up, to the raised deck, and saw archers there, three of them, notching and shooting fast. Three women.

'Sky shields!' he yelled, and his men snapped their shields up over their heads, to protect them from above, as they would to approach a gate tower in a siege. Immediately he felt the strike on his shield, for the first time regretting the choice of a small one. He could take an arrow and live. He could take one and die only to be reborn. He wanted neither, especially when he could tell, from the roaring at the other end of the ship, even louder and more triumphant now, that Stromvar was about to capture his deck.

He stepped under the wider shelter of Elric's big shield. 'Split!' he cried, realising his mistake in the instant. For the smith went left, to the stair he'd been assigned – and an arrow immediately passed through Bjorn's shirt at his shoulder. There was agony as it gouged his flesh but at least it didn't lodge.

Yelping, trying to make himself as small as he could under his platter-sized shield, he ran to the right stair.

Two of his men had beaten him to it. Each got halfway up the stair before they tumbled back, shot. Bjorn rushed up, felt two more arrows pass a finger's width either side of his face – and then he was on the deck, whirling his sword in a great arc about him.

There were not many of the enemy there – perhaps a dozen, bows cast aside now, swords in hand. A dozen, perhaps the same number he led. Yet the three who faced him were women. He had learned, in the arrogance of his youth and to his cost – for it had been the first time he'd died in battle – that women warriors could be the toughest of all.

He didn't have long to take them in – an impression of long fair hair, and clothes of forest green – before they came at him. For just a moment he had all three, and only just managed to avoid their thrusts, taking one on his shield, one on his sword, one with a sharp swivel of his hips. Then his men were with him, and the fight swirled. There was one before him, and he glimpsed, before she attacked, a pretty face, twisted in rage.

She didn't have a shield. Her sword was longer even than Sever-Life, but with a thinner blade, and he guessed, suddenly and by the way she lunged at him, one arm at full stretch and the other slapping down behind her, that her weapon could only kill with its point. The observation, his curiosity of all ways of the sword, nearly killed him, as he felt the steel slide into his side when she eluded the parry he swept down with a flick of her wrist, coming under his blade. It was a good lunge, it could have killed another man, and he saw her see it, saw it in eyes he realised were startlingly green, and triumphing. But the triumph was premature – he was a god, after all – and it was almost with regret that he stepped close and punched his shield into the side of her head. He hit her hard ... but perhaps not as hard as he could have.

She fell, body and sword smacking the deck. Whirling, shield thrust out and sword raised, he checked for danger. But the fight here was over. Three of his men were dead, but so were most of the enemy, the others face down on the deck. Only one of them still had a sword in hand – a short man, with a face beaten by wind and waves; a sailor then, richly dressed in a doublet of purple, and his brown hair flowing in styled waves over his shoulder. The master of this vessel, for sure. He looked at the Northmen surrounding him, looked at his own dead men and the three felled women on the deck, then said something loudly in his guttural foreign tongue. When no one moved, or replied, he sighed, reversed his sword, kneeled, and held it out to Bjorn.

Who took it. It was the same kind that the woman had stuck into him. It had jewels on its elaborate guard and, as he discovered as he swirled it through the air, a wonderful balance that he looked forward to studying.

But not yet. Things to do first. He leaned over the railings and looked down at his own ship. As had been planned, it had disengaged, and was held on oars a boat's length away.

'Now,' he called.

Soren, his second in command, nodded, removed the lid, then dipped a brand into his fire barrel, unused till now. When it caught, he lifted then laid it on the special sacked stone in the sling. Special, because when he released the pin, when it flew in a high arc towards the town, it not only flamed but whistled, the holes bored through the rock making it shriek like a sea eagle plunging for salmon.

He'd recognised the horn as soon as it sounded. Midgarth horns were forged from brass in all sizes. Ulrich, the smith of

Askaug, was a master maker. It was one of his larger ones that had sounded in the bay.

Yet Luck still did not fully believe it. Thought at first it could be just another thing he heard, that he wished for, that wasn't there. Ever since his voyage with Sirene, his time with Gytta, that world had seemed the real one, this one the illusion. The three times he'd voyaged since had only added to that certainty. He had not seen his beloved again, hard though he'd searched for her. But he had seen other things. Wondrous. Terrible. Now, when he looked in reflecting glass, eyes that were getting blacker by the day stared back.

It was only when he noted how those around him reacted, screamed, ran, that he realised they'd heard the horn too.

His people had come.

He was not surprised. Of course they had. The men and women of Midgarth were not the kind to wait, head lowered like a beast for the butcher's maul to fall. He could imagine them out there now. Hovard the Wise and Bjorn Swiftsword. Stromvar the Dragon. Perhaps Freya too?

He could imagine them. But he could not journey to them. Sirene, in exchange for her gifts, had taken away so much.

Anazat the monk had been angry that he'd spoken to the woman from the faraway land. He'd been dragged from her sight ... but not taken from the terrace. For Anazat wished him to witness the prophecy fulfilled. Witness the power of the child, as that child was revealed to the world. Anazat, with his plans for everyone, in all worlds.

He'd seen the child before of course; twice, in his early journeys with Sirene. The child that was neither boy nor girl and was both. The child these people believed had come to redeem them all. Luck knew how important Anazat thought this day, this first revelation, was. The news of it to be carried throughout Saghaz-a, and inspire its people to conquest.

No wonder he's so angry, Luck thought, looking again at the raging monk, who was shouting commands. Midgarth's horn had spoiled all his plans. Another tale would be told of this day.

Both the terrace and the room were clearing, messengers dispatched with orders. From the corner where he'd been thrown, he could again see the young woman holding the baby. For once she was being ignored, standing bewildered, as men swirled and shouted around her.

It came to him then, with a force like a slap. Her baby was what held the people of Saghaz-a together. Without the child, the prophecy, what were they? Four tribes who had fought each other for centuries. Who would perhaps, without the belief that bound them, fight each other again? The question penetrated the dullness he found now shrouded this so-called real world. For he realised he *had* found a way to help his people in the fight.

Men ran about, shouting. No one paid any attention to him. No one noticed when he stood up and drew out his knife. For what he planned to do he needed blood. His own, then someone else's.

He dragged the blade across his palm.

Freya had kept part of her attention on the water. Hard, when there was so much fighting to be done on land.

Then she heard it, the sea eagle's shriek. Saw the flaming stone strike. *Hovard,* she said, but not with her voice. They had both sliced the palms of their hands before battle. Now she would be able to speak to him in her mind across a mountain, further, even if he were back in Midgarth. It was easy here, only fifty paces away, the noise of battle nothing.

She saw her husband look at her, look to the sky, and nod. *Do you think I am deaf, wife?* he called.

The whistling fireball plunged into the roof of a house not

yet aflame, one of the few. *Time to go,* she thought to him, and he replied, *Yes.*

They had done what they set out to. The fireball told them that Stromvar and Bjorn had taken a ship – one of these so-different ships that they must study if they were to beat the enemy that was coming. They had delayed that invasion perhaps for a time – the houses in the docks had been filled with weapons and other supplies. But more important than that, they had told these people something.

Come if you dare. For we are not afraid.

She had not had to fight much. The crowds upon the docks were not soldiers in the main and had fled in terror at the serpent ships' approach. They were almost unhindered as they destroyed what they couldn't plunder. Their ships at the dock now bore many barrels of food and ale, cloaks and jewels, strange weapons. The town burned. They had left their mark all right. They would take plunder, hope and defiance back to Midgarth.

A voice was again in her head. And if a voice in a head could sound strange, this one did. *What did you say, Hovard?* she thought, looking at him.

She could see him look up; was close enough to see his frown. *I?* he replied. *Nothing.*

And then the voice came again.

Freya.

'Luck?' She staggered as she said his name out loud. Then, resting her sword tip on the ground, she leaned on it and called his name again in her mind. *Luck! Where are you?*

Here. Up here!

She looked up. At the top of the hill was the largest building in the town. The centre of whatever they'd been planning this day, she guessed, because it was decorated with large banners, and had a huge roof terrace facing the bay, a crowd upon it. Now she could sense Luck there. It was too far up the switchbacked roads, with too many people between her and it, to reach it on foot.

On the wing though?

She looked down. Having been one so often, she understood how birds felt. How they existed beside man, yet lived in an entirely different world. Man did what he did, and the only time a bird became involved with him was when he presented an opportunity. A ploughshare turning up a worm for a thrush. A fisherman gathering herring in a net for a gull to dive upon ...

... one warrior killing another so that crows and ravens could feast.

There was a crow before her now, tearing at the guts of one of the few soldiers she'd killed. She called, and the bird turned its blue-black eye onto her. And then she was gone, the crow's resistance to her nothing, only a caw of frustration as she flew him away from his meal.

She landed on the low wall that fronted a terrace. Some men were still upon that, richly dressed, pointing at the raiders in the harbour and shouting orders to others below. In the room beyond, there were fewer people. She saw a young woman, standing alone in one corner, with a baby in her arms, terror on her face. And then, in the opposite corner, she saw Luck.

Within the bird, the goddess gasped. He had never been a cockerel like his brother Bjorn, strutting with the lush plumage of colourful clothes and a gaudy comb of styled hair. But Luck had always dressed soberly, cleanly and kept his beard trimmed. The Luck before her wore a sack-like robe in need of cleaning, while his beard bushed up his face and spilled over his neck. Also, with the sharp sight of the bird, she saw that his eyes, the eyeballs themselves, had grown dark. They were blackened.

It would be dangerous to fly across the room to him. She cawed once, then bent her mind to his.

Luck. I am here.

She saw him jerk up, look wildly around. One hand had a knife in it, the other dripped blood, where he'd cut himself to speak to her.

Here. On the terrace wall.

His dark eyes focused on her.

This is a joy beyond all price, she said. *Come now, for we have done what we set out to do and now we return to Midgarth.*

Hovard? Bjorn?

On the dock and in the harbour, awaiting us. Come here beside me. I will lure a mate to this bird. Let us fly.

He did not take a step towards her. *No. I cannot.*

You can, and swiftly.

He took a step towards her. *No, I cannot. I have lost the way of it.*

'What?' She cawed the word aloud, the shock of it was so great. It was as if he'd said he had lost the ability to breathe.

Another voice intruded. Hovard's. *Freya, we must leave, now. They are starting to muster their forces. We must save our men and women.*

I come, she replied. But she didn't fly off, bent her mind again to Luck. *If you cannot,* she said, *then I will leave this bird and we will walk together to our ship. Hovard awaits.*

It is not possible.

I understand that you cannot fly. So we'll walk ...

No. She saw a sigh ripple through him. *I cannot leave here.*

She saw him anew then, the dark eyes. What he'd said about the drug that she'd seen him drop onto the glass back in Askaug half a year before. How ... it began a craving in him. *Luck,* she said, *we will go back. I have potions that will help you leave this ... darkness.*

No, that's not it. He swallowed. *There's something ... something I must still do here.*

When he thought this to her he looked away. She saw where

he looked – to the woman with the baby, standing in the corner.

Freya! Hovard's voice in her head was a shout. *Come now!*

Luck heard it, or sensed it. They both could also hear Midgarth's horn, sounding the summons of recall. Three short notes, one long. *Go,* he said.

But …

Freya, you know I am not a warrior. I can help us best here. Here is where my fight must be.

She had trusted his judgement in most matters for centuries. Now was not the time to doubt him, even with the darkness in his eyes.

Be careful, she called, then raised her wings, and flew. She heard his voice as she swooped towards the dock.

What is the point of that? she heard him say. Within the crow, even as she flew, she smiled. That was the old Luck speaking. He was still there.

She was gone. Freya whom he'd always loved. Freya, his brother Hovard's wife.

He knew he was right. He'd lied to her, of course. He was mainly staying for Sirene, her temptations, her sight, of course he was. For the chance to find Gytta again. But there was something else he could do too. He'd told the truth when he told her that he was not a warrior. But warriors' blood flowed in his veins and he could see an enemy clearly. Could see how he could change this war at a stroke, with the slaying of one.

Two, he corrected himself, hefting his dagger, crossing the room to the woman, and her baby.

Landing on the aft deck, Freya transformed to herself.

As the crow, with a last resentful caw, flew off to feed, she shouted, 'Cast off,' and her crew, who had all returned at the horn's summons, cut the lines that held them to the dock. 'Take her, Beornoth,' she called to her helmsman and she left him to get the men to their oar benches and guide her longship from the dock.

Hers led, while Hovard's was just behind and close to her left. They passed Bjorn and Stromvar's two vessels, which floated free again and swung about to follow close behind. Neither god was aboard them. Both were on the ship they'd captured, and as she passed she looked at it, the wind bellying the sails on its three masts. The rivals would set about learning all they could about the working of it from whoever they'd persuaded to captain it for them. Both would want the command of it; she fancied that, despite the wind and the drum that set the oar beat, she could already hear them arguing about it. Nothing like this had happened in three hundred years of sailing in Midgarth, all refinements to their sleek vessels having been settled centuries before.

Their land had become complacent in all ways. No more, she thought, as she turned her attention back to the town burning behind her. Though our enemies will not be so complacent now either.

Most of the houses in the town were wooden. About half of them were on fire, and the rest soon to catch, if the townsfolk, whom she could still see running like rats from an overturned nest, could not figure out how to stop it spreading. There was more fire in the bay, for Hovard had sent a flaming ball into as many ships as he could as he left. Even without knowing them, she could see that most of them were designed for war. This had been an invasion fleet, readying. And though she was joyful that they'd done those plans some damage, she also knew from the size of the vessels and the number of the people gathered there that they had only delayed, not stopped, what was ahead. How long they had, before these people came for their revenge, before it was Midgarth towns that burned, she could not know.

Still, it was a good beginning. And from the ship they'd captured, and the people upon it, they would learn much of this enemy. Enough, perhaps, to make a difference.

And Luck? He was the one who had decided to go and learn about them first. But what had he achieved? She had been shocked at the changes in him. The ones she saw. The ones she felt, when their minds were joined. His body and mind were equally ragged. Yet he was still Luck, the wisest god of them all. He could have come with her, somehow they'd have made it out. But he'd chosen to stay. Told her that he could fight best where he was. She hoped it was wisdom that guided him still, and not the smoke, blackening his mind as it had his eyes.

Luck? she called a last time. She waited, but got no response. He was about his own work now, so she set to hers.

No one noticed him as he crossed the room. No one noticed the dagger in his hand, nor the intent on his face.

People passed in front of him, running, shouting, now blocking the mother and the baby from his sight, now revealing them. He stopped when he was halted, moved when he could, step by step closer to his destiny. Nothing less than the saving of his whole world.

He had never liked to kill. Even animals he took only to eat, to feed others, or to study how a body worked. Necessity had always driven him. It drove him here.

He reached them, standing in their corner. The woman was so different from any he'd seen before. She had skin the light-dark colour of tanned deer hide, and as smooth, though it was streaked in paint she must have mostly rubbed off. Her eyes were narrow, shaped like mussel shells, a darker brown. She was of a height with him and he was, of course, small for his race. Perhaps she was tall for hers.

He had learned some things about her. Anazat had told him

a little, and whenever he'd mentioned her to others their eyes would grow light, they would stare above him in joy. But that was nothing to the rapture all expressed when they talked of the baby. The one born in a far-off land. The one born to save them all. The one who was neither boy nor girl and was both.

The One.

She – he – looked only like an infant in her arms. Squirming, fussing, disturbed by all the noise, the scent of burning, the cries of people killing and dying in the harbour. The woman was trying to attach the baby to her breast, exposed from the side of her robe. It was many years since Luck had seen a woman's breast and many more since he had seen a child offered one. Since Freya had suckled the last of her daughters, Raika, then refused to have any more. For, she'd told him, the pain of laying onto a pyre an old woman that she had raised as a baby to her breast was just too great.

As he watched, the babe sniffed milk, gave a final wail, and latched on.

That last suckling he'd witnessed had been more than one hundred years before. He'd forgotten how natural the moment was, how tender. He knew he shouldn't wait, shouldn't hesitate. If you are not one who easily kills, when you decide you must – as the few such occasions had taught him – it was best to strike quickly and have done. He gripped the dagger tighter, stepped forward.

And then the woman looked up at him. 'Thank you,' she said. She spoke in the language of Saghaz-a.

He halted. 'For what?' he replied in the same.

'For giving me …' She looked away, hesitating, seeking a word, before her eyes were on his again. 'Hope,' she said. Then she sat on the floor and turned her attention fully to the baby at her breast.

Hope, Luck thought. This child is the prophecy of hope to

this land. This child has united these four tribes behind that hope. This child offers them the world to conquer. He could end that hope with a thrust.

And yet ... It came to him suddenly, what Gytta had said to him in that garden, in the vision Sirene had guided him to. His wife had said, 'You may be the only one who can stop what is to come.' But she was the gentlest soul he had ever known. She had spoken to him of love. And this that he'd thought to do, this killing of a baby, he realised, suddenly and certainly, was the opposite of all that she had meant.

Sheathing his dagger, he lowered himself to the floor beside the mother and the child.

Anazat sat facing the globe, too tired to raise the vial in his hand.

He'd been exhausted before he'd reached the northern port of Billandah. Exhausted from the ceaseless travelling, the effort it took to keep the Four Tribes united. This day, with the arrival of the One, was meant to end that effort. Once the child was revealed, and the word spread, there would be no more dissension. All would be truly united, and at last on more than a prophecy. On the reality. And then the plan – nothing less than the conquest of the world – could begin.

The Midgarthians had changed that. He could still smell the smoke from their burning of the town. This port, which was to have been the launch point for the seaborne invasion of Midgarth, could no longer serve. Most of the carefully amassed supplies had been destroyed. As bad, the Northmen had stolen a ship. All reports had told him that the people of that land, men, women and gods, were indulgent, self-absorbed, obsessed with their way of life, the fighting and the feasting. No reports had said that they were stupid.

Now they would be ready. They would understand far better

how to fight the invaders from Saghaz-a. So a greater fleet must be gathered than even the one planned. A whole new plan devised and ports to support it stocked.

But he had learned something long ago: that to achieve his will he must adapt. He would not have come this far without knowing how to deal with a setback. However great this one, there were ways to move around it.

In Midgarth he had his slave, Peki Asarko, who had failed to disunite the land at their gathering, failed to kill the leader that could unite them, the one who'd come and burned the town that day, Hovard. The Lord of the Lake of Souls had lain low since his failure and Anazat had been too busy to work him up again. Now that time had come. He would speak to him through the smoke in the glass and force him to begin a campaign of murder and savagery, to turn the Midgarthians in, when all their attention should be out.

He would do that after. There was someone else he must speak to first.

He sighed, opened the vial, poured a single drop onto the globe. Immediately, the smoke within it began to swirl, and then clear.

The prophet some knew as Smoke appeared within the smoke. 'Anazat,' the immortal from Corinthium said.

'Lord Makron. What news?'

It was swiftly conveyed. Their army in the cave beneath the mountains had been discovered before they could break through. They were being held, for now. Makron had plans, though they might involve some further delays.

'No delays,' said Anazat. 'You must change your plans.'

The renegade struggled with the orders, knowing how they would be received by the Horse Lords. But when Anazat conveyed the necessity, in forceful terms, Makron accepted what must be.

When he understood, and was gone, Anazat slumped back. He had never needed sleep more – but first he had to speak to Peki Asarko. Another traitor to his people, like Makron, who would set his own world ablaze.

Plans change, he thought, as he reached for the vial again. But at least I now know this: though they may lose hundreds of men in the doing of it, the Horse Lords will storm through the mountains, and sweep to the Great Sea. Three weeks after that ... Corinthium will fall.

5

The Battle of the Ridge

In the tunnel, they had no need to build a barrier of stone or wood. The enemy built their own – of flesh.

They did not lack courage. They kept coming. Dying. They used large shields to stop the arrows but their stumbling over their fallen meant that there was always a moment when a shield slipped, and an arrow found a gap. There had been pauses when no one came, an hour or so at a time when Ferros was able to give his men, in groups, the chance to rest, eat, drink. He assumed the enemy would start trying different things. Every moment they paused to think of them was a moment bought for the reinforcements to come. Roxanna had ridden for the town, Tarfona, six hours before. If they assembled fast, and brought spare horses, a cavalry regiment could be here by dawn the next day. Twelve hours away. Ferros thought that he could hold the tunnel till then. If he did not run out of arrows, though the dead yielded a few every time there was a lull, when his men could slip forward and scavenge them.

'Commander! I think they come again.'

Ferros dropped his cup, and ran back through the entrance. He'd ordered holes hammered into the walls, torches pushed into them, so some were always burning, flamelight dancing over jagged stone. There was little to see, save for that gruesome pile of dead. His sentry had called him for what he'd heard.

The chant was low, the tongue, of course, unknown to him. Yet the intent was clear. Beyond the other entrance men were again preparing to charge and die.

Ferros notched an arrow. Beside him, three men did the same. He turned to a fourth, whose hand hovered over the huge weapon called the Bow of Mavros. Usually used in sieges to batter at towers and walls, its bolt, with its spear-blade tip, was even deadlier in that narrow cave. 'Do not shoot unless I say,' he ordered. They had only five bolts left – they smashed on stone having passed through body or shield, and Ferros felt sure he would need these last ones.

They did not come in a rush this time. And it was not a man that first appeared – but what looked like a raft, the height of a man and made up of logs lashed together and pushed first lengthwise into the tunnel, then swiftly spun to stand upright, its tip nearly on the roof, its base scraping over the dead. Men held it, men they could not see, men they could hear, uttering that same war cry. 'Wait.' Ferros said softly. 'Wait.'

The cry grew louder. The raft jerked up and down as the men holding it traversed the bodies, and targets were revealed for a moment – a shoulder, a lower leg. There was a chance to shoot, to fell one of the men. But Ferros had a different plan.

'Wait.'

The raft was past the bodies. The men were no longer stumbling. They were about a dozen paces away now and with a giant shout they began to run.

Ferros turned to the man at the Bow of Mavros. 'Now,' he cried, and the man slipped the trigger free.

The giant bolt smashed into the wood. The raft crashed backwards onto the men behind it – five, Ferros could now see, with more behind at the entrance – knocking the bearers backwards, wrenching the wood from their grip, exposing them to sudden flamelight, like beetles when a rock is turned over. Scurrying like them, but unable to escape.

'Shoot!' cried Ferros, and loosed.

Men died, some fast, some slower. All added to the pile, the flesh hill continuing to rise. The chants had ended with the smashing of wood. Only the groans of dying men broke the silence now, and then they too were gone, leaving only the sputtering of flame.

Ferros waited. Nothing stirred. 'Call me if anything moves,' he told one of his men, the sergeant of the troop, a huge warrior, a Wattenwolden from the northern forests, called Gronigen.

'Sir,' the man growled.

Ferros stepped out of the cave. The night was fully fallen. The moons rode the sky. This time of year, they approached each other like lovers in courtship, both waxing. In three weeks' time they would meet at midnight and it would be Midwinter and the beginning of the return of the sun.

There was a fire fifty paces from the cave's entrance. A pot was over it, food being cooked. He walked towards it, suddenly tired and hungry, thinking of how many night camps he had made in the deserts near Balbek, how calm his world had always seemed, under those rising moons. Yet just behind him, in the dark depths of this mountain, an army waited to destroy his world.

He saw her, sitting by the fire. He managed not to think about her while he fought. Away from battle, she took over his whole mind, and swept it in confusion. Joy was there – but a kind of terror too. She was dead, and she had returned to him.

Lara.

He studied her. She must have felt his gaze upon her because she looked up, rose, came to him. 'My love,' he said.

She stared at him for a long moment before she replied. 'Am I?' she asked.

And there it was. All that was between them. From the moment he'd discovered that he was immortal, all that had been certain about his life was gone. His career as a soldier. His love for her. No, that was untrue. He knew he loved her. He just no longer knew *how* he could. If he was destined to live and never grow old, and she destined to age and die, how could he love her?

All that had changed, now that she was immortal too. They could go on together, for ever. Yet even as he thought that, it filled him with a kind of dread. What would they be like in a hundred years' time? In three? Five? Besides, perhaps it was already too late. She had changed. He had. But in his changing he had taken ... steps.

Roxanna. He thought again about the black-skinned immortal who had bewitched him. He did not love her, not in the way he did – had – Lara. But he was obsessed with her nonetheless.

All this, in the few seconds as he stared back at her, as he thought about her question.

'Shall we walk?' he said, not answering. But she did not follow him when he turned.

'You need to eat, Ferros. Rest. The fight in there,' she gestured with her head to the cave, 'is not over, is it?'

'No.'

'Then come to the fire,' she said. 'We can talk later. After.'

He caught her arm as she turned away. 'But I need to know. How ... how did you live? And how did you learn so quickly about ... about this other part of immortality?'

'About possession?' She looked above him, at the blue moon. 'It is even better than the first, Ferros. To live a hundred years is one thing. But to love as a hundred people? Fight as them? It is something else again.' She smiled, 'As you will soon discover.'

He didn't reply, nor deny, as he had before. As he had the

first time he'd witnessed it, when Roxanna possessed that man, and then killed him, in the alley back in Tarfona. He'd thought about it, of course he had. He'd wondered if it was because he was an orphan, that he had always been entirely alone with himself. It was what kept him whole. How could he then be someone else?

And yet he also recognised something – for all his revulsion, deep within, part of him craved it too.

He shook his head. 'Listen,' he said, 'you must tell me—'

It was all he got out, before the shout came.

'Sir! Here!'

It was Gronigen, the sergeant, at the entrance to the cave. 'Do they come again?' Ferros shouted as he ran up.

'Someone does. But not in arms,' the huge soldier grunted. 'This fucker wants to talk.'

Ferros stepped into the cave. At its end, beyond the flesh hill, and the fallen wood, something moved in the light. He peered, surprised by the square of cloth, stiffened by glue, and cross-hatched in red and black. For this was the way of *his* people, when a truce was sought. Why did an enemy use it too?

'What do you want?' he called.

'Conversation,' a man replied.

His voice was refined, from Corinthium. Ferros knew exactly who he was. The wilderness messiah who was raising the tribes in rebellion. The one he'd tried to kill before. Who went by the name of Smoke, though that wasn't his true name.

The tunnel carried sound well so he didn't need to shout. 'Makron,' he said.

There was a silence before the voice came again. 'You know me?'

'I have been … *told* of you.'

'Roxanna.' The man laughed. 'I wonder if she has told you *everything* about me.'

'She told me all I need to know – that you are a traitor to the empire.'

Ferros knew that to make an enemy angry was to make him weaker. But Makron wasn't angry. Instead he laughed again. '"A traitor to the empire",' he echoed. 'Some might see it that way. Or some might say that I have simply found a greater cause to be loyal to.'

'Every traitor's justification. You lead an army against Corinthium.'

'Lead? No. The men you are killing are called the Horse Lords, by the way. They are great warriors and will not be led by me. I am simply he who prepares the way. I serve a greater purpose. And you, Ferros of Balbek? What do you serve?'

'You know me?'

'I have been *told* of you, yes.'

'Then you know that I am a soldier, loyal to the empire you seek to destroy.'

'Ah, but you are so much more than that, Ferros. You are … like me. And because you have become like me you will soon learn that it is not an ideal of empire you serve, for that died centuries ago. It is a corrupt and greedy elite who run the world only for their pleasure.' There was a pause and Makron continued, 'I am sure Roxanna has already taught you something about pleasure, has she not?'

He gave another, different laugh, and Ferros put his hand against the cave wall and gripped it hard. Roxanna *had* told him some things of this man. Not just that he was immortal too but how, a century before, Makron had been her husband. That was what was in the laugh. Knowledge. Complicity. Provocation. His enemy trying to make *him* angry. He took a deep breath, another, released the wall, spoke. 'What do you want?'

'Peace. It is peace I am helping to bring to the world.'

'By bringing an army to kill us?'

'People resist peace. Those who run the world for themselves especially. Lucan and the rest of the immortals in the Sanctum will sacrifice tens of thousands of lives to preserve their own ... *lives*. Their way of living.' He paused, and when he spoke again his voice had lost its fervour, was gentler. 'They have already sacrificed the life of one that you loved, have they not?'

Ferros started. How would this man know about Lara? Their ship had sailed from Corinthium, as had the one that brought Lara. It seemed unlikely that a spy from her ship or theirs would have brought the news so fast across the mountains. Still, even if he knew about her death he would not know yet about her ... life.

Makron continued, his voice low, persuasive. 'Think of this, Ferros. You and I are not the only ones of our *kind* who see the corruption at the heart of empire. Who want to return it to its founding ideals. How it was at the beginning. When the gift of immortality made us shepherds, not tyrants. Now we have been offered that chance again. Offered hope, in the coming of the One.'

'That baby in the glass?'

'The One.'

Ferros remembered the baby, an image of it appearing in the smoke-filled globe that this man had produced to show to the Assani tribe, seeking to win them over with magic and prophecy to fight against the empire. He, Ferros, had put an end to that, or delayed it at least, his javelin shattering the glass. He had destroyed it on instinct, recognising a threat. And instinct was what it had been, years of conditioning in the army to obey orders and fight Corinthium's enemies. Yet the time he'd spent among the immortals in the Sanctum on the Hill – learning more of them, of how they ruled the world – had sickened him to much of it.

Perhaps his silence now gave Makron hope, for when he spoke

again his voice was even more soothing. 'Ferros,' he called, 'save your men. Save yourself. This life, and all the lives to come. Lay down your weapons and join us. You can't win here.'

Ferros looked ahead, saw the pile of corpses blocking the far entrance to the cave. Then he looked back at the four huge Wattenwolden soldiers, who perhaps were not following all that was being said, but stood ready to fight hard for him because it was what they did. Fight, without questions. Those were asked by politicians when the war was over. Not now. Not by soldiers during a battle.

There was something else too, on the fringes of his mind. He sought the memory ... and found it.

He'd chased Smoke into the vast cavern beyond the tunnel. For the first time, he'd seen his enemy. But it had not been just soldiers he'd seen. Soldiers had not hollowed out the mountain, nor dug this tunnel. Slaves had. He'd noted the ribs sticking from their chests, seen the scourge marks on their backs. The One advanced his cause on the labour of slavery. And for all the empire's faults, there was not one slave from the hill of Agueros to the sands of Balbek or the grasslands of Cuerdocia.

It decided him. Questions were indeed for after a battle, not during. So he laid his hand on the Bow of Mavros beside him. 'Win? Perhaps not. But neither can you.'

There was a long silence. Makron's voice, when it came again, had lost all its sweetness. 'You are so, so wrong,' he hissed.

There were a variety of smells in the tunnel, most of them nasty. Many men had died there. Blood had flowed, guts had been opened up. Shit and blood – the scent of every battlefield Ferros had ever been on. Yet now he noticed something else. It had been there a while, he realised, but because he'd never smelled it before, he had not taken it in. Now he did because now it dominated everything else – sharp, eye-watering, like distilled liquor but without any flavour.

Ferros looked around for its source. Saw nothing on the walls, on the corpse pile ahead. Then he looked down in time to see a narrow column of liquid run from the dark ahead, and swirl around the base of the Bow of Mavros. He bent, put his fingers into it, raised it to his nostrils. Coughed and swung his head away.

The liquid was the source of the pungent scent.

He felt it, before he knew it, the peril suddenly there. Knew it before the voice came again, gloating now. 'You know the old expression, don't you, Ferros? "You can't find smoke without some fire."' He laughed. 'So since you have the one, here's the other.'

A hand appeared at the tunnel's end. It held a flaming brand. Released it to fall upon the pile of the dead.

'Out!' Ferros was turning as he yelled, one hand on Gronigen, shoving him – as the tunnel behind him exploded in flame.

He made it out, though he felt the singe on the back of his head, on his bare legs, and smelled his crisping hair. He rolled over and over on the hard sand, then sat up and ripped off his boots, which were aflame. Beside him Gronigen and two other soldiers did the same. The fourth one was not there; but then, as Ferros rose, shouting for help, he appeared from the cave, a staggering, screaming human firebrand, collapsing in a shower of sparks to the ground just before the entrance.

Soldiers ran up. One had a horse blanket which he threw over his burning comrade. But yellow tongues of fire were thrusting out of the entrance along with waves of heat that Ferros felt upon the parts of him that were burned. 'Away with him,' he shouted, and four of his soldiers lifted the man, ran him twenty paces back from the cliff face.

Ferros turned from the dying to the living. He'd just lost another man; five, including these men's officer, Gandalos, in the tunnel fight; another five were wounded, cut on arms, shoulders. That left thirty able-bodied warriors. Thirty ... plus Lara.

She was standing a little apart from the group. What they made of her, of her sudden appearance among them, he could not know. The Wattenwolden were famously terse of speech.

Everyone looked at him, expectant. That the situation had changed was clear to all. The tunnel had been their advantage, to hold the invaders within it. Hold them, until Roxanna returned with the garrison of Tarfona. Ferros looked at the cave's entrance, from which flames were still gushing forth as if from the mouth of the huge desert lizard, the lascaro, said to spout fire. But even as he watched, the fire lessened and then, suddenly, ceased. Immediately, smoke gushed out in a spiralling column, as if from a chimney laid on its side. It bore the foul scent of cooking flesh. All was being consumed within the stone walls, including his Bow of Mavros. When all had been, the enemy would come.

In the tunnel, these horse-lord warriors had been at a disadvantage, able to attack only in small groups, their long swords unsuited to the low roof. Still, they had kept coming, as the dead pile showed. They did not lack courage, and they would not again. From the cave entrance they would emerge in twos, two more to replace the first that fell, two after that. On and on, and Ferros knew that he did not have enough arrows for the army he'd witnessed in the great cavern in the mountain. They would kill more with their swords – but again, not enough.

Like all battlefield decisions, this one had to be made fast.

On the ride to the mountains – Gods, was it only yesterday? – Ferros had noted things. One was the speed of one of the Wattenwolden, the smallest man in the troop. 'Bavringen,' he called, and the man stood to attention. 'Ride for Tarfona. The Lady Roxanna will have reached there by now and roused the garrison. She was meant to have joined us here with it but that,' he glanced at the cave's entrance where the column of smoke was already diminishing, 'is no longer the plan. Tell her and Governor Doukas—'

He paused, again thinking back to the ride. There was a ridge they'd ridden up and over, about a thousand paces from the town gates. Not much of one, it barely slowed the horses nor sped them on the downward slope. But even a slight elevation gave an advantage to the occupier. It was better than trying to defend the town walls, which were of no great height, and anyway in need of repair at too many points. If the enemy came in numbers, as he was sure they would, it would be better to meet them as a solid body, on that ridge.

He took the soldier aside. Got him to repeat the instructions before sending him off. Then as he watched him gallop away, he remembered the territory through which he was sending him, filled with Assani tribesmen whose loyalty to the empire was wavering. He would send two more, each an hour apart. One would get through, he could only hope. And speedily. Roxanna and the general would need all the time available.

Time that he and his remaining troops would have to buy them. At the cost of lives and blood.

'Listen, men. This is what we do.'

Five nights later ...

Ferros reined in on the crest of the second-to-last hill before Tarfona. The very last was only three hundred paces away, but he was so stupid with fatigue he could not tell if the darkness on that hill was cloud shadow or not, and the flames fireflies or campfires. He stared at it for at least half a minute before he decided – when a horse there gave a neigh, and a moonbeam through the cloud-wrack silvered a soldier's helmet, suddenly vivid and bright.

One at least of his three messengers had gotten through – for unless his tiredness was making him see things, that was the town's garrison encamped upon the ridge.

He looked around him. Some of his men were slumped upon their horses' necks, already asleep. Many, including Ferros, had slept as they rode and more than once they'd had to go back for a man who'd fallen off. Most stared forward, hunger in their eyes. For rest at last, and the pure hunger for food. The last of their field rations had been finished the previous dawn and it was hard to keep fighting, tired and on an empty belly, as they'd had to do.

Of the thirty men he'd kept at the mountain, only ten were left. He'd lost five at the cave's entrance, when the enemy had finally assembled enough men to climb over the charred flesh mountain of their dead and charge out. One by one the others had died in the days and nights of retreat that followed, as they delayed the local tribesmen with ambush and raid. But most had been killed the night before, when the first Horse Lord appeared.

The enemy had got their horses through the mountain.

They did not have the numbers yet – perhaps two dozen. And there were probably no better horse warriors in the world than the Wattenwolden. But tiredness told, this new enemy were riders and archers of rare ability, and his men died. It was only when the pursuit had become overkeen and they'd managed to lure the enemy into the killing zone of a high-sided gulley, that they'd shaken them off by killing them all. After that there'd been no more fighting, only fleeing. For by then his numbers were reduced to what he saw before him now, these ten men.

Ten men – and one woman.

He looked at her now. And Lara, feeling his gaze, looked up

from where she was lying across her horse's neck, tapped her mount – as exhausted as her – and came to him. 'So,' she said. 'We are here. Now what?'

They'd had no time to talk, about anything, what with the riding and the killing. When they snatched a few hours' sleep each night, they lay separately. Partly that was because of the men, still uncertain who she was, where she'd come from. Mainly it was them. He didn't know what her return meant. There had been the euphoria of seeing her alive again, she whom he'd thought lost for ever. But euphoria had passed, replaced by uncertainty. They were both so different now from the carefree lovers they'd been back in Balbek. His immortality had changed everything. Hers had changed it more.

He could scarcely think. The more tired he got, the more he relied on instinct and the simplest of army truths: deal with what's in front of you. Lara and he, what they'd been, what they were, what they could yet be, was a matter for another time. What was in front of him was what was immediately behind him too – an enemy to be fought.

'We join the others. We rest. We prepare for those who are coming.'

'Good,' she replied. She began to turn her horse away, halted the movement of her hand on the rein, turned back. Her voice came low. 'You will not see me for a time, Ferros. I ... will not be here. But I will have you in my sight.'

He knew what she meant to do. Possess someone. The idea still revolted him. 'Why?' he said.

'Why? Two reasons. Because I do not want *her* to know me,' she gestured with her head to the camp ahead where, perhaps, Roxanna awaited, 'and because,' her eyes gleamed, 'it is a delight.'

'Lara!' he said, seeking to delay her, persuade her. He did not want her in the fight ahead, wanted her safe within the town walls. But then he remembered: she could not die any more than he could. And somehow that was both the best and the worst thing of all.

She did not rejoin the troop. Instead she grunted a farewell at men who had become her comrades, tapped her heels into her horse's flanks and set off down the road ahead. He watched as she swung off the road so as to miss the camp, heading instead for the town where she could ... disappear.

Shaking his head, he called, 'Forward!' and his men obeyed. Or their horses did, for those who still slept.

Roxanna was not in the camp, neither was General Doukas. They had returned to Tarfona to rest, he was informed by an officer of engineers, Sepoloumos, who'd been left in charge. He was young, nervous and, wide-eyeing the blood on Ferros's armour, deferred to him immediately. Through closing eyes, all he could see was that almost no work had yet been done to reinforce the small ridge. Walking the length of it he commanded that a trench be dug, and three emplacements hollowed out then reinforced with wood to house the Bows of Mavros they would need.

His horse had been taken. But the groom had left his horse blanket and saddle. He fell to the ground, pulled the blanket over him, and was asleep moments later. Though those moments were filled with a name.

'Lara,' he murmured.

On the second morning after her return, near dawn, she was roused by a deep, distant sound.

Lara awoke refreshed in spirit, tired in body. Though, she realised immediately, it wasn't *her* body that was tired.

For a moment, she tried to remember where she was, who she was with.

Who she was.

She raised herself on her elbows. The man beside her didn't look familiar. He had a chubby, pockmarked face and smelled of sweat, tar and seawater. Most likely a sailor then, unsurprising in the port city of Tarfona. She must have met him in one of the dockside taverns she'd visited last night.

She flopped back, groaning. It felt like miners were hacking at a coal face inside her head. Memories started to come – a series of taverns. In one of them this man beside her, whose name she still could not recall. This room above the last drinking hole. The man must have paid, because she knew she'd spent the contents of the woman's purse on liquor, hard and cheap liquor by the pounding in her head. She knew she could end it, and leave. She would have to soon, anyway, for her possession – Rablania, that was her name – was stirring within. Soon, she would be trying to reclaim herself.

The first time she'd gone into someone, the feeling of a person within her, lost in their own dream, fighting their way to wakefulness, desperate to repossess themselves ... was the strangest feeling in the world. As if ... as if the whole of her insides were itching. In the half-dozen times since, she'd learned: the stronger the will, the shorter the time she could stay within them, even though experience had taught her ways of delaying the takeover. The first time she'd taken someone had been a dock worker back in Corinthium. She'd needed him to get her onto the ship bound for Tarfona. He'd been a strong-willed brute, and had thrown her off in hours. He'd also been handy with a knife – the first time she'd discovered that there was always one thing you could take from a possession – a desire, a skill, even a memory. She, who had laughed at Ferros whenever he tried to teach her blade-work, could now handle herself in a fight.

This was what she looked forward to, each time. While she was in another's body, while she still possessed them, she needed to understand all that they were. And thus all that they had left her.

So she didn't leave Rablania immediately, despite the pain in her head – which was matched, she realised, by one in her loins. An ache there, for the man beside her had been rough in his desire last night, she felt, though she could not remember. Then one memory did come: that Rablania had urged him to be rough, losing herself in the oblivion of that, as Lara had lost herself before in drink.

Why? she thought, sinking deeper within. A possession's memories were like long and twisting corridors to run down. Most of the images flew around, were not attached to anything solid that she could grasp. Until one suddenly was – some skill, like the knife-fighting. Some lust, some … memory.

It was as if she'd left the rank room above the tavern, the fetid darkness. Walked into a sunlit field. A man was there, scything wheat. She saw him notice her, turn, smile. 'Rablania, my sweet,' he said, 'See what I have for you?' He sat and held out a circlet made of many different, small flowers – white and mauve, yellow and red. When she came to him, he laid it on her head, placing it like a crown, calling her his queen. She put her hand – her tiny, girl's hand – into his, climbed into his lap. There amid the wheat stalks he told her stories of the fairies that lived in each flower in the wreath.

Lara stood up. And it was Lara that stood, now beside the bed and looking down at the sleeping couple. His name was Mikos, he wasn't a sailor but a shipwright, and they were occasional companions. He wanted more, she didn't; wanted nothing save these encounters to seek the oblivion that would help her forget the crown-maker, her father, the man who'd died suddenly when she was ten and set her on a life of trying to find a love that could never exist again.

She stared down, at Rablania's eyes fluttering into wakefulness. Lara knew that she would be only another memory to her, added to the stock, an image from a dream. But she hadn't used the woman, as she used some, for transport, for fighting. She'd just gone along with her and, for a time, lived her life.

She'd said it to Ferros. He saw only the horror of it, that using of someone. Or the pleasure. No doubt his black goddess had shown him only that. The truth was, this was the joy of it, this gift that came with immortality. It was, she felt, the far more important part. Not living for ever, or dying to always be reborn. But to experience another? To learn their lives for a time? It was no more, no less than a privilege. For a time she was able to be a witness to lives lived, testify to all sorrows, all joys, and everything in between.

Rablania opened her eyes and looked at Lara. She wasn't startled. Thought she was still in a dream. 'Who are you?' she asked drowsily.

'A friend,' Lara replied. Then she leaned down and whispered, 'You should marry Mikos. No one will ever love you more than he does. And he loves you so much.'

Rablania turned and rested her hand on the man's shoulder, closing her eyes. He stirred, rolled into her. Lara, shutting the door softly behind her, descended the stairs, left the tavern by a side door. An alley led her to the street – and into chaos.

She'd been so lost in another person's life in that room, she hadn't paid much attention to the noise beyond it. But there were many people about, unusual for this hour so close to dawn. Rushing people, townsfolk pushing laden carts of goods, soldiers wearing the yellow armbands of imperial messengers running with purpose.

A man with a cart piled high with stone jars and bread rolls paused close by to wipe his streaming brow. She stepped close. 'What's all the activity, friend?' she asked.

He stared at her, eyes wide with surprise. 'Did you not hear it?'

'Hear what?'

'That!'

She heard it now – the deep and distant call of a trumpet, blaring a summons. She remembered now, it was the sound that had actually woken her.

'They're coming! They're coming,' the man shouted, bending to lift the poles of his cart, grunting as he shoved off.

She watched him go, then lifted the bread roll she'd filched. He did not need to say who was coming. The trumpet told her.

Chewing, she set out the opposite way to the man, towards the Horse Lords.

Ferros peered at the ridge ahead, three hundred paces from the one on which he stood. He had three mounted sentries upon it. He knew that they looked into a series of gentle valleys that dipped down behind it; they would be the first to see who was coming. He wouldn't see them until they crested the hill on which his scouts waited. Yet he could already feel them. A vibration moved through the earth into his feet. And he could hear, though the sound was as yet only a whisper. It would build to a shout, when horsemen finally rode onto that ridge.

Two thousand at least, his last scout had gasped, the only one to make it back from the six he'd sent out, his mount near uncontrollable and whinnying from the pain of the arrow stuck in one haunch. He'd been tempted to ride out himself, count with his own eyes. Until he'd realised that in the end it did not matter. They'd fight however many came, in the manner the terrain dictated. He was more use where he was, preparing for the battle.

He looked all around. He'd walked the length of the summit – if such a paltry rise could be said to have one – to reach this, the uttermost right flank. It was almost identical to the one on the extreme left from whence he'd come. Engineers had built him square emplacements, ten paces across, with baskets filled with stones on their walls, and gaps through which to shoot the Bow of Mavros that each one contained. There was another emplacement halfway down the ridge, in the middle of their lines. That one was smaller, only had a front wall. There was nothing he could do about horsemen riding around his flanks, so the wings of his army had to defend themselves as if they were in a tower in a city under siege.

He'd taken all the precautions he could. Ordered shallow pits to be dug irregularly over both slopes, then bedded with sharp stakes thrust up and concealed with mats of woven grass. The trench that ran the length of the position was wide enough to be fought both ways, with shooting steps cut into it every twenty paces for archers to mount, and larger stakes, sharpened and thrusting out like quills on a porcupine. But if the enemy swept all the way around to the middle of his lines, and attacked from both sides simultaneously and in numbers, the battle was probably over.

Ferros had walked the front slope to reach the emplacement. So he started back along the rear. Looked down at the men preparing in their own ways. He had few regular soldiers, less than five hundred, the garrison of the town, so these he'd spread out the length of the line to provide an armour-clad core for the thousand or so men of Tarfona's militia – who only had long spears and thick padded knee-length coats to protect them – to gather around. The garrison troops wore breast- and backplates of metal, tubes of chain mail up their arms, skirts lined in brass, tall boots of supple, reinforced leather and the standard empire helmet, a cone of leather with crossed bars of iron to resist the downward blows of mace or sword. Every fifth man hefted a bow. The rest had a sheath of javelins, a shield, and their curved swords. They were all cavalry trained. But the early reports of the enemy's numbers had told him that to fight a cavalry battle, much as he desired to, would be swift suicide. He had seen, in his brief glimpse of them in the huge cave under the mountain, that the enemy were all horsemen. They would come as those, fight as those. So the only way to stop them, with his fewer numbers, was to fight as infantry.

And how much do I know of that? thought Ferros, the smile for his men concealing his doubts. For he too was a cavalryman, had fought from horseback all his life, in pitched battles against the tribes of the Sarphardi deserts, and on foot only when he made night raids on enemy camps, ghosting through tent lines to kill silently, move on, kill again. His knowledge of static war, of siege and defensive position, was confined to the texts he'd studied for the tests he needed to pass for his promotions. His position this day was based on a defence conducted against those fierce northern warriors the Wattenwolden, when they'd swept down from their forests, seeking to storm a Corinthium weakened by plague. All the officers had been killed, by sickness or enemy blade. But an ordinary foot soldier, not immortal, his name Andronikos, had picked up the dead general's sword and taken command. They had been outnumbered five to one. But they'd broken the mounted Wattenwolden on a line much like this one, above a village called Kristun, on a day of snow and blood …

… three hundred years before.

As he neared the centre of his lines, making for the group of people who stood on a slight lift of land, he glanced to his left. To his reserve, his only one. Made up of those same warriors that had lost the day at Kristun – Wattenwolden, now soldiers of the empire. A hundred men, for they'd lost twenty-five in the fight at the mountain and the harrying retreat from it. Still, if there was comfort to be taken this morning it was in the sight of them, standing among their tough tawpan horses, men and beasts alike wearing the armour known, in the empire, as lamulin – alternating hand-sized squares of leather, iron or bronze, stitched together to make a light, flexible coat. He would have preferred to wear his, found fighting in it far easier. But among the choices he'd had to make this day was the one to stand out. He was the leader, and he had to be recognised to lead. So he wore breastplate, a plumed helm and a red cloak.

Though he was not the highest-ranking officer. A mere captain when there was a general on the field. Who was also the governor of Tarfona. His name was Doukas and Ferros could see, as he approached, and hear too, how well the usurpation of his command sat with him.

'I tell you again, lady,' he was whining, 'the boy knows nothing of the Assani and the other tribes. While I have been fighting them all my life.'

Ferros halted, a dozen paces away, to listen to Roxanna's reply. 'I so agree, general,' she said, her voice a caress, 'but as I was telling you, it is not the tribes who will be the core of our enemy this day, but someone else. And Lucan of the Council has trained our young friend especially to fight them.'

It was a lie, and necessary. For a few things had been established quite quickly since his arrival. The first that Doukas was a coward, and had let the Assani and other tribes be roused by the prophet Smoke because he refused to swiftly move against them when they rebelled. The second, that he had run down the town defences because he'd embezzled all the money meant for their rebuilding, forcing the decision to fight beyond walls that could not be defended. Thirdly, that he'd spent all that he had stolen on expensive wines and whores, with the former rotting his mind and the latter his body.

Ferros heard Roxanna add, 'General, your cup. It's empty,' and then the splash of liquid into a goblet. Sighing, he came forward. Roxanna saw him first, and raised her eyebrows, moving her head to the general. He had clashed with Doukas earlier, the man's arguments for caution infuriating him into anger. Roxanna's look reminded him to keep his temper.

He would – and would provoke the other man's. He wanted Doukas nowhere near this battlefield. He had problems enough, without having orders countermanded, or an early retreat called – perhaps at the first sight of the enemy. 'Governor Doukas,' he said, omitting the military title. 'I suggest the time has come for you to retire.'

'Retire? You puppy!' The older man had eyes of quite distinct sizes, the larger one bulging from his florid face. 'How dare you suggest such a thing? I am here performing my duty. Come to inspect my forces, eh!' He had taken a lurching step forward, and pulled himself up now two paces from Ferros. 'They are all to assemble before the trench here. Full arms.' He tried to snap his fingers, ended up waving his hand instead.

'I would remind you, sir, of your duty to the citizens of Tarfona—'

'You would remind me!' he exploded. 'You dare to … *remind* me. Well, I'll remind you who is the general here and who the … puppy!'

'General,' said Roxanna, stepping in to take the man's arm and halt his swaying. 'Forgive our young friend. He is rash and probably nervous before his first battle. Not like us calm, wiser, *older* ones eh?'

Ferros had been there when Roxanna let slip her age. Not being one of the immortals, Doukas had a servile reverence for them. Yet his respect warred with his wine-provoked lust. She might be three hundred years old, but Roxanna had the type of body that sculptors would take as a model for a goddess. And as ever, much of it was on display.

Both his bulbous eyes were now fixed on her breasts, scarcely held down by leather straps. 'Youth,' he muttered, staring. 'Ever rash.'

'And didn't you say, General,' she continued, 'that you would hold the city's fortress, give your forces here a second place to fight from if they needed it? Is that not right?'

'Did I?' he muttered, dragging his gaze up, scratching patches of stubble on his chin. 'Oh yes. Yes. Hold the fortress, for the inevitable collapse, eh?'

'Yes, and besides, sir, do you not hear?' She cupped a hand to her ear, exaggeratedly listening. Ferros heard it again too – the drumming of hoofbeats, already much nearer.

Doukas heard. Fear came first, before the covering bluster. 'You are right. The citizens need their governor to inspire them. Guards!' The four men who wore the white robes of the city guard, emblazoned with the portcullis and ship of Tarfona, came forward. 'To the fortress.'

They helped him to his horse, got him up. He sprawled then sat almost straight. He gazed down at Ferros, looking like he was summoning one last piece of advice or contempt. But then he belched loudly and his mount took that as a sign to take off, and did. He wobbled in the saddle, straightened, then kicked his horse into a canter.

'Well rid of him,' muttered Ferros. Then he turned to look at Roxanna. 'You should go with him.'

'I? Why?'

'I have enough on, without worrying about you in the fight.'

She tipped back her head, and laughed. 'I think you'll remember, Ferros, that I never needed any looking after … in anything.' She reached up and tapped the javelins strapped across her back. 'Aim true, my lover. I will be on the left flank, as we agreed.'

He took her arm as she turned away. 'Roxanna,' he said, 'if we … if we fail here … as soon as you see that, ride for the port. There will be ships awaiting the result of the battle. Ready to sail if we've lost. Take one. Corinthium will need to know all that happened here. Know too what exactly is heading their way next.' He turned, to look at the crest of the next hill. His sentries were still upon it, but even as he noted them, he saw all three rise up in their stirrups, drop, turn and gallop towards the lines. 'As we are about to learn,' he added, releasing her, taking a step away.

It was her turn to delay him. Gripping his arm, she said, 'If we fail, you should think of coming too. No immortal will fare too well if Smoke gets hold of them. Especially you.'

He watched her mount and canter away to the end of the line, where she had the command. Watched and thought of her former husband – Smoke, as the renegade immortal Makron was known. Actually, Ferros was looking forward to meeting him – as long as he had a weapon in his hand; though, of course, he couldn't be sure of what he'd look like, or who he'd be.

The thought of possession made him think of the one other immortal nearby. Lara. She'd been gone in Tarfona for two days, about what business he could not know, and did not wish to. Would she come to the battle? Would she stay in the town? He hoped she did – or else every man he saw fall on the field he'd think was her.

He climbed to the top of the small rise that Doukas had vacated. It gave the only view of the whole field. The three gallopers found the twisting marked passageways through the stakes then soared across the trench. But they were still a way away and by the time they approached him he didn't need their report. He could see for himself ...

... when an army rode over the hill.

They came in waves, and they kept coming. The first wave halted about fifty paces down the slope, spreading its length. Tribesmen, not the horse warriors he'd seen in the cavern. He did not know the local tribes as he did the ones near Balbek, at the far end of the Great Sea, where he'd served. He recognised the Assani by their yellow cloaks, because he'd worn one as disguise on the mission to kill Smoke. Yet yellow was just one of the colours displayed. A garrison sergeant, Hilragos, had told him that the tribes were similar in beliefs and customs, and could only be distinguished by how they wore their hair, the patterns they stained on their skins, and by the colour of their cloaks. Ferros saw before him now, in the jostling of horses, a misaligned rainbow of blues, greens, yellows, reds in various shades; Danari, Wobelani, Mishrani, just some of the names he recalled. Overlapping and blending here, all roused by the preachings of Smoke the Hermit to fight the empire together as they had fought it separately – and fought each other – for years. Imperial strategy was divide and control, the oldest law. Here it had been broken, and Ferros looked at what he thought were close to fifteen hundred horsemen from half a dozen different tribes, who would usually slit each other's throats over a strayed goat, but were now united by hate and prophecy.

Yet that was not what worried him most. It was not their numbers, not much greater than his own.

It was their silence.

He'd known tribes, had fought them, all his life. They were different in many ways, but similar in this: they made a lot of noise when they went to war. Ululations, war cries, speeches of great length shouted out, venerating ancestors, praising gods, threatening pitiless slaughter; trumpeting past glories and future conquests. *Trumpeting!* Where were the horns of war, the huge bladder pipes, the drums? He could see, with his keen eyes, that these tribesmen had them. All hung untouched from saddle horn, or across backs.

It was worse than any war noise. He glanced at the men before him in the trench. Each looked as if they were scarcely breathing, many had sweat on their brows although the morning was cool. At intervals all along the line, figures rose and made for the shit pits set fifty paces back, the only noise in the stillness the growl of sergeants trying to stop them, and even these tough men cutting off, as if embarrassed at breaking the silence. Ferros noticed one man rise from his squat, look around, and then set off at a run towards the distant town walls. He knew he should send after him, bring him back, execute him on the spot as an example of what happens to deserters. But like everyone there he could only turn again, look ahead. Because this wasn't an ordinary silence, neither for the tribesmen nor the watchers. It was a silence waiting to be filled.

And was, when the men that Makron had called the Horse Lords rode over the hill.

Ferros had seen them waiting in their giant cavern within the mountain. A glimpse only, before he and Roxanna had to flee. An impression of warriors beside their mounts. Even that one brief look had told him much – that these were cavalrymen, like him. That they would rather go to war naked, without sword, javelin and armour than without their horse. It had given him his little hope, for the tunnels were narrow, and the stallions he'd seen could not get through them.

But they had. He guessed that they had killed scores of the slaves he'd observed to achieve the necessary widening. Still it would have been a slow passage. It had taken a day, and then another to ride here. Three hundred had made it through perhaps, no more. Enough though, he feared.

For the first time in an age he wished he too could turn and run for the shit pits, keep on running to the town – then beyond it, all the way back to Balbek.

Yet he could not. Quelling his bowels, he turned and mounted his own horse, held by a groom just behind the rise. The battle had not started but it had begun. Silence was the enemy's first blow. It had to be countered. 'Sound,' he said, to the men who stood beside him.

Six trumpets were lifted into the air. Six men raised batons either side of the huge ox-hide drums strapped to their chests. At a signal from their leader, the lead trumpeter wearing the white coat of Tarfona's city guard, they struck and blew.

It wasn't the loudest sound ever heard upon a battlefield. But Ferros had ordered them to play the march written to celebrate that other victory against overwhelming odds: the triumph at Kristun. He knew that his Wattenwolden cavalry might not be so pleased at the memory it evoked of their defeat. But Ferros was not concerned about professional soldiers who would do their duty. It was the others, the garrison troops who had seen little action in years, the militia who had seen almost none. Perhaps they could be roused by remembering a day when Corinthium had been saved.

Perhaps they could be inspired to save it this day.

He began to sing. He knew he had a terrible voice but that was not the point. Words went with the tune, words that every child of empire learned along with their first prayers to Mavros and Simbala.

> 'When all was lost, that winter night,
> And death lay all around,
> Andronikos rose from the soldier ranks,
> And raised the sword he'd found.'

It was a simple song, a simple tune. But it stirred the hearts of every child of Corinthium. And it stirred the soldiers singing it now.

Trumpets, drums and words carried across the valley to the silent listeners. It ended with Andronikos's final shout, called three times.

'Victory or death! Victory or death! Victory or death!'

The tribal horsemen shifted in their saddles. Some shouts came, and then a tide of them. Men pulled mounts onto their rear legs and released their pent-up, wild ululations. Then a single horn blew from the ridge crest, a single drum was struck. Silence returned, but only for a moment, before a horseman rode down from the ridge. He bore a huge white banner that streamed behind him – a dragon, spouting flame. He rode straight through the tribesmen, out towards the centre of the hill where Ferros stood. With a huge shout, the mass of warriors spurred their horses and followed.

Before he turned to the business of death, Ferros noted that the Horse Lords on the hill did not come.

'On my signal,' he shouted, raising his arm, moving his horse forward till he loomed above the Bow of Mavros in its pit. It was a weapon designed more for siege, for the shattering of an enemy's walls, than for a battle on a plain. But part of a conversation he'd had with one of his tutors back in Corinthium had stuck with him – General Parkos had interesting ideas for open warfare. Remembering one of them, Ferros had ordered the adaptations made.

He saw the master shooter's hand, shaking just above the firing pin. 'Wait,' he growled. He glanced to his left, saw Roxanna turned to watch him at her emplacement, her hand also raised. To his right, at the other extremity, Sepoloumos was also facing him, waiting. He looked to the front again. The leading horsemen were at the base of the slope, their first arrows were flying up.

He threw down his arm. 'Now,' he cried.

The shooter jerked out the pin. The Bow of Mavros released its broad-bladed arrow, but not only the arrow – for attached to bolts just behind its head were lengths of chain carefully furled into buckets either side of the Bow. As the arrow flew these unspooled, stretched to their length, weighted as they were at their ends – and scythed into the enemy ahead to the width of three men's stretched arms either side of the bolt.

As if knocked over by a backslap of Mavros's own hand, men and horses went down, chinks opened in the charging lines. A swift glimpse showed him similar carnage at each trench's end. But most of the enemy would not have seen it. They came on, screaming. Some fell into the pits he'd had dug, some to the arrows now steadily pouring from the trench. Few made it to the line of sharpened stakes and those that did died fast.

The charge broke. Then, like a wave hitting a boulder on a beach, they flowed around the trench, overlapped it, headed for its rear.

And the second wave came.

They were less bunched, so the second volley from Mavros's three bows caused less damage. Most of the pit traps had already claimed their victims and been exposed. These charging tribesmen – the majority, Ferros noted, in the yellow cloaks of the Assani – did not try to leap or ride between the stakes. They rode just up to them, halted, drew arrows, shot, again and again. At a glimpse, Ferros saw that it was the same the length of the line. Their hill's slope was slight indeed, and the man on the horse had the height.

He pulled a javelin from his saddle quiver. Aimed, threw, killed. A second, and another tribesman died. Then he dismounted, pulled his shield from its strapping and his sword from its sheath. A Wattenwolden groom came and led his horse away. Turning to the trumpeter he said, 'Now!' and the man blew a distinct, three-note call that Ferros had played again and again the night before. The length of the trench, he saw men do as he'd done: draw sword, heft shield. And then, like him, leap from the trench, and run down the slope. Though the moment before he did he looked again at the opposite hill.

The Horse Lords had still not come.

The suddenness of the attack surprised the Assani. Many died surprised, too slow to exchange bow for sword. Ferros struck. Not at the man before him – but at his mount, cutting down on the long nose. It broke his heart even as he did it, for he loved horses more than he loved most people. But fighting on foot against cavalry it was the only way. He had taught his raw troops the way of it and the air was pierced by the terrible screams of rearing horses.

The stallion he cut bore a man holding some sort of standard, a pole with mink furs dangling from the tip. The horse rose up on its rear legs, tried to dash him with its front hooves. He dodged and weaved around them; then, as four hooves hit the ground again, he leaped and thrust his sword into the rider's armpit. The mink-tail banner fell. Ferros grabbed it with his shield-arm hand, used it to deflect a downward scythe of another warrior's sword, jabbed the tip into the man's face, cut him as he fell, then jammed the pole tip into the ground, and stamped on the shaft, snapping it in half.

He could not know whether the standard-bearer had been a leader. But he sensed something change. It was often thus in a battle – soldiers reacting to what they couldn't see, an instinct of the whole, like a flock of birds suddenly changing formation in flight. He saw the lines of attackers and defenders shift apart, standing distinct. Then, almost as one, the tribesmen turned their horses and fled, back across the valley. Those without horses ran, staggered, or crawled while wounded horses galloped, whinnying and kicking, in all directions.

Ferros turned to the rear. The enemy who'd flowed around the hill had caught the collective spirit and fled too, though several bodies were on the ground before the Wattenwolden.

He turned back. Men were cheering all along the trench. Some had run halfway down the hill in pursuit of the fleeing enemy, and sergeants were among them, hitting them with batons, driving them back. Others were in a frenzy, stabbing enemies on the ground who were already dead. Still others, not just the wounded, sat and wept.

Ferros strode the length of the trench, pausing to command a dead or injured man to be pulled from it. The worst-hurt he ordered sent back to Tarfona, sparing the lesser wounded to take them. But these raw soldiers had not done badly, and many more tribesmen lay dead before the trench than his men within it. He sent some out to collect arrows – they were already running low – others to bring back the wounded or dispatch the dead. Though always he kept one eye on the summit of the other hill – where the Horse Lords still had not moved.

'Have we won?'

Roxanna was standing before her horse, the bridle in one hand, a bloodied sword in the other. Aside from that one sign, she looked no more heated than if she had come back from a morning's gallop, such as the one they'd taken but a few months before outside the city of Corinthium.

'No.' He came to stand beside her, looked again across the valley. '*They* still have not come.'

Roxanna looked too, and licked her lips. 'I cannot wait till they do.'

Ferros shook his head. He killed when he had to, as a duty. But he did not take the pleasure in it that he sensed she did. It angered him, as so much about her did – not least a desire for her he could not shake, even now. 'Why do you not fight as someone else? Could you not take one of the Wattenwolden to be your ... plaything?'

She smiled. 'I could. But I do not know that I would find one as gifted with a sword as I am.' She raised hers, glancing along its bloodied planes. 'Besides,' she turned again to look across the valley, 'Makron is there. And I want to see the look in his eyes when he sees me as myself.'

'Makron. Your husband.'

'The man who was one of my husbands for a time. Many years ago, when I was younger and foolish.' She looked at him, the thin line of one eyebrow raised. 'Are you jealous, Ferros?'

He turned away. 'No,' though he knew that there was a part of him that was. 'So you will confront him?'

'If we win, I will. Not if we lose. I do not wish to be his prisoner.' For the first time there was something other than cool confidence in her voice, though it came back with her next words. 'As he would not wish to be mine.'

Ferros shuddered. There was still so much he did not understand of this world of immortality. And that thought reminded him: Lara! He looked back to Tarfona's walls. Is she within them? he wondered. Or is she here? He looked down at a man counting arrows. She could be him. Or the soldier next to him. Or one of the Wattenwolden. Or . . .

He shook himself. He would not, could not know. These two women who he had . . . *loved* were the same yet so different. And then, as a single trumpet sounded from across the valley, he realised that these were matters for another day. Deal with what's in front of you, Ferros, he said to himself. So he turned . . .

. . . and watched the Horse Lords come down from their hill.

They came at a slow walk and in silence. The pale sun gleamed on armour he saw now was a deep crimson red. Every step nearer revealed more detail of it. Theirs looked similar to the Wattenwolden's lamulin, though the overlapping plates of stiff leather, lined, he suspected, in steel, were smaller, less than a hand's breadth. The suit would be light and immensely strong. He could see the tips of bows rising from their backs, quivers filled with arrows hanging from their saddle horns. Each rider held a lance in their right hand, its butt resting in a holder at their stirrup. In their left hand, they each held a sword, a curved steel blade, all catching the light – as did their helmets, leaves of steel rising from the neck to a metal cap, crested across its width in horsehair, cut like a brush. The horses were as armoured as their riders.

Heavy cavalry, he thought, unlike the lightly armoured tribesmen who had come before. They would come in a charge, using weight and speed to sweep all before them. But he'd prepared for that, just as Andronikos had done three hundred years before at Kristun. For how could they keep their formation, which was their power, with stakes still thrust out like hedgehog spines on the crest of the hill?

He looked sideways, along his trench. He could sense the fear, smell it in a sudden waft of rank sweat. Men hefted their weapons. He shouted, 'Hold! Hold! Do not shoot!' Calling it again and again as he ran back from the left to the centre, heard his cry echoed by junior officers all along the line. When he reached the emplacement at the middle he dropped into it. The man in charge had reloaded the Bow of Mavros. They had only had time to make three of his chain-dragging arrows for each weapon. The last one was in place. 'On my command,' Ferros said, then looked again.

The Horse Lords had halted in the valley bottom. Still silent, they stared up. Something had changed with them. It took him a moment to notice what it was.

Every second man no longer held a sword in his left hand. He held a rope.

It puzzled him. 'Ready arrows,' he cried, looking left. He turned right, cried the same, though this time his words were lost in the yells from below.

The Horse Lords still did not move. But the tribesmen – Danari, Wobelani, Mishrani, Assani – rode screaming through the red ranks and charged again up the hill.

Ferros snatched up the bow he'd laid down, shot. Arrows flew down. The Bow of Mavros was discharged. Men died, but the tribes did not bunch as they had before, stood off about twenty paces, shooting their own bows again and again. As many arrows flew up the hill as down, a hailstorm of bone-tipped, iron-tipped death. Ferros shot again and again. Then he noted red blurs passing up through the tribal mob. Something flew out from it, right before him. And he realised suddenly what the rope was for when the lasso dropped over the tip of a stake, and tightened.

He stood, dropped his bow, drew his sword. Then he was knocked back, as three arrows hit him near simultaneously in the chest. They did not pierce his breastplate, but they stopped him and he could only drop back down into the trench, watch as the stakes twisted and jerked and were finally yanked from the ground and dragged away.

He saw the stakes twist and go, all along the line. The pits he'd had dug before had already been exposed. With more yells the tribesmen peeled away, left and right, revealing the last of the Horse Lords returned to the ranks, the stakes behind them. The lassos had gone. Re-formed, they drew their swords again, hefted their lances, and charged.

There was only one hope now, one small hope. Ferros turned, sprinted to the Wattenwolden, flung himself on his horse. 'With me!' he cried. Raising his sword in his right hand, his shield in his left, he kicked in his spurs.

One hundred men from the northern forests couched their lances and followed him in the charge.

The two lines of heavy cavalry smashed together just before the trench. Ferros glimpsed terrified faces below. He gave his mount her head over the gap for, like the Horse Lords, he did not even hold the reins. Then he was too busy, trying to kill, trying not to die, to notice much else.

There was a lance driving at his chest. He leaned hard to the side, lifting his sword up and hard across, guiding the long, narrow blade past him, bringing his weapon up fast and parallel to the ground. It slammed into the Horse Lord's neck, did not cut through his neck armour, did not need to, the neck snapping. Another lance came from his left, he got his shield up in time to save his head, but not to stop the razored edge slicing across his forehead. Blood flowed into his left eye. His opponent's momentum had brought him close, and Ferros thrust hard at his chest, his tip skittering off the red, linked plates. He was too close to bring the sword back for another cut. So he dropped his elbow, punched the sword's guard straight and hard into the face. It was enough to knock the man off balance and open him to Ferros's next cut, which he smashed into the helmet's side.

Momentum carried them past each other. He was deeper into the chaos, in the place where thought no longer mattered, only instinct. He blocked, cut, hit, missed. He lost his shield at some point, when his arm was sliced. He felt steel enter his thigh. Saw a sword raised high above his head.

And then he was down. His horse had stumbled into one of the pits. It saved his life, the curved sword passing before, not into, his face. But he could not stop his own tumble, over the horse's head. He slammed into the ground, all his air gone. He looked up, tried to catch breath. The cavalry fight was thinning, too many men dead, Wattenwolden mingled with Horse Lords on the reddened earth. But their smaller numbers meant that it was always going to be a last, faint chance and he saw that it had failed, even as the lance entered his back.

Lara turned away. She had seen enough of the fighting. The Wattenwolden cavalry had been defeated, the final defence broken, it had turned to pure slaughter and she had things she must do. Her last glimpse from Tarfona's gate tower, where she'd stood throughout, was the town's garrison and militia fleeing back to the safety of walls. Few would make it. The tribesmen, in their coloured cloaks, were riding among them, slaughtering at will. Beyond them all, on the ridge where Corinthium had made its stand, riderless horses picked their way among the dying and the dead. The living, she could see, in that last glimpse, were already being gathered in bunches by red-armoured men. As Gandalos, the young officer she'd possessed so as to be close to Ferros, she'd seen the Horse Lords' cavern and their hundreds of slaves. She had no doubt that these Tarfonans would be digging soon enough.

As she ran down the stairs, and pushed her way through milling crowds of wailing townsfolk consumed with terror, it was those prisoners who, strangely, gave her what little hope she had. Slaves were property, and useful until they died. Up there on the hill, if Ferros lived, he would be one of them for a while. If he had died in the fight, he would be reborn and become one, perhaps. To be with him, to follow him still, she would become one too.

It was why she had not possessed a soldier and fought. With the experience she had as Gandalos, she had retained enough of the soldier to recognise a near hopeless cause when she saw one. One more soldier fighting in that trench would not alter that. And she'd learned that one needed to recover for a time before trying to possess again. It wasn't effortless. She'd possessed that woman to learn more about a subject of which she knew so little: love. Now she'd rest, wait, so she could learn something about slavery.

She was twenty paces from the gates when they burst open. She pressed herself into a wall, as men and women screamed and did the same to avoid the charging horses. Three of them. Two of the riders she did not know. The third she did.

'Roxanna,' she breathed.

She did not see Lara. There were four more soldiers waiting for her just inside the gate. She did not pause to greet them, simply rode on and they went before her, scattering people as they rode hard and straight. Lara knew where they were going. To the port, to the only escape from the falling city.

It wasn't part of her plan. She'd thought to wait as long as she could before possessing a soldier, becoming a prisoner, finding Ferros. But on a whim she now began to run after the horses before the crowds closed up behind them.

Many of the panicking people were also making for the port, and though the soldiers spared neither whip nor club in pushing them from their way, though men, women and children were trampled or knocked aside in the rush, the horses could move no faster than she could run behind. The town was shallowly built, spread along its shoreline, and they reached the port fast. Gates were closed on the docks themselves, people pressing them, arms thrust through the bars, beseeching. But men with clubs, and a troop of archers with bows raised, drove the mob back. The gates opened enough to admit the riders – and about twenty people, mostly men, who scattered into the side alleys and warehouses. The guards did not pursue them, concerned with shutting the gates again and keeping the mob out.

Lara was one who got through. The horses sped up in the short distance to where the boats were tied but she soon caught up, to witness the horses being led away, and Roxanna boarding the largest vessel there. On the one beside it, sitting on the deck amid a jumble of goods, she saw Doukas, the governor, who she'd last seen riding back from the hill before the battle. He was weeping.

There was a sailor coiling rope beside the larger ship's gangplank. 'Heh,' she said, and he looked up at her, frowned. It had only been a few hours since she'd left Rablania and she was not sure if she had the strength to possess another. But she discovered she did, when the man grunted, and was gone. She could feel a distant part inside of him fighting her immediately.

She would not be able to keep him long. Long enough perhaps.

The moment of possession was the strangest – and the best. Every part of her feeling every part of him. His limbs, his aches, his scars. The sudden flash of terror as he was taken over, diminishing fast, like the wail of someone falling off a high cliff. Then his mind was only hers and she knew his passions, his fears, his memories. All to be explored, used, later. His name was Danlos and one thing she noted immediately was that, like her, he was from Balbek. For the plan she'd made, such as it was, that was good.

Someone on the deck called Danlos a dozy bastard and ordered him aboard. Casting off the last of the ropes, she ran up the gangplank. The last to do so, and as soon as she did, it was pulled in behind her and the ship began to drift from the dock.

Someone commanded her to coil the mooring ropes. She began the task assigned, dragging the rope with her as they turned away because while she was still ashore, she'd seen Roxanna go through a door set in the centre of the vessel's raised rear deck. Slowly, she worked her way nearer. By the time she reached it, the ship was well under way, the houses that lined the narrow bay of the harbour passing by. The open sea was not far off. She did not have much time.

Someone came out of the door. Before it swung shut, Lara dropped the coil and slipped inside.

Ships were compact, even one this large. A short, narrow passage led to the rear of the vessel, where the bigger cabins would be. At the passage's end, a door was ajar. Through the gap she heard soft singing.

Pushing her head cautiously in, she saw the singer. Roxanna was on a narrow, railed balcony at the very rear of the ship, the other side of a low wooden wall which separated it from the cabin. As Lara watched, the Corinthian pulled off her blouse, the last of her clothes. Dropping it to the deck, she sighed, stretched her arms to the sky, opening herself to the late afternoon sun.

Lara had to admit: her body was magnificent. That ebony skin, those taut, full breasts, hips a perfect oval above long, muscular legs. For a moment, feeling the sailor within her stir, she felt his lust, and understood, just a little, how Ferros had been unable to resist this woman. Wondered, for a moment, if she would have been able to resist, though until now she had never considered a woman in that way. Then she remembered what else this woman had done. Remembered how Roxanna had killed her, at the cult of the immortal, on the feast of Simbala.

Roxanna seized a rope, and hauled up a bucket of seawater. Raised it and tipped it over herself. Lara could see the red flow off her – blood from her latest victims. That these were enemies, killed on a battlefield, did not move Lara at all. She had begun to wonder whose side she was on in the fight to come, the fight that had begun.

She closed the door behind her. Roxanna must have noticed something – a soft sound, a draught cut off, because she paused in her second hauling, let the bucket fall, turned. Her eyes narrowed when she saw the sailor there. 'Get out!' she yelled.

'I'll leave,' Lara said, her gravelly voice the man's, the tongue from the docks of Balbek. 'Once I have told you something.'

'You dare?' Roxanna swivelled, put one leg over the low wall. 'I'll have you flayed and thrown to the sharks.' She bent to snatch a dagger from the belt she'd dropped to the floor, stood straight. 'Perhaps I'll start the flaying myself.'

'You could try,' Lara replied, drawing the knife from Danlos's sheath. 'I've learned that I am handy with a knife. Maybe we'll kill each other. And then, I suppose,' she took one step closer, 'it will just be a question of which one of us is reborn first.'

She'd wanted to see surprise in the other woman's eyes. She

did. Though shock was still to come. Roxanna's plucked eyebrows rose high. 'You are ...'

'I am.'

'But who? Have we met? Are you ... a newcomer?' Roxanna stepped closer, lowering her knife.

'New enough. And yes, we did meet. Once. Only once.' She took a long pause before she continued, 'On the night you killed me ... Carellia.'

In the other woman's eyes confusion came, before the shock that Lara had been waiting for. 'Then you are ... you are—'

Behind Roxanna, Lara saw the last of the houses to either side, could feel the ship breasting the chop where the bay gave way to open water. It was time. She'd got what she wanted, this moment. So there was only one more thing. 'Listen,' she said, moving around the stunned Corinthian, 'I have this last to say to you.' She stepped over the low wall dividing cabin and balcony, turned back. 'Ferros is mine. And I will kill you for him one day.'

'You will ... ? Stop!' yelled Roxanna, rushing forward. Too late. For as the ebony arms reached for her, Lara smiled, turned and dived into the sea.

She was still smiling as she swam to the headland. Danlos was a powerful swimmer, as nearly everyone from Balbek was. It was why she had been so glad to find him. She doubted that he would be glad, when he woke up back in Tarfona, with the city about to fall to the Horse Lords. She felt guilty about that for a moment. Only a moment. Guilt was something she'd had in her old life. Now that she had *lives*? Well, she was learning to manage without it.

6

The Maiden and the God

All Atisha knew was that she knew nothing.

She'd learned things, of course she had. Had set out to do so, from the moment she'd been captured by the Horse Lord Korshak and the Huntress Gistrane, back in Ometepe. Learned more from them, and from the monk aboard the ship that bore her away from her home, towards the land where she now was, the Land of the Four Tribes. First, she had been determined to learn their language – *tolanpa-sen*, the tongue they used in common , even though each tribe had its own, too. In the four-week journey across the waters, she had made sure she studied every day. All three who'd come to Ometepe to fetch her – and Poum, especially Poum – spoke some of her tongue, which made learning easier when words could be translated. But she stopped them speaking her language, tried to speak only theirs. By the time they'd reached Saghaz-a, she could follow conversations, if the talk was slow enough, engage in some herself. Because she'd realised that in ignorance lay her danger.

So she learned – but still did not know.

It was the same on the journey through the land, away from the seaport where she'd arrived. That had been attacked, she'd been told, by murderers, thieves and rapists from the northern lands, so she was moved swiftly, the next morning, in case of further danger. They travelled in a convoy of coaches, pulled by more of the fantastic creatures she'd first seen, and been terrified by, that Korshak had ridden: horses. The roads were smooth, tended, quite unlike the mountain path in Ometepe she'd taken to the City of Women, so travel was not the terrible lurch and bump of that rock-strewn roadway. Still, she kept finding excuses to do what she'd done then: walk, always carrying Poum, sometimes in her arms, sometimes in a sling around her back. Walking, she could talk to people who walked too – soldiers, servants. On occasion, Gistrane would be beside her. On others, though rarely, Korshak, even if he hated to be anywhere other than astride his horse. She talked, listened, learned more of the language – and of this new world, its history. She discovered that the Four Tribes had fought each other for years, in brutal, never-ending conflict. Discovered the reason why they stopped fighting, the reason why she was there.

The reason in her arms.

It was the only thing she truly knew: that the Seafarers, Warrior Priests, Huntresses, and Horse Lords had only ceased slaughtering each other because of a prophecy – that 'the One' would come to save them all. The One that was neither man nor woman, and both.

The One who was her child.

And knowing that, she knew one thing else, had one certainty: she had not saved her baby from the tyrant-king, her lover Intitepe, and his terror of one prophecy, to have Poum's life ruled by another. It was that one piece of knowing that made all her other learning worthwhile. Because if she learned who these enemies were – enemies because they planned a fate for Poum that neither Poum nor she could have any say in – she might one day know how to stop them.

There was one other person she had spoken to on the journey – only once, and briefly, before Gistrane moved her away. The man who had given her some hope, back at the seaport, before the attack. Though very different, he was like her in one thing – he'd named everyone else as their enemy. She wanted to find out more of that. For he too was from another land – in fact, she discovered in their one conversation, the same land where those *savages* from the north came from. He didn't look like a savage to her, though. Of her height, and therefore dwarfed by the Horse Lords and Huntresses. Of a different colouring than she had ever seen, with his pale skin, reddish-brown hair, and beard. He walked with a slight limp because, she could see, he had one leg a little shorter than the other; one shoulder higher than its counterpart too.

He was a man, for all that. But the true difference was in his eyes. There was a blueness deep within them. But they looked to her like night stealing over water, for the darkness that was filling them.

It wasn't until they reached their destination in the mountains, and had slept a week in the stone fortress that was named 'the Keep', that she discovered why – and learned something else.

Luck waited a week before he acted. There were two reasons for his caution.

The first was that he knew he would have only one chance, so must take it when all in the Keep were distracted – as they would be this night. For it was their great feast – the greatest, he'd been told, that had ever been given on this always special day.

Every year the coming of the prophet – *azana-kesh*, 'the one who comes before' – was celebrated. It was a story Luck had taken trouble to learn. He had always tried to understand his world; and the stories of how a people began, what had shaped them, told him much of who they were, how they thought

– how they could be fought. In Midgarth, his own people's story began with twins, one immortal, one not, separated at birth then reunited by Gudrun, who gave them the gifts. Not knowing they were siblings, they loved each other, and founded a race of both immortals and mortals. Exposed then killed because of their incest, they became the twin moons that watched for ever from the skies, meeting and loving again once a year.

It was a simple story for a simple folk. The story of *azana-kesh* was more complicated.

He – or she, for the prophet had appeared differently to each of the Four Tribes – had appeared but a hundred years before and told of the coming of the One, urging the tribes to unite behind the belief. To persuade them of this truth, he – or she – had performed miracles. For the Huntresses, a goose they had killed was reborn, killed again, reborn again and then finally sacrificed and eaten in a sacred feast. For the Seafarers, a sunken ship had risen to the surface, its drowned crew alive. On the Sea of Grass, a white *azama-klosh* had been born, a bull calf that had led the Horse Lords to a hidden valley and a huge herd of its kind that, for the first time, they did not slaughter but penned and raised. Whilst in a cave on a mountain, where the Keep now stood, a cowled woman came to a hermit called Sandaz and showed him a plant in the forest, guided him on how to distil a liquor from its roots, which allowed certain chosen ones to travel far, in visions brought by smoke within a glass. Both that plant and the methods used to extract the liquid that became Sirene were secrets known only to a tiny few.

Secrets that Luck was determined to learn.

For decades those who believed had persuaded – or enslaved, or killed – those who did not. When they were finally, fully united, the One had come. The joy of that would be expressed in a day of solemn ritual with, as its climax, a huge feast. The elites of all the tribes, the leading men and women of Saghaz-a, had been arriving at the Keep all week for the celebration.

This day. Luck had watched from the battlements, from sunrise and on, as ceremonies were enacted in the vast courtyard.

Now, with bells tolling and the noise from the huge hall growing ever louder, enough to reach him in his distant cell where he lay, he glanced across again at the second reason for his caution, looked away sharply, clutched the sides of his cot to stop himself rising, and chewed his lip.

The second reason for his caution was Sirene.

She sat on a table in the corner of the room. The seeing globe. The vial of the liquid drug beside it. The fluid was what he thought of as her. She lived within it, his guide, his blessing, his saviour.

His ruin.

He wanted her. Yearned to take her hand again to be led to … wonders. Away from himself and his lumpen body. Away from the prison of the Keep and the prison of himself, of his mind, forever questioning. With Sirene, there were only answers, there was only ever freedom, and joy. For though Anazat had said that all was at the whim of Sirene, and that he had never been taken to the same place twice, more often than not Luck was; and so went many times to Gytta's garden, to sit with his dead wife, alive again. It was not a dream. He, who had leaped both sides of the veil of things as they seem all his long life, knew the difference. Dreams were random, jagged. They did not flow, you could not touch, or be touched, although you thought you could. But guided by Sirene, he could hold Gytta, laugh with her … make love with her, with the only woman in four hundred years with whom the act had made any sense.

Though he also knew this: that just as life was constructed of illusions, an acceptance of what seemed real, so Sirene and where she led him was only another seeming. Thus, as his eyes darkened, moving towards the deeper blackness that he'd seen in Anazat and in some others, he knew that he was coming to a moment of final choice. To surrender entirely to that world of joy, give up this one that had caused him so much sorrow. Or to choose sorrow, live in this world – and try to save the land and the people he loved.

And so it was that, despite the agony of it, the hourly craving, he had not gone to the table and taken Sirene's hand for this whole week.

Anazat had left the globe and drug for him, where before he'd been denied them. He knew why – his people's raid upon their port had changed all the black-eyed monk's plans. No longer did he think that Luck would be the key to unlocking Midgarth. Now it was believed that he could be subverted like Peki Asarko had been, the Lord of the Lake of Souls doing the Four Tribes' work, betraying his people and his land. He was a tool still, to be kept and used; and so it would be better if he were fully tamed, fully dependent. Thus Sirene was left – to be withdrawn, no doubt, if Luck should prove resistant.

But I've shown him, Luck thought, his legs scissoring across the blankets. Rarely looking at the one who called him from the corner. Forever hearing her call. For this week, this purpose, I shall show I can resist her. And when my purpose is done …

He looked now, kept looking, couldn't help himself. The smoke swirled within the glass. Joy awaited. He knew, in his heart and in his mind, that before too long he would have that joy again. He had bargained with himself, as he resisted. After tonight, he'd promised. After I've proved myself to myself.

After I've seen *her*.

For all his plans, his self-denial, were about Atisha.

Toparak, the monk who he'd befriended, who'd taken him riding, and had tended him ever since, had let slip her name, when all others referred to her only as 'The Mother' or 'The Mother of the One', or sometimes as 'Holy Mother'. Toparak had not seen her himself, just heard whispers about her, in the gossip that swirled about the halls where all the visitors gathered. From him, Luck also learned exactly what part of the Keep she was in. Who tended her – the Huntresses, the tribe that was made up only of women. When Luck learned her name, and where she was, he had begun to make his plan.

Atisha, her child, they were the centre of everything. The world had been changed entirely because of them. His world of Midgarth and every other, these new ones of which he'd learned. The land where she was from, called Ometepe. High-towered Corinthium to the south. Saghaz-a, from the stormy coasts to the Sea of Grass, a land so vast the seasons were different north to south. All compelled to change because of a prophecy that had spoken of a saviour, who was neither man nor woman.

Whose mother was named Atisha.

And if she was the centre of it all, it was to her he must go ... and act.

When his brothers and Freya had provided the distraction of their raid, he had thought that he would kill the child. He'd real-ised that was wrong. It wasn't simply the killing of an innocent. He might not believe in their prophecy, their destiny to rule the world under 'the One', but he did believe that this world, his and all others, were utterly changed by the baby's coming. All his studies, his examining of how the world worked, had led him to this point. The child was his fate, as much as they – she or he, or both – was everyone else's.

If four hundred years of life had taught him one thing, it was this: fate was never something you had the power to turn away from.

There was one other thing. He had lost something, sacrificed something rather, in exchange for the joy he'd found. And he was reminded, even as he remembered it, when a sparrow came, perched upon his windowsill, and began to peck at the

145

breadcrumbs he'd left for her there. For ever since he'd been lost to the sweet smoke, he'd also lost his ability to possess the birds and the beasts.

He swung his legs off the cot, sat up to try now. Since he had discovered the way of it, in early childhood, after his first death and rebirth – he'd fallen from a boat when he had five summers, had drowned, woken on the shore a day later, possessed a seagull – it had always been as easy as thought. Until he'd come to the Keep, taken Sirene's hand. He thought now, sensed the bird, its heart, its breath, tried to push beyond ...

There was a moment he felt feather, a faster heartbeat, saw the cell from the windowsill. Then ... no. He was back in himself. The sparrow gave another chirp, flew off while he sank back onto the bed. Held back his tears. Clung to his hope. He'd been close.

He heard footsteps. As they reached his door, he threw himself off the bed, and vomited again into the wooden bucket.

'Sir?'

Luck looked up from the floor. Toparak was standing in the doorway, his concern clear in his greying eyes. 'Still sick?' he asked.

'Worse,' replied Luck, bending to vomit again, though this time producing little but bitter bile. There was no faking needed. The root he'd found in the forest, that was called 'stringen' back in Midgarth and that he gave sometimes to a person who needed to be purged of some harsher poison, had proved just as effective in Saghaz-a.

'It is time though,' the monk said, the worry clear in his voice. Luck saw that he was wearing not his usual simple brown robe but a new one of deep blue, fringed in a dark fur. 'The feast is about to begin and Anazat requires you.'

'Tell him—' Luck turned and voided more bile. Then he raised his head. 'Tell him that if he wants me, he will have me

146

thus.' He wiped his mouth. 'Though I suspect he will not want a puking Northman to spoil his decorous ceremonies.'

Toparak hesitated, then shrugged. 'I am sorry to hear this. Can I bring you anything else?'

As he said it, he glanced into the corner, to the table. Anyone who had ever journeyed with Sirene always knew exactly where she was, all the time. Luck saw desire come into the man's eyes. Dark, but not the black of Anazat's. Probably not even the darkness of his own. The man's journeys were limited, the drug rationed, as it had been for Luck. No doubt the monk was puzzled by the freedom Luck had with it now. Yet perhaps not so ... for both men knew how Sirene could bind those who took her hand. And Toparak, who had taken him riding several times, who was the closest Luck had to a friend in this land, now looked both desiring, and sad – for he knew the cost of the freedom Luck enjoyed.

'I will tell Anazat that you cannot come, and why. He will be disappointed.'

'As am I.'

The monk bowed and went. Luck waited till his footsteps had receded up the spiral stair, before rising and walking over to the table. Amid the jumble was another root, which counter-acted the effect of the sick-making one. He chewed it, felt the rumbles die away. He did not linger; the temptation in the corner would be too great if he did. Snatching up the globe and its stand he put it into the satchel he'd brought all the way with him on the journey over the mountain from Midgarth. The vial followed, though he was reluctant to let it slip from his fingers.

He stood at the half-open door, listening. He had been told enough about how the ceremony and feast would proceed to work out, by the sounds, what was happening. Music played, made upon pipe and organ. They would already have begun on the food, a series of dishes that would take at least two hours to get through. It would climax with the sacred goose, three dozen hunted and slain by the Huntresses, eaten this night in memory of that holy, resurrected goose that had shown them the way of the One so many years before. Only at this conclusion would the reason for it all appear – Atisha with her child, the babe naked no doubt, to show the assembled leaders what they had been waiting for, the reason they had given up all their hatred and united to conquer the world.

Two hours. Not long. It would have to be enough.

Passing the bag strap over his head, Luck slipped out the door.

'There! All is done. You are magnificent.' Her attendant, Lanane, stepped away and Atisha's reflection stood alone in the tall looking glass.

She wondered who it was who looked back. It couldn't be her. Atisha was not this tall woman with hair gathered in a topknot and a single golden tress halfway down her back. Atisha did not have skin the colour of buttermilk, nor saucer eyes. Atisha did not wear a dress of rich, red velvet, its hem sweeping the floor in lynx fur, buttoned up the front and to her neck in silver. She sometimes wore a necklace of seashells, never one of pearls. At her wrists there might be bracelets woven from grasses, not spun from gold.

This could not be her. And yet, she realised, it was. She recognised herself in one thing only. The women who attended her – maiden Huntresses – had altered her height with boots, her hair with dye, her eyes with paint. But they could do nothing about the fear in them.

From the moment she awoke she had been prepared. She'd been told what for – this great day of ceremonies and celebrations. Far greater than the first revelation at the seaport, which had gone so wrong. She would take no part until the climactic moment, the one when she walked into the hall with Poum in her arms.

She was not to be who she was. They did not want her reality. She was a function only. She was the Holy Mother but only in the way they saw such a one. Hence the dress, the paint. And Poum?

She looked in the mirror. The child was on the bed behind her, rolling about on furs. Another attendant sat beside her, amusing her by shaking rattles, making bird sounds. The baby was the real reason all had gathered, Atisha merely a decoration, a symbol on the side. Important as part of the story they had made up, but not truly vital. Her child was, though Poum had also been prepared for what lay ahead by not being prepared at all. All that was required of her was to be herself. Their – her and his – naked self.

As her baby rolled about, in the reflection Atisha glimpsed the mystery at her core. She kept thinking that something there would change – that Poum would become one thing or the other. By the organs, the child could be a girl or a boy. Atisha knew that things changed as children grew. But there had been no one she'd met who knew anything about this, save for the midwife at the birth who'd said she'd seen it once before – and Atisha had never seen that woman again. Though she also knew that part of her wanted change, wanted certainty, in the world in which she was now that could only be dangerous. Everyone wanted Poum to be both sexes and neither. Their unity, their whole future was based on that. So she knew that only in Poum's *difference – their* difference – was there some small degree of safety. For both of them.

She realised that she'd been staring a while. That the women who watched her, the servants, the Huntresses, all expected some sort of acknowledgement from her. What could she say about her transformation? They didn't want her truth. They only wanted her obedience.

She gave it to them with a nod.

Immediately Lanane took her arm, led her to the chair beside the table. 'Eat, lady. Drink. There is time yet.'

Time, Atisha thought. Time before we are on display.

She looked at Poum. *They* were fidgeting, making mewing sounds like a cat. If she was not hungry, her child was. And she realised that, before they were both paraded to the world, forced to be something for others, she wanted them to be just for themselves. 'Leave please,' she said.

Lanane looked at the two other Huntress-attendants. 'We stay, take care—'

'I want alone,' Atisha snapped, then calmed, closing her eyes. 'I feed my baby.'

She watched them, the conflict on their faces. Must be hard to contradict the mother of a god, she thought. Eventually saw them yield. 'We go,' Lanane said. She turned her head to the music coming from the courtyard. 'We will watch the ceremonies for a time and return.'

Atisha nodded, and the three left. They locked the door behind them. *Where do you think I am going?* she thought sourly, kicking the pinching boots off, then unbuttoning her gown. When her breast was bare, she lifted Poum from the furs, and the child fastened on eagerly.

Atisha listened to the music – strange to her ears, so unlike the music from home which always seemed to flow from the features of the land, imitating the wind moving through rock canyons, the surge of waves on sea shores, the crackle of lava spilling over the lip of Toluc, god and volcano both. The music of this land had a steady beat, and to her ear was as cold as the stones of the castle which was her prison.

She had just moved Poum to her other breast when she heard

the key turn in the lock. So soon, she thought, glaring. She was readying herself to shout, to demand more time, when the door opened and the small man entered.

He supposed it was because they were about to meet their saviour that everyone in the castle was so distracted, hurrying to find a viewpoint on the courtyard, to hear the music, see the parading warriors of the Four Tribes. He'd glimpsed them from windows as he'd passed – the Seafarers in all their peacock finery, with feathers in their cocked hats, red doublets spilling lace; the Huntresses, clad neck to toe in tight-gleaming leather, shooting fire arrows over the castle walls; the Horse Lords astride their huge stallions, bare-chested and tattooed from nape to belly, pounding curved swords into their shields. Even the usually sober monks were dressed up – all, like Toparak, having exchanged their black robes for blue ones, carrying the weapons with which Luck had seen them training in the court-yard – spears, double-handed swords, wheat flails with razor edges. They performed as they walked, as agile as acrobats, executing somersaults from standing starts, springing from one another's hands to swoop and soar, slice and stab.

He saw them only in glimpses, did not linger to marvel. He knew his enemies, their power. What he did not know was the strength of those who might oppose them.

He'd thought he might have to bluff his way past guards, to argue, persuade. He'd had no true plan, just the determination that he would reach her. In the end there was no one in the corri-dor that led to her chamber. There was only a locked door – and even that had a key in it. Turning it, he pushed the door open.

The woman, Atisha, was sitting in a chair, her baby in her arms, the same way he'd seen them that first time – feeding. But as he entered, she rose, plucked the baby from her breast, tucked herself away. 'You,' she said.

He bowed from his waist, his hand across his chest. 'Luck,' he announced.

'I remember. Atisha,' she replied, tapping her own chest. 'Poum,' she said, lifting the baby.

There was the child, naked. This child of prophecy that had changed the destiny of the wide world … because of what was at the child's very centre, which Luck, for the first time, studied now.

He thought he had seen all there was to see in his deep explorations of man and beasts. He had never seen this. This nothing. This everything. This … One. For there was the core of a man within the folds of a woman. Or perhaps it was the other way around.

Truly, he thought, the baby is neither, and both. Not single then. He and she are … *they*.

Destiny or not, to Luck's inexpert eye the baby looked as if they were about to burst into tears at the interruption of the meal.

Perhaps Atisha sensed that too, for she fussed the child, playing with its nose, then lifting it high into the air, swooping it down, swinging it. Poum gave a little laugh, and Atisha lowered the child back onto the furs, taking a root that lay there, that looked already well used, and placing it in the babe's mouth. Poum rolled about, content. Atisha stood straight and, buttoning herself up, looked at him. 'Why?' she said.

He knew what she meant. Why was he there? What did he want? What could they do? There was an immediate understanding between them. It had been there from the beginning, when he'd crossed the room to kill her child and she had looked up and thanked him for giving her hope.

But there could be no true understanding when each only spoke a little of the common language. Not in the short amount of time they had. For that he had another plan.

He came to the table, laid his satchel down upon it, reached in, and pulled out the globe.

As he placed it on its stand, she came to stand beside him. 'This,' she said. 'This on ship. I saw monk talk.' She laid her fingers on the glass. 'This for talk, yes?'

'Yes. And no.' He looked at her, their eyes level. They were of a height, which did not make her very tall. 'Also to see,' he gestured out of the window, which looked not inwards to the courtyard but out onto the valley below, 'far.'

'How far?'

'Through all the world.' He tapped the temples above his ears. 'Beyond this world also.'

'That far?' She smiled, then frowned. 'Explain.'

He shook his head, then laid a finger on his forehead. 'Not enough words here in *tolanpa-sen*,' he said. He pointed outside, and placed fingers behind his ears in the attitude of listening. Though this window faced away, the music was still loud – and growing louder. It was strange to him, coming from a land where music was made with horns, drums and tree-bark flutes. But he could tell that this was swelling, building. It told him that they didn't have long. So he said that. 'Not enough time. So this.'

She nodded. 'How?'

'This,' he said, pulling the vial from the bag. He held it up to the light, so she could see into it.

'Empty,' she said.

'No,' he replied and, with his thumb, levered the cap off.

Over his hundreds of years, he had explored almost every plant in his land. Found those that his people could use, for food or medicine. Set aside those that would harm, or even kill – being an explorer who could not die was an advantage. Consumed them in different ways – dried, raw; distilled, when their properties deserved it. He had helped his people in countless ways with the medicines he created – eased childbirth, soothed limbs, took the pain away from wound or disease. He had made cordials and liquors, brewed tastier, stronger mead or beers, though he drank few of those himself. He had also found some plants – plants of vision he called them – which could take a person from this world. There were many types of mushroom that would do this. One, red of cap, which he called 'Farsight', he would reduce to a liquid, daub onto himself at nostril and armpit, then use to journey beyond his body. It was not like Sirene, not close to that clarity. But one of the main things he'd learned was how much to take for the journey he wanted.

Dosage was all.

Sirene was so different. Far more powerful than anything he'd ever encountered, when taken to its limit. But it could also be used, as he had just told Atisha, not to travel but to see.

He smelled it, that acrid sweetness. He yearned for it, to lose himself. But he knew that it would be almost impossible to resist. Perhaps later, back in his cell, he finally would yield. But here, the purpose of the journey was different. So he'd left only a little in this vial. The same amount that Anazat had used when he first brought Luck into Sirene's embrace, and showed him the world. 'Breathe,' he said, and tipped it, three fat drops, one after the other, onto the glass.

One drop to talk. One to see. One to listen, hear, and understand.

Atisha didn't hesitate, bent, drew in the sweet smoke, gasped. Just before he did the same, Luck slipped a chair beneath her and she fell into it.

When he'd first tried it, Anazat had been the guide, he the one led. Now, he was the guide. And one of the things he'd learned in his journeying was that language was no longer required. He thought it was to do with the fact that, when they possessed an animal, the gods of Midgarth communicated words in thought. He could do that here. Atisha was standing beside him in the swirling smoke, and he did not need to struggle to speak to her.

Atisha, he thought, *are you all right?*

She turned to him. *Yes. Yes! And I do not need to find their words to tell you that.* Her eyes went wider in wonder. *How can that be? What is this?*

We do not have the time. They will be coming for you soon. Besides, words in any language will not explain it. But without words ... I can show you.

Show me what?

Everything.

She laughed. When had she last laughed? *That much?* she thought.

Yes. What they are, what they intend to do. With you. With your baby. With the world.

She nodded, laughter gone. *Yes. Show me that.*

He'd been right about her. She did not fear. No, that wasn't true. She did. But she had learned what had taken him hundreds of years to learn: courage was not absence of fear. It was fearing, and still acting.

He took her hand. *Come,* he said in both their minds, and together they stepped into the smoke.

When they came for her, it took a moment for her to stand up. The Huntresses were concerned – was she sick? Lanane wrinkled her nose, as if detecting the faintest waft of smoke still in the air. But Atisha steadied herself, rose, bent to pick up Poum, who gurgled in her arms.

'I am ready,' she said.

She followed them, but set the pace, moving slowly, gathering herself for what lay ahead, still partly in the world she'd left behind. Not the cell. The one she'd journeyed to, with Luck.

She was in the corridors, on the stairwells, crossing the great courtyard. And she was elsewhere too. With him. They had stepped out of the smoke together, but the way their minds had been joined, the intensity of the connection, made her feel connected to him still. She couldn't speak with him but she could sense him …

… sense him back in his cell. Feel what he was doing.

She knew the smoke was different for him than it had been for her. She had been drawn to it, even in that one, sweet-bitter inhalation. This she knew, though – she would be no protector of Poum if she yielded again to that delight. It had given her what she needed – a clear vision of what she had to oppose. She understood the why of it. It was the how that would take some working out. But she knew it was to do with him, this man, named for chance.

If he did not sink too deep into Sirene's smoky arms.

They paused before the great oak doors. Trumpets sounded in the hall, the doors swung in – and the roar from five hundred voices knocked her back on her heels. Lanane took her elbow again. But she shrugged it off. She needed to stand on her own.

She nodded – to herself, and to Luck, in his cell. Ready, she strode into the hall.

7

Being Other People

Ferros woke to agony.

Every part of him burned. From the nails on his toes to the hairs on his head. He remembered the pain of his first rebirth. This was ten times worse.

Why?

The question itself was a blow within his skull. He realised he was panting, managed to slow his breaths, till he was taking longer, deeper ones. It helped, a little. The general burning lessened. The agony settled in specific places.

That is why, he thought. The first time I died was from an arrow in the eye. One death blow. Here, there were many.

He tallied them. Thought gave him focus and distracted, if only a very little, from the pain.

His arm, sliced near in half by a sword. His head, where the blood had flowed so much that if he wasn't immortal he would have bled to death. The same in his thigh, where steel had entered. The worst wounds were on his back. He remembered vaguely being unhorsed, rolling on the ground, a lance thrust down. Whoever had stabbed him once had done so again and again as he lay. There were half a dozen wounds, three so deep any one of them would have killed a mortal.

Yet within the agony he could feel the healing. There was no arrow embedded in his skull, nothing needing to be removed as it had that first time, the removal killing him again. That time back in Balbek, they had kept him in the embrace of the poppy till all hurt had passed. How he wished he was in her lulling arms now!

With a wrench of his mind he took himself from his pain to his present. Opened his eyes – to darkness. Realised that it was not night or a windowless cell that was the cause, but the bandage across his eyes. When he reached up, ran his fingers across it, someone spoke.

'So you are back with us, Ferros of Balbek. It has taken longer than usual. But your wounds were ... unusually widely spread.' The man – Makron, Ferros recognised his voice from the tunnel – laughed, and continued, 'But what else could be expected from such a fearsome warrior.'

Slowly, with every part of the movement burning, Ferros took the bandage and lifted it from his eyes. Instant flaring light made him squint – to take in a large room with stone walls and a high ceiling. The light was right above him, from multiple candles in a wide holder; also from each side, where torches burned on sconces. There was light beyond the room too, through three tall, part-shuttered openings.

'Where am I?' Ferros croaked.

'Tarfona. The governor's house.' Makron reached to a flagon, poured some wine into a cup, drank, smacked his lips. 'Excellent!'

Amid all the pain, his mouth was an inferno. 'Wine?' Ferros asked.

'Of course.' He smiled. 'As soon as you put your blindfold back on.'

'Why?'

Makron laughed again. 'Obviously because of them.' He waved a hand and Ferros noticed what he hadn't before – men, dressed in the simple tunics of house servants, standing in each corner with heads lowered and their backs to the room. 'How tempting it would be to leap from your present wreck of a body into something more ...' He thrust out a lower lip. 'Pleasant.'

'I would not.'

'I do not believe you.' Makron raised an eyebrow. 'Why would you not?' He studied Ferros for a moment, then shrugged. 'Still, later for that. First, wine – when you put back your blindfold.'

Ferros did. In a few moments someone was above him, raising him from the bed. Bolts of sheer fire shot through his body. The wine, which he gulped, helped a little, before he was laid back down.

'Go,' Makron called and Ferros heard the servants leaving the room. When the door closed, Makron said, 'You can take off your bandage now, if you wish.'

Ferros did. The first thing he saw was the wine goblet on a small table beside him. He pushed himself onto an elbow, reached, groaned, drank. Then looked at the man now standing behind the desk.

He'd seen him before, at the gathering of the Assani. He'd thought to kill him there, the one he'd known as 'Smoke' – until Roxanna had recognised him as Makron, her former husband and, like them both, an immortal. Unlike then, he was no longer dressed in the flowing white robes of the wilderness messiah but in a silk tunic such as he would wear in Agueros, the immortals' Sanctum on the Hill in the city of Corinthium. His hair, which had flowed over his shoulders, was tied behind now; the beard that had occupied half his face was shorter, trimmed and shaped.

His study must have given away his thoughts. Makron ran his fingers over his chin. 'It is a relief not to have to be "Smoke",' he said. 'The prophet's work is done, for the time being. The Assani, the last of the tribes to win over, have been won. And immediately rewarded. If you'd woken a day earlier, you'd have heard them, with the other tribes, enjoying themselves on the city streets. They took their time. But even they are sated with savagery now. While I,' he lifted the goblet, looked into it, swirling the wine, 'no longer have to content myself with fermented mare's milk.' He shuddered, drank, smiled. 'Doukas! He treated himself so well. This is some of the finest Tinderos wine I've ever had. Only a man steeped in corrupt practices could have paid the price required to bring it out here.' He sipped again, then, putting down the vessel, leaned on his desk. 'Such a man will have no place in the world we are creating.'

Taking a deep breath, Ferros swung his legs off the bed. He swayed, steadied. 'What world?' he muttered.

'The world of the One, of course.'

Back in the tunnel under the mountain, this man had talked about the sickness at the immortal heart of the empire – an attempt to persuade Ferros to surrender, and join the cause. Would carry on doing so, no doubt. It was not something he needed to deal with now. Not when he was this weak. He took another sip of wine. 'The battle?' he said.

'You lost. Though it was surprisingly close. You did well, Ferros of Balbek. Very well, considering that it was, I suspect, a very different fight than those you were used to against the Sarphardi. Of course, you based your defence on Andronikos, at Kristun?' When Ferros nodded, Makron whistled between his teeth. 'Another hundred Wattenwolden and you might even have won it.' He came with the goblet and poured more wine into Ferros's mug. 'I see why Lucan and Roxanna were so happy to have found you. Especially now.'

'Now?'

Makron returned to his desk. 'When you might be one of the very few things standing between them and the ending of their world.' He smiled. 'Though of course, I have you now.'

'You have me. But what do you plan to do with me?'

'That, young Ferros, will be up to you. Because if I can persuade you to join us—' A soft knocking at the door interrupted him. 'Who's there?' he called.

'The doctor, lord. Says it is time to see his patient again.'

'Wait!' Makron reached and handed him the blindfold. 'Put this on again. We don't want you trying to possess the doctor.'

Ferros stared at the cloth. 'I have told you, I have never done so, and would not now. It is an abomination.'

Makron laughed. 'Oh, Ferros of Balbek! You have so much to learn.' As the younger man tied the mask in place, Makron said, 'Come!'

'Come!'

The shout was muffled by the thick oak door, although it wasn't simply the wood that reduced the sound. The doctor was old, and a little deaf. It was the first time she'd gone into an older body; all her possessions had been young and strong before. It was … interesting. The man was experienced, educated – and with a strong will. Lara had felt him tugging at the edge of her consciousness, trying to break her hold on him, for a few hours now.

It did not help that she was tired. The sailor from Balbek, who she'd used to confront Roxanna, had been a good swimmer, as most from her city were. But even his brawny arms had been tested by the swirling tides where Tarfona harbour met the open sea. They'd barely made it to shore, and he was unable to move further once they had, sunk in exhaustion. She'd left him, trekked the byways into town – and been halted far short of it by all those fleeing in the opposite direction. The tribes who'd won the battle were pillaging the town. There was rapine and slaughter. To go in and search for Ferros, as she had planned, would have been too dangerous. And she'd learned again, with the sailor who'd ejected her as much as she had left, that you had to have a break between possessions, preferably of a few days. A tribesman would have given her the cover she needed. But she did not have the strength to take over even the little girl who took pity on her and gave her some water from her jug, let alone a warrior.

She'd slept, hidden in a ditch within sight of the city's seaward fortifications. An hour or so before dawn, when almost all the screaming had stopped, she'd crept through a gap in the walls.

The violence had slackened, no doubt when the tribes had drunk all that they could find. The results of it, though, were everywhere to be seen in the streets she passed through. Bodies of men, women, children too, many lying in the twisted, absurd postures that death often bequeathed. Among them lay sleeping tribesmen, in their various coloured cloaks, unconcerned about sharing the reddened ground with their victims.

Lara had no true plan, except to get to Ferros. She assumed that he would either have been taken prisoner or died in the battle on the ridge. If the latter, she guessed he would be reborn in the city. During their fighting retreat from the mountains he had told her of their enemy, Makron. The rogue immortal would know who Ferros was, and would be taking special care of him.

As she approached the centre, the governor's house, the body count got higher – and ended in a flesh wall. Whoever had taken command of the building ahead had had the ground before it cleared of dead enemies, piling them up around the perimeter of the centre square. Lara slipped into an arcade, her view part blocked by bodies, and peering over them confirmed at least this much: Tarfona was now under the command of the Horse Lords.

They were no longer in the full lamulin armour they'd worn

for battle. But the sunrise reflected off red breastplate and helm. There was order here, with soldiers emerging from the building and riding fast away – messengers, no doubt, taking news of how well the first stage of the invasion of Corinthium had gone back across – through – the mountains; summoning more troops. But she'd already decided that she cared nothing for the empire. That she cared only for Ferros.

Slumping into the shadows of the arcade though, her body exhausted still, she wondered, as she had wondered so often since waking in a grave, how much in truth she did. Yet he was all she had left, certainly in Tarfona. She also knew that her answers would not be found away from him. So she had to find a way to get close.

Almost immediately an opportunity had presented itself.

Which was why she was standing outside the door now, wearing the green robe of a Tarfonan doctor, a man who'd survived the sacking of his town. In his memory, which she now possessed along with the rest of him, she saw him hide in the cellar of this very building, after the governor, Doukas, had left without his personal physician. Horse Lords had found him, not tribesmen, and perhaps they had been forewarned that men who wore a certain coloured robe were to be kept alive. She'd recognised the robe too, when he came out of the building to go into another one nearby to fetch more medicines. His Horse Lord guard had been distracted by some drunk tribesmen who'd wanted to fight. While he dispatched them, she'd taken her chance. Possessed the physician.

Too soon, she realised, leaning her head against the door she should be going through.

'I said, "Come".' The command was repeated from within. Lifting the doctor's head from the wood, she entered. Her shadow, the blood-spattered Horse Lord, came a step behind her.

She'd known, of course, having seen through the doctor's memories, that Ferros was his patient and that he'd been badly wounded. Killed, in fact. But it was with her own eyes she saw now – and let out a small gasp, stumbling a little. No one had bothered to change Ferros's tunic – and the wounds he'd taken were vivid through the rents the weapons had made. Even if they were already part way to healing, the red-mouthed gashes gaped, oozed.

'Are you all right, doctor?' Makron was studying him closely. Lara knew they'd only had brief talks before. Smoke wanted his charge healed swiftly – even if most of the healing was done from within, flesh was flesh, she'd learned, and immortal recovery could be speeded, and the pain of it eased, by mortal means.

Lara drew himself up. 'Yes, sir,' he replied. 'I haven't slept. Others needed my skills.'

'I do not want you distracted by anyone else, doctor. I need our young man here ready to ride as soon as possible.'

Both Lara and the doctor frowned. 'That may take many days.'

'It must not.' Another red-armoured man came through the door and barked something in his own tongue. Makron nodded, rose, then continued. 'Even if he dies again. Yet if he does, he will eventually be reborn, whereas you …' He paused by the doctor on his way to the door, leaned down, whispered, 'Whereas you will not be, will you?'

Oh, I don't know, thought Lara, as she watched the man leave. Two guards stayed, including the one who'd brought her. She looked at them, each similar – long hair held in a topknot, pale eyes expressionless. She fixed on one. 'Will you open the shutters?'

The man shrugged, did not move. 'Do you understand me?' The man shrugged again. She looked at the other. 'Do you?'

Maybe he understood a little more because he shook his head.

But he didn't go to the shutters so she assumed his knowledge was small. She went to them herself, opened them. The guards did not object to that – but they did when she came back and reached for the bandage over Ferros's eyes. Both growled, took a step forward, grunted words she didn't understand, their meaning clear.

She dropped her hand. Did they know about the power of possession? She doubted many did. The power would surely only be useful to immortals if it was secret. But, whatever reason he'd given, Makron must have commanded that the blindfold stayed on. Very well, she thought, fingering the blood on the cloth that followed the line of the wound beneath, before she spoke. 'Young man, does this hurt?'

His reply came slowly, from depths. 'It does. But the rest of me hurts more.'

'I see why.' He'd leaned forward, revealing the terrible wounds on his back. Blood and pus mingled with the yellow salve that the doctor had applied earlier. She bent to him and, when her head was by his ear, said softly, 'I am going to tell you something, young man. But you need to promise me that when I do you will show no surprise, nor react in any way. Do you agree?'

The blindfolded face swung a little towards her. 'I do.'

She looked up at the guards, who stared back expressionless . . . and something surged in her. Her – his – body convulsed. The doctor swayed and grabbed first Ferros's shoulder and then the back of the chair. 'Doctor,' Ferros said, 'are you all right?'

Lara looked at him, his head turned in that listening angle of the sightless. And for the first time she felt that she was seeing with her eyes, not the doctor's. She knew this feeling, a possession struggling to be free. Never had she felt such a surge before. Even Danlos the sailor hadn't been this strong. Be quick, she thought, straightening. 'It's me,' she whispered. 'Lara.'

One guard hissed – whispering was prohibited too. But Ferros spoke, at a normal volume, his voice calm, only a tremor in the hand that rose and fell betraying emotion. 'It is you. You ... and someone else.' He shuddered. 'Why have you come?'

'To get us out of here.'

'I see. How will you do that?'

'I will ... think of something.' Another convulsion went through her and she added quickly, 'But not now. I must go now. I—' She swallowed. 'I just wanted you to know that I was close. That I will never be far away. That—'

The door opened. Makron entered. 'I am sorry, doctor,' he said, returning to his desk. 'This conquest of the world. So many little details to deal with.' He smiled. 'When can he travel?'

'This young man,' she began. But her voice was a squeak and she had to force it into the doctor's deeper tones. 'This young man is healing remarkably fast. A week of bed rest ...'

'Two days. Two days and I need him astride a horse.'

'Impossible. These wounds—'

'In a wagon then.'

'Sir, we need him in our care.'

It was like she was speaking in chorus. Makron frowned at her. 'We?'

'The school of physicians,' she slurred. She took a step to the door. 'You will forgive me. Not ... not feeling so well myself.'

'Doctor?' Makron stepped from around his desk. 'What is wrong with you?'

It was the same, going in and going out. Separate then seamlessly together in a thought. Together then seamlessly apart.

The doctor and Lara were standing side by side. Until the doctor collapsed to the floor. She was the least shocked person in the room, apart from Ferros, unseeing behind his mask. Certainly she was the first to react, stepping over the doctor's body, staggering to the door.

'Stop her,' Makron cried.

The guards grabbed her, twisting her arms up behind her back.

'Well, well,' said Makron, 'now who do we have here?'

Behind his mask, Ferros had heard the doctor fall. Heard his voice change to her voice. His love, crying out. Ferros jerked off his blindfold. No one protested because they did not notice. The guards were looking at Makron who was looking at Lara, lifting her by her throat, with one hand. A strangled whisper came from her throat. She could barely breathe.

'Aren't you a prize?' Makron gloated.

Ferros didn't say anything. Only stood and, summoning the tiny strength that he had, used it to punch Makron in the face.

At least he dropped Lara. Then the guards fell on Ferros and since he'd put his small everything into the punch, he couldn't resist them. He had no defence, no way to prevent his tumble back into the darkness.

He awoke to the same, and the same level of pain. What was different was that he was in motion – a wagon, he could tell by the sway. His hands, he discovered, were bound and attached to the wagon's side, so there was no chance of removing the mask. But he could hear. And above the rattle of carriage harness, the distant grunt of horses, he could hear breathing. 'Lara?' he whispered.

There was no reply. But he knew it was her. How many times had he lain beside her at night, or near dawn, listening to her breathe? Her breath here was ragged, and Ferros recalled Makron's fingers on her throat; the last thing he remembered.

Where are we being taken? he wondered. Away from the sea, or they'd be on a boat. Inland. To the tunnel, the mountains, through them? Makron still considered him of use, otherwise he'd be dead, they'd both be finally dead, he and Lara. The traitor to Corinthium had two immortal prisoners now.

The carriage swayed and jolted over the rough road. It was uncomfortable, with his arms tied before him. Yet beneath that ache and strain he could feel something else – his immortal's body healing the death wounds he'd taken. He was being born again.

For what? he thought. What did Makron, also known as Smoke, have planned for him? For them? When the wagon suddenly jerked to a stop he thought he might find out. Canvas was pulled back. He heard whispered commands. Then someone freed his hands from the wagon sides, only to tie them immediately behind his back. He was pulled out, set on his feet. A command was given, in a language he did not know but a voice he did. *Bring him* is what Makron must have said, because Ferros was seized by one arm and dragged forward.

Not far. Another command, and he was forced to his knees, his blindfold pulled off. He blinked at a group of men in the moonlight, Makron in the midst of them. Ferros could see the effects of the punch. Fading, but it was as good as his memory of it. One of Makron's eyes was black and half closed. 'Yes,' he snarled, seeing Ferros's gaze, 'you did this. You dared to strike me. Me!' He shook his head. 'It is near a hundred years since I was last struck. By a man you know. And that blow made me turn my back on Corinthium and find another loyalty.'

'What man?'

'Lucan.' Makron spat the name. 'Leader of the Council of Elders. Representing all that is rotten at the heart of Corinthium.' He nodded. 'Yes. Lucan turned me into what you would call a traitor. What will your blow do?'

'Are you going to kill me?'

'It is tempting. But no, at least not yet. Because you are young and stupid, I am going to give you a chance.' He bent till his eyes were level with Ferros's. 'You will do what you called an abomination back in Tarfona. You will possess someone.' He looked around at the guards. 'One of these.'

'I will not.' Ferros leaned forward and spat between Makron's legs. 'You can kill me but I won't.'

'It is not you I'll kill if you don't.' He looked up, said something. Two guards ran off – and returned almost immediately, dragging a bound and blinkered Lara between them. They threw her down between the two immortals. 'It's her. She will die for your stubbornness. I'll have her head cut off in front of you now. Did you know that an immortal's head can survive being removed from the body for a few hours?' He laughed, a sound without mirth. 'She won't be able to speak to you. But you'll be able to see the pleading in her eyes as she dies.'

Ferros closed his own eyes. What choice did he have? It was everything he hated. But he had let her die before, thought he had lost her for ever. He could not lose her again.

He opened his eyes, studied the four Horse Lords. 'Which one?' he asked.

Makron smiled. 'It does not matter,' he replied. 'Because whoever you choose is going to kill all the others – and then himself.'

'What?' Ferros gasped. 'You wish me to kill them all for your pleasure?'

'Not for my pleasure – for all our protection.' He jabbed the toe of his boot into Lara's back. 'This one betrayed the secret of the immortals. The only way we have kept our deepest secret over the years is that no one,' he glanced briefly around, 'no mortal has ever seen us – *return* to ourselves. These four did. I persuaded them that she is a witch, that what they saw was magic – the sudden appearance of two people where before there had been only one. Fortunately they are a primitive people, their lives filled with a dark magic. But,' he paused, looking around again, 'they will tell others. Others who may not be so ... gullible.' He stood straight, stepped away. 'So you will choose one, Ferros of Balbek, and then you will kill the others.' He bent, seized the back of Lara's tunic and began to drag her away. 'Or you will watch her die.'

He had no choice. 'Which one?' he asked again.

'I told you. It does not matter. The one who frees you would be the easiest. Just look him in the eyes ... and want it enough.'

Makron threw Lara against a large boulder, bent over her, unsheathing a dagger, crouching. Then he called out, and one of the guards immediately came to Ferros, bent over him, took out a knife and began sawing through the bonds at his wrists.

How was it possible? It made no sense. He looked at the man's eyes, his tongue protruding between his lips in concentration as he cut the strands. He had fought these men in the Battle of the Ridge. He would happily have killed them all that day. But to possess this one? Murder the rest? How could he?

Then he heard Makron laugh. Looked across. He was tapping his blade on Lara's shoulder.

Ferros was a soldier. He obeyed orders. And he had to save her life. So when the bonds parted he said something to the man bent over him. The guard looked up, Ferros gazed into his eyes – and wanted it enough.

For just a moment the man looked startled – and then the man was gone. No, Ferros realised, *he* was gone. And yet that was not true either. He was alive inside someone else. And now he felt it, what Lara had talked about, Makron, Roxanna. The possessing of the other, the absorbing of all he was in an instant – this man's memories, his loves and hatreds, his worship, his kills. And this Horse Lord had killed so many: men, mostly, but women and even some children too. Killed because it was what he'd been taught to do from the moment he could walk.

Not so different from me then, Ferros thought, as he reversed the knife, took two paces and stabbed it down into the second Horse Lord's neck. The third turned to him, even raised a hand to block the knife as it slipped in, failed, took it between the ribs, into the heart.

The last lord was ready, had his own knife in his hand, lunged; and Ferros-in-Pershak, for that was his name, twisted far enough not to take it in the chest, not straight in, only let the edge open up his ribs. He grabbed the thrusting arm of the other man – his own brother, Borol – who grabbed his. They twisted each around the other. But Pershak was bigger. Had the weight, the height, the slope. The desire. Wrenching his arm clear, he slashed his edge across his brother's throat. But he didn't wait to see life leave, for the body to fall. He whipped around and began to sprint to where he'd last seen the other immortals.

But Makron had moved, stepped closer. He also had a sword now, not just a dagger, and Pershak ran straight onto it.

Ferros looked down onto the blade that passed through him. Then he was looking up from the ground, into Makron's eyes. Back in his own weakened body. For a moment before agony returned, he missed Pershak. Being *in* Pershak, the Horse Lord bleeding out beside him.

Makron looked down at him and smiled. 'You see, Ferros,' he said. 'Magic.'

8

The Meeting of all Worlds

When Hovard woke in his own hut, in his home town of Askaug, he wondered if it would be the last time he ever did.

It was already light outside. But that did not mean it was anywhere near dawn. In Midgarth the sun only briefly set near midsummer, now but two weeks away, as it only briefly rose in midwinter. Still, he hadn't slept much and he doubted he would any more, seeing as when that sun briefly set again, he could be dead. Not just as a god, to be immediately reborn. Finally, forever dead.

He looked across at Freya. Her eyes were closed and she was breathing gently. She had always been blessed with easy sleep. He'd envied her before and he did now. For what he had to do this day, he wished he was not so tired.

He got up carefully, so as not to wake her. Went to the window and looked out.

Askaug slumbered. It looked so peaceful. Only animals moved – goats on the turf roofs of the houses, cows and pigs in the pens. He looked at a thrush perched on a gable, singing its bold song to the risen sun; wondered briefly if he should go outside and possess it, fly to the fjord, study again the odds he faced there. But possession, however exhilarating, was also tiring, and he was tired enough. He'd need all his strength for what was to come.

'Have you slept?'

He turned to her. Freya was sitting up, leaning on one elbow. The bed furs had dropped, showing her nakedness. They had made love, a rare thing since the trouble had come to their land. Forgot the trouble in what became a frenzy, almost as wild as when they'd first been together.

Everything ends, even for gods, he thought. Hundreds of years of love-making. Those countless times. And this, perhaps, the very last. 'Not much,' he admitted.

She pulled back the furs, exposing more of herself, and the space beside her. 'Then come here, and try again,' she said, adding, 'there's time before dawn.'

'Time for what?' he said, sliding in, pressing his nakedness to hers.

'Whoa!' she laughed. 'Do you think you're a god or something?'

She pulled his head onto her breasts, stroked his hair. He settled, relishing her touch. After a few moments, she spoke. 'I was thinking of Luck.'

'Have you tried to speak to him?'

'No. I thought I'd save my strength – as you did when you considered that thrush.' She pushed her fingers up through his hair. 'But I was remembering when he refused to join me and escape the town we raided. How he told me he was staying to fight in the way he knew best. It gives me hope.'

'And me. Though what I wish most is that my brother was here now, advising me what to do.'

'He is certain that you already know what to do.' She lowered his head onto the bolster, raised herself above him. 'And you have done it. United a stubborn people. Led them to the fight.'

'Which ends today? I don't know. Sometimes I fear,' he

shook his head, 'that all I have led the people to is more death before the end.'

'There is no end, Hovard. Life will go on, whatever happens today. This is one battle. It is not the war.'

'It could be if we lose.'

'No. Bjorn and Stromvar are still out there somewhere, harrying the enemy. Einar the Black and Petr the Red fight Peki Asarko and his bandits around the Lake of Souls. Those fights will continue, whatever happens here this day.'

As ever, she had roused him. 'You are right. And I have a few tricks up my sleeve yet.'

'Sleeve?' she said, and ran her fingernails up one bare biceps.

'Hmm. You know, my heart, since dawn is still so far away . . .'

She lowered her breasts onto his chest, bent to kiss him – and then they both heard running feet, followed by a cry on the path.

'They come! They *come!*'

Hovard wrapped a fur around himself, rose and opened the door. One of the cliff guards stood there, Torval. 'Is it an attack?' Hovard asked.

'N-no, Hovard. Uh, sir, *Sire!*' No one really knew how to address him since he'd taken on the mantle of Haakon the Great, the old king, though he had not yet been crowned. 'They are waving that flag, the one they did before, the square red and black one.'

Hovard turned. Freya was already dressing. 'Another parley?' she said. 'What more have they got to say?'

'Let us find out,' said Hovard. He dropped his fur, reached for his breeches. 'But before we do, Torval, there are some messages you must run for me.'

The new envoy was different to the one who had shouted and threatened before. 'Ramaskor,' said the man, sweeping his elaborately feathered hat from his head, and bowing low over his thigh-length boots. 'King Hovard. Queen Freya. A pleasure to meet you.'

His accent was thick, but he spoke their language well. He called from the aft deck of his vessel. It floated level with the jetty that they stood upon, oars plied on each side to keep it in place. The envoy was but twenty paces away, and his voice carried easily in the still morning air.

Hovard looked around, at the half-dozen men from Midgarth, leaders all, and mortals. None flinched at the titles he and his wife were named with. It had been agreed, since the enemy set such store by them, that he should be a king, and Freya his queen, even though there had been no coronation.

There was little point in politeness. Beyond the man's vessel, in the open waters of the fjord, Hovard could see the ships of the immense invasion fleet making ready. At the Askaug end of the harbour, his own much smaller fleet was doing the same. 'What do you want, Ramaskor?' he asked.

'Only to offer in friendship what my foolish compatriot, the last ambassador, offered in threat.' Several teeth in his smile flashed gold in the morning sun. 'It would be so much better for us not to fight. How many men and women on both sides will die? And your town, after your defeat?' He raised his eyes to look at Askaug's wooden walls at the top of the cliffs. 'Many women and children in it will then die too. My brothers,' he waved one hand over his shoulder without looking, 'are always allowed to do anything they please with a town that resists us. But if you surrender, join us—'

Hovard swallowed, kept his temper. Losing it would not help him at all here. 'I thought you said you were not here to threaten?'

'I am sorry, that did come across as a threat, did it not?' He smiled, glinting again. 'I meant only to talk about the benefits ...

175

not of surrendering – I know you are too proud a people for that. So … the benefits of joining us. Joining in the great future that is upon us. Brought to us by …'

'Your predecessor has told us already. After the threats, he told us again of this "One", this child that comes.'

'Has come.'

'Has come, then.' Hovard nodded. 'And we told you that we want nothing to do with your mad prophecies.'

'You might not.' The glint was in the man's eyes now. 'For you are already a god. It would cost you too much to have another god, a far greater one, eh?' His gaze shifted to the mortals on the dock. 'But your mortal subjects might.'

'May I, Hovard?'

It was Ulrich the Smith who spoke. He had known Hovard all his life, and there was not a chance he was going to address him by any other word than his name.

'Of course.'

Ulrich stepped forward. 'We heard your other man offer, before his threats. We told him and we tell you – those of Midgarth surrender to no one. We want no holy child to rule us. We have our order and we will fight to keep it.'

Ramaskor shrugged. 'Fight and die. You see the odds you face.'

'Odds? I spit on odds.' Ulrich did, and continued, 'You've never fought a Northman with his back against the wall. And if we die,' he looked around at his fellow mortals, 'we know where we are bound. To a paradise that has nothing to do with your One. Where no baby rules.'

The other mortals grunted agreement. 'Thank you, my friend,' Hovard said, and turned back. 'So you hear how we are bound. We will fight, mortals and gods united, and defy your odds. Remember how we raided your home town three months ago, destroyed so many of your ships? And we've learned a trick or two since then, from the one we captured.' He gestured to the enemy vessel, at the centre of Midgarth's small fleet. 'Also we have friends coming to our aid, this very day. So I would not be too sure of your triumph.'

'Friends,' the man echoed. 'Ah, well, I suppose that is also what I am here to tell you. Sadly, that hope is gone as well. You see,' he turned and nodded at an officer behind him, 'we have your friend.'

There was no mistaking the man the officer and three men dragged out onto the deck. His size, the bush of red hair at his massive, naked chest. Mostly his bellowing, clear despite the sack over his head. 'You cowardly fuckers!' Stromvar yelled. 'Just give me one look at you. You'll be done, finished. I'll eat your guts raw. I'll—'

Another nod, and the officer raised a baton and clubbed Stromvar hard across the back of the head. The Lord of the Seven Isles pitched forward onto the deck. He was dragged back up, hung suspended between the gripping arms of two guards. The officer jerked off the sack. Beneath it, a bloodied bandage covered his eyes.

'We caught him three days ago. He snuck aboard my own vessel to murder us all in our sleep. Well,' Ramaskor shrugged, 'he did murder quite a few. But then he fell down some stairs ... and we had him.' He leaned down, grabbed Stromvar's hair, raised his head. 'Of course, one of the things we've learned of you so-called gods is that, though it is hard to kill you, it is not impossible. Is it?' He let the head fall again. 'So do you wish your friend to live – or would you rather see him be the first to die?'

As he spoke, he gestured again, and another man stepped forward, almost as big as the Dragon Lord. He held a huge sword.

Hovard looked around. To the fleet behind the Seafarer. To

the mortals on the dock. Lastly to Freya. Who nodded. He turned back. 'The thing you need to understand about immortals, Ramaskor, is that living for ever often makes us yearn for death.'

'So be it.' At another nod, the swordsman hefted his weapon. 'Are you certain?' the envoy asked, eyes and teeth glinting. When Hovard did not answer or move, the man simply nodded again, and stepped away.

The blow was swift, precise. The head was on the deck before the body. Hovard heard it, did not see it. He was too busy lifting his horn from his waist, putting it to his lips, giving one long blast, then turning and following Freya and the mortals running ahead.

He caught up to her as they rounded the first house on Askaug's small dock. 'A new task for you, wife,' he said.

'I know it, husband,' she replied, as they reached the small rowboat they'd left on the shingle beach. He and Ulrich pushed it out, she leaped in, and began to row. 'I will take my ship to board Ramaskor's – and see if we cannot reunite Stromvar's head with his body before life leaves both.'

When they reached her ship, she called, 'Good hunting, King Hovard,' before she and the smith scrambled up the boarding net on the side.

'And you, my queen.' He took the oars, pulled hard for his own vessel – the one they'd captured in the raid. It stood tall above the Midgarthian vessels, so when he reached its forward deck, he could look down on all his people's serpent-prowed craft. Fifteen ships only. While ahead the enemy had forty at least. But this was Askaug, he knew these waters, and he was fighting for his home, for his people's whole life. And, as he'd told Freya that morning – he still had a few tricks up his sleeve.

Closing his eyes for a moment, to see and feel Freya's kiss on his naked arm just an hour before, he opened them again, as his rowboat nudged into the wooden wall. Tying it swiftly, he climbed up to the deck, drew his sword, waved it above his head and bellowed, 'Oars and sails!'

Midgarth's fleet had been held on oars like war hounds on leashes. Released, and with a cry roared from hundreds of throats, they surged towards the enemy.

Freya had heard her husband's cry over her own crew's preparations. *May the gods guide you, Hovard*, she prayed, glancing at his ship. *And me*, she thought, turning her attention and sight elsewhere.

Ramaskor's vessel was perhaps a little smaller, sleeker, but it was still like most of the Seafarers' ships – built for mighty ocean waves and winds full in the sails. It had oars, for dead calm, and manoeuvring. But the waters at the end of Askaug's fjord were shallow, and the wind was blowing off the land. The enemy wallowed as they tried to get that wind in their sails to rejoin the rest of the invading fleet. Oars – rowed by slaves, she had learned – were being plied to shrieked orders and the crack of whips.

His vessel was side on to her as her own oars, powered by free men, drove her sleek craft straight at its middle. Study of the ship they'd captured had shown that its weakest point was exactly halfway between its mighty oak prow and its fortified aft. So they'd adapted their own craft accordingly.

'Double time!' she yelled, and her men and women responded, rising then falling back onto their benches, using all their weight as well as the strength in their arms. The *Eagle* swooped at its prey. She let her have three more strokes, then wrapped her own arms around the raised rear after-stem and shouted, 'Ship and brace!' The oars were raised from the water, drawn fast through the portholes. The crew bent over their knees, wrapped their arms over their heads, and the oak ram, taken from those used to batter down a city gate in a siege and affixed at the water line to her prow, smashed into the enemy's side and stove it in.

Freya just held on. Many of her crew, braced or not, were flung forward by the force. Some groans came from her deck – but shrieks came from the ship ahead, from the hole broken in its side, through which water was already pouring; and from the deck above, where men clustered at the rail and stared down in horror.

For the moment stares were all that came. But Freya knew projectiles would soon follow. 'Now!' she yelled and her crew, trained for this moment, responded. Some threw grappling hooks to fasten the foe even tighter. Some nets, to hook onto the ship's side and aid the boarding. The keen-eyed, already chosen, had bows to hand and were sending the first arrows up before any came down. Most, like Freya, snatched up shield and spear, axe or sword.

She was about to lead them up the ship's sides, as planned. But the hole they'd made in the side, through which water now poured in and wails of terror poured out, was wide enough to allow two people, side by side, entrance. 'Ulrich, with me,' she called. Then louder, 'Up! Up for Askaug!'

'Askaug!' came the cry. The smith, who had decided to make Freya's back his special charge and ward it in this fight, helped her pull away the few broken planks that blocked them and stepped through beside her.

Into hell.

It was dark, the screams louder in the space where light only came through the oar holes and the new gap. Stank too, a brew of piss, shit and vomit that had both of them thrusting a cloak edge over their faces. Mostly the sounds made it seem like a region of the damned, of those condemned to live for ever in the frozen caves of hell. Moans, shrieks, pleas.

Freya's eyes adjusted and she saw the damned, in rows on benches, held to them by ankle shackles, with chains that passed through each one the length of the deck. Water was flowing fast in, raising things she did not want to consider to bang against her feet. From the deck above she heard the yells of combat, blade on blade. She thought to rush along the central walkway to the doors she now saw at the end, burst through them, take the enemy in the rear. End the battle fast so she could find Stromvar's body and head and reunite them. It was why she was there and she didn't have much time.

Yet compassion told her she couldn't leave these chained men and women to drown; while instinct told her that slaves would welcome both their freedom and their liberator. 'Ulrich, the chains,' she said.

The smith ran to the end of the gangway, near the far door. A bare-chested man there rose up, sword in hand. He fell to one swift blow of the smith's huge smelting hammer. The man whose life was metals then found the point where the long ankle chains were fixed. Blows fell – and the slaves were swift to turn themselves into free men and women the moment they'd run the chain through the bolts that locked them to their benches the length of the ship.

Freya had already joined Ulrich at the door. She had taught herself a little of the enemy's language, from talking to the crew of the vessel they'd captured, and the slaves they'd freed then. One word she'd specially learned. 'Freedom!' she cried, then nodded at Ulrich, who wrenched open the door.

They emerged into the chaos of the fight. Outnumbered though they were, the fighters of Askaug had arrived with shock and purpose. They fought in a body, a moving wedge of shield and blade, and the foe was falling back.

An arrow scored a line of blood across her forearm. Arrows were still flying from above – the raised rear deck where she'd last seen Ramaskor. He was still there, and with archers beside him, shooting down, finding targets. Freya tapped Ulrich with the flat of her blade. 'There!' she said, and pointed. They ran around the edge of the fight which had bunched in the middle of the deck – a deck she saw was now sloping towards the hole she'd made, like a warrior folding himself over a wound.

Unnoticed in the tumult, they made the stairs to the raised deck. Ramaskor was distracted – by his ship, obviously sinking now. Then by the great cry as men and women, naked and covered in filth, burst up from the deck below. She was close enough to see his expression change from defiance to fear. Then to panic, as he looked around for a way to escape.

She ran up the steep stairs. The archers swung to face her, but she had metal and they had yew. When the last fell, she turned to Ramaskor. He at least had a sword in one hand – and Stromvar's head, hanging by his red hair, in the other.

Ramaskor held the sword out and the head away, down the slope which had become pronounced, towards the water. 'One step nearer, bitch,' he said, 'and he's in the sea.'

The blindfold had fallen off the eyes of the Dragon. Perhaps no one had thought it necessary to retie it, seeing as his huge body was on the other side of the deck. Yet she knew, as all the gods of Midgarth knew, that even when beheaded they could live on a while. Stromvar knew it, for his eyes focused on her. He could not speak of course, with a severed throat. But his lips could still move, and did, shaping unmistakable words.

'Fuck him,' Stromvar said.

There was a moment of stares. And then the ship lurched, something giving, failing deep within it. Ramaskor looked away – and Freya lunged, at full stretch, the point of her sword passing swiftly through the man's throat. He was dead even as he fell, and as he fell he released what he was holding, sword and head. And Freya, letting her own sword go, dived and caught

Stromvar with both hands, just before his head rolled off the deck. He looked at her, and though his lips did not move, she could tell what he was thinking by his raised eyebrow.

The ship was listing hard over. In a few moments it would roll. All sounds of fighting had ceased, as everyone else realised too, and the fighters looked to save themselves. She could hear bodies hitting the water, slaves and sailors abandoning ship. She slid down to the guard rail, such was the angle now, leaned over it to see many of her crew rowing hard back, withdrawing the ram from the ship's side. Even as she looked, with almost a groan it came loose, and the vessel beneath her righted itself a little, just for a moment.

She turned. 'Ulrich,' she cried, 'his body.'

The smith nodded, bent, lifted Stromvar's huge, headless form, and stepped off the ship into the water that was now only his body length away.

'Here we go,' she said to the head. Stromvar closed his eyes.

They sank for a moment and then she was swimming, holding the head above the surface – though with no lungs she was not sure he needed to breathe and missed, even in that moment, Luck trying to explain it.

Her crew were looking for her. She and Ulrich were hauled aboard. 'Row for the jetty,' she called, and was obeyed. She took Stromvar's head to his trunk, laid the severed parts together, pressed hard. There was an instant bonding, and the great chest rose in a breath – that whistled out through the god's lips.

She had to get him away. Somewhere quiet. A place where the healing could happen. Not in the middle of a sea battle.

'Row for the dock!' she called.

She kept the pressure on the body. But she was able to look over the shoulders of her rowers, to the open sea beyond, where the gap between the two fleets had nearly closed.

'Fight well, my love,' she said. But only in her own mind. To speak to his would need strength, focus, and she needed both of those to keep the Dragon Lord alive.

'Shoot!' yelled Hovard, from the deck of the ship he'd taken on the raid. He'd fitted one of Luck's slings to it. But it had not had the same success as before. It appeared that the enemy could learn as well as he.

He followed the flaming arc of the ball, watched it strike. But again, as had the previous shots, it struck high boards specially erected as defences. They might slow the ship, block – not channel – the wind. But they deflected fire away from the deck. Only one missile had bypassed them, set the sails of one ship alight. It had steered away to battle the flames alone. Ramaskor's own vessel was behind him somewhere and he could only hope Freya had dealt with it, and rescued Stromvar. But thirty-eight vessels came on.

Thirty-eight! Hovard looked either side of him, to the fifteen of Askaug and their allies. Bjorn and Stromvar had taken another five each with them, to harry the enemy. Others had been pledged and had not come. Although he'd been acclaimed at the Moot on Galahur, and the decision made to rally behind him as leader and fight under his command, many lords had chosen to stay in their own lands, where they believed they were safe. Despite what Freya had said that morning, he had not united his people as much as he had hoped.

He looked again at the fleet ahead. Much more than double his numbers, and each vessel nearly double the size. So the enemy had close to four times his manpower. Still, he thought, looking down at the faces of his own crew, even if I see fear there, there's also determination. This is an invader coming to conquer, to change our whole way of life. No matter the odds, they would be fought.

And there was a tactic he'd thought of to change those odds.

To maximise the resistance. Turning to the bugler beside him, he said, 'Blow the call.'

He did, the notes rising and descending in a run that he'd made familiar to his fleet in the weeks they waited. The call was picked up and repeated the length of the line. He'd thought to save it for later, when the battle would be at its height and it might be needed. But with only one of the foe's ships damaged from his fireballs, there was no later. There was only now.

They had trained for this. And he noted with pride how the men and women of Midgarth acted on that training.

His own captain, Ture – commanding the vessel itself, to leave Hovard free to command the battle – only needed to do what he had been doing: slowing his boat, keeping few sails up, so with wind off the land in them his vessel did not surge ahead of the fleet. Now he bellowed for a mainsail to be lowered, the ship slowed still further – to allow the other ships all to come to him, gathering round him like chicks around a hen. There was an order to it, a place for everyone. The furthest came in last, slotted into the final place. Now all their longboats were shields in a shield wall. In moments, what had been a scattered fleet had become a floating fortress, lashed together with ropes – and hope.

A fortress – but also a compact target. On the ship he'd taken, he'd found what looked like a huge stationary bow. But it came with no similarly sized arrows. No doubt it was awaiting its supply for the invasion. Like the enemy, he'd made some preparations to counter what he expected would come: reinforced the sides of his ships with stout oak panels. Lined them with cloth bags filled with earth. The extra weight slowed him; but he'd gambled that in the fight he would need strength over speed.

Someone cried, 'They shoot!' and Hovard saw projectiles flying towards them. Heard their whistle in the air, felt the thump as they hit. The panels absorbed some force, the earth bags some more. But many passed over, or found gaps. Masts were severed and fell. He saw a man cut in two.

There was nothing they could do but take it. Volley after volley came, bringing destruction, death. When it finally ceased, Hovard looked up to see why.

The enemy were now too close, their high-sided ships making the angle of shot too steep. Too close – and close enough for a response.

On every ship the captains yelled, as Ture yelled on his, 'Bows!'

Arrows flew, the first volley aimed straight and clearing the railings, the second high in the air as they would shoot over a shield wall, to drop down onto the enemy's decks like metal-tipped raindrops. Then arrows were returned, with four times the payment.

'Shields,' came the cry and crews dropped bows to raise shields over their heads.

Hovard had his own shield bearer – young Torval, who'd brought the message to him that morning. The tall youth sheltered both of them from above, leaving Hovard free to look everywhere, see, then shout, 'Brace!' and grab a guard rail himself, just before the first of the enemy's ships drove into them.

The fortress shuddered, everyone upon it feeling the blow up through their feet. It was just the first, blow after blow landing, like fighters with fists. Hovard, from beneath the lee of the held shield, turned in a full circle. The enemy had swept wide and come in on all sides, just as he would have done.

There was a last shudder, then only waves moved them again. A few more arrows thumped into the shield above him, then these too ceased. For a moment there came ... not silence, for people were wounded all around, dying, crying, praying. But a hush anyway, waiting to be filled.

And was as, with a great cry, the men who Hovard had heard called by a word they did not have in Midgarth, 'pirats', came pouring down from their ships.

His leadership was ended. He'd brought his ships to this place and given his people all they ever asked for – a fighting chance. Nothing was left for him to do except join them in that fight.

'Enough,' he said to Torval, who lowered his shield as Hovard picked up his. He already had his helmet on. Now he drew his sword.

The first pirats were already on his deck – big men with short-bladed swords and small round shields. Hovard ran at the nearest one.

The man swept a cut down to his head. Twisting to avoid it, Hovard let the blade pass over the length of his body, before putting his own through the man's chest. He fell, Hovard put his boot on him and pulled his sword out, in time to use it to block another high cut, from another huge pirat. He let his wrist slip, allowed the man to follow the force of the blow down, hit him with his shield between the eyes when their eyes were almost level. The pirat stumbled back, arms wide. Stepping close, Hovard opened his throat with a slash.

He stepped over the body. More of the enemy were arriving, by rope, by swung nets, by ramps, sliding on their arses down steep slopes of wood. The press thickened and it got harder to swing his sword. He saw now why the enemy chose short-bladed ones. There was one at his feet and he bent and snatched it up. He was not his brother Bjorn, but four hundred years of fighting had taught him a thing or two. This was a weapon for the close fight, more cleaver than sword, a thick, heavy blade, not much of a point. So he used it accordingly.

He did not think, anticipate, choose. He reacted, to what came at him, to any opening he saw. Even gods grew tired and he did, as did all around him, blows coming in more slowly, misplaced. Even the noise slowed, as if people could not get out the words, the screams.

And then he heard it, felt it – something give. A trumpet called, not a Midgarth horn, but a strange high pitch. Immediately, the pirats on his deck began to run back to their own, climbing ropes and nets, fleeing up steep slopes. Many fell, were dispatched. Most got away.

Hovard made it to the highest point of his deck, tried to peer through the debris of smashed wood and dangling bodies. Then he saw it, as one enemy ship pulled away, managing to disentangle itself. A bigger ship, standing off. He had not noticed it before – its wide front platform, the three huge sideways bows upon it.

He thought again as a leader, not just a fighter. The opposing commander had reconsidered the fight where his numbers did not really count. He was pulling away to shoot more and more. To batter the enemy before coming in again. He knew he was right when more of the enemy began to hack themselves clear. He wondered if it was time to do the same – run for the port, make the next fight on land, at Askaug's walls.

Then, as he was about to start shouting commands, a strange thing happened to the ship standing off. It … shuddered, keeling over hard before levelling again.

Something had struck it. Men on it were screaming and pointing to the water, others trying to swivel the giant bows.

Suddenly Hovard knew. And for the first time in what seemed an age, he smiled.

'Bjorn,' he said aloud.

He'd only been a whale once before. In truth, Bjorn preferred birds, the freedom of flight; or bears with their ferocity. Swimming was hard work; though for a time, in his early hundreds, he'd sought out and inhabited sharks. The great white ones were the best, with their mighty jaws, their razor teeth, their hunter's eyes and nose. But if hawks or bears were hard to stay within, fish were harder. Something about the brain refused to yield for long. It was why he had followed the pod of great blues so close to the entrance to Askaugfjord. It was fortunate that their yearly migration took them in the wake of the invasion fleet, the one he and Stromvar had harried all the way down the coast. They'd had successes, cut out and savaged enemy vessels at night, killed their crews. They had reduced them by ten. But they'd lost most of their own – three sunk, five more too damaged to continue. So when it was only him and Stromvar, Bjorn had wanted to return, to help in Askaug's defence. The Dragon was defiant, sought one last attack, to sneak aboard the largest enemy vessel as they rode out a storm in a bay, kill its captain and crew. They'd quarrelled and Bjorn had sailed south alone. But a mast wrecked by storm had forced him to hole up and the enemy had passed him again. He followed. He didn't know what had happened to Stromvar.

But when he saw how the battle was going, and the whale happened to be passing ...

His head hurt. A giant blue had a skull like a boulder but he *had* just driven it into the rear end of a wooden hull. He'd been aiming at the rudder, missed it. He needed to try again – if the whale didn't muster all its will and pop him like a cork from a bottle filled with winter ale. He hoped not. He liked swimming even less as a man – and Hovard's fleet was a long human swim away.

Something entered the water and passed before his face. It stopped, floated back up. A huge arrow. Fuckers were trying to shoot him.

Can't have that, he thought, and dived.

The other thing he'd forgotten about whales was that they

could sense things under water. Things that were beyond sight, hearing, scent. It was ... something else. He could sense the ship now – not see it, smell it, hear it. He knew where the ship was – to his right, about five hundred paces from where he swam. He even knew it was facing away from him. So, using his mighty tail to drive himself through the water, he gained speed, aimed up – and smashed into the aft of the vessel, destroying its rudder and opening a gash the size of a wagon.

This really hurt! And the whale had had enough. Bjorn fought to control it, rode it like he would ride a wild horse ... trying to *steer* it, aiming it down the fjord, towards Askaug ...

And then he was gone! Shot out sideways, fortunately close to the surface. Not so fortunately, perhaps, as the whale leaped from the water and then fell back again, missing him by only its own body width, sucking him down into a whirlpool. He made it back to the surface a second time and with no air. Gasping, rolling onto his back, Bjorn began to kick.

Hovard watched the ship sink fast, men tumbling into the water. Perhaps the commander had been on that one. Perhaps he was just furious. Because the order to stand off was reversed, and the other ships began sailing back in for the grapple.

'Clear away the wounded and the dead,' Hovard called. 'Arrows ready!'

His men were ahead of him, as were those on other ships. The second stage of battle was about to begin.

Then he heard it.

It was a sound unlike any he had ever heard before in four hundred years of life.

It was akin to a trumpet – but not one ever sounded in his land. And by the startled reactions of such of the enemy he could see, not from theirs either. The note was so deep it felt like it was wrenched from the centre of the earth, violating the air, not going through it.

The enemy ships had been regrouping but they had not yet started to return. There were gaps between them, and through those Hovard could see to the open water at the mouth of the fjord. See the new ships that had appeared there now, twenty at least at a glance. Some were like those of his enemy. Some were not, and of a type he'd never seen before – lower in the water, even sleeker than the sea serpents of Askaug. Something else was different too. Huge flags were at every mast pole, spread by the wind off the land. They flapped, came, went, some symbol appearing and disappearing. He couldn't quite tell what it was.

Until a gust of wind straightened one – and he made out what he was looking at, something he'd never seen before. Like the trumpet's call, it was not something of their land, of any land he knew.

On the flag was a cone-shaped mountain, belching fire.

Intitepe stood on the foredeck of the *Toluc*, the first ship he'd captured, the one he'd renamed for his brother god the volcano, and made his own. In the four-week voyage, he'd learned the ways of the vessel, so different from the low, fast ones he'd mastered three hundred years before in the seas off the coasts of Ometepe, when hunting down the last of his sons. Many of those had made the voyage with him, though he'd lost half a dozen on the way; their crews and, worse, the warriors they transported.

He looked now at the survivors. First there were the seven tall-sided ships, like his, returned to the seas from which they'd come. They'd been sent to attack his realm. Instead, he'd captured them, and was going to use them, with fifteen of his own. Captured pirats, the ones who were freed slavs, had helped him alter them, make them fit for the longer sea voyage – to attack their world.

Though this wasn't their realm, was it? That was further east.

Sekantor the Savage, the pirat he'd freed to be his captain, had taught him much more than sailing skills. He – along with the three munke – had revealed the world he came from: Saghaz-a, the Land of the Four Tribes. A criminal from the tribe of Seafarers, he was delighted to fight against the ones who'd chained him to a bench. As were all the other slavs, from the other ships they captured one by one, as they arrived off Ometepe. It was such a simple solution, to turn slavs to masters, masters to slavs. He'd had a fleet ready to sail – and a pirat ready to share with Intitepe all the secrets and plans of his world.

Such plans! Once Intitepe had learned of these other worlds, he felt the joy of destiny found. Ometepe was always going to be too small a place to contain the ambitions of an immortal god. He'd realised that he'd been bored for over three hundred years, waiting for … exactly what had happened. After all that life, he'd thought he was incapable of surprise. And then to learn that the prophecy he'd always feared – that just as he'd killed his seven sons, so a son of his would kill him – was connected to a prophecy in those new worlds?

He smiled. His child – his and that bitch Atisha's – was going to rule the world. Not a son, not a daughter. Neither. Both.

He laughed again as he thought of it, the wonder of it. Servants and sailors, awaiting his command, raised their heads. He had arrived in the new world – and the first thing he saw was a battle.

He had always enjoyed those.

There was the thump of boots on the stairs, and a moment later Sekantor stood beside him. His face was speckled in blood. Not his. He'd been below decks, encouraging the slavs. *He* always enjoyed that.

The pirat went to the front rail, peered ahead. 'Lord,' he said, without turning, 'we come interesting time.'

As well as learning the ways of the water and the new worlds, Intitepe had studied the language of one of those worlds. The munke had taught him. He and the pirat could speak, after a fashion.

'What is?'

'Battle.'

'This see.' He waved forward. 'Who fights?'

'Seafarers. My people fight Midgarth.'

Midgarth. Intitepe had been especially interested in that land, once he'd learned that there were immortals there too. Fellow gods, though these savage and primitive. There were no gods among the Four Tribes, though there was another land to the south that had some.

What he had yet to decide was whether he wanted to share the world with other gods ... or return to being the only one. 'Who wins?' he asked, peering. A small group of boats, all somehow joined together, were surrounded by a much larger number of Seafarer ships – though even as he looked one of those seemed to leap in the air, then rapidly to sink.

Sekantor shrugged. 'Seafarers. Too many for those of Midgarth.'

Intitepe turned to look at the pirat. 'So who side we join?'

Sekantor frowned. 'Hate Seafarers. They have friends chained to oars below.'

'You like Midgarth?'

'No. But—'

Intitepe raised a hand, and the pirat shut up instantly. He had learned it was best that way, so he didn't lose any more teeth. 'Tell all ships. We fight.'

Sekantor nodded, then raised his eyebrows. 'Who fight?'

Intitepe turned to look ahead, and smiled.

*

Hovard saw the chance – and took it.

The new arrivals decided him. They had to be reinforcements for the Seafarers. The prisoners they'd taken on their raid had not talked about another tribe of enemies who flew the banner of a fire mountain, and sailed strange ships. But who else could they be? Half as many again as the enemy's fleet, that was already more than double his before. Midgarth could not win on the water – but on land?

The sudden sinking of their largest ship must have spooked the Seafarers. Or perhaps they were waiting for the newcomers to join them. Either way, they had not recommenced their attack. Giving Hovard his chance.

He called to his bugler. 'Sound Breakaway!' he cried. The notes came and the word was shouted everywhere too. Ropes were unlashed, the boat fort swiftly dismantled. When all floated free, Hovard called again. 'To Askaug.'

The enemy used oars, but they were really ships of the sail. Though he'd learned from his study of them that their ships could harness an offshore breeze, it was a cumbersome process. His oarsmen were already pulling hard for the strand beneath Askaug's cliffs when the first vessel had enough sail up to give chase.

As soon as his vessel grounded on the pebble shore, Hovard was over the side. Everywhere men dropped, waded, carrying their weapons and their wounded.

'Husband.'

Freya was running down the pebbled strand towards him. He stopped, and she was in his arms – only for a moment. She pulled away and they both continued walking towards the cliff path. 'Do we flee?' she asked.

'No. At least, not yet. They are good fighters on the water. But there will be few in the world who are as good on both water and land as we are.' He grinned, then saw her arm, its bandage. 'Bad?'

'Not so much. An arrow glance and healing fast.'

'Stromvar?'

Freya grinned. 'He's in the mead hall. The wound heals, but he must not move for a while.' She glanced back, at the enemy now under full canvas. 'Do we have that while?'

'I do not know. I hope. Did you see the new arrivals?'

'I did. More enemies?'

'Who else?'

They reached the clifftop, ran swiftly along the path and through the town gate. He had left instructions for the town to be prepared for siege, in case the water fight failed. He had been obeyed.

He climbed the stairs of the gate tower. From there he could see into the bay – and the sight there stopped his breath.

The Seafarer ships had sailed as close as they could without grounding. And the new fleet sailed between them, grappled them, and men began to board.

He supposed it was the surprise of it, the confusion of some ships being like their own and others not. Maybe the men of the fleet who had been in battle were simply exhausted. But few resisted – and he could see those few that did being swiftly dealt with.

'What is happening?' murmured Freya, taking his arm.

'I do not know. But the newcomers fight our enemies.'

'Does that make them our friends?'

'I do not know.'

Whatever happened, happened fast. There was noise, and the screams went on for a while. And then there was almost a silence.

He looked down. The last of the warriors of Midgarth were straggling up the trail. He could see the dark folk of the southlands, the red hairs of the north, interspersed with his own fair ones. Many of the peoples of his land *had* united. For a time. But for how long could they stand?

The last of them limped through the gates. He was about to call for the bar to be lowered when he noticed one final straggler – not walking, but crawling. His eyesight was not as keen as in his youth four hundred years before. But even he could see the distinctive topknot of red hair.

He ran down the stairs, out of the gate, to the figure who had given up crawling and rolled onto his back. 'Need a ride, brother?' Hovard asked.

'I'd be grateful, brother,' Bjorn replied. 'I tell you, it isn't easy being a whale. My head hurts!'

His eyes rolled up. Hovard bent, hoisted him onto his shoulder, carried him through the gates, lowered him carefully so that his head rested against a hay bale. 'Husband,' Freya called from the tower above, 'you need to see this.'

Patting the slumbering Bjorn on one cheek, Hovard ran up the stairs.

The sight had changed. For one, all the ships had taken in their sails. For another, the low, sleek ships that he'd noticed at a distance had pulled away from the fleet. To the beat of a single drum, a dozen of them swept forward on their oars. At each mast, the burning-mountain flag flew.

'Are those ships made ... made of straw?' Freya muttered.

They passed the grounded Midgarth ships. Ghosted onto the strand.

It was hard for warriors to disembark from a vessel anything but clumsily. These men managed it. Thirty at least from each ship, moving ten paces in from the waterline, halting there, forming two ranks.

They did not look like any human anyone on the walls had ever seen. They wore armour made of slatted wood, lined in metal. Helmets also wooden and surmounted with feathered crests from birds which did not fly in Midgarth – iridescent greens, violets, deepest blues. Each had a bow and quivers across his back, a stabbing spear in one hand, a short sword in the other.

Every man there had skin that was the brown of fir bark.

They stood silently, though some kind of drum beat slowly on, as if they waited for a signal. Or for someone. Perhaps the man who dropped now from the ship at the very centre of the fleet and strode through the shallows to the shore. He was dressed similarly, though his helmet was crested in gold, and had no feathers. The cloak he wore did though; indeed it seemed to be made of them, flashing every colour in the rainbow.

This man passed through the ranks, stopping five paces beyond them. For a long moment, he gazed up at Askaug on the cliffs. Then he drew his sword, hefted his spear, and cried out a single word, his voice as deep as the horn that had announced his arrival in their world.

'Intitepe!'

Four hundred men answered him. Four hundred men followed him up the path.

Hovard turned to Freya. 'Get everyone out the back gate. Disappear into the forest. Meet where we planned.'

'Can we not fight?'

Hovard shook his head. The last time he'd felt fear like this was when he'd fought Ut the Slayer on Galahur. Before that it had been three hundred years, when the bear he'd possessed was attacked by another and he'd been too stunned to escape. The fear he felt now was worse than either of those times.

'We could hold Stromvar and one hundred men from the Seven Isles at this gate. Perhaps a few hundred of those pirats. Not these. Go. I will fight for a while to cover you and then I will follow.'

'Stromvar cannot move. Bjorn barely can.'
'Fling them both on a cart. Then run, Freya. Run!'

9

From the Dark

It had been three weeks since his journey with Atisha. Luck had not been able to see her again – though something of their connection lingered with him. Especially when he travelled with Sirene, which he tried to resist – failed to resist – too often. He felt her then, a presence in the shadows of the world, just around the corners of his sight.

It was hardly surprising. He'd learned that Sirene reflected the world *as was, as is, as might be*. In these days, Atisha and her child were the focus of that world – of all worlds, for all those that had thought themselves separate and alone were now linked by the prophecy of the One. It was no wonder baby and mother so dominated all thought.

And Luck had realised, with his near four hundred years of experience of seeing beyond the veil of things as they seem, that such power, focused on a child, could not be stopped by that child's death. He'd thought to kill Poum, end it all with a fall of his knife. Now he knew, he could see, that such a terrible act would only have accelerated the destruction of Midgarth. Of … everywhere. What would replace it, he could not know. From the end of one world would be sown the seeds of the next. But the interim would be suffering on a scale none of the worlds had yet witnessed – and he knew each had already seen too much.

It was in this mood that Anazat found him. Open to ideas – though perhaps not quite in the way the black-eyed monk thought.

'Do you travel with her?'

Luck opened his eyes. He'd been slumped at the table, the vial of the drug in his hand. Unopened. He'd sat, held Sirene, trying to resist her call. Then Anazat was there, and Luck suspected he would have to resist no more. 'No,' he said, as he sat up. 'I was waiting for you.'

'How did you know?' Anazat came further into the room, looked down. It was always a little hard to tell with a man whose eyes were all black. But he was tired, that Luck could see. Exhausted even. He drew out the other chair at the table, fell into it, rubbed the twin darknesses of his eyes.

'I knew because you had not been to see me for a while. Knew that you were busy in the world.' Luck waved at the globe, the smoke shifting within it. 'And even though I have not seen it directly, I know that world is in torment.'

'You are right.' Anazat scratched at his chin, which rasped. Luck had never seen him unshaven. This close he could see that the bags beneath his eyes were nearly as black as his orbs. 'Things have not gone entirely to plan.'

'You wish to show me?' Luck kept the edge of excitement from his voice. But his hand shook as he lifted it towards the glass on the table.

Anazat moved his hand from his jaw, swept it over his head. Shaven, except for the monk's circlet of hair which, even in the weeks since Luck had last seen him, appeared to have shaded from grey to white. 'Yes,' he replied. 'I'll show you. Because the time has come, Luck of Midgarth, for you to choose. Not to betray your people, as you thought I wished you to do. To save them.' He ran his tongue over cracked lips, revealing his black teeth.

He did not reach for Luck's vial. He fished within his cloak, pulled out a larger bottle, uncorked it – and Luck held his breath. What he wanted to do was soar throughout the world beyond. So he hoped the monk would pour a big measure. But Anazat tipped and released just three drops. Enough to see, if not travel. Luck's disappointment held but for the moment it took to realise what he was seeing: Askaug – and immediately also seeing that his hometown was a smoking ruin.

He gasped. 'Is this true? Have your armies already destroyed my home?'

'No. It was never our intention.' Anazat raised a finger, pointed. '*He* has.'

The smoke shifted again – and Luck was looking at a warrior standing before the burning walls of the mead hall. The man made him think instantly of Atisha. They shared a look – brown skin, almond eyes. Though his eyes reflected flame – and shone in triumph.

'His name, in his own tongue, is Intitepe. He comes from Atisha's land. He is her husband, though he has many other wives. Has *had* many others – for he is as long-lived as you, Luck. He is an immortal, the only one in Ometepe.' He grunted. 'That is not quite true. He is the only *male* immortal.'

'Then why is he standing in my town?' Luck growled. 'Why has he come so far to destroy it?'

'Why?' Anazat echoed, licking his cracked lips. 'We thought we knew. Thought he'd come for the child. For the One.'

Luck frowned. 'What's the child to him?'

'Intitepe is Poum's father.' Anazat spoke louder over Luck's gasp. 'And in his world, it is prophesied that he will be killed by a son. So he kills all sons as infants.'

'But Poum is not a son. He ... she ... *they*—'

'You presume to understand the logic in a savage's mind?' Anazat snapped.

201

'Wait.' Luck looked away from the globe for a moment, though that was hard to do. 'You said you *thought* he'd come for the child. What has changed?'

Anazat took his gaze from the globe too, looked into Luck's eyes. 'Now we think he has decided to conquer the world.'

Luck could not help his laugh. 'What? Like you?'

'No, not like us. We sought to bring the One's light to all—'

'By invading our land,' Luck shouted, slamming a fist on the table, 'and murdering my brothers and sisters?'

Instead of shouting back, Anazat said softly, 'We have had this argument, Luck. It is one for another time. This is different. *He* is different.'

He gestured again at the globe and Luck looked. This … Intitepe was striding away. Soldiers were following him, dressed similarly in what looked like wood-slat armour, helmets, and cloaks decorated in feathers, though not so extravagantly as the one who led them. 'How many men does he have?'

'We are not sure. Maybe five hundred.'

'To conquer the world? Then he is mad, and my brothers will eat him for dinner.'

'Ah, but they could not. Because he is not alone.' Anazat swallowed. 'Many Seafarers have joined him.'

Luck squinted at the glass. Now the feathered men had passed he could see, outside the smoking mead hall, other men nearly as flamboyantly dressed. Feathers again, but held in cocked hats, like the men he'd observed coming to the ceremony where Poum was hailed. 'I thought all in your land were united in belief.'

'Not all.' Anazat's voice cracked, and he coughed. 'The Seafarers were the hardest to convince. Their lives had always been about fighting, raiding, stealing. Only when all three of the other tribes united and came for them did they submit. Many, perhaps most, adopted the belief of the One. Some missed their old ways and caused trouble.'

'So what did you do with them?'

'We killed them,' Anazat replied. 'Or we made them row the loyal Seafarers' ships.'

'You turned them into slaves?' Luck shook his head. 'Do you not see the contradiction in your philosophies of love?'

'No.' Anazat leaned forward. 'In forty years we have restored peace to almost all our world, to peoples who fought for centuries. Most people now live free, with hope. With love. And we would bring that love to everyone, everywhere.'

'Yes, yes, I have heard all this before, Anazat.' He pointed at the globe. 'How many are the ones who disagree?'

'Not too many. But enough to delay all our plans. The invasion of Midgarth has failed.' He grunted. 'Another invasion has pre-empted us. Which also means that the fleet we sent to conquer Ometepe has been ... turned.'

Luck leaned back. 'Your plans have not gone well indeed.'

'A brief setback only. In the south, we are winning. Corinthium will soon fall. It is an empire of a size that makes Midgarth and Ometepe look like fishing villages on our coast. Using all its vast resources of wealth and manpower, we will turn again north, west. Conquest – unity! – is but delayed. The people of the One will triumph.' He looked again at the globe, so Luck did too. 'Meanwhile ...'

'Meanwhile?'

'How would you like to go home?'

It was not a thing that Luck had expected him to say. He had set out from Midgarth to learn of his enemy. He had done that, and far, far more. But what profit would there be for the man who sat opposite him to send him back now?

He thought it, asked it. 'Why would you let me go? Do you think I will do your bidding there?'

For the first time, Anazat smiled. 'As you have learned of me and mine, Luck, so I have learned of you and yours. You are not like your brothers. You see the whole world differently. You know that there is more than fighting, drinking, on and on, life after life.' He raised a hand to prevent Luck's interruption. 'And I do not even ask for any promise save one: that you go back and rid the land of the scourge that has come upon it.'

'Rid it of this Intitepe, so you can then come and conquer us anyway?'

'Perhaps.' Within their dark, Anazat's eyes glinted. 'Or perhaps you, Luck the Lame, will finally realise that there can be a different world ... for everyone in it, everywhere.'

Luck sat back. Even the globe could not pull his attention now, as his eyes went inward. To go back was what he most wanted. Yet he'd had that chance in the northern port, with Freya, and he'd stayed. He'd thought, and told her, that it was because he felt he could fight their enemies better from within. But that was only a partial truth.

He had also stayed because of Sirene.

He loved her. Loved her taking his hand and guiding him where she would. Often to Gytta, his beloved, dead wife. Sometimes to visions he would never have seen even in an immortal's lifetime. But he knew that he had to loosen her hold on him, if he was to do all he must. Loosen – but not let slip entirely. For in what lay ahead he would need her, in ways he could not yet know. So of this he was certain: he could not allow Anazat to control him by controlling the supply. If he did, even if he was not chained to a rowing bench, he would still be a slave.

He looked again at the globe. Enemies, old and new, swirled in smoke within it. His land was under threat again, from something he could not understand. But something else had also happened – he had learned again to hope. Hope had come with Atisha. Strangely, it had also come with what Anazat would call the *world's* hope. With Poum.

Not something he need share with the man before him. Nor what he intended to do about it before he went.

'I will go. On one condition.'

'Name it.'

Luck pushed his vial towards the monk. 'That you show me the plant where Sirene is born.'

Black eyes narrowed. 'That is impossible. Only a very few must know this. For if that secret were to escape into the world …'

'It will not. But it will go with me,' Luck leaned back, 'or I will not go.'

Anazat stared at him. Luck stared back. Moments passed. Until finally, Anazat shook his head, and whispered, 'You do not know what you have asked. But I will give you this gift. This curse. And may the One take pity on you for it. I will make the arrangements.' Levering himself out of his chair, he crossed to the door, called. In a moment Toporak appeared, and the two men had a swift, whispered conversation of which Luck only caught snatches. He could hear that his riding companion was shocked by what Anazat commanded. Shocked enough to query the command. But not to disobey the repeated, hissed order.

When he left, Anazat turned back. 'It is done. Other arrangements for your departure will be made,' he said. 'Now, come with me. There is something you need to see.'

Luck followed Anazat from the cell, along corridors, down stairs and across the courtyard to a door. This the monk opened with a huge iron key and, picking up a basket placed just inside, led Luck into this other building, the one in the castle he'd never explored, the only one forbidden him, though he'd seen guards go into it from time to time and wondered what they did within.

They continued down three flights of stairs. It was lower

than he'd ever been in the Keep before, far beneath the ground. Winding corridors with earth floors were lit by torches every twenty paces. These shone on wooden doors, with closed iron grilles in them. From behind some came noises, growling. Moaning. Once, a scream; once laughter, though it had no humour in it. On they went, down. The doors were fewer, the torches too.

The oppression made Luck whisper, not speak. 'Your prison?'

'Yes,' came the reply, 'for very special prisoners. But none as special as ... these.'

He'd halted before a door, bigger than the others they had passed. He used another key and the door opened onto a circular gallery, one side of which was earth. The other was latticed wood. Torchlight flared, lighting the woven struts from within. 'Look,' said Anazat, beckoning Luck forward.

He stepped to the lattice, peered down ... into a pit, a circular cell, perhaps six paces wide, the height of two men below him. It was sparsely furnished – two cots, two chairs, a table. At that sat two people. One was larger – a man, muscles showing through the rents in his tattered, filthy tunic. The other was slighter, probably a woman.

He couldn't tell their gender by their faces though – for both wore helmets made of metal which covered everything above the mouths – though there were narrow bars across the front which he assumed meant they could partially see. Thick leather straps held the helmets firmly to the head. 'Feeding time,' said Anazat and, springing a latch in the lattice before him, he swung a section open, then lifted the basket he'd brought, attached it to a rope that hung there on a pulley, and lowered the basket into the cell.

Luck watched the two prisoners. They had been alert, their heads tipped up when they heard noise above. Now the man got up and carefully walked to the basket, bent, picked it up, carried it back to the table with the rope still attached, where the woman reached swiftly in and pulled out its contents: a wheel of bread, a jug of liquid, some apples. They began to eat, fast, cramming the bread and fruit in, taking turns to drink deep.

'They are hungry,' Luck said.

'They haven't eaten for three days, so—'

'You starve them?'

'We keep them ... dependent.'

'Why are they wearing those masks?'

'Because without them they would be dangerous.' Anazat nodded down. 'Like you would have been, before we first talked.'

'You mean,' Luck reached to grip the lattice before him, 'they are immortals?' He studied them again. He was certain they were not from Midgarth. He'd sense something if they were. 'They can possess animals? So you prevent them fully seeing so they cannot?'

'It is why we mask them. To prevent them possessing. Though it is not animals they can possess,' Anazat turned to look at him, 'but mortals.'

Luck took a step away from the lattice. Something cold played around his heart. 'That is impossible,' he breathed.

Even in the faint torchlight, Anazat's black eyes gleamed as he answered. 'Not in Corinthium.'

Corinthium. Luck had learned something of the city-ruled empire far in the south. Guided by Sirene, he had glimpsed the land sometimes – so vast it spanned forested mountains, grassy plains, deserts, a huge inland sea five hundred times the size of Midgarth's Lake of Souls. But only once had he seen any of its people. It had been when he arrived at the Keep, when Anazat first led him into Sirene's embrace. His vision had included a young man, a mounted warrior, leading a troop of horsemen to the fight. He recalled how something in the young man's face, in the determination he'd read there, had given him hope.

Anazat spoke, as if to his thoughts. 'His name is Ferros. The woman, his woman, is Lara. He led the fight against us in the south. He lost. Now he is here and we are going to … *persuade* him to join us. Join in the glory of the One.'

Ferros. It *was* the same young soldier he'd seen, of that Luck was certain. And nothing he'd even briefly observed in that young man led him to believe he was *persuadable*. He felt an excitement suddenly. He thought of an old Midgarth saying: the enemy of my enemy is my friend. But he didn't say that. Instead he asked, 'And this young man can possess another man, you say?'

'Man or woman, yes. As can this Lara. Which makes them both dangerous. Which is why we keep them masked. Like you of Midgarth, they do it with a look.' Anazat turned and jerked the rope. The basket fell from the table and he used the pulley to drag it across the floor and rapidly up the wall.

The young man turned and shouted something. 'What did he say?' Luck asked.

Anazat shrugged. 'I do not think it translates directly into your tongue. It is to do with certain acts that should never be performed – with cattle.' He set the basket on the floor. 'Hmm. Perhaps it will be five days before they next are fed.'

Anazat swung the lattice shut, picked up the basket, ushered Luck out of the gallery and locked the cell door. They retraced their steps up and out of the dungeons. When they stood again in daylight, Luck asked, 'Why did you show these people to me?'

The monk turned to him. 'For the same reason you were chosen. For your curiosity.' He smiled. 'Midgarth was always going to be too small a world for your intellect. But the world out there may just be big enough. Corinthium. Ometepe. You can help us bring peace to it all. The peace of the One. With you, Luck of Askaug, as one of the wisest in all the worlds.'

With that he turned and walked away, leaving Luck standing by the door. You are right, he thought. Midgarth, what it was, has been changed entirely. This new world is so vast, so different. You have given me a vision of it, of so many things. But you are mistaken in how I see them.

He started across the yard – but stopped in the middle, where the four paths met, and turned slowly, looking around the entire Keep. Anazat wanted him to leave there; leave this land, return to Midgarth; save his land from this new invader, this Intitepe. Though truly what the black-eyed monk wanted was for him to save his land from one enemy and thus lay it open to conquest by another – the Four Tribes.

Well, he would leave. But he knew, in that moment, that he would not leave alone.

He continued to his cell. As soon as he entered, he saw it.

On his table was a cloth sack that had not been there before. It was the kind he'd seen the Keep's gardeners use to move plants from bed to bed in their herbal gardens.

This sack had earth in it too. He saw that when he opened the neck of it. But it was not sight that overwhelmed him. It was smell. His knees gave and he sat down suddenly in the chair, nearly spilling off it.

The liquid Sirene had an odour, mainly of the liquor used in its distilling, and some botanicals it was blended with. In its depths though was something else, something of the forest in autumn, a rot that was also a bloom. This bag of earth stank of that, the bass note of the drug amplified a hundredfold. It made his stomach heave, his head swirl.

Undistilled, unfiltered, what he smelled here was the essence of Sirene.

For centuries he had sought edible roots, and mushrooms on

rotting stumps, among dead leaves, coiling up certain special trees. Some were for eating, some for medicines. Others, like the red-capped one he called Farsight, gave him visions, allowed him to explore beyond the veil of things as they seem. None were as powerful, nor as uncontrollable, as Sirene.

This he also knew, in that first, terrible inhalation: that it was unlike any other of the thousands of scents he had ever smelled in this world. It was not just new. It was entirely different. Which could only mean that it came from somewhere ... *other than this world.*

He gasped, overwhelmed by the realisation. Groping for the bag, he sealed the bag again. As his head and stomach settled, his mind worked. Whether it was roots or spores within the earth in this bag, he would find them, cultivate them, extract their essence. He would distill Sirene. It would take time back in Midgarth, time he was not sure he would have, in that threatened world. He only had time ... now.

He looked across at the globe, the smoke swirling within it. The vial beside it. He knew what he must do. He longed to do it, to revisit Gytta's garden, to lie there with her fingers moving through his hair. But that was not why he crossed to the table, sat down. Anazat had used a few drops to show Luck what the monk needed him to see. Now he needed to see for himself. Had a question that must be answered, fresh born in a scent that was not from his world.

He opened the vial and tipped onto the globe five times the dose Anazat had used. In half a heartbeat, he was gone.

He hoped for it, and it happened. He was in this same place – the forest path that led to Gytta's garden. And the intense nausea that had come when he inhaled Sirene raw, that also came because he'd visited her twice with little time between, passed in the wonder of being there again.

Oh, the aching beauty of the place! The temperature the

perfect warmth of a summer's evening when the fierce heat of day is gone. The towering trees swollen with blossom, their scents mingling with those from the profusion of bushes and flowers. Caressing breezes passed through the laden branches and birds swooped among them, calling in wild harmony.

The path before him ended in even greater delights. At his love. He could already hear her soft crooning. In a moment he would inhale the sweet scent of her hair.

He took a step, the first before he broke into a run. Oh, to run to her! Back in Midgarth, he never ran. One leg was shorter than the other, one shoulder larger so he lurched whenever he tried to move quickly and children would laugh. In this place, everything was balanced – legs even, body straight. To run was one more delight. He'd reach rapture all the quicker when he did.

He lifted his foot – then held it there above the path. Held it with the thought that came, the memory of what had brought him here this time. The memory of who he was: Luck the Lame. A man – a so-called god in his own land – who had scarcely glimpsed happiness in four hundred years of life but had worked out his world every single day. With thought. He could do that here, even in paradise.

He lowered his foot. Looked around again. Everything was perfect – proving this place false, because life never was. She was not there, his guide. Sirene. She was also everything there. That flower. Gytta's song. All his joy.

'Answer me this,' he called.

She appeared in an instant, ahead of him down the track. Her back to him, her hooded cloak moving as it had when he'd met her before, shifting colours swirling in a breeze.

'What is it you would know?' she said, her voice clear and low.

The last time he'd seen her he'd asked her, 'Who are you?' It was the obvious question. Now he knew it had not been the correct one. The correct one was what he'd asked everything, large and small in the world, from the moment he could think for himself.

'Why are you?'

'*Why?*'

Sirene turned. The folds of her hood covered most of her face. He could see her mouth though, and full lips in a face as pale as the moment of dawn now shaped a smile. 'No one has ever asked me that. In this world. In none of the worlds beyond.'

The worlds beyond? Luck knew that she did not mean the black-eyed monks. That the worlds she spoke of were indeed *beyond*. Like the scent of the plant from which these visions came. 'Which world are you from?'

'*From?*' Again the word came with the slightest emphasis. 'I am not from anywhere. I belong nowhere. I am everywhere. I am Sirene.'

Luck felt a stirring of anger. Anazat spoke like this sometimes, answers given as a kind of riddle that Luck was too ignorant to solve. He swallowed it down. Anger would not help him here. Would not begin to answer his questions. The next of which was, 'Are you a god?'

There was a pause. 'No.'

'Immortal?'

'Yes.'

He was getting somewhere. But he also understood that this sort of questioning could not last long. 'Do you control all who voyage with you?'

'I do not control. I see a hunger and I feed it.'

'Hunger for what?'

'For knowledge. For power. For certainty.'

Luck thought of Gytta. He could still hear her singing down the path. It took all his will not to take that step towards her. 'For love?' he asked.

'For love most of all,' she whispered, then turned back to the path, pointing ahead. 'Come.'

But Luck did not. Instead he took a deep breath then spoke again. 'First answer my question: why are you?'

He could sense Sirene considering. The voice changed. It was no longer a woman's. It was not quite a man's. It was neither – and it was both. 'I am sent to watch.'

'Sent?' Luck frowned. 'Who sent you?'

The world shivered around him on her reply. 'Those whom you would call … gods.'

Luck did not believe in gods. He was called one in Midgarth, as others were. But only because of his differences – that he was immortal, reborn again and again; that he could become a beast for a time. Yet from the moment he could reason he had believed that he had been given those powers, those differences, randomly; like others born with green eyes, not blue, or with legs shaped to run faster. He thought of Poum, the child hailed as a new god, because of *their* difference at their core.

Careful, Luck, he cautioned himself, and stepped closer. 'So I ask again: why? Why did these *gods* send you?'

'I told you. To watch.'

'To watch what?'

There was a longer pause. Finally Sirene answered. 'The gifts.'

'Gifts? What gifts?'

Another pause, shorter. 'Immortality. Possession.'

Luck thought back to the tales heard first when he could barely walk. 'It is said that they were brought to Midgarth by one called Gudrun.' Luck remembered a conversation he'd had with Anazat. 'That someone named Andros the Blind brought them to Corinthium. Taz— no, Tasloc left the gifts in Ometepe.'

'The gift-bearers were different as peoples were different,' replied Sirene. 'Sent by those who send me now.'

Gifts? Ten years before Luck had decided that immortality

was not a gift, but a curse – on that day he laid Gytta's sickness-withered body on a pyre and watched until the flames dissolved her. Gytta, who sang to him now from further down this path. Once again, the urge to run to her, to lose himself in … the *illusion* of her, nearly overpowered him. Once again, he resisted. Resisted too the lure of easy anger, mastering his voice as he mastered his desire. 'These gifts?' he said. 'Why did the gods give them to us?'

'To see what you would do with them.'

'*Do* with them?' His echo was incredulous. Sirene's words made him think of his life in Askaug. How over the centuries, in his quest to understand life, all life, he had trapped animals – squirrels, certain birds, deer, wolves, mice – to test them in different ways. With food, with fear, with … desire. 'Are you telling me,' he said, his voice rising, 'that these gods are … *experimenting* with us?'

Sirene had paused before. Now she took so long to reply that Luck thought her gone, with only her shadow still standing there. The world around them – this dream of his happiness – began dissolving at its edges. Birdsong went from harmony to discord; flowers and leaves drooped, browned. Finally, though, she did answer, with one word.

'Yes.'

The dam of his anger broke. 'Show me these gods,' he cried.

The sky clouded over, warmth fell away, birds ceased singing, Gytta ceased singing. Yet something like a laugh shuddered through the cloaked back. 'You are not ready for that, Luck of Midgarth. Not close to ready.'

His anger went cold. 'You underestimate me, Sirene. Others have before you, and it has cost them.'

At that, Sirene turned again – and this time through the folds of her hood he could see her eyes. He'd seen them once before and they'd been pure white. Now they were of a black so deep they made Anazat's look like suns. 'In all my journeys,' she said softly, 'begun in a time when stars were yet to be born, across the wide universe, no one – *no one* – has ever *threatened* me.'

Luck stepped back. He didn't feel fear exactly, though the power coming from the hooded figure was as great as he had felt in a lifetime of explorations. And yet? There was something about what Sirene had said – or rather how she'd said it. There was no anger to match his own. Instead, there was ... there was a kind of wonder.

A trace of it remained in the voice when she spoke again. 'You have many journeys still to take. And when you have joined with the *one*,' again, there was the slightest weight on the word, emphasised in the way it often was, back where his crooked body lay, 'then you will have your answer. At a time when you may be able to understand it. At a time when you may even be able ... to use it.' Lifting a hand from the folds of her cloak, she continued, 'But until then ...'

Warmth returned to the forest, light to the sky, singing in the trees – and from further down the path.

Gytta. Now, more than ever before, he yearned to run. Oh, to lie in her lap, feel her fingers in his hair, dissolve into her love!

Yet he did not take the step – because it was what Sirene wanted. He saw that clearly now. She wanted to feed his hunger. It was ... part of the experiment.

He turned away, instant tears blurring his vision at what he must say. 'No.'

It was all gone on the word, in less than a heartbeat. The forest and everything in it. Sight, sense, touch, delight. He was in the darkness again with nothing but a voice. From far away. Whispering within his ear.

'You surprise me,' Sirene said, and was gone, taking the light with her.

He was lying on the floor of his room. It took him a long time before he found the strength to grab the edge of the table, heave himself up, fall into the chair. On the table before him was the vial. There was some left. He could demand more.

He picked it up. Without his bidding, his thumb rose to the edge of the cork. He could change his mind. Go back, even now. Touch her. Be touched.

He stood, stumbled to the window ... and hurled the vial out onto the mountainside. From somewhere far below came the faint sound of it smashing.

He lurched to his bed, toppled onto it. Immediately, he began to sweat. Gripping the blankets beneath him, he coiled the cloth into ropes, and wept.

One week later ...

Atisha lay in her new cell, watching the ceiling shift in dappling moonlight. They had moved her that day, her first room considered too lowly for her status. The leading men and women of the land – Seafarers, Monks, Huntresses and Horse Lords – those who had been unable to attend the great ceremony, were going to be arriving at the Keep over the next weeks. Each would be presented to her – though truly to Poum. Each would then return to their parts of the land with the fire of faith in their eyes – to spread that fire over the mountains and beyond the furthest seas.

Beside her, Poum had finally fallen asleep. Fitful as ever, and Atisha's own sleep ever disrupted because of it. She couldn't blame her – teeth were coming in, and hurt, despite tinctures the monks had given her to ease the pain. Also Poum was always responsive to her mother's moods – and Atisha's had been dark for days now.

What was she going to do? What power did she have to do anything?

None. All her life now was in the role they'd given her – as holy mother to the holy child. People barely looked at her, their fervid sight consumed by the baby in her arms. So all she could do was affect the child. Deny her milk? Fail to clean her? Her only power was in not being what she was, a mother. And so was no power at all.

She thought again of the last time she'd had a little hope, given to her by that strange man from another world. Luck was his name – *bura* in her tongue. Yet did he have any more *bura* than she did? Another prisoner, yet held by stronger shackles even than hers, of powerlessness. He had shown her those, through the sweet smoke. Through Sirene, he had helped her see the world, hers and others, the threat to it all. The threat centred on the babe who lay beside her, fussing again.

She scooped her child up, put her to a breast. It calmed, though she doubted Poum was hungry. As her baby suckled, she tried to seek out Luck. For a while after they'd been joined in smoke, she'd felt connected to him still; but that connection had swiftly faded, and with it her small hope.

She heard a cry. Not from Poum, still attached; but from the maiden who slept now in this new cell on a cot at the base of her bed. They would never leave her unattended, even for a moment – though this girl was a deep sleeper, and only a shout would rouse her.

Careful so as not to disturb her baby, Atisha rose up in her bed to watch the girl dream, envious that someone could. And then she saw that it was not a dream that had made her cry out ... but a snake.

It was settled on her neck and even as Atisha watched it struck, fangs fixing into flesh. The girl rose up, reached for her throat, gave a strangled cry, fell, her eyes rolling up in her head.

Atisha dropped Poum on the bed. The baby yelled, but Atisha did not. This was one danger she could deal with for she would not have survived long on the hillsides of Ometepe if she had not learned the ways of serpents.

There was a stout stick in the corner of the cell. She leaped, grabbed it, turned fast, raised it high …

Over the man crouching over the woman on the floor.

'Please don't,' Luck said, arm lifted to protect his head.

Atisha kept the stick raised, stared, unbelieving. She had not heard the cell door open. She looked. The bolt was still shot. How could he be there?

Then she saw the snake, slithering away fast to the door. She cried out, took a step, raised the stick higher. 'Stop,' commanded Luck, then rose and put his hand beside hers on the wood. 'She should not die for doing my bidding.'

'What?' said Atisha. Somehow, she *must* have fallen asleep. Everything that was happening was as random as her dreams – a man, a snake that stings. So she let him take the stick from her. Since she was sleeping, it did not alarm her. 'You travel in dream as well as smoke then, Luck?' she said.

He frowned at her, then laid the stick down next to the Huntress maiden. 'No dream, Atisha. Come, we have … little time.'

It was the sort of thing that someone might say in her sleep. 'Time?'

'For escape.'

She shook her head, tried to clear it. When awake, escape was all she thought about. To be in control of her own life again. To decide for her and for Poum. The idea made her believe she still dreamed. Her one hope, this small man. Her one desire, to be free. So this *had* to be a dream.

She closed her eyes, swayed. He laid his hand on her arm, shook her gently. 'Atisha,' he said. 'We need to move quick.'

She opened her eyes – and all her questions, her thousand questions of how and why, of a snake that had struck and even now slid through the gap under a bolted door, none of it mattered. Not when he talked of all that she wanted. 'How?' she said simply.

'Bring things. It is—' He pointed to the window, pretended to shiver, words in their only common tongue, the tongue of their captors, failing him. 'Food here?' She pointed to the table which, as ever, was covered in things meant to tempt her. He nodded. 'Bring all.'

He went to the door, gently slid the bolts. She did as he said. There was so much food: bread, cheese, dried meats and fruits. She tore a blanket from the bed, made a big pouch, filled it. Then she wrapped Poum in the sling she'd fashioned for her.

She joined Luck at the door. He had it open, and was listening. 'Come,' he said.

They left, pausing at the tops and bottoms of circular stairwells, descending each swiftly. At the door that led to the courtyard they had to wait, as two night guards passed. When their footfalls had completely faded, Luck opened it, and led her to the stables.

By the flickering light of a lantern, she saw a horse was saddled, with bags dangling from its horn. 'I ... cannot ride,' she said.

'I can, with you and the baby before me.'

Outside, the bell tolled four times. It was the first call to prayer, and monks would soon be about. 'Then let us go swiftly,' Atisha said, stepping to the animal.

But Luck did not join her. He was looking at the door, chewing his lip. 'Something I must do first.'

'No!' Now this chance, this faint chance was before her, she did not want any delay. 'Nothing matters, except we go away.'

'One thing matters,' he replied. He picked up an iron mallet, that would be used for the hammering in of horseshoe tacks; moved to the door. 'I come back fast.'

'Wait!' she said, but he did not. He was gone, and all she could do was sit, and hope that he was as good as his word.

In the lowest dungeon of the Keep, Ferros was awake. It was hard anyway for them to sleep, for there was no angle either could take on the straw mattress without the metal cage of the mask biting into their head. They'd discovered the only way was to sleep in turns, the sleeper's head cradled in the other's lap.

Lara's was in his now, his back against the wall. She was restless, little moans escaping from her cracked lips, beneath the rim of the mask. The eye-slats of his mask prevented him seeing the whole of her, and he turned his head slowly to take her in piece by piece. The miracle of her, restored to him. No matter how dire their circumstance, no matter that they were prisoners, and hope was a memory, still he had her, whom he'd thought lost for ever.

He knew why she moaned. Four days of no food, and the water in the bucket used up two days since. He wondered about starving – was that a way an immortal could die? He seemed to remember that back in Agueros, the Sanctum on the Hill, he had learned of some hermit that had tried a hundred ways to kill himself and starvation was one. He'd failed, lived. Lived and suffered.

As Ferros did now. Was it his curse on his warder that they were being punished for? A pathetic act of defiance bringing this punishment of starvation? His desert mouth, his knotted stomach, made him regret it. Mostly, he regretted it because he knew that his love suffered as he did.

A louder moan and she turned in his arms, slept on. He looked down at her – and his neck, already rubbed raw from his trying to prise off the strap, was rubbed again. He winced. They had attempted to remove the masks, their own, each other's. But the device was well made, and the small brass lock unbreakable.

The monks had carefully prepared to keep immortals powerless.

They needed to. His anger came again and with it, something else. Desire. He had resisted everything to do with being an immortal, saw it as a curse placed upon him. When he'd learned of their special power, the ability to possess another human, he'd thought it an abomination.

No more. Not since he'd been forced to do it by Makron. It *had* been as easy as thought – while everything that first Roxanna and then Lara had told him about the joy of it was true. He knew, given the chance, he would do it again and again. To save himself and those he loved, yes. But also for the sheer delight.

He had drunk ale and wine over the years as a soldier, occasionally to oblivion. But he'd never found the escape in it that others did. Even the smoke of the poppy that Ashtan, his brother in arms and life if not in blood, had made him inhale, which had given him wild and vivid visions, was not an experience that had tempted him to repeat it. But possession?

He growled, felt a hunger greater even than the one that tortured his belly – the growl echoing there in a long, low murmur. Lara stirred, and he soothed her with strokes on her neck.

A noise came from above. A door opened, but far away, at a higher level. It could be another prisoner being brought down. He'd heard faint cries before, like bat squeaks in the night. It could be his guards. They came to check every night, or day, whichever it was – time had no meaning in a world lit only by lantern-light. In the days since their last feeding they had come, renewed the lamp oil, left.

A nearer sound – a key in the lock to the door above. The guard coming to check … or perhaps, at last, bringing food?

221

He didn't want to hope. He wanted still to defy. But his belly wouldn't let him.

Lara woke. 'Do they come?' she asked, her own desire clear.

'Perhaps,' he said, and they both sat up, looked. Through the slats he could see a shape moving beyond the latticed screen. Lower to the wall. A different, smaller guard.

He could not help the growl but he contained his whisper. 'Let me see you for but a moment,' he said, trying to prise up the mask again, in vain.

Luck looked down. Both of the prisoners were swaying their heads back and forth, trying to see him through the slats of their helmets. Without those on, Anazat had told him, they might attempt to possess him.

They were immortals. That he could understand. Once he'd learned of worlds beyond Midgarth – the Land of the Four Tribes, Ometepe where Atisha and her child came from, Corinthium where these prisoners belonged – he'd accepted that there must be immortality elsewhere too, just as there would be birds and horses. It followed that with immortality must come the gift of possession. But of mortals? Another man or woman's life? Since he'd been told, he'd spent much of his time trying to understand the *why* of that. What would it do to a people, a world, its gods? He had not understood and realised he did not need to, not yet. These of Corinthium had that ability, where the Four Tribes and – Atisha said – those of Ometepe did not. Which was why Anazat caged them.

Which was why Luck would set them free.

My enemy's enemy is my friend, Luck thought, setting down the mallet he'd brought. It was now stained red. Not being gifted at the use of weapons he'd hit the prison guard too softly the first time and then, he suspected, too hard the second. He'd had to. The man had opened the door from the courtyard without questioning, then had objected when he saw who it was that forced himself in. Thus, the double hitting. There'd only been the one night guard for the prison, which was just as well. Luck didn't think he'd be able to surprise another.

He went to the part of the screen that opened, unlatched it. The faces swung to him there. He wondered if they had any of *tolanpa-sen*, the common tongue of the Four Tribes. 'Friend,' he called, then lifted and threw down the rope ladder.

'Friend?' the man – Ferros was his name – queried. Then he lowered his head, saw the ladder. Giving a little cry, he crossed to it, climbed.

Soon they were both there, staring down at Luck. 'Come,' he said and led them from the chamber.

They climbed back up the dark, twisting corridors, the two that followed touching the walls to help them in their part-blindness. When they reached the guard, Luck was happy to note that at least the man was breathing, though he had lost some blood.

Luck held up his hand. 'Wait!' he said, and opened the door a crack to look out. Some monks moved in the courtyard, crossing to the great chapel for their morning worship. But these were the tardy, for he could hear the chanting had already begun. When the courtyard was again deserted, Luck led them swiftly across it to the stables.

Atisha came from behind the saddled horse. 'Where you been?' Then she saw who followed him. She stepped away, clutching Poum. 'Who?'

'Friends,' Luck said, then led the two into the next chamber, where a farrier's tools lay about. He picked up a hammer, showed it to Ferros, tapped at the side of his own head, at the place where the prisoners' brass locks lay. Ferros understood, reached for the hammer. Luck held it away for a moment then raised a finger to his lips. 'Shh!' he went, sweeping his gaze beyond the walls.

Ferros might or might not know much of the language but Luck's meaning was clear and Ferros grunted, took the hammer, beckoned Lara to lay her head on the stone shoeing-block. Squinting through the iron bars was awkward, and it took three blows to strike off the lock. Lara did not hesitate when she'd taken off her mask. Took the hammer in her turn and used just one hit to knock off his. He stood, removed the helmet, and both of them then turned.

Four people from three different worlds stared at each other for a long, long moment.

Luck broke the silence. He pointed at himself and Lara, then outside. 'Enemies,' he said.

Ferros gestured beyond the walls then tapped his chest. 'Enemies,' he echoed.

'Good.' Luck pointed at the horse. 'We go.'

It was Lara who answered, nodding. 'We go.' Then she pointed at her mouth, patted her belly, and moaned.

Luck understood. He remembered that Anazat had planned to starve the prisoners. He turned to Atisha. 'Share our food?'

She did not hesitate; opened the bag. With a cry, Lara reached in and pulled out a hunk of bread, tore at it. Ferros took some too – but then stopped. 'Danger?' he said, pointing again outside.

So the man from Corinthium does speak some of the common tongue, Luck thought. He nodded. 'Yes.'

Ferros took a bite of bread, then grabbed a sack from a horse stall, threw the loaf into it. 'Yes?' he asked, pointing into Atisha's blanket.

'Take half,' Luck said, and Ferros and Lara obeyed.

When the food was divided, Ferros looked around at the stalls, the horses in them. 'We go,' he grunted.

'That would be a fine idea. And fast.'

Luck said it in his own tongue. Ferros may not have understood the words, but he got the meaning. He said something to Lara in their tongue, and the two of them moved among the stalls till they had found the mounts they wanted. Swiftly, they harnessed them, grabbing sacks of oats to tie to their saddles for horse-feed while Luck tied the bags he'd brought from his cell to his chosen mount.

At the stable door they paused. The distant drone of male voices came. The devout worshipped, the rest of the castle still slept. Luck led them, but not to the main gate. There was a side gate that gave onto the forest. Toparak had taken him through it when they'd gone riding.

They stopped at the corner of a building. While Lara and Atisha held the horses, Ferros and Luck peered round the corner at the gate, twenty paces away. 'Guards,' Luck said.

There were two of them, leaning against a wall. Once again Ferros understood – and understood what must be done. Hefting the hammer he'd kept, he walked swiftly to the gate. There was a challenge, and then there were grunts, one cry, blows. Ferros whistled, and the three of them joined him at the gate. Luck looked down, and shuddered. There was no question of whether these guards were dead.

They walked their horses a little way into the dark forest – though it had already become lighter. They halted at a clearing, a crossroads of trails. By the sun rising in the east, Luck knew his direction. 'We go,' he said, pointing north.

'We go,' replied Ferros, pointing the opposite way.

A silence came, as each stared at the other. So many questions, Luck thought, and no time to ask any of them.

Though Lara did not think so. 'The One?' she said, but in the language of the Four Tribes, pointing at the baby in Atisha's arms, still sleeping as Poum had through everything.

Luck supposed that, whatever tongues they understood, that phrase meant something to them all. And he suddenly remembered the instinct he'd had the first time he'd seen Poum: that if this One was there to lead the Four Tribes to the conquest of the world, a way to end it might be to … end the baby's life. He felt a sudden fear. Who were these people? This fierce warrior who killed with such ease? He took a step forward, to stand just in front of Atisha, though he knew there was almost nothing he could do to protect her and the child.

It was Lara who had spoken, Lara who reached out … and laid her fingers gently on the baby's crown. She murmured something – and again, a blessing sounded the same in any people's tongue.

Luck mounted, Ferros boosted Atisha, holding Poum, up before him. They all looked at each other. Then Luck remembered something else he'd wanted to say. He lifted one of the sacks he'd tied to the saddle, opened it and pulled out his globe. He pointed back the way they'd come. 'Enemies,' he said. Then he circled his hand around them all. 'Friends,' he said, adding, 'we fight them, yes?'

They must have had enough of the common tongue to understand. They both nodded and Luck continued, though he was at a loss how to explain this. 'This for talk with friends. Do you understand?'

'*I* understand.' It was Lara who pointed, at the globe and at herself. 'Need …' She made a pouring motion in the air.

'Need this.' Luck pulled a vial of Sirene out. He'd realised that his defiance of throwing the last of his drug onto the mountain had been foolish. He'd asked for, and received, a little more. 'You find and we … talk? But,' he said, pinching his thumb and forefinger and rubbing them together above the globe, 'little, little.'

He didn't know how to explain dosage in this tongue. But

Lara nodded, as if she understood. 'We find and we talk,' she said. 'Then, we fight … enemies.'

As Luck tucked the globe back in, cushioning it among the many scrolls of paper he'd also stolen, that he'd used to study the other wonder of this world, writing. As he lowered the sack again, he remembered something else that Anazat had said to him when he first came to the Keep: that the monk knew where the globes were in the world, and who was with them. He wasn't sure how to warn about this. 'Enemies,' he began. 'Uh, enemies see us with this too.' He tapped the sack with the globe and gestured in a circle at all of them. 'Careful.'

Ferros and Lara both nodded. Then, with all the words still unspoken, they rode their opposite ways.

My enemy's enemy is my friend, Luck thought, watching them till the forest hid them. He knew, wherever Ferros and Lara went, they would fight. As would he … and Atisha.

Though he could not see it for the trees, he looked back in the direction of the Keep. Nearly half a year before he had climbed over a mountain to find out who was killing the gods of Midgarth. He had learned who, and so much more. If he had some answers, if he knew now who his enemy was, he came away with so many more questions – not least about the contents of the other sack tied to his saddle, filled with earth and spores. Questions about the sorrow and the joy he had found in Sirene. Questions above all about these gods she'd told him she watched for, these gifts they had given.

All questions for another day.

The silence of the night was suddenly broken by a bell. Clanging loud and harsh it told that escape – theirs', the others' or both – had been discovered.

'Hold fast,' he said, leaning over Atisha's shoulder, wrapping his arms tight around her. There was something wonderfully comforting in touching her, and the child. 'Fast, brother,' he said to the horse, and tapped his heels into its flanks.

The horse understood him, broke into a gallop, and ate the forest floor.

10

The Fall of Corinthium

Three months later ...

Like everyone else on the sea walls of Corinthium, Roxanna stared into the impenetrable mists and prayed.

Unlike everyone else, she prayed to no gods. She believed in none. Not Simbala, Goddess of Birth and Death. Not Mavros, God of War and Light, nor any of their offspring, the lesser gods who ruled various aspects of life and so the minds and superstitions of those who stood near her. She'd always believed that she and her kind had all the attributes, and most of the powers, of gods. Immortality, for one. So she prayed, as always, to herself.

'I will be true,' she murmured. 'I will live through all that is to come. Die and be reborn. I ...'

She faltered. She'd always had a total belief in herself and her kind. She'd seen immortals die, of course. Over her hundreds of years of life, she'd killed a few herself – cut off their heads, or dissolved them in fire. Enjoyed it – the horror in their traitor eyes as they realised this time they would not come back. But none had ever died from mortal causes – disease, age, accident.

Until Lucan. Until she'd returned from her mission to Cuerdocia to discover that her father had simply lain down at the docks and died.

229

It had weakened her, that knowledge. The thought that she too could be subject to Time's laws eventually, like any fisherman or stone mason. And the one thing she did not need now was to be weak. Not when whatever was approaching through these sea mists finally arrived.

Grey choked sea and land. She could see for thirty paces each way, no more. If what she saw was repeated beyond her vision, any fears would dissolve. For here in the tower that was the central gatehouse and sea entrance to the city were gathered the finest of that city's warriors. Of the empire's warriors, truly. The elite of the Wattenwolden from the forested north, of the Sarphardi from the western deserts and Assani from the eastern plains; the tall thin fighters from the southernmost province of Xan, black-skinned as her; the tallest, strongest men from the seven hills behind her. All merged into one force by the uniform of the imperial guard – the leather armour moulded to each torso with eagles at both shoulders clutching in their talons the javelins that crossed each chest; the purple tunic, lined with strips of steel, reaching to the knee; the bronze greaves below, the indigo cloak about their necks, the full-face steel helm, crested in a horsehair comb, dyed red. Every man had his razor-edged short sword at his side, each held a stabbing spear in his right hand. Strapped to the left arm was a great wooden rectangular shield, edged in gleaming bronze. Barbed throwing javelins were in a sheath on the back. Every warrior bore the broken nose and scarred face of a man who had fought in countless battles, and triumphed in almost every one. With an army of these, it did not matter what came through the mists, they would be defeated. With an army of these, she could retake the empire that had fallen.

She had three hundred.

Beyond them, lost to grey, were lesser warriors. Some experienced, those who had managed to escape the doom of the provincial cities like Tarfona or Balbek. Five hundred perhaps. But most of the men who manned the walls were artisans – cobblers, builders, weavers, stable hands and scribes. For Corinthium had neglected its own defences for too long. What need was there, when the only enemy were far away on the fringes of empire, savage tribes who could join together to mount a raid but never stay together long enough to take a city? The army had been kept small because of that. Small and efficient and mainly recruited from those same tribes, who were then sent off to fight others like them. Desert warriors in the forests, woodsmen on the sands. Kept small, too, because the money could be spent better elsewhere. On the glory that was the city. Especially its heart, the highest hill, Agueros and its sanctum of immortals, the city within a city. All men of age were required to train for a time with the militia. Some women volunteered. Few did service, only the poorest and dumbest who had not the money to pay the bribes to avoid it, nor the wit to send some idiot in their stead.

It was a mistake, she knew now, that neglect. A mistake made over hundreds of years, ever since the first immortals had gathered at the fishing village with its superb harbour, and transformed it into the city of Corinthium, that gave its name to the empire it made. Compounded by every immortal who had come since, seduced likewise into neglect by the pleasure of what they had discovered. Failing to realise that everything changed and aged, even if they, the immortals, did not.

Her father, Lucan, had been one with vision. Had realised that things must alter. But he was dead – a dead immortal! – and she, his daughter, had managed only a few changes since her return.

But would they be enough to deal with whatever was soon to appear through these mists?

Roxanna swivelled, staring north now, into the fog that also gripped the city and the home she could not see. There were six hills between her and the Sanctum on the Hill, each filled with mortals who had become less and less biddable as rumours of what was coming grew louder. What she'd realised – again too late – was that the threat wasn't somewhere distant, it was already there, and had been there for years. This promise of 'the One', of a god who would supersede all the others, who would bring freedom to all. This message that Makron – her husband one hundred years before, a traitor known as 'Smoke' now – had been spreading on the edges of empire for years. Whispers of it had arrived on every boat that docked. Had grown to mutters and then shouts. She had quelled much of it, the discontent. Using the old methods – coercion, bribery, imprisonment. Murder. She'd possessed some leaders, as she'd done the year before with Maltarsus, the dockers' leader, to end his strike. Him, she had merely disgraced. But the men and women who stood in taverns preaching the word of 'the One' she'd killed, as had other immortals she'd recruited. Streone had been distressed to be commanded to go into his special field, the theatre, and kill there. But over the centuries theatre had become almost a centre for the spreading of lies and discontent. Surprisingly, the fat poet had discovered both the skill and an appetite for dealing death. Between them all, they had dealt with the most prominent of the malcontents, the rumour-mongers, the ecstatic. But it was like the seven-headed, fire-breathing lizard of myth, the Lascaro. Cut one head off, and from the ground it died upon another reptile sprang up.

In a way, she thought, turning back to face the sea, it is good that whatever comes, comes now. Another month, and she was not sure she would have the strength to possess and kill as many as she would need to. There would be too many lizard heads. And exhaustion made the time required between possessions ever longer.

She looked again to the sea. Still nothing emerged from the fog. Yet phantoms writhed upon it, made from her fears – men and women with the twisted faces of the mob, pulling down the red marble towers on Agueros.

'My lady.'

Lost to grey and to her fears, she started, turned. 'General Olankios. What news?'

He stepped in beside her, leaned on the wall. She could see that he was also exhausted, as well he might be. When Balbek fell, he had been almost the last man out, the commander of the imperial forces there, staying to fight to the end with his men. He had been killed – twice – first at Balbek's donjon when it was taken, again when some sailors mutinied on that last ship. Loyal soldiers had saved him, and he'd been reborn to deal with his slayers. When he'd arrived in the city, he had only just over one hundred men left from his provincial command of a thousand. But he had arrived, and was by far the most experienced commander in the army, so he had taken charge. Hence the exhaustion. He might be immortal but he still needed sleep – and hadn't had much in three weeks, once he'd realised the rundown state of the city's defences.

'News?' he muttered, rubbing his grey face and pushing knuckles into eyes already swollen. 'None from the water. Not one of the fast sloops we sent out have returned.'

'I know that. Why do you think I've been standing here all day?' She snapped the reply, took a breath. 'I meant from other parts of the city. You've been making a tour of the defences, have you not?'

If he noticed her temper, he didn't react, or chose not too. She'd taken over as leader of the Council of Elders from her dead father. Except in the actual field of war, she was *his* commander. 'They are, as we know, not good. If you would look here?'

He turned to the soldier who was his secretary, and pulled a tattered roll of cured calfskin from the young man's satchel. There was a long table set back from the walls upon which lay spare sheaves of arrows, javelins, water jugs and rolls of cloth for bandages. He crossed to it, cleared a space, and unfolded a detailed map of the city. 'The waterfront is narrow,' he said, running a grubby finger along the line of the wall on which they stood. 'And these forts I ordered built under the Twins, on the end of each cobb, will take some passing, with their Bows of Mavros, and the underwater stakes.' He tapped down. 'Hence the relatively few forces I have here, for now.' He traced the lines of the western walls, along the left side of the map. 'The hills and ravines here make all attacks hard. But the walls have always been dilapidated there and we have not had time to rebuild them substantially. So I have had to place more soldiers than I can truly spare at towers along them.' He yawned. 'Excuse me, lady.' He laid his finger on the other side of the map. 'In the east here, the cliffs are high – except here and here, where the river gorges cut down to the sea. The walls are a little better – but these wide beaches mean that you could land a substantial force quite quickly. It is where I'd attack if I were them, rather than head on here – and we can only assume they have some traitors in their ranks who know the terrain, hmm?'

He glanced up at Roxanna, but she didn't change expression beyond a tightening of the jaw as she thought of Makron. Did everyone now know of her treasonous husband?

Olankios looked down again. 'So I have more men, better men, on these walls, here and here,' he tapped both beaches, 'and my main reserves between them, uh, here.'

She looked down, then up at him. 'In Sevrapol? What if you are wrong and they do attack us here, in the harbour, in strength? Sevrapol is quite far north.'

'It is central, lady,' he sighed. 'And I stationed them there because the north may be where we need them most.'

She looked at those inked northern walls, and beyond them to the sketched fields and forests. It was her favourite riding country – where she had raced Ferros all those months ago. But no one was riding there now – or rather no one from the city. 'Have they moved?' she asked.

Olankios shrugged. 'The Wattenwolden shift their camp every week or so. Once they have hunted the woods out, and the stench from their shit pits gets too much. But they are, as always, in sight of the walls.'

'And they still have not sent back our envoys?'

'No. Nor sent any of their own.'

She looked at the map again, seeing other shapes in the inked trees. The Wattenwolden, the fierce warriors from the forests to the north, had come in numbers to Corinthium. In numbers, it was said, such as they had not brought since they tried and failed to storm the city three hundred years before. Then, after an army went north and broke them at Kristun, there had been peace between Corinthium and these barbarians, more or less. Trade. The Wattenwolden supplied mercenaries to fight on the other side of the empire, in the deserts of Balbek, or the grasslands of Cuerdocia. A hundred or so stood in the uniform of the guard on each side of her now. 'Do these know,' she said softly, 'that their brothers are waiting beyond the northern walls?'

Olankios shrugged. 'Perhaps. A renegade may have slipped over the walls to tell them. Which is why I have my northern mercenaries here, facing south, and my southern soldiers – Assani and Sarphardi mainly – facing north.'

'Enough of them?' Roxanna asked swiftly, feeling a chill pass through her.

'It depends.' Olankios shook his head. 'Three hundred years ago the Wattenwolden failed to break our walls because they didn't have enough ladders and enough men. Will they have learned that lesson, do you think?'

'Have you not sent spies to find out?'

'Of course!' the general barked, then closed his eyes. When he opened them and spoke, his voice was again calm. 'But like your envoys, lady, none have returned.'

'I am sorry, sir,' she said, squeezing his arm, 'it is this mist. It is playing tricks with my mind.'

'With all our minds.' Olankios stood, rolled his shoulders. 'Until it clears we will not know if this,' he gestured back down to the map, 'is sufficient.'

'It will be, general. For Mavros favoured us when he sent you back here. Praise him.'

'And Simbala too.' Olankios murmured the stock response with about as much fervour as she had. She suspected that, like her, he was one of those immortals who did not care much about gods. And what else is he? she wondered. He'd studied her body, as all men who admired women did. As ever, she'd made no effort to conceal her charms, her breasts bound in straps of leather, her long legs swathed in the same, her black skin shining. Should I fuck him, bind him even closer to me? If all else fails, if these walls fall, I will need him and his soldiers to get me out. So ...

She still had her hand on his arm. She squeezed it lightly. Yet when she looked into his eyes she saw not lust, but curiosity. And strangely he spoke of someone who she'd just been thinking about. He often came to mind when she thought of fucking someone. 'That young warrior from Balbek I sent you last year? The new immortal, Ferros? Was he worthy?'

'In all kinds of ways.'

He didn't pick up on her tone. 'You say he did well, out there,' he waved a hand, 'in the grasslands of the Assani?'

'He is a born general ... General.'

'But no word has come of him since Cuerdocia's fall?'

'None.' She took her hand away. 'Why do you ask?'

'I don't know.' Olankios rubbed his eyes again, then looked at her, his gaze suddenly intense. 'Yes, I do. Because I sensed something about him. Your tales of him confirm it. And I believe I would rather have him standing here beside me on these walls than five hundred more of the imperial guard.'

As would I, Roxanna thought, but didn't say. Yet was it only tiredness that made her breath catch a little as she thought of Ferros? Three hundred years of men, and only one other had made her breath catch like that. Now both of them were out there somewhere, beyond these mists.

Which, even as she looked at them, began to fray. The sky had got lighter above them, the waves a little clearer below. 'General! Lady Roxanna!' Olankios's aide who'd gone to the wall came running back. 'The mists! They are clearing …'

'We can see that, boy,' the general growled.

'There's more.' The young man halted before them. 'The men of long sight have spied a shape in the mist.'

The three strode back swiftly to the wall. When she reached it, Roxanna realised she didn't need long sight to see the shape, or tell what it was. Tell also what bad condition it was in. 'Ready three longboats!' she called down to the pier below, where runners waited. 'Get out to that ship and speed the captain and his news to us.'

Though Olankios's voice was calm beside her, she could hear the edge in it. 'Keep your boats at the dock, lady,' he said. 'His news follows in his wake.'

She glanced at him, then again to the water. Even in the time she'd looked down to shout orders, the mists had frayed further, were a tattered curtain now, not a rolling bank. Then, in a moment, it was as if that curtain was torn away by an unseen hand – perhaps by the Twins' hands, for right beneath the giant

237

statues that guarded the sea entrance to the city was where all the grey suddenly vanished.

'Mavros!' muttered the young aide, leaning forward to grip stone.

She had no gods to call upon. But if she had, Roxanna might have chosen Simbala, of birth and death. Especially death. For it had come to Corinthium, in five hundred ships.

'Messengers!' Olankios ran back to the table and started scribbling notes there with a charcoal pencil as fast as his fingers could move. 'This for the Sevrapol reserve. Tell Stipol to bring First and Second City squadrons down here at the run. Third and Fourth to march double time to the northern towers.' He clapped the first man on the back, shoved him away, scribbled, spoke to a second as he wrote. 'Follow him with this. Go to the western towers. Tell Malvrouko to send a report immediately. If no enemy appears within the hour he is to come here with half his command immediately. Run!' he bellowed. 'You'll need to take the same basket on the Heaven Road.'

'General, should we not bring the entire reserve here? Look!'

He glanced briefly, then wrote another note. 'No, lady. Trust an old soldier. This is the main attack, I am sure. As I am also sure the Wattenwolden will hear of it and attack too. Only a show of strength may deter them. I wish I could be in two places at once.'

'Who commands there?'

'Sofran. A Sarphardi.'

'An immortal?'

'No.' He smiled briefly. 'I shoved a sword into his arse when I captured him twenty years ago and it took him months to heal.'

'A good general?'

'Good enough with horsemen. He's never fought on a wall.'

Roxanna nodded. 'Then write me the command.' She saw him hesitate. 'Do it, Olankios. Because I fought the Wattenwolden

238

at that wall three hundred years ago. It was my first battle. And, trust me, I have picked up a few things since then.'

'By Mavros, were you there? So was I. Young and shit-scared, before I knew I was immortal.' He scribbled as he spoke, folded the note, passed it to her. 'Sofran may object, despite this,' he said.

'He may. But I can be ... persuasive.'

'I am sure you can,' Olankios said, but over his shoulder, as he strode for the front wall.

Roxanna headed the opposite way, to the stone staircase. She was halfway down them when she heard a universal, anguished cry. Not from the imperial guard behind her, silent and staring, but on each side further along the walls, where the armed citizens were.

'The Twins!' all shrieked, a rising moan.

She frowned but it could not slow her. The Twins were the guardians of the city, their hands crossed at the harbour entrance. One, a warrior, was 'strength'. His brother, a scribe, was 'wisdom'. Where their hands met was inscribed 'peace', the peace they made between them.

There was a legend that if the Twins ever fell, so would the city. None but the weak-minded believed in such tales. But such was the force of fear she heard in the cry that she stumbled as she reached level ground, before running on towards the platform of the Heaven Road.

What could be happening to the Twins? she wondered.

Ferros turned away. He'd had enough of staring into the mist. It was playing tricks with his eyes. As if the rolling grey was a wall in Xan, the city in the southern deserts he'd visited once to recruit, where storytellers used lamplight and wooden puppets to make stories from shadows. They told of ghosts and monsters, gods and heroes from their ancient world. Here he saw people he knew – or had known, for many were dead: Ashtan, his Sarphardi comrade, who'd been there when Ferros died and was reborn for the first time, and had died himself soon after; Tamin the One-Eyed, the kidnapper and rapist he'd killed that day, one of his first as an immortal. All those he'd killed since. The mists had presented a parade of his victims. He was a soldier, killing was his trade. But slaying a foe in honourable battle, in an equal fight, was one thing; murdering someone while possessing another's body was quite something else. In the grey mists he saw the surprise in the eyes of the three Horse Lords he'd killed. Though the surprise was strongest in the one who'd hosted him, Pershak, as the Horse Lord's body was thrust through by Makron's sword.

He shuddered, then slumped down to put his back to the boat's railing. There was little space, so crowded was the deck with soldiers from all over the world – Seafarers, Horse Lords, Huntresses, Assani and other tribesmen. Dotted here and there, standing out, a black-robed monk. Much tattier were the people from the captured cities. Like them.

'Anything?' asked Lara, as his shoulder touched hers.

'No,' he replied, and turned slightly to study her.

Study *her*. Lara, as she had ever been, yet different too. He had seen her as so many others, in the months since fleeing the Keep. In the long ride south through Saghaz-a to the tunnel under the mountains, and especially when they reached it, they'd needed to possess again and again to make good their escape. To begin with they'd both taken over others at the same time. But it had nearly cost them their lives when they had been challenged by a Horse Lord just after they'd returned to themselves, and been too exhausted to possess again, whether him or any other. Ferros had killed the man, knife to knife, taking a killing wound himself. He'd been reborn, of course. His victim hadn't. Since that scare, they'd alternated possession when it was required – she the lord, he her slave. He the merchant, she his whore. They'd got by, possessed only when they were forced to. Saved their strength.

He stared at her. She did not look at him; would not, and he sighed. He knew why. It was not only what possession took from the body. It was what it left on the mind – for him, those faces in the mist. Because possession wasn't just of the body. Possession left memories, of another's life. Of those they'd hated, or loved. Of those who had loved them. Those memories lingered. For her? It was why she would not look at him now, lost in the recall of her last possession. In a Huntress's terrible memories.

He focused on his drawn-up knees. At least the memories of her possession had saved them a huge journey. For when they reached Tarfona, the city they'd defended and lost three months before, the plan had been to take ship to Balbek, their home city. To find Lara's family, mother, father, sisters. But they'd swiftly learned the news, shouted in drunken triumph in the city's taverns, up and functioning again to entertain Cuerdocia's new masters. The Four Tribes and their native allies had paused only long enough to take and sack Tarfona before they'd moved swiftly down the southern coast of the Great Sea, a fleet growing with each conquest. Every small town had surrendered fast. Only Balbek held out, commanded by Ferros's old general, Olankios. But even his skill could not keep the enemy out for long. So the Huntress's memories had showed a city ravaged, its people slaughtered or enslaved, those who did not flee into the deserts.

Where the Huntress saw glory, Lara saw horror. She did not actually *see* her family, know their fate. So she'd still wanted to travel on there and find them. But he would not go.

'The fate of the empire will be decided at Corinthium,' he'd said. 'The city is where I must be.'

They'd quarrelled through a night and a long, slow dawn as the invaders' fleet, boosted with all the vessels they'd captured at Balbek, readied to sail. She'd deployed every argument – that they, above all others now, knew the corruption at the heart of empire, the corrosion of immortality. That all that mattered now was family – hers, for he was an orphan and she was all he'd ever had. He'd replied that the army *was* his family. His brothers and sisters fighting now to defend the empire on the walls of the great city. That every moment of every day of his life since his orphaning at seven had been devoted to that cause. However corrupt and corroded, he could not abandon it now.

'So you choose your love for empire over your love for me?' she'd spat.

'No. It is not a choice, Lara,' he'd said. 'I go where I must. You, where you must. And we will find each other again.'

'How? In a world gone mad, how exactly do you think we will do that?'

'If the city stands, you will find me there. If it falls, and I live, I know where you will be.'

'If the city stands,' she'd replied, her voice rich with venom, spitting out her last argument, 'then you'll be standing beside *her*. Or should I say, lying under?'

It was there again, as it had always been, from the moment Lara knew of them. He and Roxanna. His betrayal. And though he protested that he didn't love Roxanna – he didn't – though he declared that he loved only Lara – he did – yet the dark queen of Corinthium was ever between them, and before him. He might not love her – but he was obsessed by her. It was her face he saw, more than any other's, in the mists before the ship.

He knew Lara knew that. So in the bitterness of that dawn, when the last words were hissed out, and the fleet made ready to sail, and rendezvous with the one from Balbek, she had chosen to go with him, though the bitterness was between them still and had been in the two weeks' sailing. At least, in the chaos of that boarding, and the crowds upon every deck, they had no need to possess anyone. Makron, the immortal traitor, was the only person who could have recognised them and he was on a huge ship with other leaders in the vanguard of the fleet. So they'd slept beside each other, back to back, as themselves. They'd barely talked. All the words had been spoken that could be. All fates would be revealed, in the place beyond these chill mists that had settled over the fleet for the last two days of sailing.

As he looked away from her, as he looked up from his knees to the sails, still bellying in the strong southerly, he saw beyond them that the sky, hidden for two days in grey, had lightened. Even as he noticed, the cries came, as others saw it too. Lara stirred beside him and they both rose, just as everyone on the deck rose. Gasps came, the same gasps they'd given when they'd first seen the wonder of the world – the city of Corinthium, heart of the empire named for it, vast towers against the sky. Nearer to, more gasps came for the Twins, those colossal statues, arms joined over the entrance to the harbour.

It may have been a shock to most aboard – and most ashore too, the sudden appearance of such an enemy. But one man aboard another ship was not shocked, had seen it all before. And that man, that immortal, that traitor, Makron, had a plan.

Even as they watched, the huge vessel – of the empire's fleet but manned by Seafarers – together with five more beside it, all swung side on to the Twins, and the cobb ends on which they stood. Arrows from dozens of Bows of Mavros, captured at Tarfona and Balbek, flew at the small forts set up there. A pitiful few came in reply.

'What are they doing?' Lara murmured, seeing what else was happening – the scores of small skiffs, dropped from the bigger vessels' sides, rapidly filled with men, rapidly rowed towards the plinths from which the Twins' huge feet were carved.

'I am not sure.' Ferros's voice was weak, and he coughed to strengthen it. 'But I fear—'

'Ascrami! All of you. Ascrami! To me!'

The man who called was a Horse Lord. Shorter than many, his lack of height was made up for by a protuberance of belly. But the word he called was an Assani word, and one all aboard knew, all over the empire. Depending on the context it could mean 'mad fighters' or 'crazed heroes'. But Ferros knew it by its other usage.

Expendables.

Those who shifted at the call, and tried to avoid the Horse Lord's gaze, were exactly that. Some had been brought from the caves where they'd dug a tunnel. Some had ridden the grasslands. Most were what Ferros and Lara purported to be – residents of the fallen cities, who'd surrendered at their conquest to spare themselves death, to eat from the conquerors' stores. All were kept alive, expendable, for this purpose: to lead the first wave in any attack. To fill a breach in a wall with their bodies, to weaken the sword arms of the enemy so that they would fall more easily to the actual warriors that followed. There was a cult around them, like the suicide cults that had plagued Corinthium when people sought immortality. For any ascrami that survived the assault was rewarded with a herd of goats, or a plot of stream-front land.

Few ever lived to claim either prize.

The Horse Lord gestured and other men dumped piles of weapons onto the deck. In a swift glance, Ferros could see the poverty of the rusty blades, the patched-up shields. Yet while others hesitated, he went and picked out the best of what there was for himself and Lara. Poor enough, for an officer of the

Ninth Balbek Riders but still their only slight advantage in what was coming.

They would have to be ascrami. Even possession was not an option, not there on that crowded deck. Besides the only ones to be possessed were other ascrami. They might as well fight as themselves.

He came back, handed the lighter and better of the two swords to Lara. She took it with a grunt, swung it through the air, testing its weight and balance. She might still look like the slim young girl from Balbek but she'd been within a half-dozen fighters now, and had learned from every one.

'Stay close to me in what is to come,' he said, holding out the better of two shields.

'And what do you think that is?' she asked, taking it.

He was about to reply that he didn't know – but then he realised he did. Realised it in the screams that had grown louder and louder, which he'd first mistaken for the seagulls that flocked over the cobb ends where, in times of peace, boys cast their lines for fish. But it was men and women who cried now, as they fought and died. His glance confirmed it, as a bolt hurled from the fort passed through the mainsail above him. As did the pot-bellied Horse Lord, bellowing now, 'Over the side now, ascrami! For glory! For glory!'

They were not the first wave of expendables to be sacrificed, Ferros saw as he straddled the railing, and dropped into the skiff tied up below. Many, perhaps all, had died in that first wave, corpses floating face down in the waters, or broken on the rocks that surrounded Strength's plinth, beneath the walls of the small fort that had been erected since the first time he'd come here. A fort already battered by the arrows of Mavros from the fleet, logs split and wrenched asunder – gaps defenders tried to avoid, for the arrows from smaller bows flying through them. A breach had been made – and it was their wave of ascrami that was being sent to storm it.

Wrong, thought Ferros, as he dropped onto a bench and lifted his shield above his head – for some arrows were flying the other way too – they were not expected to storm the breach. They were expected to kill a few then die in it providing a flesh bridge for better, less expendable warriors to storm across.

The calmness he always felt in combat came to him. That cannot happen, he thought, as arrows jerked the wood above his head, and less protected men and women around him screamed and died. So when the boat struck the rocks at the Twin's feet, and the first of the ascrami leaped screaming upon them, he dropped his shield and sword, wrapped both arms around Lara, lifted her, and hurled them both the other way, into the water.

For the moment of sinking there was silence, a blessed pause. But arrows shot into the water near them, passing close and fast, losing their velocity, floating up, as they must. The two of them broke the surface and the cacophony of war returned in full measure. Lara had never learned to swim. He had, as part of his army training. As she flailed, spitting water, gasping air, he pulled the shield straps from her arm, wrenched her sword from her grip, tucked his hand under her chin and kicked hard, on a line parallel to the cobb.

The tide that had brought the invading fleet was coming in sets of waves, the last of each set huge. One caught them now, drove them hard in towards the boulders at Strength's feet. Ferros managed to plant his feet on a submerged rock, take some of the wave's force, use it to pivot sideways. Fortune or the gods favoured them; there was the smallest of coves, pebble-floored, boulder-walled. They fell onto its stony ground, and the wave tried to suck them back out. Wedging his feet, thrusting above him with his hands, with Lara still choking across him, he managed to resist the tug. When the water receded, they scrambled and crawled a few paces into the tiny cove.

They lay there for a time, each wave that came lapping at their feet, the last and biggest all but dragging them out again. But Lara had regained her breath, and did as he did, digging in her feet. The wave left them, and Ferros took the opportunity of smaller ones to scramble to the sea's edge, and look up. He came back, crouched where Lara lay. 'We are directly below the Twins. The attack goes on, and the next ships – with real soldiers this time – are coming in. We haven't got much time.'

Lara coughed out some more water. 'To do what?'

He jerked his head left. 'The cobb dips in that way, towards the city. I'm no sailor, but I think the tide is starting to go out.'

'So?'

'So after the next big wave breaks, we wade and stagger and swim when we must before we scramble up to the roadway.'

'Then?'

'Then?' He reached and pulled a strand of seaweed from her hair. 'Then we run to Corinthium.'

'Sounds easy,' she said. She leaned over and blew water from both her nostrils, then she too came up onto her haunches. 'I am ready.'

They waited, shaking with cold. When the water began to recede from their ankles, Ferros led them out. Without looking up to the source of the terrible sounds above them – blending into the single, high-pitched shriek of war – they staggered, and floated, holding fast to rocks when they had no choice. But it was slow-going, with the attackers' overshot arrows still clattering off rocks around them. Halting, gulping air, Ferros looked up. 'It'll will be easier to move up there. Also, I fear—'

'What?'

He'd turned to the sounds behind them, not far away. 'The

247

fort is about to fall. When it does,' he rose to a crouch, 'we will have company upon the cobb.'

He began to scramble up the boulders, Lara following. When they reached the roadway, they looked back. They had not come far, perhaps one hundred paces. They could see clearly.

The fort was not about to fall. It had fallen.

Defenders were already running from it, passing them without a glance. Beyond what remained of the structure, the tall ships had come close, and their Bows of Mavros had reduced the fort to a shambles of broken beams. A glance across at the base of Wisdom, the other Twin, showed the same scene. Whatever the commander in Corinthium intended with these defences had failed.

It did not take much thought, and only one word. 'Run,' he said.

They did, though wet clothes slowed them, almost as much as their exhaustion. Soldiers of Corinthium – city militia, Ferros could see – overtook them, throwing off their breastplates, dropping any weapons they had, terror widening their eyes and giving their feet speed. They needed it – for behind them came the conquerors fresh from conquest, blood up and crying for more. In the swiftest of glances, Ferros had seen members of each of the Four Tribes, and their allies from desert and grassland. Distinct among them, the black robes of the Warrior Monks, with their tall, scythe-tipped spears.

Arrows fell, shot by the Huntresses whose skills Ferros had admired. Men tumbled, screaming, plucking at the shafts suddenly sprouting from their backs. They were a hazard to feet, Ferros and Lara vaulting the dying, even as these reached up and tried to grasp them. Looking through the seething mass ahead, he could make out a solid body of men near the city end of the cobb. They looked so far away.

Somehow the two of them got closer, close … and then

stopped, as the fleers bunched before the blockage, a sudden gathered mob, an easy target, cattle in a pen with Fate's lottery casting for its victims. Either side of Ferros a man died, each turning to grasp him as they fell, a last appeal in their eyes. Another arrow scored a line in red along Lara's neck, and she cried out in agony, falling into Ferros. She sank into him as she would in love, as she had not done in an age of longing. He held her tight, and for the moment all that was bitter between them was gone. They could die here, clutching each other. And even if they were reborn, who knew what world they would be born again into, and if they would be together in it?

Cries now from behind them, death there too, and Ferros looked up to see arrows passing over from the city's soldiers ahead and into the enemy. The mob before him gave, they were stumbling forward again, towards what he now saw, by their purple tunics, were members of the imperial guard. They were drawn up across the width of the cobb in ranks of shield and spear, ten men wide and many files deep, with shield men in every second rank to ward them against death from the sky. But what had caused the survivors of the forts to stumble forward again was the parting of the ranks, opening files for the mob to stream down.

There was bunching again at each entrance, with men striving to push forward until they couldn't move. The press shifted slowly, but at least only a few arrows now fell among them and he and Lara were getting close.

Then someone yelled, 'Those two? Who are they?' and men found a little space to move away from them. They stood isolated, different from the soldiers in their dress from the provinces.

Ferros was aware of spears being hefted, bows lowered. 'We are of Corinthium,' he cried. 'I am an officer of the Ninth ...'

He got no further. 'Seize them! Seize them both!' Men came forward, grabbed them by their arms which were twisted and bent behind them. Then they were brought at a run down the ten-deep file to the rear, flung onto the ground, pinned there.

An officer, distinguished by the red of his horsehair crest, grabbed Ferros by the shirt at his neck and raised him a little off the ground. 'Who did you say you were? Speak fast, because I have no time for foolishness.'

'You never did, Malthoros. Though there was that time in the oasis near Kumam …'

The officer jerked his head back, as if to see the face before him more clearly. 'F … Ferros? By the gods, how …?'

'I will explain if your men would only let me go.' The officer nodded, and both his arms and Lara's were released. Ferros stood. 'Though truly, Malthoros, I think neither of us have time for talk.' He squinted back along the cobb, where the enemy had pulled back beyond easy bow range but were clearly gathering; looked across at the other cobb, where a similar scene was developing; finally glanced at the city walls. 'Who commands?'

'Our old general, Olankios. Though,' he coloured slightly and continued, 'the leader in name is the head of the Council of Elders. That woman.'

'What woman?' It was Lara who asked the question.

'The Lady Roxanna.' He went on, before Ferros could speak. 'But she is not here at the port. She's gone to the northern walls, to face the Wattenwolden.'

'What do you mean?' Ferros gripped the man's arm. 'The tribes of the north attack us too?'

'We do not know. They have not yet. But there's an army of them and—'

'Never mind. There's much I need to find out.' He glanced back to the cobb, where more and more of the enemy were gathering. Mavros's balls, he thought, they've already landed some horses. 'I'll go to the general,' he said.

'I'll see you with him soon. Once he saw the size of their

fleet, he knew the Twins' forts would not stand long. He only ordered me here to save as many as I could before returning.' He looked past Ferros, whitened. 'Gods' jaws, have they got cavalry?'

'They are fine warriors, Malthoros. Better than any Assani we fought. They will use javelins,' he thought back to the battle on the ridge, 'and nooses, thrown to grab men and break up the ranks. Have men with knives ready to cut rope. And do not leave your retreat to the walls too late.' He turned. 'Come, Lara, we'll—'

He broke off. Because Lara had gone.

He ran forward, scanning the backs of the mob of survivors now stumbling towards the town. He couldn't see her. Though it was possible, of course, that 'she' was no longer there.

Cursing, he ran towards the city.

He had just reached the gates under the main tower, was halted by a crowd again trying to push in, when the cry came. Different from all before it. Not the cries of fleeing men and women, or the shrieks of the dying. This was like the city itself spoke … moaned, in one voice, just a few words.

'The Twins. No. No!'

Ferros turned, stepped away to the pier, so he could see out to the open water. 'No,' he moaned with the rest of them.

He'd known that many of the enemy's ships carried not soldiers, but miners. The same slaves he'd first seen carving a tunnel through the mountains into Cuerdocia. These must have been landed as soon as the cobb forts were taken. For he could see that the Twins, which had stood upright ever since they were erected hundreds of years before, were starting to lean.

He turned and pushed to the gates once more, was halted there by the crowd. He knew the legend, as they all did. And if the Twins did fall, could the city be far behind?

There was still no sight of Lara. Yet since he could not see her, nor know what she was about, he realised he could only do what he had always done: follow the soldier's creed. Deal with what was in front of him. Fight this fight now. Fight all other battles when they came. Including the one with her.

Finally through the gate, he ran up the stairs to report to his general.

As soon as she'd heard the name, Lara knew that she must go to her.

Roxanna. Roxanna was why she was there. She did not believe in the empire, as Ferros still did. If she ever had, that belief had gone when she saw the rot at its very heart, the corruption of which she'd become an unwilling part.

Immortals. They kept the world in chains, it's people pets for their pleasure. She knew the joy of it. Not the dying and being reborn. Not the rapid healing from any wound. Not the living for centuries. That would have been unbearable: one life, for ever. No, the pleasure lay in the *many* lives that could be lived.

Possession. All those people, all those memories shared, all those skills learned, all that ... *humanity* that an immortal could be a part of. For a time. Long enough to be the best of a person. Not so long as to be forced to live the heartache at the core of most lives.

The old god who brought immortality – Andros the Blind, he was named in legend – he had not brought a gift but a curse. *She* was cursed. It was like those who sank into the embrace of the Poppy of Sleep. They lived a dream in the beginning, until the dream was all they were, turning soon enough to a nightmare from which they could never wake.

But on the voyage back across the Great Sea she'd made up her mind. For one last time she would yield to the joy – and then she would be done. Some escaped the poppy's hold, and she would escape this. This last time, that had begun even now:

when she'd realised it would take two days to reach the northern walls on foot through a city that was about to fall, through mobs of the desperate. So she'd possessed a messenger at the port entrance to the Heaven Road.

She did not care what urgencies were in his satchel. The empire's fate did not matter to her. All that did was who waited at the end of the ride.

Roxanna.

On that voyage she'd asked herself again and again: was it only revenge she sought? The immortal had killed her to steal Ferros – or thought she had. But she had realised her desire was greater than mere vengeance – or even the taking back of Ferros. After all that had come between them, she was not sure it was possible for them ever to be together again. No, this was personal. Like finding the man who had first corrupted you with the poppy, and killing him. Roxanna had corrupted her. In her immortal life she had possessed – used – hundreds. For them, for herself, the dark queen of Corinthium must die.

As the basket rose over the hills, she moved till she could better see over the basket's edge. When she'd taken the Heaven Road that first time, she had been unable to even look down, so frightened was she of the drop. But this man she possessed – Bratan, just twenty, a fisherman's son – was not frightened. So she was able to clearly see, through his eyes, all the chaos below.

Each district she passed over, spread over the seven hills of the city, had terror at their hearts. Soldiers marched here, marched there. Citizens gathered goods onto carts depending on the tide of rumour – though where they thought they could flee, with the sea before occupied by the Four Tribes and their allies, and the forests behind filled with Wattenwolden, she did not know. Many had recognised the futility and in parts of every district – and all over the fourth hill where Sevrapol, the entertainment district was – people rioted. Looted and fought, drank and fucked. Burned. All the theatres she'd passed when she'd followed Streone to the district – the first time she'd seen the globe filled with smoke, and men talking across the world – were aflame. Weeping and laughter found equal voice in the doomed city.

Only where there were soldiers was there any order. From the tower over Sevrapol, the middle hill, she could see almost to the limits every way. On the western walls, the towers were held. To the east, soldiers marched along beaches fronting bays, though none of the enemy were in them. The fight was in the south, with the fleet she'd arrived on now fully in charge of the bay, though they had not yet begun to storm the walls. And in the north?

She turned, saw … the sun, which had finally dispersed the mists, was beginning its fall into the west, its beams flaming the red-walled Sanctum on Agueros. It also reflected off the backplates and helms of the soldiers who held the northern-most walls, a thousand glittering points of light. But she could also see, distinctly, a separate glow beyond, on the open fields between walls and forests. A mass of light that, even as she watched, started to slip forward like a wave over sand.

Each stop was brief, enough to disgorge whoever needed to descend. When it pulled away from Sevrapol, there was only her and one other, both bound for the final destination, Agueros. She looked to it, until a distant shout from behind turned her, and she looked back at the port. 'No,' the other messenger moaned. 'By Simbala, no!'

The young man she possessed had the far sight, much better than her own. So she was able to see, clearly, the Twins, joined as they were at the hands, falling. To her it seemed that the warrior, Strength, fell first, pulling his brother Wisdom with him into the sea.

She turned her back to it. She had already decided – the fall of the Twins, even the fall of Corinthium, did not concern her. Only one fall did – that of her enemy ahead. And that could not happen until she reached the seventh hill.

On the central tower of the northern walls, Roxanna stared out at the Wattenwolden – and the Wattenwolden stared back. Apart from a burst of archery two hours before, with three score arrows shot high to drop on them from the sky, that had wounded only two men, they had not moved – according to the Sarphardi general Sofran who had, after reading Olankios's note, and with ill-concealed temper, ceded her the command.

She counted them again, as far as she was able. A rough gauging – ranks ten deep and two hundred paces wide – gave them two thousand warriors. All men, for the forest tribes left their women behind when they went out to fight. And what did she have? She looked along the walls, both ways ... perhaps a quarter of that, five hundred men. Four hundred were the Sarphardi soldiers, who fought for the empire for the pay they were given, and the rewards of conquest. Loyal enough, when both were offered. Neither were this day, for this fight, she knew. She could only hope that their years of service, and the one hundred imperial guardsmen positioned among them, would keep them in place if – when! – the attack came. Hold the walls long enough for the reserves Olankios had ordered to reach them. Two squadrons of city militia, three hundred men and some women, plus one more hundred of the guard, was not a huge reinforcement. But it would have to be enough.

She looked away from the silent enemy before her – reluctantly, because she had this strange feeling that it was only her stare that was holding the tribes in place – to the streets behind. The spine of the city, the Stradun, was a wide avenue that rose all the way from the port to where she now stood. Usually it was choked with people and carts, stalls with vendors selling everything from pigs' heads to bolts of cloth. All that had been cleared away, by imperial order. Those reinforcements should be marching up it now. But even if they marched double time, they would not be here until an hour after sunset at best.

Which was upon them. She could see far over to her right the last beams leaving the red towers of Agueros. Faces that had been clear fifty paces along the battlements were now blurred. And before her ...

She turned back, and could not contain her gasp. The Wattenwolden still had not moved – but everything had changed. Because behind the very last rank, every twenty paces, a bonfire now burned.

'They have lit their campfires for the night.' Sofran, who'd stormed off when she'd usurped his command, had returned, unnoticed. Roxanna glanced at him, his brown eyes reflecting flame in the dark brown face. 'So,' he said, 'I can stand most of my men down, rest them, feed them.'

'Not yet,' she replied. 'The fires may not be for their rest.'

'Then for what, *General*?' The inflection on the word was clear, mocking.

'Perhaps they think to try to burn us?'

Sofran snorted. 'I've fought these bastards for twenty years. They know two ways of it: ambush columns in a forest or charge the enemy in a shouting rush, preferably on a horse. They only use fire to cook, and to jump through when they are drunk to make themselves feel brave.' He nodded. 'They don't like fighting after sunset either. Something to do with their demon gods being blind in the dark so they can't find them and take them to paradise.' He leaned forward and voided the contents of both nostrils onto the parapet before him. 'So that's what they'll be up to now,' he continued, wiping his hand on his cloak, 'which means I can stand my men down. Is that not right ... *General*?'

He'd added the title after a pause, and with the same inflection.

Roxanna felt fury constrict her throat. She spoke through it, taking his wrist, twisting it, 'Listen, you—' she began.

And did not finish. 'They move!' came the warning shout from near her, echoed all down the wall.

She whipped back. Flame was spreading down each file ahead, men bearing torches from the rear, moving swiftly to the front. Every warrior took flame as the torch passed until every man appeared to hold a firefly. But how they held it she could not see.

Until she did. By then it was too late.

'Arrows!' she screamed, her cry lost in the cries of many as every single man in the Wattenwolden host raised a bow and shot a flaming missile into the sky. Two thousand arrows fell, and if many fell short or long, at least a thousand descended fast onto the walls – and into those who had not managed to raise a shield, or make themselves small where front wall met the parapet floor.

Sofran would mock no more. He'd raised his head to stare into the sky, to bellow commands, and an arrow had stopped his words, entered his mouth, flame snuffed in his throat. He stared at her, incredulous, his eyes each side of the shaft, then tumbled off the wall into the yard. Leaping, she grabbed a dropped shield, held it over her head, looked out through a crenel – and watched as the Wattenwolden, with a roar, shot a second volley, and then charged. Even in the dusk light she could see that in every fourth file, men carried ladders.

They'd learned another lesson since they'd last failed to take Corinthium.

'Archers!' she cried, turning to her left to see, not the armed warriors she needed … but men hurling away their weapons and running for the stairs, all along the battlements. It was the same to her right – Sarphardi, militia, even guardsmen, all had caught the terror. The staircases were jammed, men fought to flee, stumbled, fell. Some were crushed, others used the bodies of their comrades to slide to the ground. None stopped there, but sprinted off down the streets, to disappear into the empty stores and warehouses.

There was nothing she could do. The wall had fallen. So there was but one hope now – that she could reach the reserve marching to them, and divert them to the only place a stand might yet be made: Agueros. Hold that hill, and hope that Olankios had broken the invaders at the port, and would march then to their relief.

When she'd arrived at the Sanctum from the southern wall, Roxanna had gone to the stables, saddled Shadowfire herself, then ridden him to her command. He was tethered just behind the main gate – which, even as she reached him, was thumped with a dozen heavy axes. Ladders clattered into the crenels above. The first of the enemy appeared and, unopposed, leaped over, shrieking, stabbing any of the wounded left behind. Stabbing the dead too, just in case.

Roxanna threw herself onto her horse's back. But the animal, terrified by screams and flames, bucked, nearly threw her. For a moment, she lost the stirrups, had to fight to get the stallion under control. She'd just planted his four hooves on the ground when three huge warriors, their bodies swathed in bearskins with their own heads under the beasts' jaws, ran at her, shouting. She let Shadowfire have his head, and the stallion again rose onto two hooves, front ones dashing the air. The warriors ducked and weaved about her. She snatched for a javelin in its sheath by her leg, missed it, grabbed another, was too off balance to throw it, so jabbed it like a spear into one man's face. He fell, a second man was caught by a flailing hoof and reeled back, but the third stepped away, and raised his bow.

As the front hooves hit the ground again, Roxanna leaned

back and threw, just as the man shot. Arrow passed javelin. Both found their mark.

Roxanna screamed, as the arrow passed through her arm – though the archer took her javelin in his right eye. Yelping, Roxanna got one foot into a stirrup, kicked hard, and used thigh and reins to guide Shadowfire away. He went, as ever, into an instant gallop and she managed to cling on, despite the agony in her left biceps. The shrieks, cries of triumph and despair, faded fast behind her. Soon the only sound came from the steel of horseshoes on cobblestones, and her moaning, as she fled one lost cause in search of another.

They had repelled three assaults. The first wave had been ascrami, reluctant warriors, and their bodies lay in heaps beneath the sea walls. The second wave had followed a barrage from the ships, more Bows of Mavros than had ever been assembled in one place, many shooting flaming bolts with glass jars of oil attached, exploding on impact. Many were aimed high, over the walls, and Ferros had had to take dozens of warriors to fight the fires that burned the port warehouses and threatened to cut off their retreat, should they need to make it. He'd succeeded, though much still smouldered. But when he returned to the gate tower he found that the second assault had only just been beaten back – and that the general was wounded.

'I'd tell you it was nothing,' gasped Olankios, 'but I'd be lying.'

He grimaced as he raised himself a little off the cot, in the sentry room at the tower's rear, showing the bloodied bandages wound about his middle, and Ferros saw both where the injury was, and that the stain was still spreading. The general confirmed his fears. 'Gut shot,' he moaned as he fell back down. 'The doctor here,' he nodded his head to a man in healer's robes in the corner, 'wants to give me the poppy, send me back to

Agueros. But I cannot leave my post here – besides, I think the journey would kill me.' A faint smile came. 'I was killed at Balbek, you know. Then again aboard ship. Dying's hard for a man of my years.'

Ferros kneeled by the bed. 'Sir, could you not—?'

Their eyes met. Both men knew what Ferros was asking. It was the very thing that Olankios had been going to tell Ferros the first time he died and was reborn, at Balbek. Of the gift of possession. But the general just shook his head, even that little movement causing a groan to escape his lips. 'I never have.'

'You have not? Why?'

'It always seemed to me,' he closed his eyes, 'an abomination.' He opened them again, looked into Ferros's. 'You have?'

'I … I have. I was forced to. Like you I thought …' Ferros looked away to a wall, seeing the Horse Lords he'd killed that first time – and Pershak, he would never forget his name, who he'd possessed, bleeding out on the ground next to him. 'But once you have it's …'

Again he ran out of words. Olankios nodded, and with difficulty reached out a hand and laid it on Ferros's forearm. 'Irresistible? That's what I understood. It is why I always … resisted.' A spasm shook him, and he bit his lip till the blood ran, then focused with new urgency. 'Others feel like us, lad. Immortality does not have to be this … curse. Find those who think like you. Lead them. I will—'

War trumpets drowned his words. They were not of Corinthium. Cries followed that were. 'They come again! They come!'

Olankios tried to rise, couldn't. 'No,' he said, 'I'm done. It's you, Ferros. Under the cot. My baton of office. Take it.' That little smile came again. 'You know, I said to the Lady Roxanna only today, that I would rather have you here than five hundred guardsmen. I got my wish.'

'General, Roxanna is—' But Olankios no longer heard him. He'd lain back down and closed his eyes. Ferros felt for a pulse, found none. 'Good fortune for the journey,' he murmured, then reached under the cot and pulled out the general's baton of office. Looked for a moment at the bronze eagle at its tip, clutching lightning bolts. Stood, and walked out into the air.

They were different from those who'd come before, the warriors now in ranks upon the beach. If the first wave had been reluctant soldiers, wheat for the scythers of Corinthium, and the second wave the tribes, horsemen who had the courage but not their horses, this third wave was made up of the strongest warriors of Saghaz-a, who'd journeyed from their far-off lands, through the mountains, across the Great Sea. Ferros knew that they'd fought each other for centuries, these Seafarers, Huntresses, Horse Lords and Warrior Monks. Each was hardened from generations of constant war. Now all were united under the banner of 'the One'. And that banner flew above them now, right in the centre of the host. White, fringed in gold, surrounding a single, all-seeing black eye.

Though united, the ranks were divided by tribe. The first rank were the Seafarers, and Ferros noted the weapons they carried, the small round shields, the short, thick-bladed swords – butcher's cleavers, truly, and perfect for close combat on a deck. Behind these came the Horse Lords, dismounted here – though there were one hundred mounts held by grooms at the rear of the host. Then, the smallest number of them, thirty or so Monks in their black robes with their long spears that had a scythe blade, hammer and hook at their tips. The last rank were Huntresses, and he knew they were at the rear not because they were lesser warriors, nor fearful, but because their greatest skill was with the bow.

He looked from the silent enemy to his equally silent command. Spread along the walls were the best of the city's militias, which was not saying much in terms of their training. He'd interspersed squads of imperial guardsmen to keep courage up, keep them on the walls. Yet it was in the tower where he stood that he was surrounded by the very best, men he'd been delighted to find when he first arrived: twenty of the Ninth Balbek Riders, his own regiment. Twenty left of one hundred. Though none were as close to him as Ashtan had been, these were still the comrades he'd got drunk with in taverns, competed with at lance and bow, who he'd ridden thigh to thigh with into battle. Demetrios, Haldan, Eurokos, Glaman … all of them. They'd escaped the fall of their city and now they would fight for him, their standard, their general, their empire, as they always had. Die for it, if necessary.

It was the subject of the general that Demetrios addressed, when Ferros stepped in beside him. 'Olankios?' the old veteran asked.

'He sleeps. Regaining his strength to rejoin us here.'

The man glanced down, saw the baton, nodded at it. 'And for now?'

'For now …' Ferros jumped up on a crenel, swaying there for a moment – Mavros, what if he'd fallen? – then gave a shout of 'Corinthium!' and waved the baton each way. All along the walls, men growled. He jumped down, and pointed with his chin to the enemy, spread out along the wooden docks and jetties one hundred paces away. 'How long have they been standing like that?'

'Not long. Boats kept landing them, and others marched in from the cobbs. They've only just separated into their ranks.' The man reached up and ran a finger under his helmet's chinstrap. 'We've left them alone, as you commanded.'

He'd ordered that no one shot. Most of their arrows had been spent on the previous two assaults. Their three Bows of Mavros had but two bolts apiece. But he'd ordered that all bodies be scrounged for what had killed them, all shafts that had found wood, or skittered off stone, to be gathered and hammered out, or new bone tips fitted. He had … not enough. But some. Some that could be spared to perhaps provoke the enemy into coming a little before they were fully ready.

He had his own bow, as did the rest of the Balbek Riders. All along the walls, only the champions of city or guard had been issued with bows. He cupped his hands over his mouth. 'Archers of Corinthium,' he shouted. 'Three arrows. On my command!' He repeated it the other way then raised his own bow, nocked an arrow, lifted the weapon, drew string to his ear. 'Now!' he bellowed, as he released.

His arrow preceded three score others. No aiming was required, only the parabola calculated. He was always good at that, and though he did not look to see, being occupied with nocking and drawing again, he knew by the cries of warning and then of pain that he and many of the others had struck true.

Sixty more arrows flew. Sixty more. It did provoke, as he had hoped. Arrows flew back, many hundreds. He assumed it was the Huntresses but did not look to see, hunched down as he was behind the battlements while the steel-and-bone rain fell. Almost none found targets in the sheltering men.

The downpour slackened, then ceased. He raised his head to peer through a stone gap. Provoked, the enemy was indeed coming.

He did not need to cry the call to arms. Along the length of the walls, archers slung their bows, and picked up their blades. Then everyone stood up.

There were gaps in the ranks that were running forward and as soon as the rear rank cleared the docks, Ferros could see the damage done – perhaps a hundred bodies on the ground, some moving, most not. But at least a thousand ran forward towards his five hundred, shouting as they came, that same simple word again and again.

'One! One!'

He noticed now what he hadn't before – the Four Tribes had others in their ranks, and along the length of them. Men in loincloths, tribesmen perhaps, or slaves. Scores of them anyway, and each group of six carrying long ladders. Then he also noticed that right in the centre of the charging enemy, twenty men pushed a wheeled battering ram. 'Bows of Mavros!' he yelled each way, the order needing to be passed in shouts down the walls to overcome the tumult, already so great. It was Olankios who'd anticipated this part of the assault and had a small red flag on a stick shoved into the gravel fifty paces before the gate, so small few who were not looking for it would see it.

The men who operated the great bows needed no further orders from him. When the front rank of screaming Seafarers reached the flag, the three Bows of Mavros shot – and the battering ram exploded, scattering splinters that killed or maimed dozens.

It was a brief triumph, briefly acknowledged with cheers from the defenders. Most of the enemy could not have seen it, occupied as they were by running on to reach the wall. Scores of ladders slapped down along its length.

Three ladders were on the tower itself, at the crenellations. With Demetrios and Haldan, Ferros seized the prepared ash staves, their ends carved into splayed, split hooks. He guided the hooks onto a rung – not the top one, he knew that those could too easily snap. Four down, and just visible through the gap. Laying the poles along the stone, the three men bent their knees, gripped tight and pushed forward.

It took a moment, the weight of all those climbing hard to shift. Slowly, slowly then suddenly quicker, quicker the ladder rose, went upright, fell away. He heard the cries, swiftly drowned out by others – along the tower, an ash pole had snapped, a ladder was set, and a Seafarer stood in the gap of stone, cutting down with his cleaver.

A thrust of spear, and the man fell back, screaming. But another was in his place immediately, a Horse Lord with his long curved sword. The first Rider who ran at him fell to it. The second had his thrust turned aside with the shield and only just ducked the blow that countered him. There were half a dozen men between Ferros and the threat but he could still reach him. Drawing a javelin from the quiver on his back, he put it through the Horse Lord's throat.

The man who came next was all in black, and used the scythe-blade of his spear to clear a gap on the platform into which he leaped. He was a blur of movement, shaft as deadly as the steel, and three men fell to wood and metal.

Ferros drew a second javelin, threw but it was as if the man had a dozen eyes, could see everywhere. He dodged sword and missile simultaneously, spun and struck. More ladders had slapped down to join the first, Seafarers in their feathered finery at two of them, a black robe at the third. The defenders were too distracted by the one, still-whirling monk.

Gripping his sword again, Ferros charged. Ducked the swung wood, which would have stove in his head, dodged the thrust point that nearly impaled him. The hook on the back of the weapon snagged the edge of his breastplate and the monk drew him hard in ... exactly where he wanted to go. Using the momentum, he somersaulted along the ground, rolled up and thrust his sword into the man's chest. Such was the force of his arrival his weapon went all the way through.

If a man whose eyes were entirely black could look surprised, he did. He was dead before he fell. Ferros put his foot on the monk's chest and drew out his sword. Raised it over his head on guard immediately. But no other attacked him. Indeed the attackers were gone, the enemies swept from the walls, the last ladder being pushed out and away even as he looked.

'Clear them away! Clear them!' he cried, waving his sword at his own fallen, the dying and the dead. Obeyed, he ran left, for the nearest side of the tower, looked the length of the walls. They had held; he could see ladders smashed on the ground amid splayed and crumpled bodies. Some men of Corinthium were among them, and more were wounded or dead on the parapets. But the enemy was running back to regroup, and those of the city jeered at them as they fled.

Maybe we can do this, Ferros thought, turning to cross to the other, western side. Maybe.

An arrow passed a hand's breadth from his ear. Shot from the wall just below him. He ducked, but one swift glance had told him enough – the western wall had dissolved into a series of isolated combats. Corinthians still fought there – but the enemy was up, and more of them were arriving by the moment.

He went to the front again, peered through a gap. Where they had failed, the enemy were retreating. Or repositioning – for a breach was a breach, and the western wall, however hard the defenders might still be fighting, was about to fall to overwhelming numbers.

He looked at his men, his closest comrades. Five of his Riders were dead. Fifteen were left, though some had taken wounds. He could stay where he was and die with them. Or he could try to get them and as many other soldiers out, to fight again elsewhere.

Agueros, he thought. The last stand will be at the Sanctum.

The western wall was gone. There was nothing he could do for the men upon it. But they could help him save the rest by their sacrifice. 'Demetrios,' he called. The man, like Ferros himself, was an army orphan, following the flags since he was six. Like Ferros, he'd started out as a bugler, and had retained the skill. 'Sound the retreat. But only out to the eastern wall.'

'The western men?'

Ferros shook his head, and the man nodded, went to the left side of the tower, raised brass to lips and blew.

There was nothing more that Ferros could do. 'Ninth Balbek to me!' he shouted and led them to the back of the tower, waited till all had preceded him down the stairs before bending to lift a groaning Glaman. With the man's arm over his neck, he took the stairs, even as another ladder slapped onto stone behind him.

His men were already mounted by the time he reached them. To the east, those who could run were heading into the city. From the west still came the sounds of battle. It killed him that he could not stand and fight with his command. Yet all he would do here was die with them, and there was another fight ahead.

Heeling his mount's flanks, he led the last of the Ninth Balbek Riders towards Agueros.

It had been easy for Lara to arrive in Agueros the first time. The last stop of the Heaven Road was right in the centre of the citadel, after all. But once she'd delivered her messages – her duty as the young messenger she'd possessed and one that enabled her to reach the centre of the Sanctum – she had swiftly discovered that her quarry was not there. She learned from a servant that Roxanna had paused only long enough to collect a horse, then ridden to take command at the northern wall.

Getting in a second time was not easy at all. Because, as she'd found out when she'd journeyed there, still in pursuit, that wall had fallen, and the Wattenwolden were looting and slaughtering their way ever closer. Most of the inhabitants of the city's upper hills were now trying to gain access to the seventh and northernmost, all at once. Thousands crammed the main gate, hundreds were at each of the smaller ones – Lara knew, she'd tried them all; tried to force her way through, shouting that she was an imperial messenger on Sanctum business, but few gave way for her, many cursed her, and she'd had to give up. Then she noticed that the Heaven Road was still moving, and she made her way through the mobs and ran down to the next hill, Perilinos, and its platform.

Every basket coming from the south had five in it when it should only have three, each journeyer's face the same mask of terror, eyes forever cast back whence they'd fled. Night had fully come now, and a light rain was falling. It was doing little to diminish the fires that blossomed in every district of the city south of where she waited.

Another full basket passed, with another hollow-eyed load. She'd risen again as it came, lay down when it passed. Because what was disturbing her most was a restlessness within. Possessions always fought back, from the moment when they were taken, and this one was young and strong. It had been weeks since she'd last possessed someone and, rested, she'd have kept him for a day at least. But she was tired from the day and her quest, and she did not know how much longer she could go on. It was like when she was within the doctor back in Tarfona. She did not want suddenly to become herself again.

Another basket approached. She rose to her knees, peered. Four! Four men in it, though all of them large. Her young man was large too, but four meant some space, however small. She would force her way in. She had to. With all the fires, the Heaven Road could not stay open much longer, surely?

The basket clattered through the last stanchion. She made ready to leap, staggered, nearly tumbled off the platform … because a young man was suddenly sprawled below her and she was swaying above him.

It was as if he'd awoken from a deep sleep. 'What?' he mumbled, reaching up, grasping her hand. 'Who?'

All of those who approached had their faces turned away, were staring back at the burning city. As the basket came level, she wrenched herself from the messenger's grasp, and hurled herself into it. It swayed wildly, the occupants shrieked and cursed her, she was lying with her nose on the floor and her ankles in the air – but she was aboard. Once she'd righted herself, and the men had left their cursing, she looked back. The young man – Bratan – was standing, staring after. She wished him well. He had fallen in love for the first time with a goldsmith's daughter. He loved as she remembered Ferros once loving her. She hoped that, despite it all, Bratan would find his love again.

'Where have you come from?' she asked one of the men who'd help right her, who all wore the uniform of the imperial guard.

'The port,' he grunted.

Ferros, she thought. 'Does it hold?'

'Hold?' The soldier gave a short, disgusted bark of a laugh. 'It's gone, like everywhere else. We were lucky to get out with our lives.'

It turned out to be the final basket. When it reached the platform in Agueros, just as she, the last passenger, was stepping out, the ropes on which it travelled suddenly went slack. With an almost human sigh, the machinery ceased moving.

From the platform hill, she could see down into all of Agueros. The rain was less here and the night well lit by torches. Every road of the citadel stirred with armed men, while vast hosts squeezed the main gates, beseeching entrance. Few were admitted.

Almost directly below where she stood was the most beautiful building there – the Sanctum on the Hill. The heart of

Immortals' Corinthium blazed with light and, like a heart, the red stones appeared to pulse, as if blood flowed through them. Lara knew that whatever was being decided for the empire would be decided there.

She would be there.

Guards were on every door. She knew she would not be admitted, dressed in the rags she'd worn ever since her capture in Tarfona. But she knew one other way in, that perhaps would be less guarded.

Circling, she made her way to the stables.

There were three entrances to it – a side one for servants to come and go, the main one on the street, and the one that led back into the heart of the complex. That last was the way she'd been taken on her very first visit, all those months ago. She could enter the inner Sanctum from the room above the kitchens.

She moved down corridors and through the servants' quarters, all eerily deserted, as if someone had just stepped out to take some air. In the kitchen, there was even a pot still bubbling over the fire. The liquid in it was almost gone, the pot about to scorch and, without thinking, she found a thick towel and swung the pot from the rack. Heat came through the towel. She put it hastily down, wiped her hand on her breeches and then walked into the yard.

This was the place where she'd first seen them together. Ferros and Roxanna. Had been able to tell, in a moment, that if they had not already made love, then they were on the brink of it. There was heat between them, as they stood between horses that also steamed. Ferros was wet, he'd ridden into a river. He quivered as he leaned into the bitch queen of Corinthium and Lara had seen that it was not only from the cold.

She shook her head clear of memories, and listened. This was a back way into the Sanctum but even so, people knew of it and were trying to get in. There was a constant hammering on the tall wooden gates, and pleading through the wood. Three soldiers stood in the small gate tower looking down, nervously clutching their spears. The walls were high and sheer, and their tops, covered in broken shards of glass, curved outwards. Still she was sure that desperate people would find a way to climb them, or break through, soon enough.

She'd just reached the door that led into the main buildings, was about to go through it, when she heard a yelp of pain from the farrier's room; a woman's voice. Curious, she stepped to the entrance.

The room was bright with light from a lamp and the banked fire. At its centre, in front of the anvil, a man stood, a blacksmith by his apron and sooted face, holding metal tongs. Seated before him was a woman.

Roxanna.

Lara took a short, sharp breath as the blacksmith spoke. 'My ... my lady, I am sorry to cause you pain. I only tend animals. I ...' He broke off, as the distinct sound of something being driven into the gates reverberated through the room. 'Let us go into the Sanctum, away from—' He gestured outside. 'Get help. Get you proper help.'

'Listen, you fool,' Roxanna hissed. 'The Sanctum is a trap from which there will be no escape. Here, with the horses, here is the only chance to get away. But I can't ride far like this. So do it, and stop blubbing like a baby.'

Lara shifted slightly to get a clearer view. Now she saw that Roxanna had one arm across the iron block – and that there was an arrow through it. 'Do it!' Roxanna screamed, rising to slap the man hard across his face. 'Do it!'

Sobbing, the man gripped the arrow with his tongs, just below its head. Then he put his foot against the block. Still, he did not pull.

'I'll do it, if he won't.'

She had spoken softly. But the man jumped, dropped the tongs, reeled round. Roxanna cried out, then focused her glazed eyes. 'You,' she said.

There was silence between them all – and then an upsurge of noise from beyond the room – wood cracking, men screaming, a bugle calling. The blacksmith looked at them both, turned and ran past Lara out the door.

The two women stared at each other. Roxanna's surprise showed no more than in the slight rising of one beautifully teased eyebrow. When she spoke, her voice was calm, despite her clear pain. 'I wondered if you'd survived.'

'I told you we'd meet again.' Lara took a step in as she spoke. 'On that ship leaving Tarfona.'

'You did. You also said something else. That Ferros was yours. That you would kill me for him one day.' Roxanna took her arm off the anvil, winced. 'Is this the day?'

'It's as good as any other.' Lara took another step. She was just four paces away now. 'But with this difference. I do not kill you for Ferros. I am not sure he is mine any longer, so he doesn't matter.' She drew the long-bladed dagger from the sheath at her hip. 'No,' she added, stepping one of those paces closer, 'now I am going to kill you for myself.'

Roxanna stood. Her left arm, with the arrow through it, hung at her side. She gestured to it with her right hand. 'With me like this? It doesn't give me much of a chance.'

'More chance than you gave me when you stood at the altar and slit my throat.'

Roxanna nodded. She even smiled. 'True. Though of course if I'd known that I was making another immortal—' She broke off. 'So ... Lara. You have experienced some of the pleasures of the gift, I have no doubt. So why this? Instead, why not let me guide you ... to more?' She stepped around the anvil, closer.

Still smiling. 'Why fight? Why not join us? Corinthium has much to offer one who has proved herself so ... capable.'

'Corinthium has nothing left to offer.' Lara tipped her head to the tumult, the bugle, the shouting, the smashing of wood on wood. 'Because Corinthium has fallen.'

'Not quite yet. You and I could still get away.' She took another step. They were just two paces apart now. 'Think of it, Lara. You and me. Two immortal queens.' Her voice dropped to a husk. 'You believe you discovered real passion in Ferros's arms? Wait until you come into mine.'

Lara stared for a moment, then laughed. 'Oh, you are very good. And me just a simple provincial girl.' She shook her head. 'No. I prefer my way. This way.'

She flicked the knife. Roxanna looked at it. 'Are you any good with that?' she asked softly.

'I have learned a few things.' She looked down. 'There was a sailor I possessed, on the ship to Cuerdo—'

It was as far as she got, before Roxanna leaped.

Only the knife fighter's instinct, inherited from that sailor, saved her life – at the cost of her ear. Roxanna's weapon, snatched out from the sheath at her right hip, with its long, thin blade, pierced her flesh, tore it. It was painful, but it was better than the eye where the strike had been aimed.

Lara threw herself to the side, just as the blade entered her. Felt – heard! – the rip of flesh before she somersaulted over the stable's earth floor, her movement halted by the anvil. Roxanna followed fast, dagger flipped in her hand, for the downward plunge. But Lara had her knees pulled up to her chest for the roll, and shot her legs out now, taking Roxanna's chest onto the soles of her feet. The dark face came close, the blade's tip closer, but it skittered off the anvil just above Lara's head, steel shrieking over iron. Gathering all her strength, Lara drew her knees in then shot her legs out, hurling Roxanna away. She crashed onto her back, driving herself backwards with her feet, then getting up on them, as Lara rose too.

Lara raised her left hand to her ear. It came away covered in blood. 'Well,' she said, 'aren't you the tricky one?' She wiped her fingers on her jerkin, then dropped into the knife fighter's stance, the right, weaponed hand thrust out above the right knee, left leg back, left hand with fingers splayed before her chest. Roxanna paralleled her, with the exception of her left arm, the arrow still through it, dangling at her side. 'Come on then,' Lara said, and darted close, flicking the point past the dark face. Roxanna swung just her head back, darted and flicked in her turn. Crouching, circling now this way, now that, moving in, leaping back, each had their eyes fixed on the other's. Both ignored the noise still rising, rising, beyond the stable doors.

Leaning onto his horse's neck, Ferros stared at the mob battering at the stable doors of Agueros. 'Again,' he said, and beside him Demetrios raised the bugle and blew another clarion blast.

It had as little effect as the previous time. The men and women had glanced up at the first call, then returned to their task of smashing in the gate. There were militiamen among the mob, and these were driving a thick pole, probably one of the ones that supported the Heaven Road, again and again into the wooden doors. They were not made for the treatment. No one had ever thought that an enemy would try to break in this way. It would not be long.

'Why not just wait?' Demetrios lowered the bugle. 'We want to get in, they are going to open the door for us.'

Ferros looked at the man. His own exhaustion was repeated in his comrade's face. 'And when the gates are down, what about those who follow?' He glanced back down the way they'd come. 'They will enter here too, and take any defence being made of the Sanctum in its rear.'

'With all respect, sir, I think any defence is fucked.' Demetrios leaned over and spat. 'If these who pursue us are anything to go by.' He shook his head. 'My advice? Ride on now, out to the north.'

Ferros looked back again. No one was coming. But that did not mean they were far behind. Some Horse Lords had caught up with them quite quickly once the port wall had fallen. There'd been running fights on every hill, the length of the Stradun. Only at the last hill, Perilinos, had they shaken them off, by ambush and a sudden charge. They'd killed the remaining ten Horse Lords, but lost five of their own in the doing of it, with two so badly wounded they could barely sit their mounts. He'd lost horses as well, and three of his men were doubled up. 'We can't ride on. With these exhausted mounts? We have to get into the stables. New mounts, hay for them. Supplies from the kitchens beyond—'

He broke off, as the noise from in front of them changed, as men shouted and, with a shriek of tortured wood and metal, the gates crashed in. He raised a hand, holding his men by him. When the last of the mob had run through the entrance – though many more were rushing up now from bolt holes up and down the street – he dropped his hand, and heeled his mount forward.

As they rode into the yard, the last of the invaders were already running into the buildings ahead. 'Demetrios, take three men and grab anything you can from the kitchens. Glaman, lay the wounded by the well here and see if you can staunch their blood – and your own. Haldan and Mikos, into the stables there. Saddle the best of what you find, and bring extra horses for provisions. Eurikos, take one other, go a little way down the hill, keep lookout.'

'Sir!' came the cries. Every man in the Ninth Balbek was

happy to obey one of their own – especially as they believed he had a plan to get them out.

But do I? he wondered, lowering the well bucket on its rope, pulling up a pailful, crouching to hold it to the lips of one of his wounded, a Sarphardi named Drakan. No more than a boy, he was of the same tribe, the same clan, as Ashtan, his old comrade. He looked like him too. Perhaps that was why Ferros had ridden back into a hopeless fray to extract him, when he'd fallen under a Horse Lord's hooves.

He drank himself, then passed the pail over to another man to refill. Forcing himself to rise – Mavros, but he was exhausted! – he crossed to the farrier's room. They would need spare horse-shoes and tack, rivets, saddles ... and hay, especially hay, if they were to escape the fall of the city. He'd made his peace with his planned desertion. When the front wall had yielded so easily he'd known that this was a lost fight. All that mattered now was survival, of those he cared for. His comrades and ...

He stopped. Can I leave though? he wondered. Without Lara? But how can I even find her in this madness?

Now that the gates were stoved in and the mob past, it was almost quiet – though there was a distant hum under everything, distant wails of despair. Closer to, though, he realised that there were different sounds – grunts of exertion, shuffling feet ... finally the snick of steel on steel.

Someone was fighting in the shadows ahead. Drawing his sword again, he stepped into the farrier's room.

It took a moment for his eyes to adjust to the light there, for night had fully fallen outside, the room only lit by a small lamp and the forge's fire. It took a longer moment to believe what he was seeing – all his wishes, all his hopes, all his nightmares, gathered before him. The two women who pulled him apart were together – and they were fighting. Even as he understood he saw Lara make a leap forward and lunge; saw Roxanna

276

stagger back into the anvil and only just parry the thrust; noted too, the arrow in her dangling arm.

He found his voice. 'Stop this,' he yelled.

Only one obeyed him. Only one turned to him. 'Ferros,' Lara said.

Before, distraction had cost her an ear. Now it cost her the fight, and then her life. Because Roxanna did not obey, did not look; just pushed herself off the anvil and drove her knife deep into Lara's heart.

'No!' screamed Ferros, running forward, catching the body before she fell. There was light in her eyes, confusion, fury before all these were swept away by death. She slumped, and he laid her gently down, then rose.

Roxanna had a wild triumph in her eyes. She'd left her dagger in Lara's chest and she raised her free hand to the ceiling. 'She tried to kill me first, Ferros. I did not want it but she—'

He stopped her words, closed her throat as he grabbed her by it, shoving her back against the wall. 'And I am going to kill you!' he screamed.

She placed her hand on his wrist, pulled him away enough to speak. 'Are you? Really kill me? Cut off my head? Throw my body in the forge fire?' She coughed a laugh. 'You will not, and you know it. As you know that she is not dead. Not yet.'

He'd forgotten. How was he expected to remember, when all the rest of life was as normal? He was a soldier and he fought. He let Roxanna go, stepped back, lowered himself to the ground beside Lara's body. 'You are right,' he said, taking her head into his lap, closing the staring, quizzical eyes. 'I will wait till she awakes.'

'Fool!' Roxanna yelled. 'Leave her! You have a city to fight for. An empire. Your fellow immortals.' Her voice softened. 'Me.'

He looked up at her. Everything he'd felt for her, all his

desire, had gone. 'No, lady,' he replied. 'The time has come when I fight for no one but my brothers and her.'

Roxanna opened her mouth to reply – but at that moment Eurikos rushed in, shouting, 'Sir! Soldiers approaching down the street.'

'Horse Lords?'

'Wattenwolden.'

'How many?'

The man licked his lips. 'Too many for us.'

'Go help with the horses. Call Demetrios from the kitchens. Whatever he has will have to be enough.' The man rushed out, and Ferros looked up again at Roxanna. 'Haven't you got an empire to save?'

She ran her tongue over her cracked lips. 'We will meet again, my lover. Have no fear of that.'

Without another word, she left. He stood, bent, hesitated ... then pulled the dagger from Lara's chest. Dropping it, he lifted her, and walked into the yard.

His men were already in their saddles, some with wounded comrades before them. Demetrios held a fresh horse for him. Ferros gave Lara's body to his comrade, mounted, reached down. As Demetrios handed her up, the soldier looked into her face. 'But she's ... she's dead, isn't she?'

Ferros took her, held her across his body with one hand, taking his reins into the other. 'Not for long,' he said, then put his heels into his horse's flanks.

They rode from the yard, just as three dozen Wattenwolden ran screaming towards them up the street. They outdistanced them in moments and Ferros led the last of the Ninth Balbek Riders through the broken northern gates, away from the fall of an empire.

*

Above the Chamber of Debate, through a secret viewing slit that her father had installed to spy on proceedings, Roxanna watched the deaths of the last Corinthian immortals.

After the final onslaught, when the combined force of tribesmen, Horse Lords, Huntresses, Seafarers and Monks had burst through the very last of the defences, there had been a great massacre. Those few who survived it were brought to the Chamber, to join those who'd already fled there. These were mostly immortals, gathered in desperation in what they thought could be a last refuge. She recognised most of them. Living so many years you got to know everyone, after all.

There were some missing. Or perhaps not. Because ordinary people had fled there too. She wondered who in the Chamber were truly mortals, and who *contained* her brothers and sisters who had sought one last hiding place – within someone else.

It did not help them. When the sounds of combat, the shrieks of the dying, finally ceased, two masked men, dressed all in black, came in. She knew who they were. Streone would always find it hard to conceal his bulk. While the other she knew, by his height and shape, by the way he walked, was her husband.

Makron.

Servants accompanied them, carrying chains. There were also five big men, each one bearing the huge, heavy sword used for decapitation. These five wore blindfolds, though she could tell that they could see through them by how they moved. So their eyes would be hidden from those in the room, the immortals in the room. They could not be possessed.

It was obvious what the two masked immortals were doing. They would stop before a soldier, or a servant, or a prostitute. They would raise their mask, stare into that person's eyes. If they possessed the person, vanished into them, they reappeared a moment later, alongside the one who'd been possessed, who staggered as if drunk before being shackled, led away. If they looked and did not enter – well, they had found someone already possessed. The hiding immortal was ordered out, and another dazed mortal dragged away.

They did not have to do that many times. One thing you learn if you live a long time, Roxanna thought, as the last immortal reappeared, is when the game is up.

Soon only immortals stood in the Chamber of Debate. And, of course, the blindfolded men with swords who, on another command, began using them straight away.

Roxanna watched the first few heads lopped. Then she walked away, to make her own arrangements. Climbed to her room in the tower. To a good place to die.

She looked around it again. The structure, of course, had remained the same, those eight walls. But it had seen many changes, as fashions came and went over the centuries. As she changed. She'd delighted in what every new conquest of empire had brought in. For twenty years the room had resembled the inside of an oasis pavilion in the deserts of Xan. A hundred years later it had looked for a time like a Wattenwolden frontier fort – if those foresters were to use gold instead of pig iron, silk instead of yak wool. Yet, after all the fads, she truly preferred it as it had been for the last century – simple, stark even, each piece in it the most perfect example of its craft, of wood, metal, fresco and weave.

She sat on the bed, ran her hand over its emerald coverlet. The love-making it, and its predecessors, had witnessed! From Chiron, her very first lover, through all the men and women since to ... Ferros, the last to take pleasure with her there.

'Ferros,' she murmured, rising, moving to the balcony, placing her palms upon the balustrade. Her left arm twinged at the movement but the arrow had been removed three hours before so that she could hold a shield at the last stand, and she was already almost healed.

Ferros had bent her over this railing, facing out to the world, his hands around her throat. She thought she'd captured him then, with drugs and bewitchment, and a type of love-making that he'd never known; bound him to her. She'd revelled in him, his youth, his strength, even the conflict within him. Relished the challenge he presented, a hawk to be trained to her hand. He'd escaped her, though, gone back to ... that little bitch who'd dared to come for her. Who'd fought her, who she'd killed for a second time. But that was out there, beyond the slaughter in the Sanctum. Perhaps Ferros would get Lara out, to be born again.

Into what world? she wondered. It did not matter. One she would not live to see.

She was prepared. When she heard the men sent to kill her at the door, she would drink off the special draught she'd prepared, from the milk of the serang, the desert snake, the most poisonous venom in the world. It would kill any mortal in moments. It would kill the part of her that was mortal for a time. She would be dead for a day and a night if left alone. So when they cut off her head she would never know it.

There! It was the first, distant footfall at the bottom of the tower's spiral staircase, her killers beginning the long climb. She moved back into the room, to the side table, where the vial stood. Lifted it – and was surprised to see her hand shaking. How many times had she died over her three centuries of life? Five, each rebirth an agony. Now there would be ... what? She had been a priestess of Simbala in her time. She had mouthed all the rituals – but she had never believed them; never thought that the paradise others envisioned to lessen their mortal load awaited her. Still, she thought, smiling slightly as she raised the glass, I am prepared to be wrong.

The footsteps halted outside her door. She hadn't locked it, hadn't seen the point. Yet she did not drink. I have never turned away from death before, she thought. So this last time I'll look my executioner in the eye, to show him how little I care.

The rolled iron hoop turned, the door swung in… and Makron stepped into the room.

He was alone. No mask, and changed from the black that had concealed him in the Chamber into a simple white robe, with sandals on his feet. He was different from the smooth, shaven politician she remembered, had grown his hair long, together with a beard, both streaked in grey. Yet his eyes were the same iridescent blue they'd always been, in a skin now burned dark by desert suns. His voice was the same too. Not the one she'd heard in Cuerdocia when he was preaching to the Assani. The one he'd used to beguile her, to seduce her, all those years before. She had not heard its soft lilt since the morning he'd left this, their marital bed, to vanish into the southern suns.

Its tone was unchanged as well – deep, mockery-tinged. 'Essence of serang?' he said, pointing at the vial.

'Tinderos wine,' she replied. 'Have a sip.'

He laughed as he closed the door behind him. Leaned against it and stared at her for three deep breaths. Finally spoke. 'Wife,' he said.

'Husband,' she replied.

He took his lower lip between his teeth and regarded her for another long moment. 'You haven't changed,' he said at last. 'A little more blood than usual, perhaps.'

She looked down at herself. Her black leather garments had absorbed so much they looked like metal that had rusted. 'Well, I've killed a lot of people today.' She studied him. '*You* have changed.'

'I have.' He ran fingers up through his beard. 'Do you like it? The desert prophet look?'

'Not really.' She considered. 'You're very clean for a prophet, aren't you? And where's the blood?'

Makron looked down. 'Oh, I try to avoid blood. I was never as fond of shedding it as you. Besides,' he smiled, 'my allies are so good at it, and enjoy it so much, I leave it to them.'

'You were always good at getting other people to do what you don't like to.'

'It is called delegation.' He took a step into the room but stopped when she took a step back. He pointed at the vial still raised in her hand. 'Why don't you put that down?'

'I don't think so. You see, I do not plan to be dragged from this room and butchered by you – or rather by those you *delegate* to the task.' She shrugged. 'At least, I will not be aware of it when I am.'

'Why do you think that is going to happen?'

'Come, Makron. I know it is rare for either of us, but let us have a little honesty, here at the end.' When he did not reply, she continued. 'I am the last leader of Corinthium. You've killed all the others.'

He scratched his beard. 'Not all. There will be a few out there who escaped the Sanctum's fall. Fugitives now. They will be caught soon enough.' His eyes narrowed. 'I wondered – you didn't see that young desert warrior, did you? Ferros of Balbek? He escaped the prison where he was held. He and his woman.'

She shook her head. For some reason she decided not to tell him. To deny him that at least.

'I wondered if he'd made it here. He's quite a … remarkable young man.' He shrugged. 'No matter. He'll show up. Immortals seek each other out, don't they? And there are so few of us left now, eh?'

'There's Streone,' she said.

'Ah. No. There isn't.' Makron smiled. 'He served his purpose. But who would want to share power with that perfumed lump?'

'You killed him?'

283

'Had him killed. The very last. He was,' Makron looked up at the ceiling, 'quite surprised.'

Roxanna nodded. 'So only I remain to call you traitor.'

'Traitor?'

'What else would you call yourself? Not only a traitor to Corinthium, but to your own kind.'

He did not reply, just moved carefully around her to the table at the far wall, where tall bottles stood. He uncorked one, sniffed it, poured himself a glass, then took a sip. 'Ah,' he sighed, raising the glass to the lamplight. 'Lucan's reserved Tinderos wine. How I have missed you!' He turned back to her. 'Now, as for the title traitor, I do not own it.'

'What do you call yourself then?'

'I prefer … saviour.'

'Saviour? You always did have a grand idea of yourself, Makron. What exactly are you saving?'

'Corinthium itself.' He shot off the rest of the wine, then put down the glass. 'To be a traitor, you have to believe in something then betray it. For close to one hundred years I have not believed in what we created here, this … *game* of immortality. This life of pleasuring and corruption for a gaggle of stupid, self-indulgent men and women who are raised above the herd only by a random gift in the blood.' He tipped his head to her. 'Leaving out yourself, of course, my love.'

'Thank you.'

'And me. You see, you and I were always the only two meant for greater things.' His eyes glowed. 'You and I were never meant to be merely the first among equals.'

'Were we not? Let me see if I have this.' Roxanna set the vial of venom down on the edge of the table, still within easy reach. 'All this slaughter, this destruction? You've done all this … to conquer an empire you despise?'

'Oh no, my love.' He smiled. 'I've done all this for you.' He surprised her with that, for she could not help the slight gasp that came. So he added, laughing, 'Together with an empire to rule, of course. The two of us. Though it's not merely an empire now. There is a world out there so vast you cannot conceive of it.'

'I see. So your allies, busy sacking the city … you have not betrayed them? Do they know of your plan?'

'Hmm, no.' He coughed. 'They don't even know I am immortal. I thought it best to conceal that. Besides, they have other concerns. Other … beliefs.'

'The One?'

'The One.' He smiled again. 'How much do you know of that prophecy, I wonder? The power of it?' He whistled. 'When I learned how that power had united four peoples who had killed each other for centuries, well … I knew I had found what I'd been seeking for a hundred years and had not even realised.'

'Something to believe in?'

'Me? Ha! No, no,' he replied, laughing. 'We are the same in that, you and I. We believe in nothing … but ourselves.' He nodded. 'Something for *others* to believe in, though? To believe in utterly, believe in so deeply, so profoundly that they will kill anyone for that belief, and die themselves for it, happily?' He shook his head. 'Can you see the power in that? The power of an idea?'

'So the One is only an idea? This child does not exist?'

'He … she … *they*, as I have come to think of *them*, exist, though I have seen *them* only in visions. In smoke within the glass. But understand this – the child is not important. Only the idea of the child is. How that idea can be used.'

'How *you* can use it?'

'Yes.'

'I do understand.' Roxanna stepped around the table. His blue eyes glowed, lit from within. Not by fanaticism, she could see. By ambition. She had never minded that in a man. He had not truly had it before, when they were married. 'Tell me this,' she said. 'What is it you still fear?'

He frowned. Took a deep breath. 'You are right to guess at that, Roxanna. For not all of those who follow the One are fools. There are leaders, capable ones. There is a monk called Anazat. There is a world in the north called Midgarth, where some men and women – immortals too and one in particular – have the ability and the guile to resist. There is also an immortal from a land in the far west who has come here and whose ambitions are as great as my own.'

'So there are immortals in these other worlds too?'

'Yes. But different from us. Very different.'

'I see.' She ran her tongue over her lips, tasted the iron of blood there. 'So these are the obstacles yet to be overcome?'

'They are. With Corinthium just the first to be surmounted on the way to my desires.'

'Ours, Makron.' She stepped closer. 'Ours, husband.' She took his hand. 'Our obstacles. Our desires.'

He looked deeply into her eyes. 'So you are with me?'

She smiled. 'Did you truly think I would resist an offer to rule the whole world?'

'An offer from me? Perhaps. We did not part well, you and I.' He laughed. 'Now come, let's toast the compact with your father's Tinderos wine.'

He picked up a bottle. But she took it from him, set it down. 'There's a better way to celebrate than drinking, don't you think?' she said, and pulled him slowly down onto the bed.

Later, much later, when he was snoring softly beside her, Roxanna rose, and went to the balcony. Stood naked at the railing, enjoying the chill air on her skin, and gazed down on the corner of the city she could see, towards the east. It was the darkest hour of the night, dawn a way off, yet there *was* light

286

in the sky from a thousand fires. Moonlight too, for the rain clouds had cleared and the twin moons – Blue Revlas, Horned Saipha – which had met to make love a few months before were now heading opposite ways. Some lovers part, she thought. Some ... reunite.

There was not much sound – she thought she could hear soft weeping, though that could have been her fancy. Even ravishers and conquerors needed to sleep, after all.

She looked back at her husband. He had astounded her, she who was not often surprised, because over three hundred years she believed she had seen everything, learned the secrets and the capacities of every man and woman she'd ever met. It was quite the offer he'd made her – to rule, with him, the entire world. A world far bigger than she could ever have imagined.

She ran her hands up from between her legs, over her hips, her breasts, finally through her long hair, unbound as he'd commanded. She shook it, enjoyed the tickle of it on her shoulders. Feeling alive was a good thing, when she'd thought that by this time she'd be asleep in serang's embrace, or with her head rolling over a floor.

On the bed, Makron muttered something and turned over. She looked at him.

He'd *commanded* her to free her hair. She'd *obeyed*.

There is one thing better than ruling the world as its queen, she thought. And that is ... to rule it alone.

She crossed back to the bed, stared down at her husband. Though not yet, she thought. I have so much to learn. Of other worlds. Different kinds of immortals. New enemies.

Of the One.

She lay down, wrapped herself around him, to warm herself. He stirred, did not wake. She smiled, as she felt his heart beating under her hand.

II

West Meets East

The mist appeared from nothing, rolled over the land, swallow-ing the world, isolating the island. Moments before Anazat had been staring hard at the small cove on the opposite shore, will-ing a boat to depart from it. None had, and perhaps now none would. If the man he awaited was as superstitious as Ganator, now muttering curses and prayers behind him, he would wait for the grey to clear. 'Sirkesami's breath' was what the cursing Seafarer lord had called it, an exhalation of poisons from the mouth of a demon, which his people would never willingly sail into. Many of those who had unwillingly done so had vanished, it was said, to live for eternity as slaves in that witch's undersea palace.

Anazat felt like cursing too – but not mists. He wanted to curse such people as Ganator who professed the end of all superstitions in the redemption of 'the One' and yet continued pleading with their old gods and devils. Curse too all those who had thwarted his plans, old allies and new enemies. But if the Warrior Monks had eradicated most superstition, they had also ended the power of a curse. There were no gods to grant it, after all. There was only the One.

With a grunt of irritation, he began to breathe deeply, rhyth-mically, slowing the pace of thought in his mind. Fury would not hasten the man that circumstance had forced him to invite to this parley. If he came. Anazat suspected he would. He had been offered the world, after all.

This world anyway. This world of snow and mists. This barbarity. This ... Midgarth. Which should have fallen long before now, despite the local gods' spirited resistance. Would have, if not for the man he awaited, whose ambitions Anazat had underestimated to his cost. It was understandable – compared to the rationality of the Monks, the man was a savage. But it had been a failure of vision and he would never miscalculate the magnitude of this enemy's desires again. Indeed the best thing was to turn them into a weapon for the cause.

A high-pitched squeal of delight came from behind him, very different from the Seafarer's continuing prayers. The large man who made it lay in the long grass beside the small folding table Anazat had brought, to hold the seeing globe. Grey as ever swirled within it, shifting like the mists, as dense and impenetrable. As with the mists, he wished that the smoke within the glass would also clear. It was vital to what he planned for the meeting ahead. Vital too that he learned more of what was happening in the far south, at the city of Corinthium. But communication anywhere had been sporadic over the last few days. Maybe the mists had something to do with that. He had poured a large dose of the drug upon the glass, though he'd swathed his face to do so. He wanted to talk, not take Sirene's hand and be led along delirious paths. But his ally in the land, Peki Asarko, had swooped in to inhale deeply with all the desperation of the deprived. His own supply had run out months before, and Anazat had not renewed it.

He giggled again, and Anazat shuddered, wondering what unspeakable things he was doing in Sirene's dark corridors. He was needed – for now. Until reinforcements arrived, Peki Asarko's forces from the Lake of Souls made up close to one third of the army. Painted fanatics, they were all in thrall to their leader, who was one of the local gods himself, yet as unlike them as could be imagined. Where they were, in the main, tall, lean warriors, he was shaped like a ball, made of rolling, soft flesh. His *pleasures* were different too. He killed as they did, as was the Midgarth way, though not for glory. He killed so he could skin his dead, embalm them, reassemble them ... display them. Even Anazat, who knew much of cruelty and cared for little except his cause, had been revolted by what he'd seen in Peki Asarko's lodgehouse.

Something shifted in the glass. Smoke swirled apart, and a face appeared. It was the one he'd sought. 'Makron,' Anazat said, stepping close, bending. 'You are there.'

'I am.' The blue-eyed lord smiled. Despite all the times he'd used the glass, the Corinthian's eyes had darkened only a little. He did not inhale more than was necessary to see. It was another reason not to trust the renegade. Another traitor to his people, like Peki, whose head would be struck from his body as soon as his usefulness was past. But that time was not yet.

Something moved behind Makron. 'Are you alone, Makron?'

'I am not. I wished to introduce you to someone.' He shifted to the side, allowing another to lean in. 'This is Roxanna.'

She had skin the colour of darkwood, eyes a deep brown within it, black hair pulled back from a high forehead. Even with the distorting effect of the glass, and even though such a thing meant little to a monk such as he, Anazat could see that she was beautiful. He'd also heard of her.

Makron, though he'd resisted Sirene's full embrace, found wine harder to refuse. Anazat had got him drunk one night at the Keep, to learn all he could of the man he would use to take Corinthium. Part of his willingness to betray his empire was the cruelty that this woman – his wife, even though she was immortal and he was not – had practised on him. 'Lady,' Anazat said, tipping his head.

Makron must have sensed the disquiet. 'I know! We'd agreed that all immortals were to be killed in Corinthium. I decided to spare just one.' He reached and ran a finger down her cheek. 'Not just for myself. Once she learned of what we are doing she became a complete convert to our cause.'

'Praise the One,' Roxanna said, her brown eyes glittering.

'Praise him. Praise her,' Anazat responded. And knew, with all the certainty of a true believer, that she was not one. Another head to roll, he thought, but said, 'Any other immortals that survived?'

'We killed most in the sack of the town. Some hid and we've dug most of them out of their holes and finished them. There's probably a few more, but the city is still burning in parts, and there is chaos everywhere. Other things to deal with.' He turned, listened, nodded, turned back. 'But this lady reminds me that we have yet to find the man you let escape, Ferros of Balbek. Also his wife,' he looked to his side again and smiled, 'correct, my love, his *bitch* of a wife.'

He laughed, and Anazat was about to question further when the Seafarer, Ganator, called, 'The boat is coming.'

Anazat looked. The mist was breaking up as suddenly as it had come. Sun pierced the clouds, and grey tendrils now streamed from treetops like rising horse tails. He could see the rowboat. Three in it, as had been agreed, to meet the three that waited. He turned back. 'This Ferros is dangerous, that much I know. Find him, kill him, and this wife also. I must go.'

'Sir.' Makron bobbed a bow from his head. Yet the last thing Anazat heard before smoke again filled the glass was a woman's laugh.

I will kill you both, he thought, his black eyes contracting. And sooner rather than later. If he'd been in Corinthium, as had been planned, he would probably have killed Makron by now, his usefulness over. But he'd had to change all his careful plans ... because of this savage being rowed towards him now.

'Intitepe,' he muttered, turning away from the globe. He glanced down at Peki, still giggling in his dreams. 'Throw a bucket of lake water on him,' he said to Ganator. 'I need him awake.'

As the Lord of the Lake of Souls was roused, squealing, Anazat stepped to the water's edge to stare. He had heard others describe the God of Ometepe, was eager to see him for himself. Gauge what kind of man he was. Though someone who could decide to sail across the world with four hundred men to conquer it was already fearsome. And mad. Now Anazat would see if he could persuade him to turn both his fierceness and his madness to the cause of the One.

The One that was this man's child.

Layers within layers within layers, he thought.

The boat was about halfway to the island – still a way away – when Peki Asarko joined him. His long stringy hair was plastered to his face and the tunic that encased his corpulent body clung to his folds of flesh. 'You had to wake me, didn't you?' he grumbled. 'Sirene had taken me to a land where only children lived. We ran through fields, hand in hand—'

'I told you I did not want you to join her today. You disobeyed me.'

'Can you blame me?' Peki's already shrill voice rose higher in complaint. 'It's been three months since I did! You promised me you would bring me more and then denied her to me.'

Anazat took a breath so he did not bite the man's head off – another head, he reminded himself, that would roll in the dirt as soon as his usefulness was past. He made his voice calm. 'The man in the boat is both the obstacle and the solution to all we need to do here,' he said, taking the other's arm, 'so I am in great need of your help.'

The gentle tone soothed. Wringing some water from his locks, Peki looked ahead at the boat. 'This man is from a far-away land, you say? Where he is one of their gods?'

'Their only god,' the monk replied, 'for he has killed all the others.'

Peki stopped his squeezing. 'Just like I will do here,' he said.

'Just as *we* will do. But first we need to get this ... god upon our side.'

'Why?'

Anazat took another calming breath. He had explained this to the Midgarthian once already. 'Because he has brought four hundred warriors from his land. Worse, he has freed the slaves that were on the Seafarers' ships we sent and many have joined him. More want to.' He looked again. The boat was nearer, but the figures were still not clear to him. His mortal eyes were ageing. One man rowed, two sat shrouded in cloaks, their heads in hoods, that was all he could see. 'We have to finish your brother gods here and now, since we have them trapped. But we cannot do that if we have to fight this Intitepe as well.'

'I thought he wants to fight them too?'

'He does. Us, them, everyone. We need to persuade him to join us and fight only them.'

Peki nodded. 'A god, eh? And can he possess animals, like me?'

'I do not think so.' Anazat shrugged. 'My spies reported from Ometepe that it was not known to be a power of his.'

'Oh.' Peki licked his lips. 'Perhaps I could teach him.'

'Do not!' Anazat shouted, then lowered his voice. 'He is powerful enough as he is, don't you think?'

'Perhaps.' Peki thrust out his lower lip, pouting. 'And you say that I must serve him?'

'*Pretend* to. For now. He has come to conquer the world. We shall give him one. This one. Midgarth. You'll be at his side – ready to deal with him when we have what we want.'

'Deal with him? I will,' Peki murmured, running his fingers up the sheath that hung from his belt. In it was a curve-bladed skinning knife. And I have a place of honour already set aside where I will display him, he thought, and gave a little giggle.

The boat was closer. Anazat leaned, lowering his voice. 'Speaking of possession – do you sense any of your brother immortals nearby?'

'No. But that does not mean one is not here.' Peki shook his head. 'If you like I could—'

'Shh!' Anazat hissed as, with a last pull at the oars, the boat ran onto the strand.

Of the three men in it the rower stayed at the oars, one remained sitting while the third rose and stepped onto the beach. His face and head were still shrouded.

'Are you the Fire King of Ometepe?' Anazat asked.

'Not me,' said the man, throwing off the hood, revealing a wind-burned, much scarred face, with a single eye, a trimmed beard and long, curly brown hair.

'Sekantor the Savage! You traitor!' It was Ganator the Seafarer who spoke, lurching forward, reaching for the sword at his hip – which was not there, as had also been agreed.

'No traitor, Ganator the Grouchy.' Sekantor laughed, then pulled one of the soft, wide-brimmed hats the Seafarers favoured from beneath his cloak. It unfolded easily and he placed it on his head, uncurling the emerald and cerulean bird's feathers on its brim. 'Rather, loyalist of another cause.' He lifted both hands, palms up to the sky. 'Lord of all horizons,' he declaimed. 'Brother of Immortal Toluc, majesty of Lava! King of all Kings, ruler of all beings! Father of water, air and earth! God of Fire! Kneel before him, all who would not die! For he has come!

294

Intitepe!' He ended in a shout then reached back, offering a hand.

The other man stood in the boat, and threw off his cloak. Then, taking Sekantor's hand, he stepped from the boat. Anazat had sent spies to observe the aliens' camp. These had warned him – the few who'd returned – that the ruler of Ometepe demanded and received respect that was no different from worship. So he kneeled, pulling Peki Asarko down beside him. Ganator sank on his other side. All three gaped.

Intitepe appeared to be made of gold. Each slat of his wooden armour that fell from neck to hip was edged in it, his knee-length tunic was sewn with it, the tight-fitting helmet on his head was a slim, beaten piece of it, with cheek guards shaped like arrowheads curving into lips that were painted gold too. His brown skin had been dusted and glimmered bright, even in the pale daylight. His eyes were deep brown orbs set back in sockets that were like almonds. These eyes were fixed on Anazat.

He put his hand to the ground to push himself to his feet – and Sekantor, who'd also kneeled, tsked. 'No, no! You must await the Fire God's permission to rise. You are fortunate that he is not demanding you lie with your face in the earth so he can walk on you. I have told him of your ways, so he is prepared to be lenient ... this time.'

Beside him, Ganator growled something, feeling once more for his hip where a sword should lie. 'How much does he know? Of our ways, of our ... situation here?'

'On the voyage, I explained much of the world. It is very different here than in Ometepe. He finds the differences ... interesting. But if you mean the situation here, in Midgarth,' Sekantor smiled, 'he is willing to hear your opinion on it, and what you will offer him.'

'Does he speak any of the common tongue?'

'He does not need to speak to understand. He is Intitepe, God of all understandings, and can read men's minds in their eyes, know their hearts without words.'

Anazat looked again into Intitepe's eyes. They unnerved him, he who was never put out. He realised part of what that was – four hundred years of the certainty of power looked back. If the god knew a little of their worlds, Anazat knew something of his, from the monks he'd had hidden there for years, and from the reports that the Horse Lord Korshak and the Huntress Gistrane had brought back along with the One. How he had slain every other immortal in his land – the males at least – including his own father and his seven sons, to rule Ometepe alone. How that ambition had been enough – until he discovered the world to be far greater than he'd ever imagined. How he had only one fear – that death would find him at the hand of his own son. He had killed any male child born, thrown them living into the lava of his brother god, Toluc the volcano. Only one had escaped him. The One, who was neither daughter nor son, and both. The fear of that, as well as his ambition, had driven him across the wide world in a quest for his destiny.

Fear and desire. They were the twin tools Anazat had worked with all his life. Tools to be used now. 'May I show the Fire God something?'

Sekantor murmured, Intitepe grunted, and the Seafarer turned back. 'You may all rise.'

They did. Ambition ... and fear, Anazat thought, and spoke. Slowly, as Sekantor translated. It was clear that the Seafarer had worked hard to learn the language of Ometepe. But some things were harder, and Anazat spoke clearly, focusing on what a fire god might want, and need and even, perhaps, fear.

Otters were smart creatures, Luck had always found. He enjoyed possessing them, had spent much of his youth, the years before he was one hundred, exploring the rivers, lakes and fjords of Midgarth in a pelt. Their will was strong though, and he could never remain in one longer than a day, whereas he could stay in a less intelligent animal – a bear, say, or a stag – for twice that time. But he'd found and possessed this creature rather than the more obvious choice of a bird ... because of Peki Asarko. The traitor-immortal would be aware of any raven or even sparrow sitting in a tree, observing. Hidden in the reeds of the fore-shore, Luck knew he would have a better chance of watching and listening, for longer.

Observe and listen he did, tried not to react, simply absorb. But he could not help the occasional gasp, almost human, that slipped from the otter's mouth. So much had happened in the time since he'd caught the black-eyed assassin in Askaug. The fall of an empire. The rise of the One. The coming of that One from across the world, brought by their mother, Atisha, wait-ing now back in the bowl of Galahur with her baby, and with the others who also waited – Hovard, Freya, Bjorn, Stromvar, together with the last three hundred fighters of Midgarth, men and gods. Waiting to hear what Luck could tell them, of salva-tion or of doom.

He listened, as the men before him debated, wrangled, finally agreed. Their conclusion: nothing less than the division of the whole world. Not what he'd considered the world a year ago, this Midgarth. The world he now knew. The mighty empire of Corinthium to the south – now fallen, he heard them say. Ometepe in the west, the land of the Four Tribes in the east. Only in that vastness, those diverse peoples, did he hear a little hope in the division being discussed. Saw it too, in how the men spoke, rather than what they always said. He had studied the common tongue hard when he'd been a prisoner at the Keep and had learned much more from Atisha since their escape, and from the reading of the scrolls he'd stolen; but he did not understand all, missed some words. What he did not miss was the movement of their bodies, their faces. Saw when they lied, noted when they told half-truths. Also, Anazat would sometimes speak in Midgarth's tongue to Peki Asarko. It part filled in what he had lost before.

By the time the men were shaking hands – it appeared that gesture of acceptance was universal across the world, though Intitepe merely nodded – Luck knew all that he needed. Knew the doom of Midgarth. Also saw the glimmer of hope, in what had not been said.

Peki Asarko suddenly turned and looked to the reeds where he was hidden. The Lord of the Lake of Souls might have sensed his fellow god sooner if he was not still partly in the land of Sirene. Luck knew how hard it was to emerge from it. When Anazat had poured the drug onto the globe, it took all his willpower to remain where he was and not rush forward and join Peki Asarko in the inhalation of the sweet smoke. Three months since he'd last done so, at the Keep. Yet every day she called to him from her cloth prison in the corner of his room. He could not answer her, not yet. Yet deep within he doubted he would be able to resist for ever. No one who'd ever known her could. He'd looked away when the black-eyed monk poured a couple of drops later, to show Intitepe something that had the Fire God shouting in his own language at the sky before he calmed and listened again to the face talking from the glass, telling things that Sekantor translated.

When Peki rose and peered, Luck slipped back into the water. Powerful strokes with paw and tail drove him back across the lake. When he reached the shore, he lay on the bank for a few moments, panting, then left the beast, and lay there a few moments more as himself. Back on the island, the meeting was over, men and gods were back in boats, paddling for different landfalls.

He didn't have much time, to do all that must be done. Limping towards where he'd tethered his horse, he mounted and rode fast for the Midgarth camp.

Atisha sat high up in the bowl of Galahur, hunched in a cloak against the light rain, nursing Poum and listening. Though Luck had taught her some of the language of his land, it was little enough. She could glean the odd word. 'Fight' and 'flee' were among those spoken. Shouted, more often, as the conversation progressed. But she understood much, even if not in the words. Desperation is clear to those who have an eye for it. She had lived with it for so much of her recent life it was easy to recognise. See, too, how it gripped different people. Some it made fearful, some furious.

One of the furious was speaking – shouting – now to the crowd sitting below her on the slopes. There were about one hundred gods, she'd been told, and two hundred mortals. All that was left of the army of Midgarth, that had fought and harried the invaders of their land from Askaug all the way south to their great meeting place in the middle of the country. Many had died. Many mortals had fled to their homes to guard their own families, despite the urging of the leaders now standing on the grass mound at the great bowl's centre, to stay and fight as one.

From what she'd heard, in words she understood, the enemy forces were five times as strong. And had moved into all the valleys that led to Galahur, trapping them there.

Trapped, she thought, as one big man, Stromvar, stopped shouting and yielded the speaking staff to another, Hovard, who took it and began speaking more quietly but with no less intensity. From what Luck had told her, though the odds against them were great, they were helped in one thing – the enemy was also divided. It had given her a moment's joy to hear that, until he told her the reason for it, which had chilled further a heart already frozen with fear – the Fire God had crossed the sea.

Atisha knew why he had done so – his reason in her arms. Intitepe feared only one thing – the prophecy of his doom. He had come to end the threat as he had failed to in Ometepe. He had come to kill Poum.

Trapped, she thought again. Yet this time it was not fear that came with the word, but fury. All these shouting men. All these plans being made around her. And she, who had never felt helpless in her life before, who had always found a way to choose her own path? She was expected to sit still and listen to these men deciding her fate? Truly though, it was not even hers they were debating. It was the babe's she held. Poum, possible saviour of one united world. Poum, potential destroyer of a king. If she ... he ... *they* ... lived.

That, Atisha thought, is all that matters. Not to them, to these shouting, plotting men, here and elsewhere. To her. And she would be the one to decide.

The voice came from right beside her, though she had not heard any approach. 'May I hold the child? Ease your back?'

She turned. Luck was there. She smiled. 'My back is good. You wish to hold the child to ease yourself.'

He smiled too. 'It is true. In all this madness, a child makes some sense.'

'Even this child? This strange, different child?'

'Especially this one.' He still had his arms open and Atisha passed Poum to him. 'Hiya, little mouse,' he said, enfolding the baby, staring into the dark brown eyes. He pursed his lips, blew out air with a whirring noise. Poum reached up and grabbed at his mouth with a delighted giggle.

'Poum likes you,' Atisha said. 'You and me alone in the world.'

'That's because we have an understanding, Poum and I.' He blew again, changing the sound to a duck's call. Poum cried out again, and mashed a hand into his nose.

She watched them playing for a while, then spoke. 'You went somewhere. Did you find what you sought?'

'I did.'

'It is ... it is not good, I can sense it.'

Luck sighed. 'Today, maybe not. But in the future, perhaps.'

'Is not this the time to speak plain, Luck?' They had talked so much on their return journey to Midgarth, they used words of the common tongue and words of their own languages, mixed. 'Because I wonder if my baby and I will see another dawn.'

'You will, if I have anything to do with it. Many, many more.' He peered down into the bowl, where Hovard's reasoning, however thought through, was having little effect on the fractious crowd. 'After I go down there and speak to them.'

He looked to hand Poum back. Atisha didn't take her baby, just held out her hand. 'Wait! You must tell me first. I don't want to hear later what you decide for me. I decide!'

Her fierceness took the smile from his face and he nodded. So he told her swiftly, what he had seen, heard, understood while he had been in an otter's skin, and what he felt they needed to do now. And when he finished, she asked, 'And Intitepe? You say he saw in the seeing glass that revolt has spread throughout his land?'

'He did. Someone there told him. What made him angriest was that an old woman led the revolt.'

Atisha laughed, a rare thing. 'I'd wager that is Besema. She helped me escape the City of Women. She is a fighter.' She broke off, a frown returning. 'So he will return to crush it?'

'So he says. Though he will help the Four Tribes conquer here first then claim Midgarth as his second kingdom – to be ruled in his absence by Peki Asarko while he goes back and reconquers Ometepe. This is the promise that Anazat made him for his aid.'

'So he will not stay to kill my child?'

'That is his first goal. He said he would not leave without it.' He swung Poum up, dropped the baby suddenly, to another yelp of delight. 'So we will make sure that he does not.'

He reached the child out. Still she did not open her arms. 'How much of this will you speak down there on the mound?'

'Some, not all. Later all, to Hovard and Freya. They are the ones who will make it work once they see the sense of it.'

'Not the two shouting men?'

'Stromvar and Bjorn?' Luck smiled. 'No. But they have different skills that will help us too.'

'What skills?'

'They will fight unto death itself. Even a final death,' he said, the smile gone. 'And that will give us the time we need.'

'We?'

'You, me ... and Poum. That future I talked about? *We* are it.'

'I see.' Finally she reached, took back the infant. 'Then I will trust you on this, Luck of Askaug. As long as you know that, in the end, only I will decide for myself and my child.'

'That much I know of you, Atisha,' he said, rising. 'And when I say "we" I mean it.' He reached and laid a hand on Poum's forehead. 'Because I have had this feeling for a while now. That, before long, it will be this one who decides for us all.'

He limped away, down the slope. Hovard saw him, ceased talking, waited. Luck climbed the ladder to the top of the grass hut which was the speaking platform. Hovard handed him the speaking stick and he raised the staff high. His voice was powerful though he did not need to shout.

'Warriors of Midgarth,' he said. 'I bring good news. We are going to fight!'

It is surprising, Atisha thought, as the men and women

302

cheered, how sometimes I understand everything. Even without words.

'Come, Soul Lord. Anazat wishes you.'

Peki Asarko smiled. He liked the name Sekantor used for him. The only language they had in common was *tolanpa-sen*, the language of Saghaz-a, that both had been forced to learn. Neither spoke it well, and adapted it freely. In Midgarth, he was Lord of the Lake of Souls. But 'Soul Lord' had a good feel to it. He had killed many in his life, taken their bodies, remade them for his collection. Perhaps he had taken their souls as well.

Sekantor was also called 'the Savage'. Peki preferred a simpler form for the Seafarer, who had done things to prisoners that surprised even him. 'I come, Savage,' he called.

The man went away. But Peki did not rise immediately to follow; stayed sitting before the cage, and stared into the eyes of its occupant. The puma stared back, eyes near as black as Anazat's gleaming in the torchlight. It did not blink, nor look away. It was … unyielding. Savage as well.

When his hunters had brought it to him, he'd considered killing it, flaying it, preparing the skin, stuffing it, mounting it, fixing carved wood in place of its eyes. He had not worked with animals since he'd discovered his passion for the art as a child, two hundred years before. Humans were just so much more *interesting* as subjects and when he'd learned to take them, body and, yes, perhaps soul, he only wanted to do it again and again. But Anazat, after his visit to the lodgehouse on the Lake, had not been delighted by the displays. He'd been appalled, and had forbidden Peki his simple pleasures. And since the black-eyed monk controlled Sirene, the drug he craved, Peki had been forced to obey. Even though Anazat had allowed him none in the three weeks he had been in Midgarth. He'd only had what he'd been able to snatch at the meeting on the island. Even that little had been begrudged.

Forbidden. Obey.

These were words he had not heeded since he first left his own people, who also had not understood his tastes, and come to the Lake of Souls.

He reached again into the leather bag at his waist. Only then did the puma's eyes leave his, to follow the movement, giving a low growl as the hand emerged clutching another piece of raw goat's liver. Peki held it in front of the cage for a moment, then threw it in. The beast stooped, snatched, swallowed, then raised its eyes to fix once again on Peki's.

It would be easy to possess it. He had not gone into a beast for a while. To his shock he had discovered he'd been unable to when in the full grip of Sirene. But deprivation had loosed her hold, and the one brief snatch of her on the island had not caught him again. He knew he could do it – open the cage door first, stare, dissolve, run free.

Kill.

But he would not. There was too much at stake. With dawn would come the final defeat of his old enemies, his fellow gods of Midgarth. They were trapped on Galahur, with just two hundred mortals. Outnumbered five to one. They would be defeated and he would be ...

What? Soul Lord still? In this new world with its new, single god, 'the One'? With this fire god, come from across the water, given rule over Midgarth? With Peki to serve under him?

Forbidden ... Obey ... Serve.

'Come!'

Savage shouted again from further away, irritation clear. Peki rose, keeping his eyes on the puma's, who continued to stare back. He pulled out another hunk of bloody meat and threw it into the cage, then turned and walked away, down the river path to the war camp. As he approached it, he heard the familiar smooth voice of the monk, though now it was raised in fury.

The cause of Anazat's anger lay before him in a bloody heap on the tent's earth floor. This Seafarer's frilled finery was torn and sopping crimson, blood running from half a dozen wounds. 'This fool,' the monk yelled, addressing Peki as he stepped in, 'has let the enemy slip away!'

'They came so fast, lord, and in such numbers. Some were beasts too. We fought hard but—'

'Silence,' Anazat screamed, kicking him in the shoulder.

Now Peki recognised the bloodied man: Ganator. He had been sent to close off the single valley behind Galahur with three hundred men, though fifty could have done the job, such was the steepness of the slopes. 'Are they all gone?' Peki asked.

'We do not know. We have scouts out but—'

Another man came into the tent. Not of Midgarth: he was brown of skin, and wore the strange garments of Ometepe. He went straight to his god, who Peki noticed now for the first time, sitting cross-legged in one dark corner of the tent, far from the lamp-spill. The man fell before him, kissed his feet, was beckoned up to whisper into the Fire God's ear. Intitepe nodded once, then rose. He beckoned Sekantor, who bowed, stooped, listened, then turned to Anazat.

'Intitepe's spies have said: not all of them have gone. One hundred remain in the bowl of land.'

Peki knew, as soon as the man said it. Other spies had reported before that all that was left of Midgarth's forces after the fight through the land were two hundred mortals and …

'They are the gods,' he said, stepping forward. 'It is only gods who have remained to fight.'

All looked at him. 'How do you know that?' said Anazat.

'There is a story, written at the beginning of time,' Peki said. 'A story of the last stand of the gods. A final battle. It is called—'

He paused. There was no phrase for it in *tolanpa-sen*. There was only one for it in Midgarth so he said it, in that tongue. 'It is called "the Coming of the Dark". It has come. They will stand.'

'Then we will bring them their dark,' Anazat snarled, then turned to Sekantor. 'Tell the Fire God. We attack with the first light.'

Sekantor leaned in to speak fast to Intitepe – who raised a hand, cut him off, spoke in his turn. The Seafarer listened, nodded, turned back. 'Do we know that the mother and baby also stand? Or are they with those who escaped?'

Anazat kicked the man on the floor again. 'Well?'

'How can I know?' he whined. 'I could not see. It was dark. I was fighting—'

Anazat cut him off. 'We cannot know till we can go up the valley. We cannot do that till we have killed the gods who remain. So the order stands: rouse the army. We attack with the light.'

Sekantor translated this last to Intitepe, who nodded, and left. The Savage, on a further command from Anazat, grabbed Ganator by the collar and dragged him out. He shrieked in pain, a noise suddenly cut off. Only Anazat and Peki remained.

The monk sat suddenly. 'So tired,' he said, rubbing his black eyes with the heels of his hands. Then he looked up. 'I do not think that Luck will have remained. He is not a fighter. And his concern will be for those he stole – the mother and the One.'

'You think he has fled with the mortals?'

Anazat shrugged. 'I think so. But we must know. And we do not need you in the fight, Peki Asarko. We need you to become a bird and find out. That is why I have denied you Sirene. For a task like this one.' He stood. 'Obey me in this, and I promise you a vial of her, to use when and as you desire, on your return.'

'I will.'

Anazat stood, and left the tent. Peki waited for a few

moments, then turned to look into the far corner, where smoke swirled in the globe. He had not looked there before, knew he could be too lost in it if he did. Now he stared, licked his lips, and smiled. *Soon, my love*, he said to Sirene. *Soon I will come to you again.*

He left the tent, moved through the mustering camp. He had his own commands and he would follow them. He would like to see Luck again, who had escaped him when he'd had such special plans for him and for his brute of a brother. He would also like to see this child that everyone was talking about. He was fond of children. They had such soft skin.

He considered the trees. He would become a bird. A falcon would be best if he could find one. Then he could hover ...

He stopped, as a different idea came to him. A bird could only watch, bring news. *Obey.*

Smiling, he walked through the trees towards a cage.

12

The Coming of the Dark

Freya stood at the tent flap, her face raised into the starlight, eyes closed. Thinking about death.

Not the death she'd experienced before, three times in her three-hundred-year life, from which she'd returned each time. A final one. That was what had been agreed yesterday in the bowl of Galahur. Agreed by the two hundred mortals and the one hundred gods, each with a single vote. In the end there was no disagreement, from either group. The mortals would live to fight another day ... while the gods?

The gods would see that they could.

When Ulrich had pointed out, quite logically and without resentment, that a last stand meant something different to those who could be reborn, or could transform to animals when all was finally lost, Hovard had agreed. When the smith had added that although all warriors believed in the immortal paradise that a good death on a battlefield would take them to, it was only the gods who had actual proof of immortality, Hovard had once more assented – and proposed something different for the morrow. The news that Luck had brought back from his spying on the island made it the only course.

'Ulrich has spoken true,' Hovard had called out. 'For all these years you have died in our battles. So tomorrow, I am ready to die – finally, truly die – for you.'

The mortals had been silent then – it was the immortals who acclaimed the decision. In murmurs, then speech, finally shouts. She had shouted too, the same realisation coming to her as it came to all the others in that one moment.

How many lives could they live? How many babies who had been held to a breast, or dandled on a knee, or taught as a youth to hunt in a forest, could be laid an old woman or man onto a funeral pyre? Almost every god there had seen families grow up and pass on. Every one of them knew these curses of immortality. Now they'd been offered a chance to rejoin their families, in the world beyond. Perhaps. They, like her, would seize it.

The Coming of the Dark.

Only a very few gods did not agree – and they were permitted to lead the mortals to safety in the night. They were younger, with younger families, who did not yet know the sorrows of immortality. There was no shame in their going, for it was agreed that it would be a sorry world indeed if all the gods were dead; that some would be needed to carry on the fight. Others, of course, had been born a god and did not know it yet, for they had not yet had their first death. So there would be light still in the dark to come. Especially if this fight was good, and the memory of it lived on.

'How does the starlight feel?'

She did not open her eyes to look at him, not yet, just smiled at her husband's voice and called, 'Come feel for yourself.'

He rose, came to where she stood, put his arms around her, looked out. After a moment he said, 'Are you sure, Freya?'

'Are you?'

'I am for myself. But the thought of your death ...'

He broke off. She raised fingers to his cheek. 'My death at your side. My rebirth there in paradise.'

He thought for a moment, then said, 'Are you sure it exists, this eternal paradise?'

She made her voice low like his. 'You know, I truly hope not.' She laughed. 'Haven't we lived long enough? Do you really want another forever?'

Hovard tipped back his head and laughed too. 'I do not. These lives were enough. Since I got to spend them with you.'

He drew her against him. Held her there, and she enjoyed his warmth against her back. Until she noticed something else against her back. 'Truly, Hovard? Again?'

'Well,' he replied, a husk in his voice. 'It is still night.'

She laughed and turned to him, reached down to grab his cock where it rose between them. 'So when you said to me "one last time" for that second time earlier this evening – you were lying, again?'

'Not lying exactly.' He shrugged. 'Just wanting to preserve *some* strength for the day.'

'Shouldn't I help you with that?' she asked, her voice still low, moving her hand up and down what she held. 'Shouldn't I let you get a little more sleep?'

'You know.' He reached under her shift, ran his fingers slowly up her inner thigh, until he reached the apex, slid two fingers inside her, then added, 'I have always thought that sleep was overrated.'

She shoved him back then, and they fell onto the bed they'd made of blankets and furs. Over the centuries they'd been together, their love-making had come and gone, settled into routine, exploded with some springs, died in some winters. Always, eventually, they'd found their way back to each other. But nothing like they had over that summer and into this fall.

He was still naked from the night. She grasped the shift at her hips and pulled it from her body. Then she straddled him, fell upon him, taking him, all of him, in an instant and deep inside her. Both cried out at that, neither moved, until he did, pulling himself up, pressing himself against her, bending to her breasts, cupping them in his hands, putting his mouth, his tongue, his teeth, upon each in turn. She threw back her head, moaned, let him have his fill of her, fill her too. Then she started to move slowly on him, circling her hips, feeling all of him within her, every last part. He fell back to stare at her, as she leaned away, hair spilling down her back now, her hands either side of his knees, changing the angle, starting to thrust down. After a while he rose again, seized her, spun her, she below now, he above. He withdrew almost, but not quite, all the way. Said, 'Let us make this last for ever, love,' and then pushed himself into her, so slowly it seemed as if he did not move at all, until they could not be closer joined. He left as slowly, returned, and their eyes were in each other's. So she saw his change, a moment of something else and she whispered, 'Yes, love, yes!' and he moved faster, faster. She called him, flooded for him, tightened on him, the sensations within her building, building, as she felt them build in him, and when he exploded in her, she exploded around him, and they held those moments, held each other, joined everywhere, eyes, bodies, minds.

They lay and did not move despite the dawn light at last beginning to grow beyond the hide walls. She did not think of many different things, or return to any worries. Today, she thought, will be a good day. A good, last day.

They only moved apart when they heard whistling, and foot-steps halting outside. 'You know,' said Bjorn, 'I could be wrong. But I believe someone has been making love around here.'

Freya pulled a fur up to her chin, looked at Hovard, who nodded. 'Come in, Bjorn.'

Their brother god thrust just his head through the flap. 'Aw, look at you lovebirds in your nest. You make me jealous that I have no one to nuzzle with at the end.'

'No one, Bjorn? From the sounds coming from your tent last night, it appeared you had your pick.'

'You heard that?'

'Brother,' said Hovard, sitting up, 'they heard it back in Askaug.'

Bjorn came in, squatted, ran his hand up and down over his head. 'It was like Oblivion's Feast at springtime but in the autumn. Extraordinary how the promise of certain death makes so many so hungry for life.' He grinned. 'Half the women gods of Midgarth seemed to want me last night. I'll be surprised if I can even walk this day, let alone lift Sever-Life and run into battle.' He yawned, tapped the grip of the weapon, in its sheath across his back. 'Yet if I am tired, do not expect to see Stromvar rise from his bed even when the trumpet sounds. For he was even more—'

A distant bugle blast interrupted him – the enemy's – and the man who Bjorn claimed would not wake shouted from outside to prove him wrong. 'They approach, King Hovard. We await you, and your commands.' He pushed his head into the tent, looked at Freya. 'What are you smiling at, my lady?'

'You look ... like you have not slept, Dragon Lord.'

'Sleep? Who needs sleep?' He dropped a hand onto Bjorn's shoulder. 'I'll sleep when I'm dead.'

Bjorn laughed. 'That sounds like the title of one of Grim the Skald's ballads.'

They all laughed then. Bjorn and Stromvar withdrew, Freya and Hovard dressed, then helped each other arm. 'Ready,' she said.

'Now I am,' he replied, snatched up her hand, kissed it. Then, side by side they left the tent and climbed to Galahur's rim, where Bjorn and Stromvar waited.

It was a day to gladden the heart – a resurgence of summer in what had been a misty, unusually wet autumn. Sunbeams turned red-leafed trees to flame, the rivers and lakes to sheets of diamonds. Mountaintops already had some snow, and those caps gleamed stark and white against the bluest, cloudless skies. This last warmth drew scent from the land, with the spores of mushrooms, the ripeness of apples still on trees, of blackberries yet on bushes and acorns in the mulch, wafting into the nostrils of those who breathed deep. It was a day to feel again the rhythms of the world, and feel how one last taste of warmth also held the promise of its return.

It is, indeed, a fine day to die, Freya thought, then turned her attention to the land before them. Three mighty rivers converged at Galahur and on each of those, ships were being rowed. Not the vessels of the Seafarers, one of their enemies, for their keels were meant for the seas and would have grounded on the riverbed. Most of the ships were their own, captured in the long fight all over Midgarth. Some belonged to their new enemy, come from the far west, this Intitepe. Made of woven reeds and the lightest of woods, they also had no draught. Hovard had marvelled at their construction when he'd captured one in a night raid near Kroken. Even dreamed that night of building one during the long winter ahead. Which now he would not see.

The ships were filled with warriors. Many more picked their way on foot between the rivers, their formations broken by streams and boggy ground. 'Oh, for five hundred more men,' Stromvar groaned. 'We could cut them to pieces in the marshes there.' He turned to Bjorn. 'What say we possess a couple of river snakes, go sting a few? I'll wager three casks of Kroken ale that I kill more than you.'

Bjorn was known to leap upon any challenge. So Hovard was surprised when he shook his head. 'Nay, Dragon Lord. We decided on our tactics and that was not one of them.'

Hovard smiled. If even Bjorn Swiftsword refused a wager

with ale as the stake, the world was indeed coming to an end. And tactics was not how he would describe their battle plan. They had but one: to prolong the fight for the longest time possible. Though they'd accepted death, they did not desire to rush into it. More glory was to be found the longer the fight went on. For every minute we buy in blood is another minute for Luck, his charges, and all the mortals to get away, he thought. Every enemy we slay is one less to pursue them.

It was what had been decided, after the last moot, when the gods had vowed to die. They had opened the trap being laid behind them just before midnight, killing all who tried to hold them. The mortals had a few hours' head start in their retreat down the valley, Luck a little more time for his journey upwards. And the longer the enemy took to get into position …

So they waited and watched as the soldiers waded through the marshes, and re-formed on drier land closer to the bowl; while the ships were rowed, and anchored unopposed at, or near, the jetty, disgorging their crews upon the beach. All the enemy would have seen were the four gods, now arm in arm upon the lip of the bowl. Hovard could see how the sight made them wary, men sent to each side to try to spy the land, and find the rest of the forces of Midgarth. But they could only go so far, and see so much, for the gods had diverted one of the rivers, the Thrallen, three weeks before, and cut trenches, the flood held back by dykes of earth. These had been broken in the night. Three sides of Galahur were now water. The only way to get to the valley behind them was over the bowl itself. Where the gods waited for them.

It took another hour, but at last the enemy were ready. They could see the separate groups within the whole – Seafarers in the main body, their feathered hats exchanged for helms, their cleavers – so useful when fighting in close quarters on ships – given up for longer swords, spears and shields. Interspersed among them were archers, mostly women, from what they'd learned was a separate tribe in the world across the mountains, the Huntresses. Black cloaks singled out the Warrior Monks, though there were few of these. Even fewer were the mounted men, tall and with black hair that fell in a coiled rope down their backs. The Horse Lords. In a mob on the left flank were about one hundred men from the Lake of Souls, their naked bodies painted in broad white stripes.

The final large group, all men, was brighter than every other, with their wooden slat armour lined and tipped in bronze, their darkwood helmets scored through with streaks of gold. They made up the centre of the enemy, spears couched over long shields. The warriors from the far west, Ometepe.

For a while, after the last of these warriors moved into place, nothing stirred, except for the banners of the enemy fluttering in the slightest of breezes. 'Excuse me,' said Stromvar, disengaging his arm from the others. 'Time for the first tactic, is it not?'

He went back down the slope behind them, into the bowl, passing through the gods who waited there, as one enemy bugle screeched again.

It was a signal and, with a shout, most of the enemy, save for those from Ometepe, kneeled and cried, three times, a single word.

'One! One! One!'

Hovard raised his sword – and on the signal, one hundred gods of Midgarth ran up the slopes of Galahur. They took two paces down the outer side, beyond Freya and Hovard, and locked their shields in a wall before them.

A murmur arose from the enemy's kneeling ranks. A command was shouted, all stood, lowered shields, raised spear and bow.

A man stepped forward from their ranks, wearing the gaudy

finery of a Seafarer. 'What?' Sekantor the Savage cried in the language of Midgarth. 'You think you few can stop us?'

'Well,' Hovard said, though he did not call it out, 'perhaps not *only* us few.'

It was then that the giant bear ran over the hill and down the slope as fast as only a bear can run, and ripped the Savage's head off. Standing on his hind legs, the bear roared his triumph before throwing the head deep into the enemy ranks, then following it. They turned from order into instant chaos. It had happened so fast, not even the Huntresses could shoot any arrows.

Petr the Red brought their shields to them. 'Now, Hovard?' he asked.

'Now.' Their tactics, such as they were, had been decided. One hundred warriors on a hill, even if they were gods, could not hold a shield wall against a thousand men, not with all the arrows that would eventually fall on them. So they might as well plunge into the enemy and see how many hearts they could cut out in the marshes.

Hovard looked each way down the line. The only time he'd seen so many gods look so happy was at Oblivion's Feast. Why not? he thought. A different kind of oblivion awaits us now.

Beside him, Bjorn was muttering. Hovard looked at him. 'What is it, brother?'

Bjorn pointed with his sword to the centre of the enemy's ranks, from which the screams of terrified men could clearly be heard. 'Are you going to let Stromvar claim all the glory?' he asked. 'Give the order, will you?'

Hovard smiled and turned to Freya. 'Ready, my love?'

She smiled back. 'So ready, my love.'

'Good.' Glancing again down the ranks, he raised his sword, then began slapping it against his shield. 'Out!' he cried at every blow. 'Out!'

'Out!' they echoed him. 'Out!'

Then, as one, the gods of Midgarth ran down the slopes to drive the invader out.

Where the narrow trail widened into a ledge, about a quarter of the way up the mountain, Luck halted. His own eyes were not that great for this distance. But the horse he'd possessed was young, and keen-sighted. There were few trees this high up on these steep slopes, so his view down into the valley was clear enough, despite the thickening mist. He could still see Galahur, an emerald oval standing out now in a sparkling, turquoise bow of water. At this height, the people upon it, and those before it, were like ants on grass. But even as he stopped he could see the smaller group, a mere line upon the crest, run down and merge into the larger.

Like the eyesight, the horse's hearing was keener than his own. He'd heard the shriek of an alien trumpet. He'd heard, as if it was a whisper, the distant cries of 'Out!' His own eyes had teared at the thought, but a horse could not reach up and wipe them away. So he let the water fall, as he watched his brother and sister gods run, laughing no doubt, to their deaths.

Because of him. Because of the news he'd brought back from his spying, and his belief that only with the course he proposed was there any hope left for the world. Not just their world, tiny Midgarth. The world he'd discovered when he'd crossed the mountains and found out both how vast it was, and how much evil was in it. Hovard and Freya, Stromvar and Bjorn had listened, and agreed; as did the rest of the gods, and the mortals, gathered in the bowl of Galahur. They were a contentious people, man and god, yet not one man, one woman, one god raised their voice against his plan. Only Hovard had changed it from a fight and perhaps an escape to a fight to the death. 'It is the hour, brother,' Hovard had said, taking his arm and gently shaking it when he tried to argue, 'and this the cause to die for. This hope.'

This hope on his back now. Twin hopes, mother and child. Which was why he was there, bearing them up a mountain, and not dying in the valley below, with his brothers and sisters, in the Coming of the Dark.

'Is it over?' Atisha called to him. He could not shape words with a rope bit in his mouth, and a horse's tongue. But he had discovered, ever since they'd journeyed together with Sirene, that he could convey some meaning in thought. Not as he could talk with Freya perhaps. But enough to say here, his mind to hers: *Not yet. Soon.*

'I understand,' she said, then added, her voice filled with his same sorrow, 'All this ... sacrifice? For me? For me and my child?'

No, he thought, *all this sacrifice for the world.*

He didn't know if she'd understood. He turned his horse eyes back, to check the three asses and their loads. Chickens protested in their wicker cages. Sacks of seeds swayed, beside a cauldron, pots, shovels and hoes. The bag of Sirene was one of the smaller ones, with the heating flasks he knew he'd need to extract her essence tied to the neck. There were weapons too: a spear, a bow for hunting, skinning knives, his slingshot. Three ewes followed, bleating all the while as his sheep dog, Ulfa, harried them. Three goats were tethered to the last ass. Every animal was pregnant, including the dog. Seeing them, he gave another swift prayer to Raina, goddess of fertility, that of the three sheep and goats, at least one of each carried a ram within her litter of three or four. Else his new career as a shepherd would be short-lived indeed.

As he watched, Ulfa whined, then left her heel-nipping to peer down into the mist that, he saw when he now turned back, had overtaken them. Galahur was gone from his sight. She barked at something in it and all the animals shied.

318

He turned again to the track, only just visible ahead now. If the gods had bought them enough time, if the enemy followed the mortals, and their own tracks were buried by the new snow Luck knew was coming soon, they would need to stay away a long, long time. They had to be prepared for it. He assumed – for no one had ever explored this high – that among the crests there would be hidden valleys, lakes, fish and some game. No mortal lived there, as far as he knew. No one who had ever made contact with the rest of Midgarth anyway. He doubted there was anyone, for the world that high up would be harsh living for anyone not as desperate as they were.

He set hooves upon a track getting ever narrower. The horse baulked, halted, stood jerking its head – his head – up and down. He could control it, but to have an animal's instincts was part of why a god possessed one. What was this animal sensing in this engulfing mist?

He looked back, could see nothing beyond the asses, hear nothing, his ears as muffled as his eyes. 'What is it?' Atisha said, concern in her voice, fingers in his mane.

Dismount, he thought to her and either the thought carried, or the swaying of the head warned her. She did, clutching Poum, and he trotted a few paces forward.

The beast parted the mist, leaping, seizing the horse by the neck. The horse, and Luck, screamed, reared, tried to shake the animal off – but claws and teeth had sunk deep. It was a huge puma, and it used its weight now to topple the horse onto the ground, where they slid down the steepness. Yet even as his mount fell, Luck left it, lay beside it, a hand's breadth from that torn neck, trying to roll away. The puma lashed out, and fastened huge claws into the neck of Luck's cloak, jerking him hard back. The horse, blood streaming, leaped up, ran whinnying into the mist. The puma let it go. It had easier prey now.

Luck tried to grab the knife in his belt but the beast was

wrenching him back and forth across the ground and he could not grasp it. He was lifted, flung onto his back. The puma reared up, jaws wide.

Something struck it, a blur passing into its open mouth. It jerked back, ripping its claws from Luck's cloak. It stopped, shook its head as if puzzled by the thing Luck saw, as he drove his heels into the dirt and scrabbled backwards.

There was an arrow in the puma's mouth, passed through its upper jaw. The animal was shaking its head hard, trying to dislodge it – when a second arrow slammed into its chest. The puma snarled, slipped, toppled back. The slope seized it, it rolled, gathering speed, and vanished into the swallowing mist.

Seconds later, from somewhere far below, they heard an almost human scream.

Luck rolled, came onto his knees, looked back. Ten paces away, Poum was on the ground. Standing above them, a bow in her hand and a third arrow notched, was Atisha. She came forward, bow still at tension, staring down the slope into the grey. 'Is it gone?' she said, when she reached him.

He sat up. 'I think you killed it.'

'Good.' She eased the string, looked down at him. 'Are you hurt?'

He checked himself. He'd felt the agony of the puma's teeth and claws on the horse's neck but when he put his hand to his own, there was no blood on the fingers he brought away. 'I don't think so,' he muttered. 'A little shaken. I—'

Poum was now rolling and crying on the ground. Atisha ran back, laid down her bow, picked up her child, cooing.

Luck limped over. He pointed at the bow. 'When did you—?'

'On the ship. A Huntress taught me.' She smiled. 'Are you glad?'

'I am glad.' He rolled his head, shook his shoulders. His

muscles were strained. Nevertheless. He stared into the mist ahead. He could only hope that the horse would return, or they would find it ahead, and that its wounds were not beyond his healing skills. Until it did ... 'Come,' he said. 'I'll make room upon one of the pack animals.'

'No,' she interrupted. 'I do not ride well. And you ... you do not walk well.'

It was true. He never had. And it irked him again, now. Was he not meant to be this woman's protector? 'I ...' he began.

But Atisha was already shifting loads on the first ass, untying, retying, and he watched her while his heart gradually steadied. At the last she slung her bow over her shoulders, then patted the blanket on the animal's back. 'Come,' she said. 'You take Poum.'

He was about to argue – then realised how foolish that was. Argue for what? For pride? Pride was one of the many, many things that could kill them in the days – the years perhaps – that lay ahead. He would set it aside. All that mattered now was survival.

The ass was small enough, so he managed to mount it not too clumsily. When he had, Atisha passed the baby up to him. Poum was awake, and he blew his lips out, making noise. The baby giggled, and grabbed his beard. Atisha went to the ass's head and took the rope bridle.

They continued up the track – which narrowed till it was carving across a slope with the plunge even steeper than before on their left, which he felt rather than saw in that blanket of grey. Luck did not distract Atisha with thoughts, as she picked her way carefully forward. Yet, just before they reached the summit, and dipped briefly down before beginning on the next, even steeper climb, another's thought did reach him. He had cut his palm before so that she could.

Luck, Freya called. *It is done. Farewell.*

It was shocking, really, how far they had got. Yet perhaps not so, for a force of one hundred gods, preceded by bears twice the height of an average man – several had followed Stromvar's example and inhabited the beasts that had been trapped for the purpose in the week before the battle – was one that few would stand against. Following tooth and claw with sword and spear, they'd carved into the heart of the enemy. So many had fled that Freya had thought for a time that perhaps they could even win this, and was surprised at both how happy and how sad that made her. She'd been ready to die. Accepted it, craved it even. Sought death on the blades of the warriors that opposed her. But those who did not care if they died always had an advantage over those who did, and men fell to her sword, again and again and again.

She had lost the ones she loved, found them, lost them again in the swirl of combat. Now, on this small river beach surrounded by reeds where the battle had somehow thrown her, just as she placed a boot in the centre of the naked chest of one of these so-called Horse Lords so she could extract the blade she'd buried in him, she found them again. Or they found her. Both at once, and driving five Seafarers before them like geese.

Bjorn was scything his blade so fast through the air she couldn't see it. The three Seafarers who tried to parry him certainly couldn't and died quickly for their failure. Hovard was slower, more precise. Took one man with a false high cut to finish him low, and the second man with the exact reverse. 'Hovard,' she called, and he spun fast, saw her, grinned. His teeth were white in the red mask his face had become.

'Wife,' he cried. 'You know, I'd forgotten how much I enjoyed this fighting business.'

'As had I.'

'Novices!' Bjorn wiped Sever-Life on the frilly doublet of one

322

of the Seafarers he'd slain, then dropped the body. 'We saw you stumble this way, Freya. Thought you might like to join us.'

'In what?'

'More killing.' Bjorn grinned and wiped blood from his eyes. 'Watch me carefully. It'll teach you both how to be more efficient.'

He started to run towards the shouting, but Freya called, 'Stromvar?' and that halted him.

'Dead,' he said.

'*Dead* dead or—'

'No, finally dead.' He stuck his sword tip into the ground to lean for a moment. 'I saw him come out of the bear when the beast took a spear in the side. Saw him seize the spear as himself, kill three men with it. Then three were atop him, six, they held him down, I couldn't reach him and …' he passed a finger across his throat. Then his sombreness passed as he added, 'His head carried on cussing them for quite a while after it was separated. It distracted them so much it made them even easier for me to kill! I was even going to try to reattach his head, when three Horse Lords rode in and I lost him.' He frowned for a moment, then smiled again. 'Come!' he said, pulling his sword from the ground and straightening, pointing to where the noise sounded greatest. 'Is it not time to join him?'

Freya and Hovard took two steps after him – then needed to go no further. For the fight they sought found them.

They came in a rush, twenty men in wooden slat armour and darkwood helms. Men of Ometepe, far from that world but led by its god-king. To judge by the blood on his armour, Intitepe had been in the thick of the fight as much as any of the native gods and he did not hesitate when he saw three before him now.

'He's mine!' he yelled, pointing his sword tip at Bjorn. 'Take the others alive.'

While his warriors rushed past him, he took a high guard, his curving Horse Lord sword above his head, his other hand thrust out, fingers splayed, as if he would grab his opponent by the throat. He looked into Bjorn's eyes. 'Give me the child,' he shouted.

Bjorn did not know what it was the warrior yelled at him. Some battle cry, no doubt. It didn't matter. All that did was the stance the man took. Seeing it, he raised his own sword in two hands and held it straight up, its tip to the sky.

Intitepe came, whirling his weapon. Bjorn waited, until a cut passed a hand's breadth above his head, then struck down hard, knocking Intitepe's weapon to the side. The Fire God was forced to follow or lose it and as he staggered he left his flank exposed. With a twist of the wrist, Bjorn plunged Sever-Life straight into his body. His ever keen blade sank deep, brought him close. Too close to Intitepe, who knew a death thrust when he saw one, felt it. But knew he also had one blow left in him. Placing one hand on the blade that had entered him, leaning away, he cut his own blade hard and fast and level with the ground, and took Bjorn's head off with the stroke.

The god's head tumbled to the ground. His body fell after. And just like his old enemy, and recent comrade, Stromvar, Bjorn cursed his enemy even as the light faded from his eyes.

They did not see their brother's death, surrounded as they were, for Intitepe's men had obeyed him, driving at Hovard and Freya, hedging them with shields. The gods struck at the barrier, or dropped to their knees to slice into unprotected legs. But there were too many, more coming all the time, and soon all around. Finally, at a shouted command, the enemy halted, five paces away on each side, spears levelled, a square container of wood and metal.

With a sigh, Freya put her back against her husband's and said, 'Is it time, husband?'

'I think so, wife.' They'd made a pact before. Luck had told them about the Keep, how enemies were masked and shackled there, beaten and starved. They had decided that they would not submit to that. Certainly not on this, the finest of all days to die. So Hovard stepped a little away from her to give them the room they would need. They had practised this, because it was more awkward than it looked. They'd laughed when they realised how fortunate it was that neither of them was left-handed.

He rested his sword flat on his shoulder. 'Now, my love?'

'A moment,' she said, then ran the palm of her left hand along her blade. Blood ran, to mingle with other men's blood there, and she thought, clearly, silently, yet as loud as a shout. *Luck, it is done. Farewell.*

She opened her eyes. Hovard was smiling at her. 'What?' she asked.

'Truly? Talking to your other lover? Now?'

'Oh pish,' she said. 'You know there has only ever been you.'

'I do.'

She dropped her sword on to her shoulder, widened her stance. 'I love you,' she said, 'for ever.'

'For ever ... and a day,' he replied. They held the look for a moment. Until Hovard bent and shouted, 'Now!' then swung his sword, even as she swung hers.

When their heads landed on the ground, there were no curses on their lips, only that one word.

Love.

Four gods lay dead in a glade by a river. One would wake in all the agonies of rebirth the next morning. Three would never wake again.

The Dark had come.

To be continued …

Here ends *The Coming of the Dark*,
Book Two of the *Immortals' Blood* trilogy.

Be ready for Book Three, the epic conclusion:
The Wars of Gods and Men.

Glossary

Corinthium:
Sevrapol – the fourth hill. Entertainment district of the city
Lascaro – fire-spouting, seven-headed desert lizard
Kristun – famous historical victory over the Wattenwolden
lamulin – a type of armour
Danari, Wobelani, Mishrani – Cuerdocian border tribes
Perilonos – sixth hill
serang – venomous snake
Omersh – island with pirates
taka – throwing knife
Sarphardi – desert peoples, made up of clans
Saipha – the Horned Moon
Blue Revlas – the Blue Moon
Maklat – famed for its brothels
Balbek – Ferros' home town
Lascartis, Gonarios, Trebans – elite families of the city
Agueros – Sanctum on the Hill
Heaven Road – skyway to Agueros
Ice wine (from Tinderos)
Cuerdocia – province
tawpan – breed of horse
Simbala – Goddess of birth and death and birth

Tarfona – capital, province of Cuerdocia
Assani – Cuerdocian tribe
Bow of Mavros – arrow artillery
Wattenwold – the northern forests
Wattenwolden – Tribesmen from the north

Ometepe:

munke – a kind of basket
bura – luck
Palace of Waters
Toluc – volcano and main city
marana – the house of Chosen Women
Bunami – language of most of realm

Midgarth:

stringen – plant, a purgative
Inge-gerd – goddess of all waters
Raina – goddess of fertility
Galahur – gathering place for the Moot
Lorken – southern town
Kroken – northern town

Saghaz-a (Land of the Four Tribes):

Saghaz-a – Land of Joy
Saghaz – Land of Eternal Sorrow
taramazak – Horse Lords; name for themselves. Literally:
    'those who hunt from the horse'
azama-klosh – a type of bison
pazamor-ash – pirates; literally: 'the devils of the flood'
paza – little doe
Billandah – northern port
tolanpa-sen – the common tongue of Saghaz-a; literally: 'the
    only word'

ascrami – 'mad fighters' or, 'expendables'. The first wave of attack

Sirkesami's breath – poisonous mist

Sirene – the drug of communication

azana-kesh – 'the one who comes before'

Credits

Chris Humphreys and Gollancz would like to thank everyone at Orion who worked on the publication of *The Coming of the Dark* in the UK.

Editorial
Marcus Gipps
Brendan Durkin

Copy editor
Elizabeth Dobson

Proofreader
Gabriella Nemeth

Audio
Paul Stark
Amber Bates

Contracts
Anne Goddard
Paul Bulos
Jake Alderson

Design
Lucie Stericker
Joanna Ridley
Nick May

Editorial Management
Charlie Panayiotou
Jane Hughes
Alice Davis

Finance
Jennifer Muchan
Jasdip Nandra
Afeera Ahmed
Elizabeth Beaumont
Sue Baker

Marketing
Lucy Cameron

Production
Paul Hussey
Ruth Sharvell

Publicity
Will O'Mullane

Sales
Laura Fletcher

Esther Waters
Victoria Laws
Rachael Hum
Ellie Kyrke-Smith
Frances Doyle
Georgina Cutler

Operations
Jo Jacobs
Sharon Willis
Lisa Pryde
Lucy Brem

ABOUT GOLLANCZ

Gollancz is the oldest SF publishing imprint in the world. Since being founded in 1927 Gollancz has continued to publish a focused selection of bestselling and award-winning authors. The front-list includes **Ben Aaronovitch**, **Joe Abercrombie**, **Charlaine Harris**, **Joanne Harris**, **Joe Hill**, **Alastair Reynolds**, **Patrick Rothfuss**, **Nalini Singh** and **Brandon Sanderson**.

As one of the largest Science Fiction and Fantasy imprints in the UK it is no surprise we have one of the most extensive backlists in the world. Find high-quality SF on Gateway written by such authors as **Philip K. Dick**, **Ursula Le Guin**, **Connie Willis**, **Sir Arthur C. Clarke**, **Pat Cadigan**, **Michael Moorcock** and **George R.R. Martin**.

We also have a strand of publishing in translation, which includes French, Polish and Russian authors. Gollancz is home to more award-winning authors than any other imprint, with names including **Aliette de Bodard**, **M. John Harrison**, **Paul McAuley**, **Sarah Pinborough**, **Pierre Pevel**, **Justina Robson** and many more.

The SF Gateway
More than 3,000 classic, rare and previously out-of-print SF novels at your fingertips.
www.sfgateway.com

The Gollancz Blog
Bringing you news from our worlds to yours. Stories, interviews, articles and exclusive extracts just for you!
www.gollancz.co.uk

GOLLANCZ
LONDON